Crimes Against a Book Club

Crimes Against a Book Club

KATHY COOPERMAN

LAKE UNION
PUBLISHING

This is a work of fiction. Names, characters, organizations, places, events, and incidents are either products of the author's imagination or are used fictitiously. Any resemblance to actual persons, living or dead, or actual events is purely coincidental.

Published by Lake Union Publishing, Seattle

www.apub.com

ISBN-13: 9781503942981
ISBN-10: 1503942988

Cover design by Joan Wong

Printed in the United States of America

To my husband, Johnny, who helped me trust my cape.

Prologue

That summer, everyone had an opinion on the Baker case. Fox News called Baker a "two-bit drug dealer" who deserved to "rot in jail." MSNBC celebrated her as a "modern-day Robin Hood, duping the rich to provide for her poor babies." Meanwhile, *Maxim* put Baker's accomplice, Sarah Sloane, at the top of its "Hot Cellmates" list, calling her a "red-hot redhead we'd love to do time with." And when approached by a reporter for WPOR's local "Man on the Street" segment, Clive Chumley of Milwaukee, Wisconsin, said, "I don't see what all the fuss is about. That Baker lady is out in California. Those Californians will do anything. I'll be glad when this sideshow folds up its tent."

Clive Chumley was about to get his wish. The Baker case was coming to an end. Secretly tickled to have so many reporters in his courtroom, Judge Hanley glowered down at Baker, commanding, "Will the defendant please rise."

She stood. The judge went on, "You have pled guilty to one count of fraud, a very serious charge. Before I sentence you, do you have anything to say?"

Smiling, she answered, "Your Honor, I always have something to say . . ."

TWO YEARS EARLIER . . .

In middle school, Annie Baker's favorite book had been Lord of the Flies. *A geeky, shy outsider, Annie had no trouble believing children could turn on each other with such savagery. She couldn't wait to reach the civilized promised land of adulthood. And for a while, adulthood* was *a paradise, but then she moved to Southern California.*

1

Annie Baker & the La Jolla Ladies' Book Club

The book club women had to sniff Annie Baker before they would let her join in their reindeer games. Annie doubted she'd pass inspection. Everything and everyone in Dawn's fabulous living room was white and looked terribly expensive. Two low-slung white couches and a matching armchair flanked an ultramodern glass coffee table, and plush white carpeting covered the floor. Soft recessed lighting bathed the room, and a white abstract marble statue stood sentry in the corner. Lounging on the couches, the five book club regulars exuded relaxed glamour with their casual, chic outfits, careful makeup, and toned figures. The club's self-appointed gatekeeper—a haughty blonde named Valerie—asked, "So you and Dawn met at Pilates, is that right?"

Annie shook her head and laughed. "No, no Pilates for me. I'm a couch potato. These days, they play sexy music when I put my clothes *on.*" The book club women exchanged horrified glances. To this hyper-aerobicized, kale-munching crowd, Annie's spare tire was about as funny as cancer or female genital mutilation. Annie flashed a meek smile at Dawn, a telepathic "you got me into this so please help me." Dawn had invited Annie, for Chrissake! But Dawn was busy refilling her wineglass. Half an hour into the evening, and Dawn was already tipsy. If Annie wanted to finally make some friends in this town, she would have to make them on her own. Annie said, "I met Dawn down at the rec center. We bonded while pushing our girls on the swings."

Valerie cut to the chase. "So do you live here in La Jolla, Annie?" San Diego had a strict caste system based on real estate with picturesque, millionaire-infested La Jolla at its apex.

Annie said, "No. We're in Carmel Valley."

Valerie simpered, "Oh, how nice for you." A smile surfaced on the lower part of her face, but it did not reach her eyes. Annie guessed that Carmel Valley was too down-market to rate much enthusiasm from Valerie. Or maybe she couldn't move the muscles around her eyes. Too much Botox. Valerie had had *a lot* of work done. Somewhere in her fifties, she was the oldest woman in the room by a decade or so.

Coming late to Annie's rescue, Dawn chimed in, "Carmel Valley has the best public schools in San Diego." Dawn could throw this bone to Annie without being disloyal to the La Jolla home team. Everyone who mattered in La Jolla sent their kids to private school anyway. Dawn went on, "Education's very important to Annie. She went to Harvard." The other women nodded. Yes, they had heard of Harvard. But Annie sensed it did not have much traction with them. With a sloppy grin—how much wine had she had?—Dawn continued, "Annie's a real brainiac. She's got a doctorate."

Crystal, a voluptuous brunette with large blue eyes, asked Annie, "You're a doctor?"

Annie answered, "Not a medical doctor. My PhD is in chemistry. I'm a chemist."

Crystal brightened. "Oh, so you work at a drugstore?"

Annie did a double take. Was Crystal joking? Did she really not know the difference between a pharmacist and a chemist? The sincere, expectant look on Crystal's face gave Annie her answer. Survey said: idiot. Annie explained, "Um, no. I don't have a background in pharmacology. I'm a research chemist."

Crystal nodded. "Oh . . ." She didn't have a follow-up question. To be fair, most people didn't. Even back in Annie's hometown, nerd-packed Boston—God, how she missed it!—Annie had found that nothing could kill a conversation as quickly as announcing that she was a chemist. It was social napalm.

Clearing her throat, Dawn moved things along, saying, "Well, now that Annie has arrived, the gang's all here. Priscilla can't make it. She's off at the spa again."

Valerie smirked, asking, "What's she having done this time?"

Dawn shrugged. "Another chemical peel."

Valerie asked, "How many chemical peels can a person have? If you keep stripping away, don't you hit bedrock at some point?"

Crystal piped up, "I tried a chemical peel once." An awkward silence followed this. From the women's faces, Annie could tell that Crystal was not popular with this crowd. Crystal was in her midtwenties. Toddlers like her reminded the other women that no matter how much they tried, they would *never* look twenty-five again. These La Jolla women had made heroic efforts to turn back the clock. They kept themselves slim, fit, and impeccably made-up. But their features were hardened and angular. Next to a juicy peach like Crystal, they looked like wax fruit, and they knew it.

The silence stretched out, and Annie felt a twinge of sympathy for Crystal. Again, Dawn plugged up the silence, saying, "I for one am glad our Priscilla takes such good care of herself. She deserves it! She practically runs the Gillespie."

Annie asked, "The Gillespie?"

Valerie explained, "It's a private school here in La Jolla. Priscilla heads the Gillespie Parents Association. She works crazy hours so that—"

"So that the rest of us don't have to," said Dawn. Dawn raised her glass. "Thank God for the Priscillas of the world! They make my half-assed parenting possible."

Annie smiled at Dawn. Groping to make conversation, Annie asked Dawn, "So, I forget, do you work?"

Dawn laughed and shook her head. "Christ, no. Do you?"

Annie nodded. Evidently, Dawn was too pickled to have retained the last five minutes of conversation. "Like I said, I'm a chemist. I've taken two years off, but I plan to go back soon. I—"

"I loved working." It was Kim who said this. Kim was a tall, athletic brunette with ruddy cheeks and a pert nose.

Dawn said, "You were a math teacher, right?"

Kim nodded. "That's right. I taught in National City."

Valerie balked, "National City! That's a tough neighborhood."

Kim smiled. "Yup, most violent neighborhood in San Diego County. Gangs, drugs, you name it. But I had some good kids there. They worked their tails off for me."

Dawn asked in awed tones, "But did you feel safe?"

Kim shrugged. "Yeah, I felt safe most of the time. We're talking middle school, not high school. Besides, National City may be bad, but it's not a war zone."

Valerie wrinkled her nose in disgust. "But why teach there? Why not teach in a *good* neighborhood? La Jolla or Carmel Valley? You don't buy into that teacher-as-savior myth, do you? I mean, I loved *Dangerous Minds,* but—"

Dawn interrupted, "Michelle Pfeiffer looked amazing in that movie."

Valerie ignored this. "Don't get me wrong, I think it's great if you can get these kids to pick up a little algebra, but understanding a few equations can hardly make a dent in their . . ." Valerie trailed off, unable to come up with a politically correct synonym for "shitty lives."

Kim said, "I don't just teach them algebra. I teach them how to listen, how to study . . ."

Dawn drawled, "Well, I think that's great, just great, really inspirational stuff. Makes me want to get out there and write a check to somebody, some do-gooder, math-teaching thing."

Annie asked Kim, "Why did you stop teaching?"

Kim shrugged. "I don't know. The usual suspects: kids, husband, all that. Andrew didn't like the idea of me working in an unsafe neighborhood. Plus, he said the job soaked up too much of my time." Kim's cheeks reddened, and she made a business of studying her nails.

Not wanting to pry, Annie changed the subject. Looking around the circle of women, she asked, "So what did you think of *The Witches' Nightmare*?" Annie'd been up half the night cramming for this little gathering. It was her big chance to finally make some female friends in San Diego. Annie's research lab was a sausage fest, and she hadn't had much luck bonding with moms on the playgrounds.

Dawn wrinkled her nose in an "ain't I cute" move, saying, "I didn't get around to reading the book this month. But then again, I don't really need to read about witches. My mother-in-law lives right next door." The group laughed obediently at this quip.

Annie looked to Kim. No luck there. Kim had read the first fifty pages, but she "just couldn't get into it."

Crystal volunteered, "I read it." She looked expectantly at Annie, as if hoping Annie would toss her a biscuit.

Annie said, "Oh, good. I read it too. I thought it was a bit sentimental, but it made some great points about power dynamics and sisterhood. What did you think?"

Crystal said, "It's the longest book I've ever read. Five hundred pages!" Crystal faltered and looked nervously around the group. Annie nodded encouragement. Crystal continued, "I liked it, but I didn't really *get* some parts of it. There was so much going on. The book was . . . dense, really dense."

Valerie sneered, "You thought *the book* was dense?" Appropriately enough, Crystal didn't seem to catch this insult.

Annie asked, "What about you, Valerie? Did you read the book?"

Valerie took a swig from her wineglass and said, "No, I'm sorry. I couldn't find the time. This month flew by." Annie sensed that Valerie was lying. Valerie had read the book. She just wouldn't stoop to discuss it with Crystal and a commoner from Carmel Valley.

Annie was angry. But more than that, she was disappointed. She had thought she was in for some innocent, geeky fun tonight. A chance to talk about something besides kids, property values, and the rest of the crap San Diegans obsessed about. A chance to *escape* and make some new friends. Annie's social life did not exactly have a deep bench. But these women had let Annie down. The book wasn't the point of this meeting. It was an excuse to get together and talk about the same old crap with booze, better food, and fancier outfits. Leaning back on the couch, Annie listened numbly as the women gossiped about people she did not know and would probably never meet. They talked about what they would wear to the next charity event, the next gallery opening, or whatever else rich people do.

As the evening wore on, Annie said little and raided the food platters laid out on the teak coffee table. Stuffing herself, Annie felt a twinge of guilt as her pants bit deeper into her sides. Short and curvy with big brown eyes, Annie knew she was doomed to spend the rest of her life looking like a colorized, chubby Betty Boop. The other women, each preternaturally thin and fit, only picked at the food—like vampires trying to pass as human. Childishly, Annie consoled herself with the thought that no matter how hard these ladies worked out, they would never be as beautiful as her best friend, Sarah. Ever since they'd met in college, Annie had taken a perverse pride in Sarah's appearance. No one could hurt or intimidate Annie too much lookswise because Annie had already befriended the fairest of them all. It was confidence by proxy, a variant of "my dad can beat up your dad." Strange, but effective.

Annie was not alone in her silence. From what the other women said, Kim was wealthy enough to fit into their illustrious circle, but she seemed distracted and said little. Crystal tried a few more times to join the conversation, but each of her attempts was met with polite disinterest. She was the first to go home. As soon as Crystal exited, Dawn and Valerie started trashing her. *"Did you see that outfit she was wearing?" "That jewelry was hideous!" "And what has she done to her hair?"*

Valerie moved in for the kill. "Was it my imagination or has our Crystal ball put on a little weight?"

Now thoroughly plastered, Dawn slurred, "Sweetie, haven't you heard?"

Valerie leaned forward, grinning. "Heard what?"

Dawn answered, "Crystal's got a bun in the oven."

Valerie's face fell. She said softly, "No, I hadn't heard." Valerie took a swig from her glass. "Excuse me. I need to use the bathroom." She rose and walked quickly from the room.

With Valerie out of earshot, Dawn exhaled loudly, blowing her bangs out of her eyes. "Aw, crap. I thought she knew. Everybody else does."

Annie asked, "Why does Valerie *care* if Crystal has a baby?"

Dawn smirked. "Because Crystal is Walter's girlfriend."

Annie raised an eyebrow. "Okay. So who's Walter?"

"Walter is Valerie's ex-husband." Annie's jaw dropped. Dawn went on, "Valerie and Walter were married for twenty years. Then, four years ago, Walter walked out. Standard midlife crisis. He got a face-lift, bought a new yacht, chased women, the works. Then, last summer, he brought Crystal back to his big new house here in La Jolla, said he'd found the love of his life. We all shrugged it off. We gave the relationship a few weeks, two months tops. Walter didn't marry her, but Crystal hung on. And now—"

Annie murmured, "And now Crystal's pregnant. But what is she doing here?"

Dawn said, "Huh?"

Annie pressed, "What are these two women doing in the same book club? It has to be torture for both of them. I mean . . ."

Dawn sighed. "You're right. It *has* been awful: a real tension convention. We've lost a few members 'cause of it. It's been hell on me. I've really had to scrounge around for new people." Suddenly, Annie knew why she'd been invited—like a seat filler at the Oscars. Dawn went on, "But we couldn't ask Valerie to leave. She's been in this book group forever. She's the one who started it."

Annie persisted, "Okay, but who asked Crystal to join?"

Dawn said, "I did. I *had* to. My mother-in-law—Her Highness Regina—has been friends with Walter forever. They came over on the *Mayflower* together or something. Walter went to Regina and whined about how Crystal's still an outsider, how none of the women in the neighborhood have really welcomed her. Blah, blah, blah. So Regina said she'd have me ask her to book club."

Annie was incredulous. "What?" She couldn't decide who was worse, Walter or Regina. Or Dawn for going along with this whole thing. Painfully shy, Annie had always had trouble making friends. But once Annie was in, she was *all* in. Annie didn't half-ass friendship, she used her whole ass. She pressed Dawn, "But what about Valerie?"

Dawn shrugged. "Well, we figured she'd quit when Crystal joined. I mean, really, it's the only thing that makes sense. But Valerie didn't leave. She didn't even confront us about it. Val can be an odd bird sometimes."

Valerie's actions did not seem odd to Annie. Why should Valerie make room for her ex-husband's trophy girlfriend? Screw that! Annie toyed with the idea of attending the next meeting in a "Team Valerie" T-shirt, but she suspected that Valerie did not want her solidarity.

Besides, Annie wasn't coming to the next meeting anyway. Friendwise, the evening had been a complete bust. Annie guessed she would never see any of these women again.

She guessed wrong.

As an only child growing up in New Jersey, Sarah Sloane had loved the Little House on the Prairie series. She had imagined someday presiding over a bustling household overflowing with happy children who babbled about gingham, calico, and boiled sweets.

2

Sarah's Baby Lust

After a year of fertility treatment, Sarah Sloane thought of her womb as her personal Dust Bowl—a desert with tumbleweeds rolling across it. Only a tough embryo could take root in such a wasteland. Still, Sarah had to try. Today was all about trying. She lay beached atop an exam table on a thin sheet of white paper. Her bottom was propped up on a pillow, and her feet were hooked into stirrups. Her flimsy blue hospital gown flapped back at the waist to bare her rump to the room's cold air. She stared up at the ceiling and tried to look unruffled while the nurse dabbed lubricant onto the folds of her labia.

The nurse was a plump middle-aged blonde named Carly. When Carly finished, she stepped back and announced in her thick Midwestern accent, "Okeydokey, you are ready for takeoff." Carly peeled off her white latex gloves and dropped them into a bright orange biohazard container. Turning, she asked, "First time trying IVF?"

Sarah grinned weakly, saying, "No. It's my second."

Carly smiled, revealing a smudge of pink lipstick on her front teeth. "Well, good for you for getting in here so young. Usually, women wait until their late thirties or forties to come in and get help. And it just breaks your heart. There's only so much we can do for them, ya know? You're what, thirty-one, thirty-two?"

Sarah answered, "I'm forty-two."

Carly's cheeks reddened. "Forty-two?"

Sarah nodded. "Forty-two."

Still blushing, Carly recovered quickly. "What can I say? You totally fooled me! Forty-two years old, and you don't have a single wrinkle."

Sarah gave the obligatory "aw shucks," saying, "Of course I have wrinkles. Look at these crow's-feet."

"You call those crow's-feet? Those aren't even crow's toes. I pegged you at thirty, thirty-three tops."

Sarah repressed a smirk. She guessed if she had one flaw, it was vanity. Another flaw was thinking that she just had one flaw. But she really did look "thirty-three tops." Everyone said so, and her mirror confirmed it. Any thirty-year-old would envy her figure. She was tall and thin with a few very well-placed curves. Her thick red hair fell to her shoulders in shiny waves. Her high broad cheekbones, full mouth, and warm brown eyes made her more than pretty. They made her beautiful. But what made Sarah more than beautiful, what made her look *young*, was her skin. Forty-two years hadn't left a single mark on her face. No droopage either. Too bad her eggs hadn't held up as well as her skin.

Carly asked, "Honey, what's your secret? Botox?" This was a casual question in Los Angeles. *Everybody* in the City of Angels injected *something* into their faces.

Sarah shrugged, saying, "No, no Botox. Just lucky, I guess."

"I should say so. Okay, Ivory Girl, I have to leave you for a few minutes. I'll be back soon with the doc, and we'll get this party started."

Carly left the room, and Sarah missed her immediately. She took a deep breath, let it out, and began to feel bad again.

Forty-two years old! One of the worst things about fertility treatment was that—in cruel hindsight—it made most of Sarah's adult life seem like a colossal waste of time. She didn't regret the four years of college, the three years of law school, or even the three clerkships. Being a high-powered lawyer required a high-powered résumé. But there was so much time wasted *before* law school, like the four years in the Peace Corps. Confident that time's passage would never affect twentysomething her, she'd reenlisted. Sure, the karma brownie points were nice, but four years? Four peak fertility years squandered teaching villagers about drought-resistant plants only to have the government build a huge irrigation system that practically flooded the place! Even worse was the great failed actress experiment. Three years blown on acting classes, waitressing, and endless auditions—culminating in Sarah's film debut as Panicky Villager #3 in *Frankenstein's Son: The Reckoning.*

So, yes, Sarah felt bad as she lay on the exam table. And then she felt bad about feeling bad. The fertility websites said that it was vital to keep a positive attitude. So happy thoughts, happy thoughts.

Happy thoughts had come easily when Sarah had first started trying to have a baby. Back then, months after she and Michael had gotten married (she'd had to kiss a lot of frogs before finding her prince, but Michael was worth it), Sarah was only thirty-seven. She'd known plenty of women who got pregnant after thirty-five. So why not her? She bought a few negligees, counted days from her period, and then lunged at a very happy Michael around ovulation time.

After a few years of increasingly desperate trying, Sarah had stepped through the looking glass into the world of medical treatment. Dr. Alpert tested Michael first and made sure he wasn't shooting blanks. Then the good doctor—Sarah's personal Mad Hatter—began plying her with powerful drugs. But Dr. Alpert's drugs were nothing like the tasty, colorful concoctions Alice took in Wonderland. Fertility drugs were no fun at all: large white suppositories jammed up inside Sarah's vagina or vials of fluid to be mixed and injected daily into her bruised thighs.

The drugs made Sarah as moody as a toddler on meth. One of her banner moments had come on a recent ovulation day. Around bedtime, she had approached Michael in a bulky T-shirt and sweatpants, saying, "Hon, it's go time." She took his hand and shuffled toward the bedroom. When they got there, Sarah pulled off her sweatpants and crawled under the covers.

Michael said playfully, "Hey, how come I don't get a show?" "Show" was Michael-speak for Sarah's lingerie fests.

Sarah recognized this comment for what it was, a demand dressed up as a joke. She said darkly, "I'm not in the mood for a show."

"Well, the show helps *me* get in the mood. I mean, I can't just order my sailor to salute. I have to . . ."

Sarah glared at him. "You have to *what*?"

Michael's eyebrows shot up. "Excuse me?"

"What exactly do *you* have to do?"

"I'm not sure I follow . . ."

Sarah went on. "What do you have to do? Do you have to pee on ovulation sticks every day? No. Do you have to take your temperature constantly? No. Do you have to get your period each month to remind you of how spectacularly you are failing? No! You don't have to do any of that! All you have to do is whip out your dick a few times a month and stick it in me. That's it!" Sarah's volume grew, like an approaching siren, as she spoke.

Michael shook his head. "No, no. I am not doing this. I can't be with you when you're like this."

"Like what?"

"Like a psych patient! Like some female version of *Cuckoo's Nest*!"

Sarah rolled her eyes. "They made that. It's called *Girl, Interrupted*."

"Thank you, Roger Ebert. Nothing makes me hornier than being corrected by my angry, batshit wife!"

Michael turned and walked out to the foyer with Sarah on his heels. She hovered over him while he put on his sneakers. Her anger morphed into panic. "What are you doing?"

"What does it look like? I'm going for a walk. I am not doing this tonight."

"What do you mean you're not doing this? Tonight is the night. It's go time."

"Yes, it *is* go time. It's time for me to *go*."

Changing tacks, something Sarah could do with dizzying speed, she tried to sound contrite. "Honey, I'm sorry. I was completely out of hand. Let's go back to bed. Okay?"

Michael shut his eyes for a moment, took a deep breath and let it out. Then, slowly and deliberately, as if giving instructions on how to diffuse a bomb, he said, "Look, I know you want to do this tonight. But I can't, not when you're like this."

"So you want to throw away an entire month because of one hissy fit. Is that it?"

"Sarah, there will be other months, other chances . . ."

"How do *you* know that? For all you know, this could be the last month I have!"

Now it was Michael's turn to roll his eyes. "You're not dying, Sarah."

"No, I'm not dying. But my eggs are! They're forty-two years old, Michael. Forty-two! They were around when eight-track tapes were popular, when lava lamps were considered groovy. They do not have much time left. They can't afford to wait while you sulk."

Michael shot back. "If it's so important that we do this thing tonight, maybe you shouldn't have treated yourself to another one of your tantrums!"

"Well, Professor, I'm sorry we can't all have your perfect composure. But it's hard to remember to curtsy when I'm pumped up with more hormones than a beef steer!"

Michael threw up his hands. "Wonderful! You get to say whatever you want because you're on meds."

Sarah countered, "Fine, blame me for us losing this month. But let's not forget all the months we've lost because of you!"

"What's that supposed to mean?"

"You're *never* here! Last month it was China. The month before that, Peru. Sorry for being testy, but it's hard to reproduce when my husband is off digging up bones in Where's-Waldo-Stan every time I ovulate!"

"Sarah, that's my work. When they call me in on a find, I have to—"

"Right, you're a big, important paleontologist. You *have* to go. God forbid a fossil that's been underground for a gazillion years should have to wait one minute longer! When they find my dried-up eggs in a riverbed a million years from now, maybe then I'll finally have your attention!"

Michael groped for a reply, but Sarah was too fast for him. She always lapped him when they got into a fight. Coloring, he stormed out the door.

Sarah fumed for a few minutes and then started bawling. She tried to calm down, but her thoughts were all over the place. Michael was a monster for leaving on ovulation day. No, wait, Michael was a saint for putting up with any of this. After all, he wasn't the defective one. He had nothing but strong swimmers. Dr. Alpert said so. Goddamn Dr. Alpert. All those tests, all that money . . . and he still could not figure out why any of this was happening. Just "unexplained infertility." "It happens." Shit happens. Shit, shit, shit.

The doctor might not say it was Sarah's fault. Michael might not say it. But still, it *was* her fault. It had to be. Michael dumped his perfect sperm into her body. That's all a man has to do, all he can do. It's up to the woman's body to use the sperm, to make it last longer than it would have if it had splashed down on a Kleenex.

What if Sarah's body continued to fail? What then? She and Michael didn't want to adopt. She felt sort of guilty about it, but she was a secret yet avid fan of her own DNA. And Michael was so handsome and brilliant—not to mention funny, giving, and sexy as hell. Who wouldn't want a photocopy? She thought about getting a surrogate, but renting a womb felt wrong somehow, exploitative. She had a vague but strong sense that some things shouldn't be outsourced.

But what would a childless marriage be like? She'd read plenty of articles about how great it was to be childless: more freedom, more money to play with, and—oh yes—a smaller carbon footprint. But how would she and Michael fill the void? By continuing to work insane hours? By traveling the world and pretending that childlessness had been their choice? Or would they play the substitution game, raising puppies or kittens? Sarah couldn't picture it. And how could Michael forgive her for putting him through that? And how could Sarah *ask* him to do that for her? How could she impose on him like that? Sarah hated to impose on anyone. No, the noble thing would be to drive him away, free him to go find another wife, one who wasn't defective. Was that what she was doing? Driving him away? Maybe so, but it didn't feel noble. It felt awful.

Fortunately, this time, Sarah only drove Michael away for an hour or so. He came back to her with a single rose in his hand. Michael always brought Sarah flowers after a fight. He needed things to be all right. He needed *her* to be all right. Sarah started to say that she was sorry, but he put a finger to her lips to silence her. They both started laughing. They always laughed when Michael made this gesture. It was ridiculously stagey. Then they went to the bedroom and tried to make a baby. As Michael moved inside her, tears ran down Sarah's cheeks. Michael gently wiped them away.

Now, weeks later, lying on Dr. Alpert's table, Sarah cringed as she replayed this little fight in her head. She was grateful when her phone chirped. It was a text from Annie. *Good luck on baby day! Think fertile thoughts. XOXO.* Sarah smiled. Annie followed Sarah's fertility quest closely. She was Sarah's most devoted fan, cheering from the stands even when the weather was terrible.

Sarah was about to respond, but her phone rang, playing the ominous daa-dum theme from *Jaws*, the ringtone for Sarah's boss, Marty Goldstein. Sarah answered, "Hello, Marty."

"Hello back, Mrs. Sloane!" Marty bellowed this—he bellowed most things—in his thick New York accent.

"What do you need, Marty?" A bit of New York crept into Sarah's voice as she asked this. She tended to mirror people.

"Why do you always assume I need something from you? Did it ever occur to you that I might just want to call to see how you're doing?" Marty always had to start every conversation with a joke. And with the client paying him seven hundred dollars an hour, he could afford to dawdle.

Sarah purred, "Oh, that's so sweet of you. Usually, we only get to chat at our knitting circle."

Marty laughed. "Knitting circle, I like it. I'm gonna use that one. So where the hell are you anyway? I saw your office was empty."

Marty did not know about Sarah's fertility treatments. No one at her law firm knew. If they did, she would be marked as a mommy in waiting and dumped into professional limbo. Fortunately, Sarah could lie fluently. "At the dentist. I should be back at the office in an hour or so."

"When you're done getting your chompers inspected, I need you to go back through the Harris e-mails." Harris was a defense contractor whom the government had accused of bribing a congressman. Harris was probably guilty. Marty's clients usually were.

Sarah asked the million-dollar question: "How soon do you need me to get to this?"

Marty sighed, "Well, I don't want you to pull an all-nighter, but I have a conference call set for noon tomorrow with Harris and his lawyer. I need to know what's out there."

Sarah's mind flashed to the three CDs of e-mails on her desk. She and Marty both knew there was no way she could read through them without pulling an all-nighter. Still, Marty liked to like himself. He thought of himself as a warm, reasonable boss, not as the slave driver he really was. Marty rewarded associates who played along with his fantasy. So Sarah played along. "No problem. I'll shoot you an e-mail on it tomorrow morning, okay?"

"That's my girl." Marty hung up, satisfied.

Sarah switched off her phone, and Nurse Carly reentered the room, this time with Dr. Alpert. Alpert immediately got down to business, injecting the embryos into Sarah's womb. He told Sarah to lie on the table for another half hour. After that, she should go home and stay in bed for the rest of the day. She should keep her hips propped up on a pillow and relax. Sarah nodded.

An hour later, she was back at her desk.

When eleven-year-old Sarah read Are You There, God? It's Me, Margaret, *she loved it whenever the preternaturally reserved Margaret let down her guard and prayed, confiding in God and begging him to make her "grow." Sarah herself didn't pray. She wasn't sure whether God existed, let alone whether he'd listen to her. Luckily, later in life, Sarah found a friend who would always listen and talk back.*

3

Phone Call

Two weeks later, Sarah got her period. Her first call was to Michael; her second was to Annie. Annie and Sarah had been best friends for more than twenty years. They'd met on their first day at Harvard, when the university threw them together in a dorm room in Hollis Hall, and they had clung to each other ever since. They made an unlikely pair. Annie was a short science nerd with strong opinions, weak social skills, and a quick sense of humor. Sarah was a tall, gorgeous redhead with impeccable manners and an almost pathological need to please people.

Their friendship worked because they complemented each other. Sarah became Annie's stylist and social coach. She taught Annie how to approach people and make small talk so that Annie could survive Harvard's pompous soirées. More important, Sarah taught Annie the value of etiquette. Annie's bohemian parents had raised her to believe that most manners were empty formalities, ways of showing off. Sarah—the product of two proper British expat parents—made Annie realize that little shows of respect and gratitude mattered, even if they were scripted.

Annie helped Sarah too. She became Sarah's anchor. Sarah was terribly indecisive. She did not know what *she* wanted, so she tried to give other people what *they* wanted. And because Sarah was smart and beautiful, plenty of people wanted things from her. Sarah attracted lots of men, and not always good ones. Whenever these suitors turned out to be shits, Annie let Sarah know. Annie was a highly effective cock block.

Mutual dependency brought the two women together, and books cemented their bond. Taking many of the same classes, Annie and Sarah grew up together—intellectually speaking. Every book was a revelation to their suggestible young minds. They both sulked through their work-study jobs after Marx told them they were "estranged from their labor." Then they acted like entitled assholes for a week after Ayn Rand told them to be selfish. Later, Charles Dickens's starving children and miserly industrial overlords made them repent.

After college, when geography and jobs kept them apart, the friends relied on the phone to keep their friendship alive. Now, when Sarah called to say that IVF had failed her again, Annie consoled her for a few minutes and then got down to business. "Did you cut out gluten this time?"

"Yes."

Annie persisted, "What about wheat and alcohol?"

Sarah asked, "What is this—a checklist?"

"Of course. I'm a chemist, Sare. Protocols are my life. What about caffeine?"

Sarah said proudly, "No caffeine. I went an entire month without Diet Coke. Do you know how hard that was for me?"

Sincerely impressed, Annie said, "Yeah. You practically live on that stuff. Crap. What are we missing? Do you want to try acupuncture again?"

"No thanks," said Sarah, but she smiled. She was grateful to Annie for taking ownership of the situation, for tinkering with it. None of

Sarah's other friends reacted that way. They didn't know what to say when confronted with news of Sarah's infertility. They had no script, so they floundered. They made sympathetic noises and then avoided the subject. Sarah knew that she should not have resented this. Her friends were trying to give her space. But Sarah did not *want* space. Between her empty womb and her unfinished nursery, Sarah had too much space already.

Fortunately, Annie was never passive when it came to Sarah. No matter what problem Sarah had, Annie always rolled up her sleeves and barged in with all the advice, comfort, and intellectual muscle she could. Annie read all of Sarah's fertility books. She used her connections to scout doctors. She even offered to be a gestational surrogate. Sarah had turned her down, saying she could not expect Annie to do that to her body. Laughing, Annie had reassured her that her body had seen better days ("It's not like you're defacing a Renoir"). To Annie, Sarah's problem had a solution; Annie just had to figure it out. So she charged ahead. "Is there anything you *haven't* tried yet?"

"Rain dances."

Annie laughed. "How about human sacrifice? We could use your boss."

Sarah groaned, "Oh, c'mon, Marty's not so bad."

Annie huffed, "That guy makes Voldemort look like a pussycat."

Sarah knew where this was going. "Okay, whatever, let's move on."

But Annie would not be deterred. "I'll tell you what you haven't tried yet. You haven't tried switching jobs. You work one-hundred-hour weeks. All that stress has to wreak havoc on your system."

Sarah sighed. They both knew that stress could be part of the problem. But what was Sarah supposed to do? Quit her job for a baby that might not even come? Sarah didn't know if she could cope with being jobless *and* childless. She said, "Look, I know I've been working long hours for the past few months, but once I finish this brief, things will settle down. I think—"

Annie broke in, "Not this again. You always tell me how things will settle down after the next brief, the next case. But nothing changes. Your hours are insane. I've seen galley slaves with cushier setups."

"Don't worry. I can handle it. I—"

"That's just it. You probably *can* handle it. You're the hardest-working person I know, and you hate to complain. But your stoicism is backfiring, Sare. Marty drives you as hard as he wants because you never complain. It's like you're stuck in an S&M game without a safe word."

Mentally folding her arms against her chest, Sarah said, "Annie, please drop it. I'm not going to quit my job, not in the middle of a recession."

The word *recession* cowed Annie. "I'm sorry. I shouldn't badger you, especially not today."

Sarah felt a tear slide down her cheek. Wiping it away, she asked, "So how about you? How're you doing? How was the book club?"

Annie sighed. "Awful. The grand ladies of La Jolla didn't like me much."

Sarah winced. She knew how hard it was for Annie to put herself out there, how easily bruised she could be. Trying to sound breezy, Sarah said, "Aw, screw 'em. You're wonderful." Sarah moved on. "How's Harry? How're my godbabies?"

"Harry's fine. I asked him to reorganize the garage, so he's happy." Annie's husband, Harry, had obsessive-compulsive disorder. He was fine so long as Annie kept feeding him home projects. Annie went on, "Oscar's having some issues, but it's nothing we can't handle."

Sarah's antennae went up. "What do you mean?"

"Oscar's teacher said he had some behavioral problems. She had the school therapist take a look at him. No big deal."

"What did the therapist say?"

"I don't know. I'm going to meet with her tomorrow to find out. I'm not worried. I'm sure it's nothing."

Annie had been skeptical about therapy since reading One Flew Over the Cuckoo's Nest. *Nurse Ratched's icy professional tyranny became Exhibit A against this "healing" profession. Annie found Exhibit B years later when she read Augusten Burroughs's memoir,* Running with Scissors, *which described how an eccentric shrink used little boy Augusten as a guinea pig. Exhibit C popped up at Oscar's preschool.*

4

The News About Oscar

The next morning, Annie strolled into an ambush. She knew she was in trouble as soon as she entered the preschool's conference room. Instead of the lone therapist she had expected, Annie found four women lying in wait for her: the preschool director, Oscar's teacher, and two strangers. The women had squeezed themselves around a small wooden folding table. Annie murmured apologies for being late and sank onto the room's only empty chair.

The director of the preschool, Tami, got things rolling. Tami was a thin, prim brunette in her late fifties. Annie had secretly dubbed her "Tami Three Times" because of her habit of saying the same thing three times over, just with different words. Tami started the meeting by assuring Annie that Oscar was "a wonderful child, a treasure, a joy." Tami went on, "Of course, you *know* Kira." Kira was Oscar's teacher. She was a middle-aged Russian expat with red hair and lively green eyes. Annie adored Kira. Annie's oldest, Maddie, had also been in Kira's class, and

Annie planned to make sure baby Rachel got her turn with Kira someday. It had been Kira's idea to have a therapist take a look at Oscar. In her thick Russian accent, Kira had assured Annie it would be "no beeg deal." Now Kira flashed Annie a tight smile.

Next Tami introduced the school's "therapeutic team." She gestured first to the blonde on her right, saying, "This is Melanie. She's our OT." Melanie looked like one of those fresh-scrubbed teenagers you find working at Foot Locker. She wore khaki pants, a blue T-shirt, and white sneakers, and her hair was pulled up into a ponytail.

Annie asked, "OT?"

Melanie said, "OT stands for occupational therapist." She had a high-pitched, breathy voice. One octave higher, and she could be Elmo's cousin.

"You mean like a job counselor?"

Melanie shook her head. Her ponytail swayed. "No. I don't work with adults. I work with children, mostly on sensory processing issues."

This meant nothing to Annie, but she let it go. Tami gestured to the woman to her left, saying, "And this is Gwen. She's a therapist, a counselor, a resource for us." Gwen smiled serenely. Dressed like an ex-hippie in a billowy purple tunic, Gwen had bushy gray hair that fell past her shoulders.

Tami said, "Why don't we begin with Melanie's assessment and then we'll move on to Gwen? Okay? Okay."

Melanie opened a spiral notebook. "I worked with Oscar for about half an hour and then I watched him on the playground with the other kids. I think he may have SPD."

Annie asked, "What's SPD?"

"SPD stands for sensory processing disorder."

Annie pressed, "Okay, I've got the name, but what is it?"

Melanie said, "Sensory processing disorder? Well, it's a disorder involving . . . sensory processing." Annie blinked in confusion. Melanie added, "SPD shows up in lots of different ways. Some children have tactile problems. They hate to be touched. Other children can't handle noises. Then there are kids with movement problems. They fall a lot, rock themselves for comfort, things like that."

Skeptical, Annie asked, "So what makes you think Oscar's got this disorder?"

Melanie glanced down at her notes. "Well, Oscar seemed very uncomfortable with noise. When some blocks clattered to the floor, he put his hands over his ears. That's classic auditory defensiveness. And Kira tells me he has trouble sitting still during circle time."

Annie asked, "Is that it?"

"Oh no, there's more!" Melanie said happily (clinical work is exciting!). "Oscar's fine motor skills are not where they should be. He can't hold a crayon properly. And his gross motor skills are not very good either. I watched him on the playground for a while, and he fell a lot."

Annie felt the blood rising to her face. "Is *that* it?"

Melanie shook her head. Again, the blond ponytail swayed. "There was one more thing. I noticed he moved a lot better when Kira put music on. The music really seemed to help him somehow." Melanie squinted as she said this, as if responding to music was inherently suspicious.

Annie felt her temper straining at its leash. Speaking louder than she'd intended to, Annie said, "Let me get this straight. Oscar doesn't like loud noise. And he's clumsy, and he fidgets during circle time. That means he has a disorder?"

"Um, yes." Melanie's smile faltered. Annie's intensity unnerved her. This was San Diego. Intensity was for workouts, not conversation. Melanie went on, "Kira also mentioned something about Oscar being grumpy a lot. That's a red flag for us. Many children with SPD have problems with depression."

Annie answered, "So now Oscar has depression because he's grumpy sometimes? What is this? Is every negative trait a pathology?"

Melanie started, "No, of course not," then pulled her neck in and hunched her shoulders slightly, like a turtle retreating into its shell.

Tami rescued her, saying, "Annie, I know it's hard to hear all of this. But we're telling you what we see. We want to make sure you have all the information you need . . . for Oscar's sake. Maybe we should move on to Gwen."

Geriatric hippie Gwen fingered the wooden beads around her neck and began, "I did not have time to do a full evaluation, but I spent about an hour with Oscar one-on-one. He's definitely on the spectrum."

Annie asked, "On what spectrum?" *Great, now there was a spectrum!*

Gwen explained, "The spectrum is a group of developmental disorders. At one end of the spectrum, you've got typical children. At the other end, you've got Asperger's and autism."

Annie reeled. "Autism?"

Gwen nodded, smiling placidly. "That's right." Gwen's serenity was galling. She looked as if she had just handed Annie a steaming mug of hot cocoa instead of terrible news.

Annie flailed, "But autism . . . I mean, the spectrum. What is . . . I mean . . ."

Gwen said cheerfully, "He's a *high-functioning* autistic, if that helps."

Annie sputtered, "That doesn't help. I mean, what . . ." Annie's throat ran dry. She could have downed a bucket of water. "I mean, what are you basing this on?"

Reading from her notes, Gwen began counting symptoms off her fingers. "One, he avoids eye contact. Two, he can't carry on a normal conversation. He doesn't listen. He just spouts non sequiturs. Three, he has articulation problems: music is 'oosic,' that sort of thing."

Annie felt panic bloom inside her. She'd noticed all this, of course. How could she not notice? Oscar was nothing like his wickedly articulate big sister, Maddie. Annie had even asked Doc Green—her chummy aged pediatrician—about it. He'd told her Oscar was a late bloomer.

And Annie had believed him, she had needed to believe him. Now, gritting her teeth, Annie asked, "Okay, is there anything else?"

Looking up from her notes, Gwen said, "Yes, I'm afraid so. I watched Oscar for half an hour on the playground. He spent all his time by himself, lining trucks up in rows. He didn't seem to know *how* to play with the other kids. That's odd because most kids his age are starting to form friendships. Kira told me that Oscar doesn't have any friends."

Annie's jaw dropped. She felt as if someone had kicked her in the chest. Annie could handle it if Oscar was quirky. But loneliness was a whole other deal. Loneliness was terrifying. "Well, maybe Oscar prefers to be alone. Some kids are like that."

Gwen shrugged. "That's possible. I'd have to run a full evaluation to figure out what's going on with him. It takes a few sessions to get at the meat of the problem."

Annie did not want Gwen anywhere near Oscar's "meat." She turned to Oscar's teacher, Kira, and asked, "What do *you* think? Are you buying any of this?" Annie knew she was putting Kira on the spot, but she didn't care.

Kira hesitated before speaking. In her thick Russian accent, she answered, "I am not expert like these ladies. I don't have degrees in psychology and things like this. I don't know name for what is happening with Oscar. He is a sweet, sweet boy. He is quiet, and I see him trying so hard to do what is right, what will please me. He is, like you say, a loner. But I don't think this is his choice. The other kids stay away from him. They think he is strange. I see Oscar watching the other kids sometimes. And I can see he wants to play with them. But he doesn't know how to. I think he is sad, very sad boy."

Annie said nothing. What could she possibly say to that?

Sarah had a habit of missing the point. As a teen reading George Orwell's Animal Farm, *she fell in love with the workhorse, Boxer. Boxer slaved in the fields to make the new farm a success, always vowing, "I will work harder." When Boxer broke down and couldn't work anymore, his corrupt animal brethren sent him off to the glue factory. Orwell meant to show how authoritarian masters exploit the masses' labor. But Sarah was too busy admiring Boxer's work ethic.*

5

Sarah Strikes Back

Sarah felt terrible for Annie. She wanted to dash down to San Diego to offer reassurance, hugs, and Häagen-Dazs. She wanted to read every book she could find on autism and sensory disorders so that she could help Annie do battle. After years of relying on Annie's support to get through her own fertility quagmire, Sarah knew that she owed Annie big-time. But for now, the debt would have to wait.

In the weeks since Annie had gotten the news about Oscar, Sarah's boss, Marty, had made Sarah work nonstop. Sarah didn't have time to go down to San Diego. She didn't have time to do anything but work, sleep, and then work some more. Marty had always been demanding, but now he had kicked it up a notch. Sarah didn't know what had caused this sudden uptick. It was as if Pharaoh had brought in management consultants to help maximize the slaves' productivity. She would have complained to Michael about it, but he was gone half the time: last month, China; this month, Nepal.

Sarah had not had a day off in months. Most nights she got out of the office around eleven. Some nights she didn't go home at all. But she did not dare complain. She was stuck. Sarah had been an associate at Burke & Goldstein for seven years. Being a seventh-year associate at a big firm is like being a forty-year-old woman in a long-term relationship. You are poised to win or lose big. It all depends on whether the one you're with decides to commit. If the firm makes you a partner, you're safe. You get the closest thing to tenure that capitalism offers. Things are less rosy behind door number two. Firms go by an "up or out" system: either you move *up* and become a partner or you're *out* of a job. Suddenly, you have to go job hunting. But lots of firms won't hire you because you're damaged goods. The taint of *not* making partner lingers for a long time. Getting a new job can take months, even years. And then you have to prove yourself all over again.

Sarah didn't have the energy to start over. She would stay with Marty, at least until she got pregnant. If Sarah got pregnant, she could deal with not making partner. For her, a baby was not a consolation prize; it was *the* prize. But Sarah wasn't pregnant, so for now she would stay where she was and hope that Marty would ease up on her—an absurd fantasy, like hoping that a crocodile would bite you gently.

On this particular Friday morning, Sarah sat in a conference room, fantasizing about what it would be like to loaf on her couch at home for just a few hours. She'd snuggle with Michael. Michael was back in town for a few days, and . . . Marty broke in. "Hello, is there anybody in there?"

Sarah blinked her eyes wide. "Sorry. I'm sorry. What is it?"

Marty smiled and gestured to his secretary, Doris. Doris stood next to the conference room table with her pen poised above her steno notebook. Marty said, "Lunch. We're ordering from Tommy's. What do you want?"

Sarah managed, "Oh, uh, same as usual. I'll have turkey on wheat with cranberry sauce. And a Diet Coke. Thanks." Doris nodded and scribbled it all down.

Sarah grinned sheepishly across the table at Joe Lipman. Lipman smiled back. Lipman had come to Burke & Goldstein's offices for a beauty contest. Marty was vying against two other law firms for Lipman's business. Marty put his hand on the armrest of Sarah's chair. He explained to Lipman, "You'll have to excuse Mrs. Sloane over here. She was up late last night finishing a brief. This lady works like a machine. I wish I had ten more like her." Sarah smiled modestly. She wondered what was next. Would Marty toss a fish into her mouth? Maybe have her balance a ball on the tip of her nose?

To Sarah, Marty looked egregiously well rested. A stocky man with small eyes and a snub nose, Marty resembled a human pit bull. As always, he was perfectly groomed. Marty spent gobs of money on tailor-made suits, high-end watches, and toupees. He used two dark brown toupees, one that was close-cropped and one that was shaggier. He wore the close-cropped one for the first three weeks of the month and then switched to the shaggier one. This created the illusion of a monthly haircut. Today, Marty sported his shaggier rug. It lent him a boyish charm that he didn't deserve.

Sarah was exhausted. She hadn't had a full night's sleep in weeks. Around eight o'clock the night before, Marty had decided that a summary judgment brief needed, in his words, "a few tweaks." Sarah had given Marty the document a week earlier, but he hadn't bothered to look at it until last night, the night before the court's deadline. Sarah stayed in her office "tweaking" the document until three thirty in the morning so that it would be ready for Marty's signature. Then she drove home and crashed for four hours next to an unconscious Michael. This was her "quality time" with her husband.

She trudged back into the firm at nine in the morning, in time to enjoy a bag of stale peanut M&M'S from the vending machine for breakfast. Two hours later, she grabbed a legal pad and walked over to Marty's office. The Lipman meeting was due to start in ten minutes. Marty leaned forward at his desk and rubbed his hands together. "So, Mrs. Sloane, you think we're ready for this thing?"

Sarah said her line. "Ready as we'll ever be."

"Well, okay, then." Marty stood and started toward the door, but then he stopped. "Oh, I almost forgot. You remember that research you did on the Myerson case?"

Sarah shrugged. "That was four months ago."

Marty smiled. "Well, I've got some good news. I was talking to Sam Edwards, and he said he'd run a piece on it." Sam Edwards was the editor-in-chief of the *California Law Journal.*

Sarah murmured, "That's great." Sarah ghostwrote three or four articles a year for Marty.

Marty went on, "Yes. Terrific, isn't it? Sam said he'll run it in Tuesday's edition. We just have to get it to him by Monday morning."

Sarah snapped awake. "*This* Monday morning?"

"Yes. That's right."

"But I have to—"

Marty cut her off. "What? Your plate should be empty now. The brief is done. That leaves this weekend clear."

Sarah said feebly, "But I was hoping I could take this weekend off. I haven't had a day off since . . ."

Marty nodded sympathetically. "I know. You've been pulling long hours. I hate to ask you to work this weekend. But this piece has to go into the Tuesday edition. Sam said he won't have space for it again for weeks."

Sarah tried another tack. "Okay, but can't we have a junior associate write this thing up?"

Marty bristled, "I can't hand this off to some toddler."

"We could use—"

Marty shook his head and smiled his avuncular smile. "Sarah, I can't put someone else on this. If you draft the article, we can get it done fast. And we can get it done right. If someone else does it, *we'll* both just end up rewriting it. You know that, don't you?" As usual, "we" meant "you." *You'll end up rewriting it, Sarah.*

Sarah exhaled loudly. She was so tired. She felt like she was watching her life on television, and she couldn't change the channel. She decided to do what she dreaded doing: beg. She said, "Marty, I know you want me to work on this thing, but I'm not sure I'll do a good job on it. I'm exhausted. I've been pulling a lot of all-nighters, and . . ." Sarah's voice broke, and she fell silent. She felt tears prick her eyes, and she sniffed hard to fight them back. She did not want to bawl in front of Marty Goldstein. That would be like offering her soft, warm underbelly to a tiger.

Marty put his hand on Sarah's shoulder. "Look, I know you're feeling a bit tapped out. But I wouldn't ask you to do this if you couldn't handle it. Okay?" This was classic Marty. Disguise an imposition as a compliment. Marty moved on, "Now, let's go wow Mr. Lipman."

They greeted Joe Lipman in the lobby, and Marty immediately started chatting him up. Sarah nodded wordlessly as the two men droned on about mutual acquaintances, golf, and how hard it was to find parking. This was not just foreplay before Marty's pitch. Marty's charm was *part* of the pitch itself. He was so darned lovable. What jury could resist him?

Sarah was part of the pitch too. Marty brought her along to represent the sort of people who worked for him, a drop-dead-beautiful associate with the right pedigree: Harvard undergrad and Yale Law. She also saved Marty the indignity of taking notes, should the need arise.

Sarah did her best to feign interest, but her mind had trouble staying tethered to the conversation. She wondered idly how the two men would react if she suddenly climbed onto the conference table, curled into a ball, and took a nap. She pepped up when Doris reentered the conference room with a bag from Tommy's deli. Marty took the bag and dealt out the sandwiches: a Reuben for Lipman, the roast beef special for Marty, and turkey on wheat for Sarah.

Sarah popped open a Diet Coke. Marty unwrapped his sandwich and made a face. "Oh, crap, this has mayo on it. I hate mayo."

Sarah said nothing. She unwrapped her own sandwich. She loved Tommy's turkey sandwiches. They always used just the right amount of cranberry sauce. Marty asked her, "What'd you get?"

"Same as always. Turkey on wheat."

Marty asked, "You wanna trade?"

Sarah shook her head. "No, thanks."

Marty pushed. "Come on. Let's trade. You always get turkey. How about mixing it up a little?"

Sarah wrinkled her nose. "No, thanks."

Marty wouldn't let it go. "Come on. You can handle some roast beef and mayo. You're skinny enough to take it. Not like me. My doc says I should lay off the trans fats."

Sarah did not answer. She stared down at her sandwich. The silence grew awkward. Lipman piped up, "Marty, you can have half of my sandwich. This thing is huge. I'll never finish it."

Marty said, "Thanks, but I don't like Reubens. I'm in the mood for turkey." Marty pushed his sandwich toward Sarah. He smiled and winked. "Come on, Sloane, let's trade."

Marty reached for her sandwich. Sarah warned him, "Don't."

Marty looked up at her. "Excuse me?"

Sarah said through clenched teeth, "Don't touch my sandwich."

Marty's jaw dropped open. He looked like he was trying to catch snowflakes in his mouth. "What?"

Sarah went on, "I said, don't touch my sandwich. This sandwich is mine. Not yours. Got it?"

Marty and Lipman exchanged looks. Marty said, "Sarah, why don't we take a five-minute break? We can—"

Sarah rose to her feet. She was trembling now. "A five-minute break? That would be the longest vacation I've had in months! You work me like a dog! I'm here all the time. Nights, weekends. God forbid I rest for two seconds!"

Marty rose from his chair and touched Sarah's arm. "Sarah, you're upset. Let's just—"

Sarah pulled her arm away. "Just what? What do you want next? Let's see—you've already taken away sleep. My social life is gone. Oh, and my husband hardly ever sees me. And now you want to take away my sandwich too? Well, screw you! I quit! Buy your own goddamned sandwich. Because you're not getting this one. This sandwich is mine. Not yours! Mine!"

Sarah took a huge bite of her sandwich. She glared at Marty as she chewed it and swallowed it. "And it's delicious!"

Sarah turned and strode out of the conference room, her sandwich clutched in her hand.

Annie had always loved Charlotte's Web, *and now she was determined to save Oscar just as Charlotte had saved Wilbur—with a brilliant PR campaign! Annie would sort out Oscar's troubles and make the world see how terrific, how radiant he was. She'd get him whatever therapy he needed and engineer so many playdates that the world would have to admit Oscar was "some boy."*

6

Oscarball

Annie didn't know what to think, and her husband, Harry, wasn't much help. Whenever Annie talked about Oscar's "issues," Harry listened solemnly for a few minutes and then started cleaning or tinkering around the house. Annie babbled about symptoms and treatments while OCD Harry swept floors, dusted shelves, and washed windows. Harry nodded as Annie rambled, and at the end he would always say something vague and useless like "I'm sure it'll work itself out."

Annie knew Harry was worried about Oscar. She knew because Harry started spending more time with his son. He helped Oscar build Lego cars. He rearranged the tracks on Oscar's train table. He read more stories to Oscar at night. No, it wasn't that Harry didn't love Oscar. It was just that Harry didn't know how to deal with mess. He'd come from an uptight home where no one had ever been gauche enough to have psychological or neurological problems. When a Champney man got upset, he would do something constructive: go for a run, clean out the garage, work on his tax return. No mental problems here, ma'am. Just a stiff upper lip to go with clenched teeth.

Without Harry to talk to, Annie turned to her other confidantes. To Sarah. And to her mother, Chloe. Chloe Baker was nothing like Harry. Chloe *loved* delving into personal matters, the more personal the better. Refusing to believe there was anything wrong with her precious grandbaby, Chloe dismissed the school's therapists as quacks. She said the preschool was a factory bent on mass-producing bland, identikit children. Annie tuned out most of Chloe's rant, catching only vague references to George Orwell's *1984*, Shirley Jackson's *The Lottery*, and the Miss Universe pageant.

Despite what Chloe said, Annie's brain kept replaying the horrible preschool meeting. The most disturbing part of it had been when Gwen said Oscar had no friends. Was that really true? No friends at all? Annie asked Oscar about it, and he said he did have friends. When she asked who, Oscar rattled off the names of all the kids in his class. Annie explained, "No, honey. I don't mean classmates. I mean friends. A friend is someone who likes you, someone who plays with you a lot. Do you have anybody like that?"

Oscar was quiet for a moment. Then, he said proudly, "Yes! I have fends. Pete and Josh! I play with them evvy day. We play Oscahball." Oscar had trouble with his *r*'s.

"What's Oscarball?"

"A game. Josh calls it Oscahball 'cause I'm best at it."

Annie smiled at her son. "That's great, sweetie. Just great."

A week later, Annie took Oscar to a birthday party. She left the girls with Harry so that she could focus on Oscar. Annie was dying to see how Oscar interacted with the kids in his class, especially his "fends" Pete and Josh. The party was held at a huge indoor facility called Pump It Up that had four bouncy structures. Kids ran amok while their parents lolled on the benches near the entrance. Parents loved Pump It Up because it gave them an air-conditioned break from their children. No worries about kids getting hurt or escaping. Just happy, contained chaos patrolled by the two or three pimply teenagers who ran the place.

At first, Annie didn't join the other parents on the benches. Instead, she shadowed Oscar, eager to learn all she could. Like a cameraperson for a wildlife program, she tried to be inconspicuous so that her quarry would behave naturally. Annie didn't see anything odd. Oscar trailed behind his two "fends" most of the time. Annie recognized Pete and Josh from their pictures in the school directory. They were good-looking boys, the alpha males of the class. Annie had never seen four-year-olds swagger before, but these two pulled it off. They were bigger and faster than the other boys. And it was obvious that they were close friends. But, to Annie's surprise, they didn't exclude Oscar. They kept inviting him along as they moved from one bouncy to another.

Watching the three boys together made Annie happier than she'd been in weeks. After forty minutes of surveillance work, Annie meandered back to the parents' bench, hoping to arrange some playdates. Since meeting with Tami, Annie had been scolding herself for not doing enough—okay, not doing *anything*—to help Oscar's social life along. Annie had never been big on setting up playdates. Playdates were so tedious. The logistics. The small talk with moms she barely knew. But now things had changed. Playdates were no longer a luxury. Oscar needed all the social practice he could get.

Annie spent a few minutes trying to charm Josh's mom, a beautician with a heavy lisp. She scored a playdate, and then went back out among the bouncys to find Oscar. She found him in a smaller bouncy toward the back of the arena. It took Annie a moment or two to figure out what was going on. Oscar was down on one knee at the center of the bouncy with his right hand over his eyes. Pete and Josh were at opposite ends of the bouncy. Each held two minibasketballs the size of cantaloupes. Josh yelled, "C'mon, Oscar! Let's go again!"

For a millisecond, Annie worried that Oscar was hurt. But then he rose quickly to his feet and yelled, “Okay!” Oscar didn’t look at Pete or Josh as he said this. Instead, he kept his head slightly bent and continued staring at the floor of the bouncy. He folded his arms across his chest and yelled, “Ready!” And Pete and Josh threw their balls at him. One of Pete’s shots missed Oscar entirely. The other struck Oscar’s left leg. But Josh had better aim. He hit the right side of Oscar’s head. The ball made a loud thwack. Oscar crumpled to the floor of the bouncy with his hands clutching his head while his two “fends” laughed. The malice in their laughter was unmistakable.

The laughter stopped when Annie yelled, “No!” She scrambled onto the bouncy and ran over to Oscar. She checked his face to see how badly he was hurt. He had a red mark on his right cheek, the promise of a large, nasty bruise. But Oscar seemed more shaken up than hurt. Tears flowed down his cheeks, and Annie could see that he was working hard not to sob. Annie sat down and hugged him to her chest. She murmured, “It’s okay. It’s okay. Mama’s here.”

Oscar cried in Annie’s arms for a while. Then someone tapped her on the shoulder and asked if Oscar was all right. Annie nodded and looked up to discover that a small crowd had formed around the bouncy. She didn’t see Pete or Josh anywhere. Eventually, Oscar stopped crying. He sniffed and tried to regain his composure. Not meeting Annie’s eyes, Oscar asked, “Game over?”

Annie nodded. Then, realizing Oscar couldn’t hear a nod, she said, “Yes.”

Still not making eye contact with Annie, Oscar asked, “Are they mad at me?”

“What?”

“Are Pete and Josh mad at me?”

Annie gaped. “What? Why would *they* be mad at *you*, honey?”

“’Cause you stopped the game. You not supposed to stop it, Mommy.”

With horror, Annie realized that Oscar didn't get it. He didn't understand what these boys had done to him, what they had probably *been doing* to him for weeks, maybe months. Oscar still thought Pete and Josh were his friends. He didn't see the cruelty in their faces. He didn't hear the contempt in their voices. All Oscar knew was that these boys wanted to play with him and somehow he had let them down. He had disappointed them by getting hurt, by not being strong enough to stay in the game.

Annie clutched Oscar to her chest and murmured, "No, honey. No one's mad at you."

When Annie read World War Z, *she never deluded herself that she'd survive a zombie apocalypse. If zombie hordes ever came, Annie had no doubt that she would freak out and do something phenomenally stupid. Though otherwise a nonconformist, Annie was highly susceptible to group panic. If a crowd ran by with pitchforks screaming that a monster was coming, she would bolt—as soon as she loaded her kids into the car.*

7

Sticker Shock

The doctors couldn't agree on what was wrong with Oscar. The first psychologist said autism. The second said Asperger's syndrome. And the third voted for pervasive developmental disorder. The only thing everyone agreed on was that Annie had to act fast. Oscar had a narrow window of opportunity. His problems were neurological, and he had just a few more years of neurological plasticity left. So get moving, now!

Treatment turned out to be expensive, terribly expensive. And insurance offered just a fig leaf of coverage. Annie and her husband would have to pay for the rest themselves: $7,000 a month. That was $84,000 a year.

Annie put these figures together for the first time during one of Rachel's afternoon naps. The shock of it—$84,000 a year!—made her reach for her telephone. She called Harry at work, and he gasped. Harry made a solid salary as an engineer, but he wasn't due for an $84,000 raise anytime soon. He got off the phone quickly, eager to call the bank and see whether they'd reverse-mortgage the house. Annie's next call was to her mother. Chloe bristled, "Eighty-four thousand dollars! That's highway robbery! Are you sure you can trust these doctors? They sound like charlatans to me."

"The doctors aren't cheating me, Mom. I think they want to load on the therapy while it will still do some good. Oscar's window is so narrow."

"My dear Annabelle, has it ever occurred to you that these doctors might have made up this 'window' nonsense to swindle you? It's a classic high-pressure sales situation."

Annie sighed. "Mom, let's not get into this again. I don't have the energy for your paranoia right now."

Chloe huffed, "Paranoia is vastly underrated."

Annie pleaded, "Mom, can we please get off this?"

"Oh, all right. I know you *think* all this treatment is necessary. I won't bother fighting it."

"Thank you."

"But still, eighty-four thousand? It can't be that much."

Annie assured her mother that it *could* be that much. She rattled off each of the treatments and their costs: $16,000 for speech therapy, $8,000 for floor-time training, $6,000 for facilitated group therapy, $40,000 for a certified aide, $14,000 for behavioral therapy. Yes, $84,000. Annie could tell that Chloe was only half listening to her as she went through these calculations. Math always shut Chloe Baker down.

When Annie finished reciting her long list, Chloe said, "My dear Annabelle, you are always so thorough." In Chloe-speak, *thorough* meant *tedious*, but Annie let it pass. Chloe said airily, "I suppose you could sell the house to cover it. Couldn't you? That should leave you with a tidy sum. You paid more than a million for it, right?"

Annie sighed, "Yes."

"Good. So you can sell the house, pocket a million dollars, and rent another house somewhere, perhaps in La Jolla. Maybe by the Cove. I love the Cove. It's so beautiful. So romantic. The cliffs there remind me of *Wuthering Heights*, only sunny!"

"Mom, we're not going to make money off the house. The market is terrible. Besides, we only put three hundred thousand down, and we'd be lucky to get *that* back. After costs and taxes, we would have to take a huge loss."

"But, sweetheart, I don't understand. You said the house was a terrific investment." Chloe feigned confusion, but Annie could hear the smirk in her voice. Chloe had lobbied hard against buying the Carmel Valley house. Chloe said that Carmel Valley was soulless. She'd warned Annie that suburbia would turn her into a Stepford wife or maybe even a Republican.

Working hard to sound civil, Annie replied, "Yes, you're right. I did say the house was a smart investment. And I still think it is. But it's a long-term investment. We won't make money off it for years."

"Well, that is a pity. But what about going back to your old job? They said they'd be happy to take you back anytime, right? I thought the plan was to take a year or two off for Rachel, then go back to the lab. Won't your salary cover it?"

Annie took a deep breath and spat out the news she'd been holding back. "I'm not going back to work, Mom."

"What?"

"I'm not going back. Oscar's treatment is going to demand a lot of work. I have to read a gazillion books to figure out which therapies make sense for him. Then, once I pick the therapies, I'll have to schlep him around to a ton of appointments. And I can't drop him off and leave because many of the therapies require parent participation. I will have to sit in on the therapy and then reinforce it at home. Otherwise, the stuff won't sink in. I can't do all that *and* work a full-time job *and* raise two other kids."

Chloe answered, "So, that's it? You're going to throw away your career? Annie, that would be a terrible mistake. You love what you do and you're wonderful at it."

"You don't even know what I do! Your eyes glaze over whenever I mention it."

"All right. I'll admit it. Your work is monumentally dull to me. I've never understood why you chose to become a chemist. It's so technical, so detail-oriented." Chloe sighed, then returned to her point, saying, "Regardless of how *I* feel about your work, we both know that *you* love it. You shouldn't toss it aside. I mean, can't you hire someone to ferry Oscar around to his appointments?"

"Mom, this isn't the kind of thing I can outsource."

"No, you're right. You can't use an average babysitter. But what if you found someone more skilled? Maybe a graduate student in psychology?" Chloe was a big believer in delegation.

"Mom, these therapies can be very stressful. Oscar is not going to want some stranger to take him through it."

Chloe brightened. "Well, what about me? I'm not a stranger. What if I take Oscar to his appointments and watch the girls until you get back from work?"

Annie blustered, "Mom, I couldn't ask you to—"

But Chloe was on a roll. She had a heroic part to play: Grandma as savior. "Nonsense. I would love to do it. It would be the perfect solution. I could come and stay at your place during the week. I'd take Oscar to his appointments, and I'd watch the girls. That way, you'd get to keep your career *and* pay for Oscar's therapy."

This horrified Annie. She loved her mother—*in Arizona*. "Mom, even if I worked full time, I wouldn't earn enough to pay for Oscar's therapy."

"You might not cover the whole amount, but at least you'd be able to make a dent in it. And you wouldn't have to feel guilty because you'd be leaving the children with someone who loves them, their grandma."

Annie flailed. "It's a really generous offer, but I can't let you do that. I mean, this is not a standard babysitting gig. Oscar is going to need a huge amount of attention. The doctors say I'll have to spend hours every day playing with him to reinforce the therapy. That's not going to be an easy slog."

Chloe chuckled. "I think I can handle my own grandson. I have experience with disabled children. I played *The Miracle Worker* eight times a week at the Weehawken Theater. The critic at the *Weehawken Daily Record* said I was the best Anne Sullivan he'd ever seen in a dinner theater production." Chloe was a retired actress with an endless list of obscure credits.

Annie said, "This isn't *The Miracle Worker*, Mom. It's not some dramatic two-hour show. It's tedious, unending hard work." Annie hoped this would chase Chloe away. Usually, offering hard work to Chloe was like holding up a crucifix to a vampire.

Chloe huffed, "I know that. After all, I raised two children of my own. And I was a terrific mother, if I do say so myself." Chloe paused for compliments, but she didn't get them. The truth was that Chloe had been a terrible mother. She had liked the *idea* of being a mother, but she'd had very little interest in the actual work of raising children.

Part of it was sheer laziness. Chloe was about as industrious as a house cat. But for Chloe, the worst things about motherhood were the boredom and lack of recognition. As an actress, Chloe Baker was used to being the center of attention. But mothers were not supposed to receive attention. They were supposed to give it, all the time. Chloe found this reality unpalatable, so she escaped. She ran off for long stretches of time to work in remote regional theaters. And when she was home, she spent her days lolling about the house reading mystery novels, watching television, and drinking wine. She watered and fed her children, but she had no interest in playing with or listening to them. Annie could not remember her mother ever reading her a story or playing a game with her. But she could remember dozens of times she'd found Chloe passed out on the couch next to a coffee mug of white wine.

When Annie didn't rush in with praise, Chloe huffed, "Oh, I know I wasn't a perfect mother. But we can't all be perfect, Annie. I can't be like you. And truth be told, I wouldn't want to be. My dear girl, the truth is that you'll never be a first-class human being or even a first-class woman until you learn to have some regard for human frailty."

Annie was unimpressed. "You stole that from *The Philadelphia Story.*"

"So what if I did? It's still true."

Annie tried to smooth things out. "Mom, I'm not attacking you. I'm saying that taking care of Oscar will be hard work. It's going to require a lot of hands-on, interactive parenting. You have to do more than be physically present. You have to—"

Chloe interrupted, "And is that all I did for you as a mother? Was I just physically present? Like a potted plant?"

A potted plant soaked in alcohol, maybe. But Annie couldn't say that. "Mom, that's not what I mean at all. I have three active young kids. And taking care of them can be physically grueling. You're in amazing shape for seventy-one, but this work is for someone much younger."

Chloe sniffed. "I suppose you have a point. I wanted to help. I wish I was a rich dowager and could just hand you the cash, but I don't have that kind of money."

Annie sighed. "Neither do I."

Annie couldn't relate to Amy Lamb, the lead character in Meg Wolitzer's The Ten-Year Nap. *Amy, a bored housewife—okay, Annie could relate to* that *part—gets a girl crush on a richer, more glamorous mom. Amy makes her hubby take her on a lavish vacation they absolutely cannot afford just so she can tag along with this rich alpha mom. Annie* hated *financial posing. She never understood why someone would brag about paying retail.*

8

Light Bulb

Over the years, Sarah and Annie had waged plenty of battles over money—with Sarah cast as the big spender and Annie as the killjoy miser. There was dinner at the posh French bistro versus the McDonald's value meal; the new couch for their first apartment versus the old one from the Salvation Army store; the trip to France for winter break versus the drive up to Montreal.

Today was no different. It was Sarah's birthday, and she had decided to celebrate by dragging Annie along on one of her shopping sprees. They met at the Saks store off Wilshire Avenue in Beverly Hills' Golden Triangle, the store that had made national headlines years earlier, thanks to Winona Ryder's sticky fingers. Sarah had not seen Annie in two months. Sarah was alarmed by what she saw. Annie looked exhausted, washed out. Her eyes were rimmed with dark circles, and a new pallor had crept into her cheeks. Cosmetic attempts to fix the situation had only made things worse. Unblended concealer and overbright red lipstick made Annie look garish and sloppy. Sarah beamed at Annie and told her she looked wonderful. Annie smiled weakly back.

Then Sarah led Annie through Saks's retail labyrinth. Annie was quiet at first, but by the time they reached the cosmetics department she'd returned to her old chatty self. While Sarah tried on lipsticks, Annie told her about the price tag for Oscar's therapy and her big austerity campaign. Annie had become a fount of depressing economies. She had gotten rid of her weekly date night, pawned her jewelry, and begun making bag lunches for Harry. She hounded her children to eat everything on their plates, turn off the lights whenever they left the room, and use both sides of their drawing paper. Annie's financial crusade reminded Sarah of the rationing programs she had heard about in World War II documentaries, only without the colorful propaganda, big-band music, or anything else that smacked of fun. Sarah sighed. "I wish I hadn't quit my job. I could have helped you out."

Annie asked, "What about you? You okay?"

Sarah winced. "Not so good. Let's just say I've got no business advising *anyone* about money. I can't believe I quit like that. It was financial suicide."

"But what about unemployment? Severance?"

Sarah shook her head. "No, you only get those goody bags if you get fired, not if you storm out in a huff."

"But what about your savings? You must have banked *something*."

Sarah closed her eyes and scrunched up her face. Thinking of her bank account made her look like she'd come across a nasty bit of roadkill. "Not really."

Annie countered, "But you were making a huge salary. The only good thing about that place was the money."

Trying on a bright red lipstick that made her look like a 1940s pinup, Sarah smacked her lips and struck a wistful pose, as if her salary was a lover she missed terribly. "Yes. The money *was* fantastic."

"So why didn't you save any of it?"

Sarah shrugged. "I dunno. For a long time, most of my money went to student loans. Law school put me one hundred and fifty grand in the hole."

Annie pressed, "But what about later, *after* you paid off the loans?"

Sarah tried on another lipstick, a maroon shade that didn't suit her. Smacking her lips together, she said, "I tried to save, but something always came up. I had to help my mom out when my dad died. Next, the wedding and the condo. And then the whole fertility mess."

Annie was dumbstruck. She'd gotten used to thinking of Sarah as well-off, almost rich. Annie blustered, "But even with all that, I still don't see—"

Sarah colored, saying, "I know. Even with all that, I still should have saved up *something*. What can I say? When you're making that kind of money, you don't worry about going broke. Why would you? There's so much money coming in all the time. It'd be like worrying about a drought during monsoon season. Besides, when you're working eighty, one hundred hours a week, spending money is your only release. I'd be at the firm at ten at night, knowing I still had a good three or four hours to put in, and I'd feel sorry for myself. I'd click on the Internet and charge a three-thousand-dollar handbag."

"So you didn't save *anything*?"

Sarah grabbed a tissue and wiped off the maroon lipstick. "No, I saved a little. I figure we should be all right for a few months."

"But what about Michael? He earns a decent salary, doesn't he?"

Sarah smiled ruefully. "Sure, for a college professor."

"Can you get by on that?"

"Yes, we can get by. We can cover all our basic expenses. But nothing beyond that. Nothing *extra*."

"You mean fertility treatment?"

Sarah nodded. "I'm pretty much screwed no matter what I do. If I stay home, I can't afford more treatment. But if I get a job at some firm, I'll be too stressed out for the treatment to work."

Annie shook her head. "I'll never understand you. You're broke. So you decide to go shopping?"

Sarah grinned sheepishly. "That's the plan."

"That's insane."

"No, it's not. It makes perfect sense. I don't have a spare twenty grand to pay for IVF treatment, but I *can* afford to drop a few hundred on a new dress. I want childlessness to look good. I call it Barren Chic."

Annie said, "You're not going to be childless forever. We'll find the money somehow."

Sarah raised an eyebrow. "Any ideas?"

Annie smiled. "How about a telethon? Can't you picture Julia Roberts asking American viewers to ante up to help two unfortunate middle-aged Harvard grads?" Annie widened her eyes and said with mock soulfulness, "For pennies a day, you can keep these two women from ever having to work again. Won't you give now?"

Sarah shook her head. "No, telethons are passé. We're probably going to have to do something a little more shady. Maybe sell a kidney on the black market. Or we could always try prostitution."

Annie nodded. "Sounds good. You could appeal to the guys who like gorgeous redheads, and I could take on the ones with a fetish for mommies with droopy tits and stretch marks." Annie dropped into a sexy, husky voice. "The principal called me while you were at school. He said you've been a very . . . bad . . . boy."

Sarah laughed. "You're a bit too good at that. It makes me nervous."

A petite brunette suddenly materialized in front of Sarah. She wore heavy makeup and had a huge beauty mark on her left cheek. Like the other beauticians working the counters, she wore a white lab coat. The lab coat implied that Ms. Beauty Mark knew things, scientific things. She simpered, "May I help you?"

Sarah mumbled, "Uh, yes." Then she gestured to a display case full of light pink boxes with silver lettering, saying, "I see you have Dermi Minérale."

Ms. Beauty Mark beamed. "It's a very popular line. It has soothing minerals."

Annie quipped, "So does foot powder."

Ms. Beauty Mark frowned but lit up again when a customer beckoned her down to the other end of the counter. She excused herself and then floated down the counter, cooing, "Ah, Mrs. Wembly. So good to see you."

Mrs. Wembly was an expensive-looking blonde. She wore a tight blue sheath dress, matching stiletto heels, and lots of gold jewelry. She was extremely fit, with well-muscled limbs and a tiny waist. Her large, surgically enhanced breasts seemed incongruous against her athletic build, as if a female tennis coach had drawn most of her body and then let a teenage boy fill in the chest. Annie guessed that the woman was somewhere in her early forties, but only carbon dating could have revealed her true age. The skin on her face was so shiny and tight that Annie could have bounced a quarter off it. The woman studied the contents of the display counter while Ms. Beauty Mark hovered. Without making eye contact, the woman tapped on the display case and said, "I'll take two of the Zalême moisturizer."

"Yes, Mrs. Wembly." Ms. Beauty Mark scurried to fetch two small white boxes from the display.

Mrs. Wembly toyed with her Dior sunglasses. Sounding bored, she asked, "I don't suppose you have any of the Repavée cream in, do you?"

Ms. Beauty Mark smiled proudly. "Yes, Mrs. Wembly. It came in yesterday."

Mrs. Wembly brightened instantly. "Really? It's here?"

Ms. Beauty Mark nodded. With great showmanship, she withdrew a small silver jar from her display case. She set the jar down on the counter in front of Mrs. Wembly, and the two women stared at it. Such a jar could not just be popped open. One must genuflect first. After a moment of silence, Ms. Beauty Mark asked, "Would you like to try some?"

Mrs. Wembly shook her head quickly, as if sampling Repavée would be somehow disrespectful. Mrs. Wembly said, "I'll take four jars."

Ms. Beauty Mark shook her head. "I'm afraid we have a three-jar limit."

Mrs. Wembly nodded. "I completely understand. Of course, I'll take three."

Ms. Beauty Mark put three jars of Repavée into a bag. Mrs. Wembly paid with a credit card and turned to leave. She looked right through Annie but broke step when she caught sight of Sarah. Sensing Mrs. Wembly's stare, Sarah looked up from the display cases and smiled. Mrs. Wembly smiled back. Then she put on her sunglasses and strode away. Ms. Beauty Mark turned back to Annie and Sarah. "Sorry for the interruption. May I get you anything? Would you like a skin-care consultation?"

Annie asked, "A what?"

Ms. Beauty Mark repeated, "A skin-care consultation. I ask you about your skin-care goals. Then I recommend products that can help you meet those goals."

Annie said, "My skin is not very ambitious. It doesn't have any goals."

Pointedly ignoring Annie, Sarah leaned across the counter, saying, "I couldn't help but overhear that you have Repavée. That's quite a coup. Half of LA is hunting for it."

Ms. Beauty Mark smirked. "I know. Would you like to try some?" She didn't offer the cream to Annie.

Sarah shook her head. "No, thanks. Repavée is a bit rich for my blood these days."

Ms. Beauty Mark smiled sympathetically. "I understand. Perhaps some other time."

Annie asked, "How much does that stuff cost anyway?"

Ms. Beauty Mark answered primly, "Six hundred dollars."

"Are you joking?"

Ms. Beauty Mark countered, "No, I'm not joking. Six hundred dollars is our price, and I think it's quite reasonable. People pay two or three times that for creams far inferior to Repavée."

Eager to smooth the woman's feathers, Sarah chimed in, "Of course, you're right. Six hundred dollars is *very* reasonable." Sarah was used to apologizing for Annie's manners. It was like having a foreign exchange student for a best friend. Sarah took Annie's arm and gently ferried her away.

As they walked into the shoe department, Annie said, "I can't believe women spend so much money on that crap."

Sarah shrugged. "*Quelle Beauté* said it's the best anti-wrinkle cream that's come out this year."

"Yeah, but you'd be *quelle* fool to buy it. There is no way that jar is worth six hundred bucks. I could probably whip up a batch of it in my lab for twenty. People are paying five hundred and eighty for a silver jar and a label. What a rip-off."

"Not *all* the creams are rip-offs. When I tried Rajeunie, I saw a definite change in my skin. The lines around my eyes faded in a few days."

"Sarah, you don't have any lines."

Sarah nodded. "Right. And that's because I use some very good creams."

"No, that's because you have fabulous genes. And let's not forget, for seven years, thanks to your job, you got less direct sunlight than a vampire."

"True."

Annie went on, "Did you see how much money that lady blew on that stuff? She must have spent two thousand bucks."

"Two thousand dollars is not so much. I remember one of my client's wives dropped six thousand for the latest La Ferme cream. They use platinum in it, either that or gold."

"People spread gold on their face?"

"Yes. They say it recharges the electrolytes in your skin."

"That's crap."

Sarah shrugged. "Probably. But I don't think it really matters."

Annie balked, "What do you mean it doesn't matter?"

"I mean legally. Legally, it doesn't matter. The government doesn't regulate most of this stuff. So long as your skin product doesn't make people sick, you can sell whatever you like. And you can pretty much claim whatever you like too. You just have to slap qualifiers on everything. You know, 'results may vary' or 'results not typical.' That kind of thing."

"So these face creams don't have to go through clinical trials?"

Sarah shook her head. "No, no hurdles. From a legal standpoint, selling skin cream is about as complicated as setting up a lemonade stand. Pretty much anyone can do it."

Annie pressed, "And they can charge whatever they want?"

Sarah shrugged. "Whatever people will pay, yeah." She looked down at the floor for a moment, her mouth slightly agape. Sarah asked, "Are you okay?"

Annie looked at Sarah and smiled. "Yeah, I'm okay. Better than okay. I just figured out how we can make some serious money."

"How?"

Annie rubbed her hands together. "We're going into the beauty business."

Annie bought Kathleen Krull's Lives of the Scientists *for its propaganda value. She hoped its funny illustrations and quirky stories would trick her children into thinking science was cool. Annie loved the book's biggest "aha!" moment: Isaac Newton figuring out how gravity works when an apple bonks him on the head. No matter how old Annie got, she never stopped hoping for her own "aha!" moment.*

9

Selling Sarah

The idea came to Annie fully formed. She and Sarah would make a killing selling overpriced skin cream to La Jolla's beautiful people. La Jolla was the perfect market. People there were rich enough to drop a few thousand on face cream with the same insouciance Annie experienced poking around the dollar bins at Target. Besides, La Jollans were so accustomed to hyperinflated prices that they had lost all sense of what things *should* cost. They were like people permanently stuck in an airport ("Four dollars for a Twix? Why not?"). In La Jolla, money was God: all-important but abstract.

La Jolla's size and location were big pluses. With fewer than forty-five thousand people, word of mouth could be a powerful selling tool. In Los Angeles, Annie and Sarah's sales pitch would be drowned out by competing chatter, but in La Jolla, their message would penetrate. La Jolla's remoteness would help too. Annie knew that Sarah would never be able to play Avon lady on her home turf. But in La Jolla, Sarah could take off her lawyer hat and become someone else. And the scheme would only work if Sarah played along.

Annie had it all planned out: She would be the chef, whipping up the face cream in her kitchen. It would cost practically nothing. She would just mix a few cheap face creams, add an ingredient or two, and then repackage the glop in a fancy jar with a French label. Then Sarah would go out and sell it. Sarah would be the face of the operation. Her looks and clothes would give her instant credibility with La Jolla's not-so-smart smart set.

But first Annie had to convince Sarah. It wouldn't be easy. Sarah could be depressingly moral sometimes. But Annie would wear Sarah down, using every pitch she could imagine. There was the social justice argument: "These people have too much money; they *deserve* to be tricked out of it." The personal power argument: "Aren't you tired of working for other people and taking orders? Wouldn't you like to finally take control of your destiny?" The duress argument: "This may be morally sticky, but we *have* to do it. You need money quick so you can get pregnant, and I need it to take care of my son. We have no choice." The utilitarian argument: "These rich people are going to waste this money anyway. We'll use it for much more valuable things." The "I dare you" argument: "For once in your life, take a risk!" The short-term argument: "This is a temporary campaign to raise money, a fund-raiser. It's okay to play fast and loose with the rules if you're only going to do it for a little while." And, of course, the "Greatest Love of All" argument: "We have to do it *for the children,* for Oscar and your baby-to-be." Cue Whitney Houston.

After a few days of haranguing, Sarah was still officially opposed to the plan. But Annie sensed some give. Absurdly, Annie imagined herself as a villain from a movie, stroking a fluffy white cat and telling Sarah, "You and I are not so different. Come join me on the dark side." For her final assault, Annie asked Sarah to come to San Diego for a weekend. Annie wanted Sarah to stroll down La Jolla's main drag and see how glutted it was with easy, fat prey. Annie wheedled Sarah, "Just come and hear me out. That's all I ask."

Sarah believed in loyalty, up to a point. When she read The Poisonwood Bible, *she understood why a missionary's family would leave the comfy United States for the wilds of the Congo. The wife and kiddies were just following dear old dad and his vision. In their shoes, Sarah would have gone to the Congo too, but she would have turned tail as soon as she ran out of hair conditioner.*

10

Humoring Annie

Sarah had approached her weekend with Annie the same way she approached the Jehovah's Witnesses who came to her apartment. She had planned to listen and then gently but firmly shut the door. But Annie was not making it easy. Driving back from Annie's grand tour of La Jolla, Annie rambled on about her scheme. Sarah folded her arms across her chest, saying, "So we should feel free to trick these people out of their money because they can afford it? Is that what you're saying?"

"Yes!"

"Annie, a burglar could say the same thing. Why not break into their houses and steal their jewelry?"

Annie said, "It's *not* stealing. What I'm proposing is a completely consensual transaction. A win-win. We get the money, and they get what every consumer wants, the satisfaction of buying powerful new stuff."

"But it's *not* powerful stuff. Your face cream isn't going to actually *do* anything."

"Sarah, *none* of the face creams on the market *do* anything. Even the high-end ones don't really work. And people *know* that. When a woman buys a jar of face cream, she knows—on some level—that the stuff is not going to make her look twenty years younger. She's *hoping* it will. She's paying for a fantasy, the fantasy that she can look younger without needles and surgery."

Sarah pressed, "So you don't see anything wrong with doing this?"

"No."

"Then why all the secrecy?"

Annie looked puzzled. "What?"

"You keep going on about stealth marketing. You said you want me to pose as some rich lady who's thinking about moving to La Jolla. A lady who *happens* to have access to this face cream and is willing to sell it to her new La Jolla buddies. If this thing is kosher, then why the subterfuge?"

"Because that's the only way it'll work. If you go up to these people's houses in a pink lab coat and announce yourself as a skin-care consultant, you won't even make it through the front door. No, it's much better if they meet you in a social context, as an equal. They'll see you, see how gorgeous you are, and then you can pitch to them without them realizing you're doing it. We make it seem like this is a sideline for you, a favor you do for a select few friends."

Sarah countered, "A favor I do for two thousand dollars a pop?"

Annie nodded. "Yes. To these people, anything that costs less than one thousand dollars is crap. If mere mortals can afford something, then it's probably not worth having."

Sarah smirked. "Well, that's convenient."

"Yeah, okay. Their snobbery helps me on this one. It means I can charge more. I looked at the other high-end creams on the market, and

I figure we can pitch ours at $500 an ounce, two grand for a four-ounce jar. Right?"

Sarah answered, "Right, if we had a well-known luxury cosmetics brand. But we don't have a well-known brand. We don't have a brand at all. We're nobodies."

With a huge grin, Annie said, "Yes! We *are* nobodies. And since we're nobodies, we can be *anybody.*"

Sarah shook her head. "Okay, you can now send out a search party. I am officially lost."

"I mean, we can say anything we want about our product. We can use one pitch to appeal to one customer and then go the opposite way with another customer. We're not hemmed in by . . ." Annie fumbled for the right word.

"Reality? The laws of physics?"

Annie shook her head. "No. What we say has to be plausible. But we have a huge amount of freedom in how we angle our pitches. We don't have to stick to any party line. It's all legal. It's—what did you call it?"

"Puffery. It's legal to puff up what a product does, so long as you don't make any specific promises. But still . . ."

"Yeah, so it's legal." Sarah folded her arms tightly against her chest.

Annie went on, "C'mon, you know I can't do this without you. I don't know anything about fine wine or high fashion . . . or how hard it is to find someone to fly my private jet."

"You've got a lot of hostility toward rich people, don't you?"

"I do not. I love rich people. Rich people are going to fund my son's therapies. They just need to be guided into doing the right thing."

Sarah rolled her eyes. "So this isn't fraud. It's paternalism?"

Annie grinned. "It's whatever makes you say yes."

"You know I could lose my law license for doing this?"

"How can they take your license away if it's legal?"

"It's legal, but it's not ethical."

"Since when are lawyers ethical?"

The friends quieted as they pulled up next to Annie's Carmel Valley house. The welcoming committee rushed to greet them. Six-year-old Maddie got to Sarah first. Dressed in a Snow White costume, she jumped into Sarah's arms and hugged her neck so tightly that Sarah had to fight for breath.

Annie's husband, Harry, came out with baby Rachel on his hip. "Good to see you, Sarah." Rachel gurgled a welcome and expressed her enthusiasm by kicking her father as hard as she could.

Oscar stood behind Harry's legs, one hand clasping the fabric of Harry's trousers. Sarah kneeled down and asked softly, "So how's my little man?"

Not meeting Sarah's eyes, Oscar smiled at the pavement and murmured, "Gordon is a very powerful engine."

Annie frowned. She had told Sarah about Oscar's lack of eye contact, his non sequiturs. Annie explained to Sarah, "Gordon's a Thomas train. Oscar got it from his grandmother, and he's pretty excited about it."

Sarah put her hand on Oscar's shoulder and said, "That's terrific, honey." Still no eye contact. Sarah rose and followed Harry into the house. As usual, toys were strewn everywhere. Annie apologized for the mess, but Sarah loved the look of happy chaos. Harry drew Annie aside to talk for a moment, and Sarah settled down on the couch next to Maddie. Maddie retold "Snow White," emphasizing that Snow White would have been fine if she had turned down the apple. That's why Maddie would only eat pears now.

While Maddie prattled on, Oscar went to the corner of the room and played with his Thomas trains. Sarah watched him surreptitiously. He looked so much like his mother: same curls, same big brown eyes, same bow mouth. Sarah caught Oscar glancing at her once or twice, but he still wouldn't look at her directly. Sarah responded by widening her eyes and craning her neck slightly, absurdly willing him to meet her gaze.

Oscar remained fixated on his trains. He didn't look up at Sarah, but he slowly inched closer to her. After a few minutes of this, Sarah laid her hand close to his knee on the floor. And, to her immense relief, Oscar held it for a moment. Then he scooted closer so that he could nestle in the crook of her arm. He smelled like baby shampoo.

Sarah decided it wouldn't hurt to at least *try* Annie's plan. For a little while.

Sarah liked Sookie Stackhouse, the spunky, telepathic heroine from Charlaine Harris's sexy Southern vampire series. But Sarah never understood Sookie's whining about her mind-reading abilities. Sarah thought it'd be a kick to walk into a roomful of strangers and instantly know their backstories and secret agendas.

11

Back to Book Club

Annie's voice boomed over the car's speakerphone, telling Sarah, "You can do this. I know you can. Now let's go over the roster one more time. Your host is?"

Sarah recited, "My host is Valerie Tilmore. She is a bitter, fiftyish divorcée whose husband left her for a much younger woman."

"And the younger woman?"

"Crystal Something-or-other. We don't have a last name on her, do we?"

Annie apologized. "No. I couldn't get one."

Sarah went on, "Crystal is a gorgeous, dim brunette who desperately wants to fit in with the other wives."

Annie prompted, "And?"

"And she's pregnant."

"Right. And who is Dawn Maris?"

"A fortyish blonde with three kids. She's the one who got blitzed last time, right?"

"You got it. And Priscilla?"

"She's the one who missed book club last time. She was off getting plastic surgery or something."

"Right. And Kim Elliot?"

Sarah fumbled for a moment, then it came back to her. "She's the one who used to be a math teacher. Her big-deal husband made her quit so she could stay home and focus on being rich. She's a tall brunette."

Annie crowed, "Excellent. Perfect score."

In the privacy of her car, Sarah smiled and straightened up in her seat. Praise was always catnip for her. Driving past La Jolla's mansions, she slowed down and peered at the street numbers until she found the right one. She spotted the numbers she was looking for painted neatly on the curbside. The house was not visible from the street. She turned right. The gates had been left open for tonight's festivities. Sarah followed the narrow driveway past a huge rose garden and came to a stop on the circular drive in front of Valerie's house. It was a sprawling two-story Spanish colonial, a "hacienda." As she pulled up beside it, Sarah whistled.

From her perch in Carmel Valley, Annie asked, "How's it look?"

"Like the house of a South American dictator, minus the armed guards."

"That sounds about right for Valerie. Are you ready to meet the girls?"

Sarah switched off her engine and checked her reflection in the rearview mirror. "Yes. But I wish you were here. I still don't like this separate-cars arrangement."

Annie sighed. "We've been through this. So far as these women know, you're a distant acquaintance of mine. I told Dawn that we ran into each other at some Harvard function. You told me you were planning to move to La Jolla, so I invited you to book club. You accepted because you wanted to meet some potential neighbors, not because you had any interest in catching up with some dumpy hausfrau from Carmel Valley."

Reflexively, Sarah objected, "Now, wait a minute. I don't see why—"

"C'mon, yes you do. We want these women to see you as a glamorous stranger. Whatever mystique you build up will be gone in two seconds if they find out that your best friend is from the wrong side of Interstate 5."

"Okay, you know this crowd better than I do, but when will you get here?"

"I'll show up in half an hour or so. At some point after I get there, you excuse yourself to go to the bathroom so I can drop the A-bomb."

"The A-bomb?"

"Your age, my dear."

"Oh, okay, so how old am I?"

"I'm going with forty-five."

"Whoa, that's way too old!"

Annie countered, "But, the older you are, the more impressive the cream will be. You can easily pass for thirty-three. So if I say you're forty-five, then these women will think the cream can shave twelve years off their faces."

"Let's go with the truth. Tell them I'm forty-two."

"Why?"

"Because if you say I'm forty-five, they'll round up and think fifty. If they think fifty, they think menopause. Suddenly, in their heads, I'm wiping flop sweat off my face with one hand while I use the other to shave my mustache. Not a pretty picture, is it?"

"No, I guess not."

"We want me to be mature enough to need skin cream but still desirable. Got it?"

"And forty-two is still desirable?"

"Yes, it's early forties. We're still in Gwyneth Paltrow/Sofía Vergara country. That's right where we want to be."

Sarah could hear Annie blowing her bangs out of her eyes. Annie sighed, "Got it. I hereby dub you forty-two. Glamorous and still highly fuckable."

"Thank you. I appreciate your support."

Valerie felt that people focused too much on sex. She was the only one in the book club who didn't like Madame Bovary. *All right, the silly cow had been "unfulfilled" by her marriage, but she could have avoided so much hassle—so much pain—if she'd repressed her passions. Valerie felt that repression and stability were underrated.*

12

Valerie's Hospitality

Before greeting her guests, Valerie sat down at her vanity table and spritzed on some extra Chanel No. 5. She'd heard that perfume could make pregnant women nauseous. Take that, Crystal.

Valerie inspected her reflection. She saw nothing amiss. As usual, her housekeeper, Esperanza, had pulled Valerie's blond hair up into a chignon. The hair extensions Esperanza had used blended perfectly with Valerie's natural hair, concealing the way it had thinned over the past two years. Her makeup was immaculate too, and her cream-colored dress showed off her well-toned arms and small waist. She topped off the outfit with pearl earrings and a thick gold bracelet that she'd bought last year at an upscale La Jolla boutique, CJ Charles.

That bracelet was the first thing that Valerie had ever bought for herself at CJ Charles, without Walter. CJ Charles had been a ritual for them. Once a year, on her birthday, Walter would take her there and ask her to choose her present. She would linger over the cases, pretending she was unsure of what she wanted. Then she would pick something. No matter what she chose, Walter would moan about how she was going to drive him to the poorhouse, but then he'd always give in. How could he resist her? She was his girl.

Valerie heard her guests mingling downstairs in the living room. Then Esperanza said, "Miss Valerie will be down in a moment. You please make yourself comfortable." Espie spoke much more loudly than usual, a coded message for Miss Valerie to get her tail downstairs right away.

Valerie hurried down the stairs. When she entered her palatial living room, she caught Espie's gaze and winked. Espie glowered at her for a moment and then slipped quickly out of the room. The guests had all arrived, except for that chubby housewife from Carmel Valley. Abbie, Addie, something like that.

Valerie made the rounds, hugging and air-kissing each of her guests. When she came to Crystal, she found that the girl had settled her now-bountiful backside (Crystal ball, indeed!) in the middle of Valerie's deep leather couch. Crystal made a big fuss of extracting herself from the sofa, but Valerie told her, "Don't bother getting up, darling. We've had enough earthquakes this season already."

Priscilla laughed at this, and Crystal smiled uncertainly. Just as Valerie was about to sit, the doorbell sounded. A moment later, Espie led a tall redhead into the room. The redhead smiled warmly at the circle of women and introduced herself. "Hello, I'm Sarah, Sarah Sloane."

Before Valerie could say anything, Dawn sprang to her feet, explaining, "This is Annie's friend. They went to Harvard together. Sarah's thinking of moving to La Jolla so Annie invited her to try book club. I said I thought it would be a great idea." Dawn said this in a great rush, eager to claim credit for this new arrival. Valerie could see why. Sarah was stunning. Long red hair. Big brown eyes. Perfect skin. A tall, thin frame swathed in a knee-length emerald-green Prada dress. The woman projected the elegance of an old movie star, Rita Hayworth or Deborah Kerr.

Valerie shook Sarah's hand. "Thank you for coming. I'm Valerie Tilmore."

Sarah answered, "Valerie, this is your house, isn't it? It's lovely."

Valerie smiled. "Thank you." She gestured for Sarah to sit down in the empty armchair next to her. Then Valerie went around the room, introducing Sarah to each of her guests.

Once introductions were made, Priscilla took over as usual. Priscilla dominated most conversations; the woman did not need her PTA president's gavel. She *was* a gavel. Her face freshly peeled and her pouty lips newly plumped, Priscilla set about impressing the new arrival. She told Sarah all about her husband's big job as a Hollywood producer, euphemistically describing him as "semiretired." It sounded better than the truth, that he had been fired. Then she moved on to the Gillespie PTA, saying, "Running the PTA may not be as glamorous as my old job in Hollywood. Did I mention that I used to be a studio executive? No? Well, I was. I got out just in time. Hollywood is not very kind to women over forty."

Valerie interrupted. "I thought that was only true for women *in front of* the camera."

Priscilla conceded, "Of course, it's hardest for actresses. There's no such thing as a happy birthday for those girls. But even when you're an executive, there's huge pressure to look young. Show a few wrinkles and suddenly they're shoving you onto an ice floe."

Sarah said, "My friends in the industry all say the same thing."

Valerie asked Sarah, "Do you have many friends in show business?"

Sarah nodded. "Professional hazard, I guess."

"What exactly do you do?" Valerie liked to know which boxes people belonged in, what labels to stick on them.

"Well, up until a while ago, I was an attorney with a large LA firm. We represented a lot of actors, producers, directors, the usual suspects." Sarah had no doubt that these women would Google her later so she stuck to the truth as much as possible. She went on, "But recently, I've gone out on my own. Now I work as a consultant to various people in the industry."

Priscilla slid forward on the couch. "Who?"

Sarah pursed her lips for a moment and said, "I'm afraid I can't tell you that. One of the reasons my clients hire me is my discretion." Priscilla nodded knowingly, as if anyone had ever been stupid enough to rely on *her* discretion. Priscilla was La Jolla's town crier.

Valerie pushed. "That's interesting. I know lawyers can't reveal what they tell their clients. But surely, once you go to court, the fact that you're representing someone ceases to be a secret. Doesn't it?"

Sarah nodded. "You're right. But most of my clients come to me because they want to stay *out* of court." Sarah winked at Valerie, and Valerie decided that she liked this woman.

The conversation in the room paused as Espie returned and deposited two large trays of sushi on the coffee table. Valerie said, "Please help yourselves, ladies. It's from Sushi on the Rock." Valerie watched as the women piled their plates high with tuna rolls, salmon eggs, and other raw delicacies. For form's sake, Valerie took a few pieces of California roll. She had no intention of eating the stuff. Sushi disgusted her. But she knew her friends loved it. And, of course, she knew that sushi was strictly off-limits for pregnant women.

Valerie watched discreetly as Crystal searched the table for something to eat. With her lower lip jutting out and her furrowed brow, she looked like a foraging ape. Honestly, what was Walter thinking? Sex wasn't everything. As if she'd realized Crystal's plight, Valerie said, "Oh, my goodness. What was I thinking? You can't eat sushi in your condition, can you?"

Crystal shook her head. Valerie went on, "Well, we can't have you starving. I'll have Espie throw something together."

Priscilla piped up, "She can have some of the miniature pizzas I brought from Sammy's. They're over there on that side table."

Valerie said, "Oh good. So no one has to go hungry." Valerie watched with satisfaction as Crystal extracted herself from the couch and lumbered over to the side table to help herself to cold pizza. Bon appétit, bimbo.

With Crystal out of the way, Valerie turned back to Sarah. "So you're thinking of moving to La Jolla, are you?"

"Yes."

"But isn't our little burg a bit out of the way for you? It sounds like most of your clients are based in LA."

Sarah shrugged. "They are. But I'll manage. My husband and I don't plan to be down here full time. We hope to split our time between La Jolla and Bel Air."

Valerie wanted to learn more about this husband. But Dawn interrupted, "Why La Jolla? I thought everyone in LA got their second houses in Malibu."

Priscilla cut in. She had to guard her turf as *the* expert on all things LA. "Actually, the 'Bu has lost some of its cachet. It's crawling with industry wannabes. My husband says he can't buy a latte in that town without the barista trying to sell him a screenplay."

Sarah said, "We *looked* at Malibu, and we liked it. Of course, I'm a nobody in Hollywood. So, unlike Priscilla and her husband, I don't have to worry about anyone harassing me with screenplays." Priscilla drank in this acknowledgment. She looked almost tipsy with self-regard. Sarah added, "But we fell in love with La Jolla. I know I'm going to sound like a real estate guide, but the Cove is breathtaking."

Nursing her second glass of wine, Dawn drawled, "And the schools are good too, at least the *private* schools are."

Sarah asked, "What about the public schools?"

Dawn giggled. "What about them?"

Kim said, "Actually, the public schools here are good. They don't test as well as Carmel Valley, but—"

Dawn interrupted. "Yes, well, we all know what *that's* about."

Sarah raised an eyebrow. "Excuse me?"

Dawn took a swig of white wine and elaborated. "La Jolla is part of San Diego Unified. So that means we have to bus in kids from other neighborhoods, less fortunate neighborhoods." Dawn made air quotes around the words "less fortunate." Valerie hoped Dawn wasn't teeing up another of her ugly rants against Hispanics. If Dawn went down that merry path, Esperanza would probably treat her to a lapful of hot coffee. Espie had "accidents" like that sometimes. She broke Walter's toe by "accidentally" dropping a sailing trophy on him hours after Walter announced that he was leaving Valerie.

Sarah asked, "So busing makes La Jolla score lower on tests than Carmel Valley?"

Dawn tittered. "Well, that's *part* of it. Actually, diversity swings the other way in Carmel Valley."

Sarah pressed, "How so?" Carmel Valley was Annie's home turf.

Dawn leaned forward, sloshing some of her white wine on the carpet. "Carmel Valley is packed with Asians. The place is like one giant karaoke parlor. And those people *live* to study." Perhaps realizing that "those people" might sound bigoted, Dawn added, "It's very admirable."

Priscilla seconded this, "Yes, admirable."

The group held an impromptu moment of silence in honor of Asian study habits. Valerie decided to push the conversation off this sandbar. "So, Sarah, do *you* have any children?"

Sarah shook her head. "No, not yet." Valerie smiled, grateful to have another member on the childless team. Valerie opened her mouth to ask another question but was interrupted by the doorbell.

A moment later, Esperanza led the woman from Carmel Valley, what's-her-name, into the room. What's-her-name bubbled, "Hey there, sorry I'm late."

Valerie rose. "I'm so glad you could make it. Won't you have a seat?" She gestured to a blank spot on the couch next to Crystal.

What's-her-name started toward the couch but then stopped. She'd spotted Sarah. "You made it!" Sarah nodded but did not rise. What's-her-name blathered on, "It's a great group, isn't it?"

Sarah said, "Yes, we've been having a lovely time." Sarah looked flustered for a moment. "I'm sorry. It's Annie, isn't it? I'm terrible with names."

"Yes, Annie. Don't worry. It's pretty hard to offend me." Annie flashed a conspiratorial look around the room, as if the other guests could vouch for her laid-back nature. Annie and Priscilla swapped introductions, and then Annie plopped down next to Crystal.

Valerie turned back to Sarah, asking, "So, you and, um, Annie know each other from college?"

Sarah answered, "Well, sort of. We both went to Harvard, but we didn't go at exactly the same time. I think we only overlapped by a year or two." Sarah turned to Annie, "You were class of '93, right?"

Annie had been helping herself to the sushi platters. Through a mouth stuffed with sashimi, she said, "Nine-nny-two."

Valerie turned to Sarah. "And you were what, class of '96?"

Sarah laughed. "I wish. No, I graduated in 1995."

Valerie nodded and tried to hide the calculations going on behind her eyes. *Class of 1995. If Sarah had graduated at age twenty-two, that would mean she was born in 1973. And that meant she was . . . forty-two years old. Holy crap! Sarah did not look forty-two. Valerie would have guessed thirty, thirty-three tops.*

While the rest of the group strained to finish the math assignment that Valerie had just completed, Annie asked, "So, what'd I miss? Did we start talking about the book yet?"

Valerie answered, "No. We hadn't gotten that far." Looking around the room, Valerie asked, "Did anyone actually bother to *read* the book this time?" Valerie tried to sound playful as she asked this.

Refilling her wineglass, Dawn said, "I only got through the first fifty pages. I'm not big on nonfiction."

With an apologetic look at Valerie, Priscilla said, "I'm sorry, but I didn't get to it either." Valerie raised her eyebrows at her friend and said only, "I see." Conversational shorthand for "I'll get you later, my pretty." After all, Valerie had slogged through three hundred pages of unrelenting doom and gloom when Priscilla had chosen Cormac McCarthy's *The Road*. Three hundred pages of bleak landscapes, starvation, and cannibalistic hordes. A literary barbiturate. If Valerie could wade through that, then Priscilla could certainly get through a two-hundred-pager on the six wives of Henry VIII.

Valerie felt annoyance well up inside her. As host, it had been her turn to choose a book for book club. Valerie hated picking books for book club. It was all about finding the one book that was just right: not too hard or too easy, not too meaningful or too flighty. And no matter what Valerie picked, only half of the book club would read the damned thing.

This time, Valerie's frustration was worse than usual because she had tricked herself into thinking that she had picked a winner. *The Six* was everything that a book club book should be: short at two hundred pages, highbrow because it dealt with English history, and sexy because it focused on a man who had humped his way through half the English court. It was also critically acclaimed by the right people, meaning that the *New York Times* loved it but the masses did not. Valerie tried to conceal her disappointment by stuffing her mouth with a cold, mushy California roll. Sarah rescued her. "Well, I *loved* it."

Valerie brightened. "Really?"

"Oh yes. I mean, what's not to love about the Tudors? All that sex and violence. Wonderful stuff."

Obviously titillated, Priscilla asked, "So wait, this was about that king with the six wives? The one on Showtime?"

Sarah nodded. "Yes, it's the same story. But it's *told* differently." Valerie nodded, a small smile playing on her lips. Sarah's enthusiasm was gratifying. Sarah went on, "What I liked about it best was the way it depicted the relationship between Henry and his first wife, Catherine. Catherine . . ." Sarah fumbled for the rest of the woman's name.

Kim spoke up. "Catherine of Aragon. Yes, I liked the section on her too." As usual, Kim only spoke about the book *after* someone else had made it safe to do so. Kim was so painfully deferential. When she went through a door, she probably let her shadow go first.

Looking at Kim, Sarah went on, "I don't know about you, but whenever *I've* seen Catherine in the movies, she's been so colorless, this drab creature with no sex appeal. So when Henry dumps her and marries Anne Boleyn, it comes across as this big, brave romantic step forward, not as an emotional betrayal."

Kim said, "Yes. I've noticed that too. And it's so unfair. I mean, in *The Six*, the author makes it clear that, for a long time, Catherine and Henry were in love. It wasn't a marriage of convenience or duty."

Sarah said, "Exactly."

Kim went on, "You know, I never thought about it, but you're right. The movies always do make Catherine look dumpy, as if she deserved what Henry did to her because she let herself go. But none of that was true. Catherine was a great beauty. Even outside the English court, people described her as 'the most beautiful creature in all the world.'" To Valerie, Kim's sudden loquaciousness came as a pleasant shock. Valerie had never heard Kim put more than two sentences together. For a millisecond, Valerie felt proud for having chosen the book that had inspired Kim's little speech. But then, Valerie realized that *the book* did not deserve the credit. Sarah did. Sarah made people want to talk, to connect with her. Kim continued, "Catherine and Henry had a *very* active sex life. Six children in eight years."

Crystal finally spoke. "Yes, but only one of those kids survived."

Kim nodded. "Okay, so the pregnancies weren't successful. But still, they had to count for *something*."

Priscilla said bitterly, "Yes, well, they didn't count for much, did they?" Valerie watched Priscilla closely. Like Catherine of Aragon, like Valerie herself, Priscilla hadn't taken kindly to being discarded by her husband for a younger model. After her divorce, Priscilla had massive amounts of plastic surgery. Over drinks one night, Priscilla had told Valerie that aging was a brutal master class on the subject of depreciation.

Sensing that she had said something wrong, Kim backed off. "No, I guess you're right."

Unimpeded by such emotional antennae, Crystal yawned loudly and stretched her well-toned trophy-wife arms over her head.

It was then that Priscilla spotted the bracelet on Crystal's right arm. Priscilla pointed to it and said, "My, my, someone's been a good girl. Let me see that thing."

Crystal extended her hand toward Priscilla, who leaned forward to inspect the new bauble.

Setting down her wineglass—for once—Dawn said, "Me next. Lemme see."

Crystal giggled and let Dawn take her by the wrist. Dawn studied the bracelet for a long moment. And Valerie peeked at it as discreetly as she could. It was a gold link bracelet with a diamond-encrusted pendant shaped like an egg. Dawn murmured, "It's gorgeous. Where did you get it?"

Crystal beamed. "CJ Charles. Walter took me there."

"What was the big occasion?"

"I'd just had my first ultrasound. Walter told me I could pick out anything I wanted. So I picked this. I loved the egg charm. It seemed like good luck. You know, for the baby."

Priscilla simpered, "Good luck for you too. Nicely done."

Crystal colored prettily. "Oh, I didn't do anything. It was all Walter's idea." Then, mimicking Walter perfectly, she added, "Nothing's too good for my girl." The group tittered obligingly. It was the first time Valerie had ever heard Crystal successfully land a joke.

Valerie forced her mouth into the rictus of a smile. She listened in a daze as Priscilla and Dawn started quizzing Crystal about the baby. Was she going to find out the sex? Did she have any names in mind? Suddenly, Valerie felt a cool hand touch hers. It was Sarah. Sarah said quietly, "Excuse me. I need to take a bathroom break. Could you show me where it is?"

Eager for an excuse to leave her guests, Valerie led Sarah out of the living room and back into the foyer. Then they walked down a short hallway to one of the guest bathrooms. Upon opening the door, Sarah joked, "Thanks. I think I can handle things from here." But then she paused. She pointed to the small watercolor painting hanging opposite the bathroom. "Where did you get that?"

"Why?"

"Because it's wonderful. It's La Jolla Cove, right?"

"Yes."

Studying the painting with real interest, Sarah said, "I've seen a gazillion paintings of the Cove. And none of them get it quite right. But this one is perfect. Who did it?"

Shyly, Valerie admitted, "I did."

Sarah raised her eyebrows. "You?"

Valerie nodded. "Yes, I used to paint a bit. Nothing serious. Just dabbling."

Sarah continued looking at the painting. "This doesn't look like dabbling to me. Do you have any more like it?"

"Yes. Quite a lot more."

"May I see them sometime?"

Valerie laughed. "Yes, if you like." She assumed Sarah wasn't being serious. Just making a polite gesture.

"How about this Sunday? Would two o'clock work?"

Valerie beamed. "You know, I think it might."

Whenever Annie saw copies of John Knowles's A Separate Peace *stacked on the "summer reading" tables at the bookstore, she felt guilty. Annie recognized herself in Gene, the bookish introvert who befriends the effortlessly popular star athlete Phineas at a posh New England prep school. Phineas's sunny disposition and genuine goodness make Gene's secret, burning envy for him even more shameful.*

13

Postmortem

Annie left Valerie's place at ten o'clock, giving her usual litany of family-related excuses. The excuses probably weren't necessary. The crowd at Valerie's did not care whether she left early, let alone *why* she did so.

Those women only cared about Sarah. If Sarah had left early, it would have been a party killer, like Cinderella's flight from the ball. Annie had known that Sarah would succeed with this flock of magpies. Hell, Annie's business plan depended on it. But the magnitude of Sarah's success still hurt Annie in an obscure way. It gave Annie a nasty case of déjà vu. Suddenly, Annie was a pimply, nerdy girl again, Sarah's disappointing plus one. Annie had spent her college years playing the dumpy best friend. It was a thankless supporting role. No matter how witty Annie managed to be, no matter how much she dolled herself up, she would never be the pretty one, never the star of the night. Annie was Rosie O'Donnell to Sarah's Meg Ryan. Since graduating from college, Annie had Photoshopped those memories. She'd tied them up in a nostalgic bow, telling herself that she'd never minded playing second fiddle. She'd congratulated herself on being too secure to get wrapped up in such pettiness. What bullshit.

The only thing that took the sting out of this evening was that—thanks to the cream scheme—Annie and Sarah were teamed up *against* these women. Annie could not wait to dissect the evening's events with Sarah back at the Carmel Valley house. But, of course, Sarah made her wait. Sarah glided into Annie's house well past midnight. Under the kitchen's bright lights, Annie could see how tired Sarah looked. Evidently, charming a roomful of snobs was hard work. Annie offered Sarah a drink of water, but Sarah wanted "the hard stuff" instead: Ben & Jerry's Chunky Monkey, straight up, no chocolate syrup.

Once Sarah had fortified herself with ice cream, she was ready for Annie's questions. Yes, she had worked in the bit about having a house in Bel Air. Yes, she'd let drop the "fact" that she had Hollywood connections. No, she hadn't said much about her husband. Annie felt herself getting excited. Fraud was fun! She asked, "So, what's next?"

Sarah smiled. "Next, I go on some playdates. Priscilla offered to take me house hunting this Saturday morning. She promised to show me the best unlisted properties on the market. She said you don't need to use a broker if you're 'in the know.'"

"And Priscilla's in the know?"

Sarah shrugged. "I don't know. I'm not in the know. But if Priscilla's as plugged in as she claims to be, I think she may end up being very important for us. She can introduce me around, maybe talk up our skin cream. She struck me as a bit of a gossip."

Annie nodded. "Yes, talking to her will be better than taking out an ad in the *La Jolla Light.* So are you going to try to sell her some product this weekend?"

"Product?"

"Yes, product, face cream." Sheepishly, Annie admitted, "I was trying to sound business-y."

"No, I don't think I should start pushing the cream yet. I think it'll be better if I sell *myself* some more. Make Priscilla think I've got some big Hollywood connections. If word gets out that I'm cozy with some movie stars, I'll have a lot more credibility when I start talking about my miracle cream."

Annie smiled. "It's the transitive theory of Aniston."

"What?"

"The transitive theory of Aniston. Jennifer Aniston has the secret of eternal youth. You know Jennifer Aniston. Therefore, you also have the secret of eternal youth."

Sarah shook her head. "A math joke at one in the morning?"

Annie beamed. She knew it was safe to let her geek flag fly around Sarah. Sarah went on, "Then on Sunday, I'm going over to Valerie's place."

"She invited you?"

Sarah deadpanned, "No, I'm planning to break in. Yes, of course she invited me."

"How'd you swing that?"

"I complimented one of the paintings on her wall. Turns out she was the one who painted it. I said I'd like to see more of her work, and she said I could come over. She was very sweet about the whole thing."

"Sweet?"

"Yes. Sweet. I got the impression that no one had expressed any interest in her paintings for a long time."

Annie brightened. "Are they terrible?"

Sarah shook her head. "No, just the opposite. She has real talent."

"What about Valerie? Are you going to try to sell her some product on Sunday?"

Sarah leaned back and stretched. Through a yawn, she said, "That depends."

"On what?"

"On whether I have any product to sell. How's the formulation coming along?"

Annie colored. "Great. I've got the basics down. Just need a few tweaks." Annie smiled weakly but knew Sarah was onto her. Annie hated how her cheeks turned bright red whenever she told a lie. She was Pinocchio with rosacea.

Sarah pushed, "What *kind* of tweaks?"

"Nothing major. I want to find something to give our cream some kick."

"A secret ingredient?"

"Sort of."

"Annie, the cosmetics companies spend millions hunting out secret ingredients. There's no way we can compete with them. I thought the whole idea was to piggyback on their research by blending some of their products together."

Annie nodded. "Yes. That *is* the idea. And I think I've found a good blend. But I still want to find something extra. Something that will make the customers *feel* like the cream is working."

Sarah shook her head. She knew how much of a perfectionist Annie could be. Annie was laid-back, almost sloppy, about most things. But when she focused on a task, she could become overambitious. Simple dinners turned into seven-course gourmet meals. A wedding toast turned into a multimedia presentation. Sarah didn't want the cream's manufacture to become too complicated. She groaned, "Annie . . ."

Annie knew what Sarah was thinking. "Look, I promise I won't take much longer on this. I want to get it right. Let's face it. Our first round of sales will depend totally on marketing—on how much these women trust you, on how much they want to look like you, *be* like you. But later on, the only way these women will buy *more* cream will be if they think it's actually doing something for them." Sarah raised an eyebrow. Annie trudged on, "We need repeat customers. It's a helluva lot easier to sell this stuff three times over to thirty customers than it is to find ninety new customers, especially if we want to keep a low profile."

Sarah rubbed her eyes. "Fine, but can you have the cream by the end of the week?"

"I think so."

"You *think* so?"

Annie said, "I may not be able to put in as much time as I'd hoped to this week. Jimmy called. He said he wanted to come visit." Annie winced as she said this, knowing the reaction it was likely to provoke.

Sarah's eyes widened. "Jimmy? You're letting Jimmy hang around *here*? Around the kids?"

Annie bristled, "Well, he *is* their uncle. They love him. They *always* have a good time with him."

"*Everyone* has a good time with Jimmy. It's easy to be good company when you walk around in a cloud of marijuana smoke."

"Jimmy hasn't touched marijuana in years."

"So what's he on now? Coke? Heroin?"

Absurdly indignant, Annie huffed, "Jimmy has *never* done heroin. At least, I don't think he has." Annie had learned the hard way that it was always better to hedge when defending her brother.

Sarah pressed, "So what *is* he on? Meth?"

Annie shook her head. "No, Jimmy would never try meth. He's too vain for it. Meth rots your teeth, makes you all skinny. There's no way Jimmy would go near the stuff." It was true. Jimmy, a handsome extrovert, had followed in his parents' footsteps and become an actor. He referred to his body as his "instrument" and had always taken great care of his looks. That was why he'd gone off alcohol. During one of his early rehab stints, he'd noticed that the coke and heroin addicts were in much better shape than the drunks.

Sarah folded her arms across her chest. "So how long is he going to be here?"

"Two, three days tops." Actually, Jimmy had said he might stay for a week. In Jimmy-speak, a week could mean a few hours or a few months. Sarah exhaled loudly and shot Annie an exasperated look. Annie said, "What? He's my brother. He called and said he wants to visit, so I'm letting him visit."

"Did he sound sober?"

Annie said confidently, "Yes. One hundred percent sober. I'm sure of it."

Sarah's eyes narrowed. "He was calling you from rehab, wasn't he?"

"How'd you know that?"

"Because the only time he calls you one hundred percent sober is when he's calling from jail or rehab."

Annie blew her bangs out of her face. "What do you want me to do? Force my relatives to take Breathalyzer tests before I let them in on Thanksgiving?"

Sarah softened. "Of course not. I hate to see Jimmy messing with your head. He comes here spewing a bunch of crap about rehab or God or AA, and you always buy into it. You get all happy and excited for him. And then bam! In a week or two, the whole thing falls apart."

Annie pursed her lips. She knew Sarah was telling the truth, but the truth was annoying. Time for a diversion. "Yeah, well, what about Chloe?"

"What about her?"

"I don't understand why you're so judgmental about Jimmy. But my mom gets a total pass. The woman has been marinating herself in gin for the last forty years. But with her, everything is forgiven. You're always on about how I need to be more patient with her. It's a total double standard."

Sarah answered, "The only reason I'm harsher on Jimmy is because of his effect on you. With your mom, you gave up a long time ago. You *know* she's always going to be an alcoholic. With Jimmy, it's different. You keep thinking he's going to change. Because he's young and charming, and, yes, he means well. But he always lets you down. You're Charlie Brown running at the football, and he's Lucy pulling it away. These visits always end with you in tears."

Annie frowned and took a huge spoonful of ice cream. "I won't go on any crying jags. I promise." Then she jutted out her chin and sniffed. "Besides, after the past few months with Oscar, I don't have a lot of tears left."

Sarah put a hand on Annie's shoulder. "Oh, Annie, that's such—"

Annie said, "Such bullshit?" Sarah smiled and gave a quick nod. Annie grinned sheepishly. "Thanks. I come from a showbiz family, you know."

"There's no people like show people."

"Thank God for that."

When Annie read The Catcher in the Rye, *she didn't identify with the angsty teenage Holden Caulfield. Instead, she identified with his devoted sister, Phoebe. Phoebe loved her screw-up brother and believed in him, no matter what. Of course, it helped that Phoebe was just ten years old.*

14

Annie's Kid Brother

Jimmy had two gears: either he tried hard or he didn't try at all. This time, Jimmy tried hard. The kids tackled him as soon as he came across the threshold of Annie's house. Maddie hugged him by the legs until he fell to the floor. Then Oscar plopped down on top of his stomach, and Rachel commandeered his head, trying to mold his cheeks like Play-Doh. She giggled, giddy with power over this giant.

Eventually, Jimmy got the rug rats off by announcing that he had presents with him—presents! He produced a huge Toys R Us shopping bag, and the kids swarmed over it like greedy scavengers. Jimmy bear-hugged Annie, saying, "Big sister, how the hell are you?"

Annie laughed and smiled goofily up at her brother. Standing six feet tall, he had a full twelve-inch advantage over her. Annie was relieved to see him looking so healthy. When she'd last seen him, eight months earlier, he'd been too thin, almost gaunt, and he'd had dark circles under his eyes. Now he'd regained the weight he'd lost, and his cheeks were pink with health. He was dressed conservatively in a button-down Oxford, chinos, and loafers. Annie was grateful for this sartorial gesture.

It was much easier for Jimmy to pass as clean when he dressed the part. Annie asked, "Any trouble getting here?"

"No, your directions were perfect. I looked for the beige house with the red tile roof. No problem." Jimmy loved to make fun of Carmel Valley's cookie-cutter homes. *All* of them were beige with red tile roofs. Annie was glad Harry wasn't around for this jibe. Harry could be very sensitive about his castle. As if reading his sister's thoughts, Jimmy asked, "Where's Harry?"

"At the office. He won't be back till nine."

Jimmy winced. "Poor guy, but, hey, that's a Capricorn for you."

Annie rolled her eyes. "You're not still on that astrology kick, are you?" Over the years, Jimmy had snacked from a huge buffet of belief systems: astrology, Tibetan Buddhism, Judaism, Objectivism, Catholicism, Confucianism, and what could only be described as Tony Robbins worship. For Jimmy, life was an acting exercise, and he needed to figure out his motivation.

"I'm not really into the zodiac anymore. But let's face it, Harry *is* a classic Capricorn: reliable, hardworking, family man, a little stiff."

"Are you saying my husband is boring?"

Jimmy raised his hands defensively. "No, no. Harry's a great guy, got a terrific sense of humor, very dry. A lot of Capricorns are like that." Annie frowned. Jimmy asked, "You're not buying this, are you?"

"No. Astrology is crap."

"Well, you would feel that way. Tauruses are so conventional." Jimmy wiggled his eyebrows, taking obvious delight in baiting his big sister. He would have gone on in this vein, but Maddie grabbed him by the trouser leg.

Jimmy worked his magic on the family throughout the weekend. He played with the kids. He joked around with Annie. He even cajoled Harry into going biking with him. Things went so well that Annie put off having "the talk" with Jimmy until late Saturday night. She asked what rehab he'd gone to this time. Jimmy said, "Answers."

Annie was impressed. "Answers? That posh place up in Malibu?"

"Yes, ma'am. Nicest digs I've had in some time."

"How'd you afford *that*?"

"Remember the Swillers ad?"

Annie nodded. How could she forget? It had been all over the airwaves for months. It featured Jimmy nodding and laughing while he downed a bottle of Swillers, not exactly a stretch for him.

Jimmy said proudly, "That thing didn't just run in California. It went national. I had so much cash, I was practically farting money. And for once I decided to do the right thing with it. Treated myself to a nice long stay at Answers."

Annie beamed at her brother. "That's great. What addiction were you fighting this time?"

"Booze mostly."

"I thought you went off booze years ago. I thought you were into coke." Annie frowned. It was hard to stay current.

"Well, coke has always been my drug of choice. But with the recession and all, I figured it made sense to switch to booze. A lot cheaper."

"Sound financial planning."

"I thought so. Besides, the coke made my nose run all the time. It was making it hard for me to get work. Can't do coke if you don't have cash."

"So did Answers help?"

"Yeah, that place is great. I worked out a lot, went to a ton of AA meetings, got a step sponsor. Got clean, you know?"

Annie asked, "What about Stephanie? Has she gotten clean too?" Stephanie was Jimmy's longtime girlfriend. She was an aging porn star with fake everythings, but her love for Jimmy seemed genuine enough.

Jimmy shook his head. "No, she's still in her disease. We broke up."

Annie tried to look grave, but it was difficult. She had never liked Stephanie. And besides, it was so good to have her little brother back, to have him healthy. Annie slept well that night. For the first time in months, her thoughts were sunny.

Her good mood vanished the next morning. She rose at six o'clock to search the guest bathroom. She started with the toilet tank. Years of living with Chloe Baker had taught Annie that drunks love to hide their booze in toilet tanks. Most people never look there, and besides, the water keeps drinks cold. Next Annie moved on to the medicine chest. It was an obvious spot, but still, the classics never went entirely out of fashion. Again, nothing. Then on to the area behind the toilet, the cupboard under the sink, the hamper. Finally, there was only one spot left: Jimmy's leather toiletry case. Inside she found a tube of Crest toothpaste, a bottle of Creed cologne, an electric toothbrush, and a Ziploc baggie of white powder.

Annie grabbed the baggie and marched downstairs to the kitchen. She was grateful that no one else was up yet. She couldn't have faced anyone at that moment. She was livid. She scarfed down a bowl of cornflakes while the baggie sat on the counter in front of her. Her mind raced. What should she do with it? Throw it out? Confront Jimmy with it? What? Annie decided *not* to decide. Get the stuff out of the way and have it out with Jimmy right now. She went to the pantry, stood on a step stool, and stuffed the baggie inside an old tin Band-Aid box that she kept at the back of the top shelf. Then she climbed back up the stairs to Jimmy's room. Soundlessly, she edged the door open. Jimmy lay asleep under the white duvet, his clean, handsome face serene in repose. Annie shook him violently by the shoulder, saying through clenched teeth, "Jimmy, get up."

Jimmy rubbed the sleep out of his eyes. He said groggily, "What? What's wrong?"

"Nothing's wrong. Nothing but the bag of cocaine you brought into my house."

Jimmy came instantly awake. "You found that?"

Annie fumed, "I sure did."

Jimmy sat up and swung his legs over the side of the bed. He looked down at the floor and shook his head. "You must be pretty angry at me right now."

"Angry? No. Try furious! I can't believe you brought drugs into my house. Cocaine in *my* house!" Annie worked hard to keep her voice down. Mad as she was at Jimmy, she still wanted to keep his lapse from the rest of the family.

"I know. It was a stupid mistake."

"A mistake? No, you don't get to call this a mistake. It's a mistake when you use the salad fork to eat the main dish. Bringing cocaine into your sister's home, your *law-abiding* sister's home packed with kids, that's not a mistake. That's a monumentally stupid, selfish, horrible thing to do."

Jimmy nodded and rubbed his temples. "You're right."

Annie was just getting tuned up. Folding her arms tightly against her chest, she said, "What the hell were you thinking? Were you planning to toke some shit during a family outing?"

"Sis, you don't toke cocaine. You snort it."

"Whatever. Excuse me for not being up on narcotics."

"I would never use that stuff here. Hell, I wasn't planning to use it at all."

"So what? You were keeping it as a souvenir?"

"Yes. I mean no. Here's the deal. Usually, when I go clean, I tell myself, 'That's it. No more drugs. *Forever.*' And that works for most people. But not for me. When I think of *never* doing drugs or booze again, it freaks me out. So I was thinking I'd take the 'just for today' angle. Just for today, I don't use. But I'm not ruling it out forever 'cause that would freak me out. I keep that baggie of coke to remind myself that I don't have to be perfect *forever*. I have to try one day at a time. It's a mind game. But it's been working for me."

Annie blustered, "That is total crap. That's like stocking your fridge with Häagen-Dazs before going on a diet. Does your sponsor know about your little 'someday' stash?"

Jimmy colored. "No, he wouldn't understand."

"Will you talk to him about it?"

Jimmy gulped. "My sponsor?" Annie could see that Jimmy was a little afraid of this man, afraid of losing his approval. That was a good sign, wasn't it? Jimmy sighed, "Yeah, I will. I promise, okay?"

Annie nodded. "Okay."

"Are you going to tell Harry about this?"

"Harry? No way! He'd never let you in here again."

"Thanks. I appreciate that."

Annie nodded and pursed her lips. She was working hard not to cry. Tears would be counterproductive now. After a long pause, Jimmy asked tentatively, "So what did you do with it?"

Annie knew what he was talking about, but she wanted to give her brother a hard time. "With *what*?"

"With the coke?"

Annie looked straight into her brother's eyes and lied. "I flushed it down the toilet."

Sarah loved the part in Watership Down *where brave warrior rabbit Bigwig infiltrates an evil enemy warren. Going undercover, Bigwig feels no guilt as he's shown around the warren because his cause is a noble one. He wants to lure away some females so that he and his friends can have children. Yes, Sarah understood Bigwig perfectly.*

15

Priscilla's Grand Tour

Sarah pretended not to notice as Priscilla smiled at her own reflection in the rearview mirror. Priscilla bragged, "Not to toot my own horn, but if anyone important moves in or out of La Jolla, I'm always the first to find out about it."

Sarah said inanely, "I'm sure you are." Then, deciding that this was not fulsome enough, she added, "I really appreciate you taking me around to look at houses. I've been on a few tours with real estate agents, but I haven't seen anything right for me."

Priscilla smirked. "Well, that's because they're only showing you the same houses that everyone else has turned down." As always, Priscilla was fashionably turned out. A silky Diane von Furstenberg halter top showed off her toned, spray-tanned arms. White capri pants advertised her perfect rock-hard rump, and strappy gold Jimmy Choo sandals revealed muscular calves and pedicured feet. She was elaborately made up and wore her long blond hair down in a glamorous blowout. The effect was almost perfect. When a breeze blew and ruffled Priscilla's hair, Sarah noticed some light bruising around her eyes from a recent Botox session.

Upon seeing Priscilla, Sarah had been relieved. Sarah knew that when dealing with the Priscillas of the world, it was best to match them on casualness and one-up them on style. The victor in such an encounter sent the intimidating message "I am effortlessly more chic than you are." Sarah wore a close-fitting purple sundress—a Roberto Cavalli knockoff—and silver high-heeled Versace sandals. The dress was just as Southern California casual as Priscilla's getup. But the contrast of Sarah's red hair and white shoulders against the purple dress made her look far more glamorous.

The first stop on Priscilla's itinerary was a seven-bedroom house built during California's tiki craze. It was a two-story rectangle with a gray cement facade on the ground floor and cedar paneling on the top level. The place was encircled by teak fencing, palm trees, and short, fat stone statues, the Polynesian equivalent of garden gnomes. The only things missing were hula dancers and a barbecue with a pig on the spit.

The mistress of the house was a tall, thin brunette with an overbite named Madge Porter. Madge was somewhere in her late fifties. She'd obviously had work done. The smoothness of her face clashed with the wattles of her neck, and her eyebrows were permanently raised so as to give her a perpetually startled look, as if she had just been goosed. Madge showed Priscilla and Sarah around the house, and they expressed appropriate reverence at its amenities. Behold the massive kidney-shaped swimming pool with Spanish tiling! Tremble before the lush back lawn with its island-themed wicker patio sets! Bow down before the plushly carpeted spa room with a huge brown hot tub sunk into the center of its floor!

At the front door, Madge offered Sarah a slip of paper with her phone number on it. She invited Sarah to please come again. Madge had lived in this house for so long. She hated to leave, but her husband insisted they trade up to a larger place in Rancho Santa Fe. It would be wonderful for Madge to know that her beloved home was going to the right sort of person. Afterward, in the car, Priscilla informed Sarah that the "right sort of person" would have to pay ten million dollars to buy Madge's house. Sarah decided she would have no qualms about selling overpriced face cream to Madge Porter.

Stop number two on Priscilla's tour was a sprawling Tudor perched on a bluff high above the ocean. Its owner, Torie, said she and her husband, Max, wanted seven million for the place. Sarah took Torie's card but had little hope of ever selling anything to the woman. Torie looked like she was in her twenties. Back in the car, Priscilla confirmed that Torie was indeed a young trophy wife. Her husband, a former hedge-fund manager, was forty years older than her.

The final stop on Priscilla's tour was a white New England–style colonial with dark blue shutters and a rose garden out front. Pulling up alongside it, Priscilla switched off her engine and asked, "Do you like it?"

"Of course. What's not to like?"

Priscilla smirked. "Yes, I thought this might be more your style than the others. There's one hitch."

"What?"

Priscilla paused for effect, then said, "The lady of the house, Natalie, doesn't *know* that it's going on the market."

"Come again?"

Priscilla leaned forward and rubbed her hands together as if she were about to sample a particularly tasty dish. "Well, Natalie's husband, Eric, is a finance guy. His group invested in San Diego real estate during the boom, made a fortune off it. Anyhoo, when the market turned south, his investments imploded. So . . ."

"So?"

Priscilla's vulpine smile widened. "So he's been borrowing money all over town. He even asked my husband for a loan. It was *so* embarrassing for Roger. Roger says Eric's finances are a complete disaster. He'll be lucky to keep his offices open for another month. And—get this—Eric hasn't told Natalie anything about it. The woman has no clue what's going on. Isn't that amazing?"

Sarah felt a stab of nausea. Priscilla had brought her to circle like a vulture over this poor woman's home. Sarah mumbled, "Uh-huh."

Oblivious to Sarah's disgust, Priscilla said, "Anyhoo, I figure this place will be on the market by March at the latest. I bet you can get a terrific deal on it. You'll be dealing with some *very* motivated sellers."

Sarah stared at Priscilla for a long moment. Priscilla had craned her neck forward, and she had an expectant look on her face. With a start, Sarah realized that the creature wanted to be thanked. Sarah forced a smile and said, "Thanks. It's so thoughtful of you to put me onto this."

Priscilla waved this off. "Oh, it's nothing. I've known Natalie forever. And I figured, why not turn one friend's misfortune into another friend's opportunity? It's like they always say, 'When God closes a door, he opens a window.'" Sarah smiled weakly. She hoped the next time God shut a door, he slammed it hard on Priscilla's fingers. Priscilla picked up her purse and opened her car door.

Sarah grabbed her arm. "We're not going in there? Are we?"

"Of course, I told Natalie to expect us around noon."

Sarah blustered, "But . . ."

Priscilla smiled reassuringly. "Don't worry. I told Natalie that I wanted to introduce you to her. She heard me talking about you at the club."

"What did you say?"

"That you were planning to move to La Jolla, and that you wanted to meet some of your future neighbors. I asked if we could drop by. Natalie's always fancied herself as something of a social butterfly." Priscilla rolled her eyes, confident that she alone deserved this coveted title. "So she said yes. C'mon. Let's not keep the lady waiting."

The lady in question answered the door on the first ring. Natalie Wilson was a short, stocky blonde with piercing blue eyes and a huge, anxious smile. She answered the door, saying, "Omigosh, you guys made it! I was beginning to worry that you wouldn't get around to me."

Priscilla asked, "I'm sorry. Are we late?"

Natalie shook her head. "No. Well, just by fifteen minutes or so. You know me, I'm always so uptight about timing. I'm early to everything." Natalie laughed in a short, staccato burst.

Priscilla introduced Sarah. And Natalie said, "Sarah, omigosh, you really *are* gorgeous. I mean, Priscilla mentioned that you were pretty, but I had no idea."

Sarah colored. Kindness from this woman made her feel like a heel. "Thanks, that's sweet of you."

Natalie led Sarah and Priscilla into the living room. It was a huge, sunny room with hardwood floors, light blue couches, and a massive maple coffee table. The walls were strewn with children's drawings and large black-and-white photographs: little girl Wilson and little boy Wilson holding hands; Daddy Wilson lifting his son up in the air; little girl Wilson jumping down from a jungle gym with a triumphant smile on her face.

Sarah said, "These photos are good." And they were.

Natalie said, "Thanks so much. One of my creative outlets."

"You're into photography?"

"Oh yes. I don't go *anywhere* without my camera. I love the way it allows me to see things, really *see* things. I've always been a very visual person. You know what I mean? Very creative." Suddenly, Natalie paused and her eyes widened. "Omigosh, where are my manners? I haven't even offered you something to drink. What will you have? Water? Iced tea? Soda?"

Sarah and Priscilla both asked for Diet Cokes, and Natalie scurried to the kitchen. She returned immediately with the sodas and a plate of cheese and crackers. She handed out drinks and then laid coasters on the table. Bustling about quickly, Natalie reminded Sarah of a hummingbird. When Natalie finally perched on the couch, she started pecking away at Sarah with questions. It was a surreal process. As soon as Natalie would ask a question, she would either answer it herself or substitute another question. Natalie began, "So, you're thinking of moving down here?"

Sarah said, "Yes, right now I'm up in—"

Natalie interrupted, "LA. You're from LA, right? I certainly understand the impulse to get out of LA. It's a zoo. Much more peaceful down here. More family friendly. Do you have children?"

"No, not yet, but—"

"I have two. Elizabeth and Grayson. I know what you're thinking. Grayson Wilson. That's too many 'sons' for one name. Do you plan to have children?"

Sarah nodded. "Someday, but first—"

"Good. So have you and your husband put in any offers on houses down here?"

"No, not yet. We're still—"

"I'm sorry. I am being so presumptuous. I tend to assume *everyone* is married. I mean, hello, you could be divorced and here I am asking about your husband."

Sarah smiled. "No, you guessed right, I am married. His name—"

"Not that there's anything wrong with being divorced. Heck, I'm divorced. My first marriage only lasted three years. But hey, if I hadn't gotten divorced from Trevor, I never would have met Eric. What did you say your husband's name was?"

Sarah began, "Michael. He's a—"

"Eric and I have been so lucky. We have a terrific marriage. I think the key is that we're so different from each other. We balance each other out. He's the big provider and all that. And I handle the kids and the artistic side of things." Sarah tried to imagine an artistic side of marriage, but she came up dry. Natalie went on. "You *have* to try some of this cheese. I got it from the farmers' market. It's amazing. Seriously, you have to have some. Otherwise, I'll eat it. And I do not need any help putting on weight. I still haven't been able to lose the weight I gained from carrying Eliza—that's short for Elizabeth. You wouldn't know it to look at me, but I work out two hours a day." Sarah felt a twinge of sympathy. In La Jolla, land of the svelte and the suctioned, carrying around an extra ten pounds actually did demand an explanation.

When Natalie paused for breath, Priscilla jumped in. "So, I've been taking Sarah around to look at houses this morning."

Natalie perked up. "Have you? Did you show her the Porter house? Oh, listen to me, 'Porter house.' Sounds like a steak."

Priscilla answered, "Yes, we saw Madge's and Torie's places. Sarah is at the start of her house search. She still needs to see—"

Natalie interrupted and turned to Sarah. "Oh yes, you couldn't possibly settle on a house this soon. I must have looked at dozens of—"

Priscilla cut in. "Yes. So I was wondering if you wouldn't mind showing Sarah around your place. I know you guys aren't planning on selling, but seeing the place might give Sarah a sense of what the houses are like in this neighborhood." Sarah winced. Priscilla was a nasty piece of work.

Natalie beamed. "Of course, I wouldn't mind!" She leaped to her feet and took them on a tour: the pool, the backyard, the sunny children's rooms, the playroom, Natalie's studio, the master bedroom. Natalie boasted that she had decorated them all. Did she mention that interior design was another of her creative outlets?

After the tour, Natalie asked Priscilla and Sarah to stay for lunch. They really *should* stay. Natalie had bought some terrific prosciutto, and if they didn't stay, Natalie would eat it herself. And that was the last thing she needed. Did she mention that she worked out two hours a day and still couldn't lose a single pound?

But Priscilla had gotten what she wanted. She piously told Natalie that Saturday afternoons were for family. At the front door, Sarah thanked Natalie for showing her around. "Your home is beautiful. I love what you've done with it. The paintings in the children's rooms, the photographs in the hallways, the color scheme. You're so creative. I envy your talent."

Natalie colored prettily. "Thank you. It's kind of you to notice. Nobody *notices* these things."

Priscilla took Sarah by the arm. "We really have to be going." The women walked down to Priscilla's car.

From there, Priscilla drove back to her place. When they pulled into Priscilla's driveway, Sarah asked, "So, do I get to meet the family?"

"Oh, Lord no, Roger is off at the club, and Chelsea's at soccer."

"I thought Saturday afternoons were 'for family.'"

"And they are, mostly. Carmelita will bring Chelsea back by four, and Roger should be back then too. That's enough togetherness, don't you think?" Priscilla winked conspiratorially at Sarah and then led her up the walk to the house. Inside, Priscilla fetched two premade Oriental salads from the refrigerator. She plated them and put them on the kitchen table. Then she retrieved a bottle of white wine. Brandishing the bottle in the air, Priscilla cooed, "While the cat's away . . ."

Sarah smiled stiffly. She was grateful that she'd arranged for Annie to call her at one. She needed a break from Priscilla. As Priscilla poured the wine, Sarah sifted through the magazines on the edge of the table. On top was an issue of *The Economist*. Below that, Sarah found what she was looking for: *People* magazine.

On the cover was a picture of Cassandra Blake, a fading movie star who'd married a man ten years her junior. Cassandra Blake had been famous ever since she had emerged in a bikini from a school carnival dunk tank in *Bisby High*. Since then, she had battled giant man-eating cockroaches in *Infestation*. She had worn pastel cardigans as an inspirational women's studies professor in *Mrs. Chips*. And she had been wooed in three smash-hit romantic comedies: *Oh, You!*, *Oh, You Again!*, and *Me, Finally!* During her long career, Cassandra Blake never seemed to age. Time refined her, polishing her the way a river polishes a pebble.

She grew shinier and more angular over the years, her skin more taut, her muscles more defined.

Now Cassandra Blake was on display on tabloid covers across the country. The young Adonis she'd married had been caught in a sex scandal. *People* published a cover photo of Cassandra Blake running her fingers through her hair in dismay; the subtitle was "Cassie's Anguish." Looking down at the *People* cover, Sarah exhaled loudly. Priscilla asked, "What? What is it?"

Sarah shook her head. "No, nothing. Work stuff."

Priscilla looked down at the *People* cover. Her eyes widened. "Is Cassandra Blake one of your clients?"

"I'd tell you, but then I'd have to kill you." Sarah winked.

"What's she like?"

"Let's say she's not too happy right about now." Then, on schedule, Sarah's phone rang. She had reprogrammed it so that when Annie called, "Cassie" would flash on the display. Sarah sighed. "Speak of the devil." She held the phone to her ear. "Hello, Cassie."

Annie said cheerfully, "See? I didn't forget. One o'clock on the dot."

Sarah fingered the *People* cover and flashed a weary smile at Priscilla. "Yes, Cassie, of course, I've seen it. I've got a copy of it right here in front of me." Sarah nodded and pretended to listen to her client rant. Sarah interrupted periodically. "Yes, I agree. I think the *People* photo was a good one . . . Yes, I saw *US Weekly* . . . Yes, I know."

Shooting an apologetic look at Priscilla, Sarah rose from her chair and walked a few steps toward the kitchen window, as if this small physical distance would somehow ensure privacy. "Yes, I understand . . . Well, of course, divorce is an option . . . First, you do the 'hurt, going into seclusion' act . . . Yes, and then after a few months, you go on *Ellen* and talk about how you've managed to heal . . . Yes, I'm sure Ellen will have you . . . No, she's not mad about that anymore. She told me so . . . What? Yes, I've gotten some more . . . Dr. Étinav sent me a shipment . . . Yes, I will bring a few jars . . . I can't bring more than three, though . . . Okay, four because you're hurting . . . Yes, okay, see you tonight."

Sarah switched off her phone and turned back to Priscilla. "Sorry about that."

No apologies were necessary. Priscilla gazed at Sarah with more than admiration, with awe. Forget about La Jolla's well-to-do, Sarah knew the ultimate people who mattered: celebrities! Not sure what to say to such a player, Priscilla silently poured out two glasses of wine and handed one to Sarah. Sarah nursed her glass slowly. She did not rush to fill the silence. She had been a lawyer long enough to know that sometimes the best way to control a conversation was by saying nothing.

Priscilla spent the next half hour trying to get Sarah to talk about her famous client. What was Cassandra Blake going to do? Would she divorce her boy toy? And what was the deal with Ellen? Why did Cassandra think Ellen was mad at her? Did Sarah know Ellen too?

Sarah played it coy. She brandished "client confidentiality" the way a Spanish dancer hides behind a fan. Priscilla backed off again and again. Finally, after twenty minutes, Priscilla hit pay dirt. Sarah wouldn't talk about Cassandra's marital woes, but—sure, why not—she would explain that stuff about the jars. Had Priscilla ever heard of a French scientist named Maurice Étinav?

Priscilla made the book club read Queen Bees and Wannabes. *She'd seen a TV spot talking about the book, about the subtly brutal culture of female teen cliques and bullying. As president of the Gillespie PTA, Priscilla felt bullying was a very important subject, and she made sure that the other book club members agreed with her.*

16

Miracle Cream

As soon as Sarah's car pulled out of her driveway, Priscilla called Dawn. Dawn picked up after one ring. She and her mother-in-law, Regina, were at Spa Hélene getting pedicures, and Dawn was bored, bored, bored. Priscilla crowed, "I had the most amazing conversation with Sarah. Guess who one of her clients is? Cassandra Blake!"

"No!"

"Yes!"

"How do you know?"

"I overheard the two of them talking."

"Get out!"

"No, it's true. Sarah was right here in my kitchen when Cassandra Blake called. She was furious about all the press coverage."

Dawn said, "What? Cassandra's mad at the press? You'd think she'd save her anger for that hubby. I can't believe he messed around with those skanks." Although Dawn had not cracked a book in years, she read every inch of the three tabloid magazines to which she subscribed.

Priscilla said, "Well, duh, I'm sure Cassie's mad at him, but the phone call to Sarah was all about the press coverage. That's what Sarah specializes in. Anyhoo, they were figuring out how Cassie should respond. You know: leave him and do the wounded lady routine or stay and talk about forgiveness."

"Uck! I hate that forgiveness crap. It's so tedious. Word to Hillary Clinton: We know you secretly hate this man! You are fooling no one."

"Yeah, well, the wounded lady stuff gets old fast too."

Dawn objected, "Not if you do it right. Like Sandra Bullock. Retreat into seclusion and adopt a brown baby to show you have grown from the whole experience. *Puh-lease* tell me Cassandra Blake is going to adopt!"

"I dunno. She and Sarah didn't go there."

Disappointed, Dawn said only, "Oh."

Priscilla went on. "Cassie and Sarah talked for a long while, and it sounds like Sarah wants Ellen to play a big role in their PR strategy. "

"Wow! So Sarah knows Ellen too?"

Pumped up with importance via association, Priscilla nodded. "Oh yes. They're good friends, and there's more."

"More?"

Priscilla couldn't resist bragging. "It took me a while to get it out of Sarah. She kept babbling about client confidentiality and all that."

"What? What is it?"

Priscilla simpered, "Let's just say that Cassandra Blake has added something new to her beauty regimen."

"Is she taking Botox again? Restylane?"

"No, not Botox. Something else. Something *new*." Priscilla paused for an imaginary drum roll.

Dawn couldn't stand it anymore. "What? What is it?"

"You remember that spy thriller Cassie did a few years back? *Four Across*?"

"The one where the missile codes are all hidden in crossword puzzles?"

"Yes. That one. Well, they shot part of it in Paris. Back then, Cassandra Blake was still hunting for a cause. She hadn't discovered teen mothers yet. So she went around to lots of do-gooder foundations, trying to find something to spark her interest. And that's how she met this French scientist, some kind of genius named Étinav. The guy was trying to develop a way to treat flesh-eating bacteria. Sarah told me all about him."

"Yuck."

"I know! Anyhoo, the guy couldn't do anything to heal skin that had already been infected. But he tried to develop a cream that would kill the bacteria before they spread onto healthy skin."

"Did it work?"

"Not really. It didn't really kill off the bacteria. It sort of slowed them down. Anyhoo, Étinav had his patients put this stuff all over their bodies. And afterward, when he removed the cream, he found that the cream had improved the healthy skin. Wrinkles disappeared. Saggy skin became firmer. Discolorations vanished."

"Amazing!"

"I know. I mean, here's a guy trying to cure some gross disease. And instead he does something way more important. He finds an honest-to-God fountain of youth."

"Wow!"

"I know. So he stays in touch with Cassandra Blake, and he tells her his cream will make her look ten years younger. But there's a catch. Even in Europe, it takes years, I mean *years,* to get this stuff approved for use on the market."

With real indignation, Dawn said, "I can't believe the government would move so slowly on this stuff. Don't they realize people's *lives* are at stake?"

"I know. So anyway, Étinav says screw it. He opens his own lab and starts secretly manufacturing the stuff. He sells it to a bunch of hand-picked high-end users, people who can fork over big money *and* keep their mouths shut. And guess who his first customer is?"

"Cassandra Blake."

"Yes, ma'am. She started using it a year ago. She's paranoid about having Étinav ship it to her house. She's got paparazzi climbing all over the place, checking through her garbage, all that. So she has him ship the cream to Sarah. Sarah starts talking to the great doctor, and they build up a rapport. Soon he's shipping Sarah cream for Cassandra Blake plus some extra. And Sarah starts selling it to her clients as a courtesy. They go gaga over the stuff."

Dawn asked, "How much is it?"

"Two thousand a jar, and Sarah's got a huge waiting list!"

"Do you think she'd be willing to get some for us?"

Priscilla smiled, pleased and slightly amazed by her own generosity. "I already asked her to add both our names to her customer list. She said she'll do what she can, but we have to keep this hush-hush. Okay?"

"Of course!"

The conversation ended quickly after that. Both women had calls to make.

Annie loved Julia Child's My Life in France, *the story of how Julia Child transformed herself—in middle age!—from a gawky Texan hick into a gawky, world-famous French chef. Julia's husband, a career civil servant, supported her every step of the way. It probably helped that they had no kids.*

17

Annie's Secret Ingredient

When Annie's husband opened the front door on Monday night, Maddie jumped into his arms and rubbed her glop-covered face against his shirt. Tensing, Harry asked, "Honey, what do you have on your face?"

Maddie beamed. "Mommy's been trying her magic potions on me again."

Annie knew she was in trouble as soon as Harry walked into the kitchen. Ominously silent, he deposited Maddie on the floor and ripped a paper towel off the roll over the sink. Then he folded the towel into a neat square and dabbed the glop off his shirt in quick, jerky motions. As he pawed at his shirt, he surveyed the wreckage that his three children had made of the house, the wreckage they made every day. The house's open floor plan enabled him to view the carnage in his living room *and* his kitchen without taking a single step. Disapproval made easy.

Watching him, Annie felt a rush of guilt spiked with annoyance: guilt because the house was in such a state, and annoyance at Harry's infinite capacity to be shocked by it. She felt like screaming, "Kids are messy. If you want kids, you want *this*." Harry was like a sun worshipper who moves to Alaska and then walks around in a permanent fit of pique because of the goddamned snow.

Laying a doily over her annoyance, Annie said cheerfully, "Hey, big spender. How was your day?"

Harry mumbled, "Fine, fine." Rachel lurched into the kitchen and threw her arms around his legs. Harry picked her up and headed for the living room.

Annie rushed to get the kitchen under control. She screwed the tops back on her skin cream jars and wiped down the counters. Then she picked up the toys that littered the kitchen floor and carried them into the living room, where Oscar was parked on the carpet watching a *Thomas* video. As Annie fit the toys back into their bins, Harry asked, "Should Oscar be watching this much TV?" *This* was how it always began. Harry never started with what he was really mad about, the mess. Instead, he took a scenic route through Annie's other shortcomings.

Still straining to sound cheerful—who the hell decided that mothers are supposed to flute every damned thing they say?—Annie said, "It's his first video today. I told him he could watch it after we finished floor time."

"How long is this one?"

"I dunno." Annie shrugged, as if she had no idea that the movie lasted a whopping fifty-two minutes, not counting previews.

Harry reached for the DVD case. He always double-checked things. It was his way. He was the kind of person who immediately reached for a dictionary whenever you disagreed with him on the meaning of a word. Annie found it infuriating. Why couldn't he understand that marriage required a bit of factual wiggle room? Harry announced, "This video is fifty-two minutes long. I thought we were limiting TV to thirty minutes a day."

Annie hated his use of the imperial *we*. "We" meant "you": "I thought *you* were limiting TV to thirty minutes a day." Harry couldn't be bothered with enforcing such limits. He was off at his precious, high-powered job.

Feeling a fight coming on, Annie stuck out her chin and cocked her neck. It was her version of pawing the ground before charging. She said, "I don't think an extra twenty-two minutes will kill him."

Harry countered, "No, it won't *kill* him. But it certainly won't *help* him. McPhail said we should limit television to thirty minutes a day."

Annie rolled her eyes. "Yes, I remember The Commandments. Thou shalt not watch more than thirty minutes of television a day. Thou shalt go on at least five playdates a week. Thou shalt do twenty minutes of floor time with Oscar at least six times a day. The McPhail God *loves* to legislate!"

"It's his job."

"Yes, it's *his* job to make up tons of rules. It is *your* job to pester me about those rules. And it is *my* job to obey."

"C'mon, Annie. These rules aren't arbitrary. McPhail doesn't just—"

Annie interrupted, "I'm not saying his rules are random. Heaven forbid I argue with the great and powerful Oz! No, what I'm saying is that his rules should not be *rules.* That way, I can aim for thirty minutes of television a day, but if I overshoot by an extra twenty minutes, I don't get yanked in front of the Inquisition."

"Annie, you know perfectly well that if McPhail *suggests* half an hour of television, everyone's going to blow it off. Hell, even when he makes it a rule, you blow it off!"

"That's not true! Most of the time I stay within his precious limits. You know that!"

Harry shot back, "You break the TV rule all the time! Heck, last weekend, you let him watch an entire movie. Ninety minutes of television in one sitting!"

"He wanted to watch *Cars.* Are you saying that we can never let him watch an entire movie again? I'm exposing him to a bit of television. It is not plutonium!"

Harry rose from the couch, saying, "Listen, you're not listening." Annie *hated* it when Harry used that expression. It was a self-fulfilling prophecy. The quickest way to get Annie to shut her mind was to tell her that she *already* had shut it. Harry went on, "McPhail was very clear on this. Kids on the spectrum should not watch TV. They need as much social practice as possible. The last thing they need is hours of sitting passively watching unrealistic characters in totally unrealistic situations. All the books say the same thing!"

"Yes, all the books *do* say the same thing! What the books *don't* account for are the pluses of watching TV."

Harry sneered, "Like what?"

"Like here we have a little boy who has trouble fitting in, and maybe, just maybe, he'll have an easier time fitting in if he knows what the hell the other kids are talking about! If the other kids are playing *Thomas* or *Yo Gabba Gabba* or whatever damned thing they're playing, maybe Oscar will be able to join in if he's seen the crap on TV. Imagine it! Unplanned playtime with actual peers! Instead of playing with Mommy or his therapist or his aide!"

Annie saw the muscles in Harry's jaw shift. She'd scored a point, but Harry didn't take long to recover. He crossed his arms against his chest. "I have a hard time believing that you are letting him watch TV *just* because you want to enhance his social life."

"You're right. You've got me! I also let him watch TV because *it makes my life easier*! There, I said it. Even though all the books are against it, I still let my kids watch TV because—guess what—I don't *live* in a book! I live here, in the real world. In the real world, kids won't sit patiently playing with their educational toys while I throw dinner together. They fight with each other. They come barreling into the kitchen to grab at Mommy and the hot stove. They want attention, and they want it *all the time*! Now, maybe you and McPhail are capable of giving three kids all the attention they want while you cook dinner, but I am not! *I need TV!*"

"It doesn't take fifty-two minutes to cook dinner, Annie!"

"No, it doesn't. But it *does* take fifty-two minutes to make dinner, clean up the dishes to appease my neat-freak husband, pack lunches for the next day of school, and decompress from fourteen hours of domestic bliss!"

"Right. I can see that you're taking tons of time to clean up before I get home!" Harry gestured around the toy-strewn living room. "And why the hell are you packing tomorrow's lunches while the kids are still up? Isn't that something you could do *after* they go to sleep?"

Annie sputtered. Now Harry had scored a point. She heard the net swish. She hated the transparency of her job as an at-home mom. At the end of the day, Harry got to come home and pick apart everything she did wrong. He got to give endless "helpful" tips. Harry was qualified to judge how well she did because *everyone* is qualified to critique a housewife. When you're an at-home mom, suddenly everyone in the world is your management consultant. The same wasn't true of Harry. Whenever he fell short at home, he always got to hide behind the opaque screen of his job. And Annie couldn't attack him on that front. Oh no, these days, Harry was very touchy about his job. Though he earned plenty for an engineer, it ate away at him that he didn't earn enough to pay for Oscar's treatment. He'd confessed this to Annie late one night—a rare moment of fatigue-induced candor. Harry had no idea how to process his shame or his anxiety about Oscar, so instead he channeled that energy into doing things: working even longer hours, cleaning every inch of the house, and haranguing Annie. Through clenched teeth, Annie said, "If I don't make the lunches before bed, they won't get made."

"And why won't they get made? What in God's name is keeping you so busy at night?"

"You know perfectly well that Sarah and I are trying to start a business."

In a voice laden with sarcasm, Harry said, "Oh yes, your beauty business. I keep forgetting. You can't be expected to do anything at night because you and Sarah have decided to play Avon ladies!"

Annie squared her shoulders. "I am *not* playing. I am trying to raise money to pay for Oscar's therapy."

"Right. By putting glop all over our daughter's face?"

"I need to make sure the cream *feels* right."

"And you think it's a good idea to use our daughter as a guinea pig?"

"I'm not putting anything harmful on her! It's antiaging cream! The worst thing that could happen is she'll look five instead of six."

The fight went on for a few more minutes until Rachel started crying. This rang the bell, so Annie and Harry retreated to their corners. They soldiered through the kids' bedtime routine, saying as little to each other as possible. Then, with the kids tucked in, Harry went to bed, and Annie trudged down to the kitchen to do battle with her face cream.

Standing at her kitchen counter, Annie tried to set aside her anger and focus. She'd already wasted two weeks concocting a fragrant, plant-based formula that would have been a big hit with the Whole Foods crowd. But she'd scrapped it because of allergies. Annie hadn't used peanut oil or other obvious allergens, but she didn't have enough data on avocado oil or mango extracts to feel fully confident. The last thing she needed was for a client's face to blow up or go blotchy just because Annie felt like getting creative. Annie kept picturing Violet Beauregarde—the gum-chewing little brat in *Charlie and the Chocolate Factory* who'd swollen up like a blueberry after sampling Wonka's latest.

No, it was best to be safe. She wound up going with StriVectin and Pond's, boring standbys that had been tested on countless lab rats for decades. She'd come up with a carefully calibrated mixture that improved both creams. Now, standing at her counter, Annie opened a jar of the stuff and spread some on her palms. Not bad. But still, something was missing.

Annie had to find that *something* fast. Sarah had come through in a big way. Her La Jolla outings had already produced orders from Valerie, Heather, Dawn, Madge Porter, and Priscilla. Even Dawn's mother-in-law had gotten into the act. And Heather told Sarah that a bunch of her other friends were also eager to buy. Sarah had whetted their appetites by saying that she would talk to Dr. Étinav and see what he could do. Étinav was very selective about his clientele. Glowing with success, Sarah told Annie that the cream didn't have to be perfect. Annie should throw together some creams already on the market and call it a day. With six sales under her belt, Sarah now seemed confident that she could easily peddle whatever swill Annie produced. Annie wished she shared her friend's boundless, unjustified optimism.

Now it was Annie's turn to deliver. She had found a good container for the cream. At least she'd managed to get *that* done. She chose a white glass jar with a silver top that she found in a tiny store on Elmira Street down in El Cajon. The jar had a pleasing, slightly asymmetrical shape. It was for a high-end Mexican bunion cream. Annie had bought twenty jars. Now the jars stood empty, twenty yawning maws waiting to be filled with Annie's magic formula.

Annie knew what Sarah wanted her to do: fill the jars with harmless goop. And that was what Annie thought she would do back when she had first hatched this scheme. But now, with actual orders to fill, the idea of throwing together some ineffectual slop seemed not just risky but stupid. It would kill any hope of repeat business. And Annie and Sarah *needed* repeat business. Twelve thousand dollars was decent money, but Annie and Sarah would need more, a lot more, if they were going to pay for Oscar's therapy *and* Sarah's IVF. And despite all the research Annie did on the face cream market—all the data indicating massive sales of quack remedies—Annie still worried that if the cream did nothing, somehow the customers would *know* it. They might not know it consciously, but they'd know it at some level. And they wouldn't want to buy it again.

The process of formulating her face cream caused Annie's attitude toward her customers to shift. Throwing together a formulation, a recipe, had tweaked Annie's maternal instincts. It was like cooking for the neighbors' kid. When he first sat down at her counter, Annie did not feel much for him. But once he tucked into a plate of her food, he became hers for a short time. Now that she'd spent weeks trying to prepare something for her customers, Annie wanted her cream to be good for them, to sustain them somehow. It should not be cosmetic junk food. Joan Collins once said that being beautiful was like being born rich and getting poorer every day. Annie couldn't make these women beautiful, but maybe she could make them *feel* beautiful.

Annie's one experiment with mood-altering ingredients had been a bust. She'd used a mortar and pestle to grind down some of her Prozac pills and then mixed the Prozac dust into the cream. She'd tested the Prozac cream on herself, but it hadn't done anything for her. No surprise there. Annie had checked online for Prozac's dermal bioavailability—how much the skin would absorb it—and the numbers had been dismal, just 10 percent. Ten percent of a Prozac's already-muted kick wasn't going to wow anyone.

For weeks, Annie had known what she should do. She closed the door to her kitchen so no kids would come blundering in, and she put on her white lab coat, goggles, face mask, and vinyl gloves. This was standard PPE—personal protective equipment, the chemist's equivalent of a bike helmet. Then she grabbed the step stool and headed for the pantry. The cocaine was right where she had left it, inside the old tin Band-Aid box at the back of the top shelf. She took down the box and walked over to the kitchen counter.

Annie had done her homework, checking cocaine's bioavailability online. And cocaine was way more skin-friendly than Prozac. The skin could absorb twice as much cocaine as Prozac. The body would absorb coke more quickly through the membranes of the nose, resulting in a more dramatic high. But the skin of the face could do the job too. Just one gram of cocaine in each forty-gram jar of cream, and the user would experience a gentle high, a little surge in confidence.

She took out a small electronic scale. Since she no longer worked in a proper lab, Annie had gone online to find this gadget. The Internet taught Annie that gun enthusiasts use high-end scales to concoct homemade gun powder. How about that? Science was everywhere! Now Annie put the scale to use, measuring out exactly one gram of cocaine onto the scale. Then she dissolved the gram into a liposome base—that's fatty solution in plain English. She hoped the liposome base would maximize the cocaine's absorption. Using a small stainless-steel spatula, she mixed the base together with thirty-nine grams of her cream formula. She loaded the mixture into one of the empty bunion cream jars and headed upstairs to face her husband.

Harry lay on his side, pretending to sleep. Annie knew he was playing possum. He was no more capable of sleeping after an argument than she was. She sat down on the bed, asking, "Are we going to talk about this?"

Harry took a while to answer. "Do we *have* to?"

"Yes, we have to."

Harry spoke mechanically, "I'm sorry I blew up at you. I shouldn't have yelled at you like that in front of the kids."

Annie nodded. "I'm sorry too. I shouldn't have yelled either. And I will try to get the house in better shape before you get home. I promise." Annie spoke in the same monotone that Harry did. If this had been a performance, the audience would have assumed they were watching two of the world's worst actors.

Not bothering to raise his head from his pillow, Harry said, "That's all right."

Annie wanted to pass out, but she knew she had wife work to do. "You want to tell me what's stressing you out?"

"What do you mean?"

"I mean, do you want to tell me why you went off like that? We both know it's not just the mess. Let's face it, this place is *always* a mess."

Finally abandoning his monotone, Harry sighed, "It's the SE chip." Harry's employer, Colfak, had sunk a huge wad of cash into developing this semiconductor chip. The last engineer who had overseen the project had botched it, so Colfak had canned him and handed over his gooey mess to its underpaid golden boy, Harry.

Annie said warily, "What about it?"

"We are two months behind schedule."

Annie countered, "Yeah, but that's not your fault! Colfak knows that. Hell, that's why they fired that other guy."

"Yes, and that's why they are *going* to fire me."

"They're not going to fire you. You're the one who's digging them out of this hole."

Harry sighed. "Yeah, well, that's not how Malverson sees it." Malverson was the company's head bean counter, its chief financial officer. Harry had had run-ins with Malverson before.

Harry went on, "Malverson called a meeting for tomorrow morning. I'm supposed to come in and explain to him and two other senior VPs exactly when we will have a perfect prototype."

Annie said, "Oh, hon, I'm sure you'll do fine." But she wasn't sure. Harry was a terrific engineer—he was great at designing projects, making them work, and motivating the people beneath him to produce—but when it came to public speaking and schmoozing his superiors, the man was hopeless. He became a ball of nerves. Annie reached across the duvet and took Harry's hand. He gave her hand a gentle squeeze. Minutes later, he was asleep.

Unfortunately, the sleep did not do Harry much good. Annie found him in the kitchen at six the next morning. From the papers splayed across the table, she guessed that he must have been up for at least an hour. As usual, he had cleaned up well. Harry was handsome in a lean, middle-aged preppy way. He wore a blue striped Oxford and chinos. He'd showered and taken obvious care to subdue his wavy light brown hair. He'd even put on cologne. Annie hoped that Malverson bastard liked it.

The trouble wasn't Harry's looks. It was his expression. Like most engineers, Harry was a whiz at counting cards, but he made a terrible poker player. He had a gazillion tells: the tension in his eyes, the way he picked at his hair when he got nervous, his defensive body language. He radiated stress and fear.

Annie sat down across from him. "Do you want to run through the spiel for me?"

"No, I've already gone through it four times. I think it's best to leave it alone at this point."

Annie nodded. Then Rachel wailed, and the morning officially began. Annie spent the next hour herding kids, but her main worry was Harry. She made her move as he headed down the hallway to the front door. "Harry, wait."

Harry turned and smiled down at her. "What is it, hon?"

"I have a favor to ask."

"Ask away."

"Well, I thought about what you said last night, about it being wrong for me to use Maddie as a guinea pig."

Harry sighed. "I'm sorry. It was way out of line for me to—"

"No, no. You were right. I'm not using anything toxic. But still, it's the principle of the thing. I shouldn't be testing this stuff on our daughter."

"Look, it's no big deal. Consider yourself forgiven. Now, I've—"

"And in the spirit of forgiveness, I was hoping you could do me a favor."

"A favor?"

Annie reached into her apron and withdrew the jar of cream that she'd mixed the night before. "This is the final formulation. I've tested it on myself. But I'd really like to test it out on someone else, make sure it feels okay."

Harry nodded. "And?"

"Well, I was hoping you'd let me put some on you. Just a little bit."

Harry shrugged. "Why not? I could afford to look a few years younger."

Annie beamed at him. She reached up and rubbed cream onto his cheeks and across the bridge of his nose. Then she rested back on her heels and said, "Well? How's it feel?"

Harry touched his face with his fingers. The cream had dissolved into his pores. He took a deep breath and let it out, as if he was deciding some great matter. Then he smiled down at Annie and said, "Great. Feels just great."

Annie went up on her tiptoes and kissed him. "Thanks, sweetheart. Now, go knock 'em dead."

Forget about Voldemort. For Annie, the biggest villain in literature was Empress Livia from I, Claudius. *Livia schemed to control the Roman Empire, and she bumped off anyone who stood in her way. Friends, relatives, even her own children! Livia's lowest point came when—after decades of marriage—she poisoned her sweet, noble husband, Augustus. The witch!*

18

Confidence Man

Annie felt like a monster. She couldn't believe that she had drugged her own husband. Doing so went against everything she stood for.

Annie had always been a rebel in a family that believed in living better through chemistry. She had spent thirty years watching her thespian parents fortify themselves with booze before every performance. And she had spent another ten years watching her little brother do the same with cocaine, alcohol, Vicodin, and whatever else he could lay his hands on. Through all of it, Annie had played the role of the self-righteous teetotaler.

When Annie's mother spiked the punch at Annie's sweet-sixteen party, Annie had grabbed the punch bowl and dumped the high-octane mixture down the kitchen sink. She had ignored Chloe's protests that it was a sin to waste perfectly good booze to make some tedious moral point. Later, in college, when Annie's lab partner tried to sell her speed, Annie had given him a look of such hostility that the poor boy had transferred to another section.

When Annie chose Harry as a mate, one of his many attractions had been his sobriety. He had plenty of other selling points too: his smarts, his kindness, his sparkling blue eyes, and that over-the-moon smitten look he gave her sometimes (Annie had always wanted a man to look at her like that—all tenderness and heat). For Annie, finding all this in one man and then discovering that he didn't drink felt like a miracle, like picking out a gorgeous, miraculously underpriced house in a perfect neighborhood and then discovering that it also came with a hot tub (a nonessential but wondrous perk!). Temperance wasn't a moral issue to Harry. He was simply allergic to alcohol; it gave him instant headaches. For Annie, the phrase "allergic to alcohol" had an almost lyrical quality. And, of course, Harry was too much of a straight arrow to use drugs. Embarrassed at his lack of worldliness, he confided to Annie that he had never even tried marijuana. He'd shrugged apologetically and said, "I figure the law's the law." Annie thought this was one of the sexiest things she'd ever heard. She almost murmured, "That's right, baby. Talk clean to me. Talk clean."

And now look at her. Just look. Her husband had confided his worries to her. And what had she done? Had she given him a rousing pep talk to boost his confidence? No. Had she assured him that—no matter what happened—she would always love him and believe in him? No. Instead, she had lied to him and spread cocaine on his handsome, gullible face right before he went into a big meeting. And who knew how he'd react to it!

Annie discovered how her experiment had gone when Harry opened the front door at six o'clock that evening. He came in singing. His tuneless, off-key voice sounded wonderful. He greeted Annie with a huge kiss on the lips and a dozen yellow roses. He said, "For my beautiful wife. Sorry about last night."

Annie asked how the meeting went, and Harry launched into a thirty-minute blow-by-blow account of his triumph. "It was beautiful. Hands down, the best presentation I've ever given. Malverson tried to stump me with system integration, but I blew right past him." Once Harry finished crowing, he sat down and played with Oscar and Maddie on the messy living room floor. Later, when Annie fed the family an uninspiring dinner of spaghetti and meatballs, Harry lavishly praised her cooking. He joked as he helped her bathe the kids, and he read them three extra stories at bedtime.

Then, once the kids fell asleep, Harry and Annie went upstairs and had the best sex they'd had in months. Afterward, watching Harry doze, Annie decided that her "special formula" might not be such a bad thing after all. She almost regretted that she wouldn't have another chance to test it out on him.

When Annie read Michael Crichton's Jurassic Park, *she giggled when the park owner bragged about the steps taken to control his dinosaur inmates. Guns! Computer monitoring! Electrified fences! Long before Spielberg worked his magic, Annie easily pictured a T. rex batting away an electric fence like a cobweb. Annie never dreamed that she'd someday act like the park owner—hoping a few magic instructions would allow her to control a different beast: cocaine.*

19

Use Only as Directed

The next morning, Annie led Sarah into her kitchen. There, Annie proudly brandished a jar of Étinav. She caressed the jar's silver top with her index finger like a model showing off a prize on a game show. As usual, Sarah proved a terrific audience. She smiled and danced from foot to foot, squealing, "You're a genius!"

Annie inclined her head graciously. "No, let's face it. *You're* the genius. You're the one who talked these women into shucking out two grand for this stuff."

Sarah beamed. "We're *both* geniuses." The women shared a moment of happy silence in their own honor.

Annie asked, "Are you sure we should call the cream Étinav?"

Sarah nodded. "Absolutely. Priscilla and Valerie *loved* the idea of buying a cream developed by some brilliant scientist to the stars. The doctor is your greatest invention."

Annie picked up the jar she'd been showing off to Sarah and placed it in a Tupperware box with five other jars. "You're going to meet with each of the customers, right?"

"Yes. I figure we can sell a lot more of this stuff if I meet with them one-on-one. One customer can lead to five or six more, you never know."

Annie let out a deep breath. "Good. You have to give these women strict guidelines on how to use this stuff."

Sarah shrugged. "Yeah, sure, whatever."

"No, not whatever. There are some important rules you have to follow in using this stuff. I mean it."

Sarah raised her eyebrows and said haltingly, "Ohh-kay."

"First, tell them they should apply the cream to clean skin. The stuff will not work if they put it on *over* makeup or sunscreen or whatever other goo they usually wear." Sarah nodded. Annie went on, "Second, they should use the cream sparingly. They should apply the cream to their faces once a day, and they should never use more than a half teaspoonful at a time. This is—"

Sarah interrupted, "Wait. Why would we want to tell them that? I mean, the more cream they use, the more they'll buy."

Annie shook her head. "No, they *have* to use it in small amounts."

"Why? I thought this stuff was innocuous."

Annie backpedaled. "It is innocuous, in small amounts."

"What do you mean? What's in this stuff? I thought you blended together some creams that were already on the market."

Annie stammered, "I did. Ninety percent of the formula is a mix of Pond's, StriVectin, and Oil of Olay."

Sarah put her hands on her hips. "Okay, so what's the last 10 percent?"

"A few ingredients I added to give the mix some pep."

"Pep?"

"Yeah. I put in some rose mint, just enough to make the skin tingle. It'll make users feel like the product is actually doing something."

"Okay. Anything else?"

Annie felt her hands start to sweat. This acting thing was a lot harder than it looked. "I put in some caffeine. It makes the muscles of the face tighten. Just a little. It's not a huge effect, and it doesn't last long. But it *is* noticeable. I figure it will make our customers think the cream is working." Annie smiled nervously. She hated lying to Sarah, but what choice did she have? If Sarah *knew* the cream had cocaine in it, she could go to jail for selling it. But if she had no idea what was in the stuff, the government would never be able to go after her. Annie had picked up this legal tidbit from an episode of *Law & Order*. Or was it from *The Shield*?

Sarah nodded. "Makes sense to me. I think a few makeup brands use caffeine already. So why not?"

"Well, it does place certain limits on use. I mean, we don't want women to use too much of the cream on their faces. If they slather the stuff on, their facial muscles might tense up too much. It could be uncomfortable."

Sarah shrugged again. "Okay."

"And the caffeine might stimulate them a bit. Not a lot, just a bit. So I think we should tell our clients to only use the cream in the morning, never at night. That way, it won't keep them up."

"Okay. That's no biggie."

Annie took a deep breath. She wasn't done yet. She said gravely, "And one last thing. We can't sell any of this stuff to pregnant ladies."

"What? Because of the caffeine?" Annie nodded. Sarah pressed, "But there's not *that* much caffeine in there. I mean, it's not like we're giving them a massive dose."

Annie recited the speech she'd practiced earlier that morning in front of her bathroom mirror. She wanted to sound authoritative but not strident—the reassuring voice of an announcer in a drug commercial.

"For a normal woman, the cream does not deliver a big caffeine dose. Only a fraction of the caffeine actually gets absorbed into the bloodstream, so she'll absorb maybe half a cup of coffee's worth of caffeine, tops. But pregnant women are different. Their pores are wide open so they will absorb a lot more caffeine. For a pregnant lady, one dose of Étinav will be like four cups of coffee. That's *way* too much."

"Got it. No pregnant ladies. I don't think that will be much of a problem. Most of our clients are done having kids."

"Good." Annie didn't want to be responsible for any crack babies.

"Any other rules? Will our customers turn into gremlins if they eat after midnight? Should they avoid sunlight and holy water?"

Annie scolded, "This is serious."

Sarah rearranged her features into a solemn look. "I *know* it is." Then Sarah picked up the Tupperware of creams and placed it carefully into her leather Hermès handbag. Smiling hugely, she wiggled her eyebrows and said, "Wish me luck, doll. I'm off to the races."

Annie smiled weakly. "Good luck."

Sarah loved the witty, beautiful heroine of Jane Austen's Emma. *Kind but conceited Emma screws up her friends' lives with her inept attempts at matchmaking. At the book's end, Emma realizes her folly and gives up meddling. Personally, Sarah saw nothing wrong with meddling—so long as you were good at it.*

20

Sarah's Rounds

Sarah felt like dancing on the way out to her car. Selling was turning out to be huge fun. Novelty was a big part of it. Sarah had known for aeons that she could write a legal brief, interview witnesses, and balance Marty's insane demands. But she hadn't known that she had a talent for selling. Finding this skill in her arsenal was an unexpected treat. It gave her a dizzying sense of possibility. Maybe she had other talents, other powers, she did not know about. It was an intense relief to discover that—after forty-two years—she did *not* know herself to the point of tedium.

The other thing Sarah loved about her sales was that they were *hers.* She had spent the past seven years in Marty's shadow. She'd write an article, and Marty would publish it under his own name. She'd develop an argument, and Marty would present it to the judge. Now, finally, it was Sarah's turn to be the "face."

Sarah drove straight from Annie's place to Priscilla's house. She wanted to get Priscilla out of the way so she could enjoy the rest of her rounds. Sarah did not like Priscilla. She reminded Sarah of the cruel popular girls she'd known back in high school. They would spew bile and then smile prettily at Sarah, assuming that she shared their views because she was one of the beautiful people too. Priscilla was another mean girl with an extra twenty years on her odometer and a much bigger bank account.

After exchanging hollow pleasantries, Priscilla led Sarah into her white ultramodern living room. There, Priscilla fished a check out of her tight pink Lululemon tracksuit jacket. "Two thousand dollars made out to Étinav, Incorporated. That's right, isn't it?"

Sarah nodded, "Yes. That's right." She had filled out the forms to set up Étinav, Inc. a few weeks earlier. Sarah accepted Priscilla's check, saying, "Thank you, ma'am." She folded it and tucked it into the outer pocket of her handbag. Then Sarah unsnapped another compartment of her bag and withdrew a jar of Étinav, saying, "Here it is." Priscilla reached out for it, but Sarah said, "Not yet, my dear. We have a few basics to cover first." Sarah settled herself on one of Priscilla's long white couches.

Priscilla sat down too, echoing, "Basics? What basics?"

Sarah explained, "As I told you, Dr. Étinav doesn't let me just hand the cream out. He demands that I personally instruct each client on its proper use." True to her word, Sarah recited each of Annie's rules perfectly. Watching the serious, respectful look on Priscilla's face, Sarah decided that Annie's rules were a plus, from a marketing perspective. They implied that Étinav was powerful stuff, not the sort of crap you picked up from the beauty aisle in your supermarket.

Sarah made only one tweak to Annie's speech. She didn't mention caffeine when she warned Priscilla to use only small doses. Caffeine was so pedestrian. What woman would pay two grand to put Folgers on her face? Instead, Sarah said that Dr. Étinav had put a patented bio-extract in the cream. Yes, *that* sounded appropriately important and scientific. With the catechism recited, Sarah handed the jar over to Priscilla.

Priscilla held it delicately in her hands, her face a mask of greedy delight. "Thank you so much."

Sarah beamed, "It's the least I can do for a friend like you."

Sarah's next stop was Dawn's place. Dawn looked different than she had at the book club. Older somehow. Part of it was the daylight. The strong California sun was less forgiving than the recessed lighting of Valerie's living room. But the bigger change was in Dawn's demeanor. Sarah had marked Dawn down as a boozy, carefree type. But now, sober, Dawn seemed oppressively somber. She crossed her arms tightly against her chest and gave a stiff smile as she introduced Sarah to her mother-in-law, Regina Maris.

Regina looked like the sort of grandmother a rich person would order for himself out of a catalog. Dressed in a light purple cashmere sweater, pearls, and gray slacks, she was a short, thin woman with perfect posture. Sarah guessed that she was somewhere in her sixties, maybe even her seventies. She also guessed that Regina must have been beautiful in her youth. Even now, she was striking. Perfectly coiffed silver hair framed her heart-shaped face. And prominent cheekbones had prevented the epidermal landslide that most women suffer in old age. Her eyes were her best feature, large icy-blue orbs fringed with long silver lashes.

After Dawn introduced her, Regina stepped forward and extended her hand to Sarah. "My dear, I am so pleased to meet you. Dawn has told me *so* much about you."

Sarah shook Regina's hand. "Wonderful to meet you, Mrs. Maris." Then Sarah turned to Dawn. "Dawn, your home is lovely."

Dawn opened her mouth to respond, but Regina was too fast. "It's not *her* home, dear. It's mine." Regina said this with a laugh, as if the idea of Dawn owning such a large spread was ridiculous.

Sarah faltered, "Oh, I'm sorry. I thought Dawn lived here."

Regina went on, "She does, along with my son. But I *own* the place. I decorated it myself." Regina made a sweeping motion, inviting Sarah to admire the opulent surroundings. The furniture was expensive and very old: mahogany end tables with delicately carved curlicues, ornate high-backed chairs, and small porcelain knickknacks. The effect was tasteful but oppressive.

Sarah enthused, "Well, it's quite *something*. So do you live here too?"

Regina waved the suggestion off. "Good Lord, no. I have always felt that it's important for young couples to have their privacy. No, I live two houses down from here. That way, I can come and go as I please."

Sarah said, "Sounds wonderful." The tired look on Dawn's face made it clear that she did not share this view.

Taking charge, Regina said, "So, have you brought this miracle cream I have been hearing so much about?"

Sarah nodded. "Yes. Of course."

Dawn broke in, "I forgot to offer you a drink. Sarah, would you like something? I have water, iced tea . . ."

Regina said acidly, "Yes, one can *always* count on Dawn for a drink."

Sarah ignored this. "Iced tea would be perfect."

Dawn turned to Regina. "Mimsy, what would you like?"

"Nothing for me, dear. And I suggest you follow my example, at least until noon."

Dawn disappeared into the kitchen to fetch Sarah's drink, and Regina gestured for Sarah to sit on the couch. Regina sat across from Sarah in a high-backed red velvet chair. She cocked an eyebrow at Sarah, a prompt for Sarah to perform and make chitchat. And Sarah knew she *should*. The customer is always right and all that. But Sarah didn't *feel* like doing it. Regina brought out something churlish in her. Sarah smiled serenely and let the silence spread out. With no performing monkey in the room, Regina grew impatient. She called out, "Dawn, what's taking so long?"

Dawn answered, "Be there in a minute." The iced tea was taking a suspiciously long time. Sarah guessed that Dawn was in her pantry tipping back a cocktail, a double. Regina rolled her eyes and sighed. Moments later, Dawn appeared with a tall glass of iced tea. "Sorry I took so long. Our ice maker is on the fritz."

Regina said, "Is it? That's strange. That refrigerator is brand-new."

Dawn colored and sat down on the couch next to Sarah. Then she immediately popped up again. "Oh, I forgot to give you the check. It's in the kitchen. I made it out this morning. Étinav, Incorporated, right?" Sarah nodded, and Dawn made a repeat dash for the kitchen.

Dawn was not quite out of earshot when Regina told Sarah, "Let's hope she won't need the ice maker this time."

Dawn came back quickly. She handed Sarah an envelope. Sarah thanked her and popped the envelope into her handbag. Then Sarah took out two jars. "Ladies, here they are: two jars of Étinav." Sarah held up one jar and handed the other to Dawn.

Taking it, Dawn said, "Thank you so much for doing this."

Sarah smiled. "No problem. But before I leave these with you, I have to cover a few details."

Regina bristled, "Details?"

"Yes. Dr. Étinav insists that I instruct each of our clients on—"

Regina interrupted, "Yes. Well, that's lovely, but I'm late for my bridge game down at the club. So I'm afraid I'll have to miss your little tutorial."

Sarah countered, "Oh, I won't keep you long, Regina. There are a few guidelines that Dr. Étinav insists I share."

Regina waved her off. "I think I can figure out how to apply face cream, dear. It's not exactly rocket science."

Sarah flashed her most ingratiating smile. "Of course, but Dr. Étinav insists—"

Regina interrupted again, "Well, surely, you can skip your infomercial with us. The great doctor is not here, and what he doesn't know can't hurt him." Regina tried to sound casual, but Sarah caught the edge in her voice. Regina Maris did not need *anyone* to tell her *anything*.

Sarah held on to her smile. "Regina, I assure you that my instructions are not long or complicated. You've paid a great deal for this cream. You might as well use it correctly."

Dawn cut in, "Mimsy, I think we should—"

Regina retorted, "No offense, dear, but thinking is not exactly your strong suit." Then, to Sarah, Regina said, "How about a compromise? My daughter-in-law can sit through your little talk, and she'll pass the highlights on to me later."

Sarah faltered for a moment. The old Sarah would have caved in to this bullying. The old Sarah was an exhausted, fearful creature who had bent over backward to please anyone in authority, or anyone with the balls to claim authority. But this was the new Sarah. She had not taken orders from anyone in six months. Sitting across from Regina Maris, the new Sarah decided she was not going to be pushed around.

Still smiling, Sarah said, "Perhaps I haven't made myself clear: one of the conditions of my arrangement with Dr. Étinav is that I instruct anyone who buys his cream on its proper use. You are right that Dr. Étinav would have no way of knowing if I deviated from this arrangement. But I would know."

Sarah took Dawn's envelope out of her purse, leaned forward, and placed it on the coffee table. Then she turned to Dawn, and Dawn surrendered the jar of cream she'd been holding. Sarah said, "Dawn, thank you so much for having me over to *your* home. I hope this hasn't been too awkward for you. If you'd like to meet with me separately, I can—"

Regina sighed, "Very well. I was hoping to avoid your sales pitch, but if it's *that* important, I suppose I can humor you."

Sarah launched into her spiel. It was over in minutes. Afterward, Sarah excused herself, and her hosts walked her to the door. Standing next to each other, Dawn and Regina made an odd tableau: the tall blond princess and the old witch who held her hostage. Sarah would have understood if Dawn pulled a Gretel and shoved Regina into an open fire someday.

Dawn thanked Sarah profusely for going out of her way and for her patience. And now that their skirmish had passed, Regina was all smiles too. She told Sarah, "I have a few friends who will be very interested in Dr. Étinav's product. May I give them your number?"

Sarah nodded yes. And then she headed out to her car. She felt hugely relieved to be away from Regina Maris. She also felt more than a little proud of herself.

The next stop was easy. Madge Porter handed over her check and sat through the product spiel without drama. With her out of the way, Sarah had one more stop to make: Valerie.

Valerie's maid, Esperanza, met Sarah at the door. She led her out to a grand tiled balcony overlooking the ocean. Valerie was seated at a table beneath a huge blue sun umbrella. She rose to hug Sarah, and Sarah caught a whiff of Bulgari's Pour Femme. As usual, Valerie wore heavy makeup, and her blond hair was pulled back in a high, tight bun. She was armored in expensive designer clothes that were far too dressy for a day at home. She looked as if she expected a team of photographers from *Ranch & Coast* to arrive any minute. She asked Esperanza to please bring out some ice waters.

With Esperanza gone, Valerie handed over a check, and Sarah ran through the rules. Then the two women sat back in their chairs and looked out at the ocean. Valerie asked who else in La Jolla had bought the cream, and Sarah told her. Valerie said, "Aah, so you stopped by Dawn's place? Was Queen Regina there?"

"Yes, she was."

Valerie shuddered. "Dawn's drinking has gotten so much worse since she moved into Regina's house. I suppose I'd marinate myself too if I had to put up with that shrew." Valerie filled Sarah in on Dawn's sob story. Dawn's husband, Joseph, had borrowed heavily from Regina to start his own tech company. Unbeknownst to Dawn, he also mortgaged their home to the hilt. When Joseph's business fell apart, Mother Regina swooped in to rescue him. Regina ordered Joseph to sell his home and move into one of the houses she owned. She also got him a job working for the family business, Maris Industries. "Now that failure has clipped Joseph's wings, Regina will never let him out of the nest."

Sarah sighed. "Poor Dawn."

"Yes. Poor Dawn. When everything fell apart, everyone felt sorry for Dawn. I think all that pity made her overplay her hand."

"How so?"

"Dawn was furious at Joseph for what he'd done. She said what hurt most of all wasn't losing the money. What hurt most was the lying, the way he'd kept her completely in the dark." Valerie laughed ruefully and shook her head. "Women always say that when their men fail." Valerie fluttered her eyelashes and did her best damsel in distress. *"It's not losing the house, the clothes, the cars that I mind. No, it's the lying that angers me, the betrayal."* Valerie resumed her usual affect. "What a load of rubbish. I have no doubt that if Joseph's little venture had worked, Dawn wouldn't have given a damn about *how* he did it. But a woman can't say, 'I'm mad because you failed and lost our stuff.' So instead we make up all this garbage about trust." Valerie shook her head again. Then she closed her eyes for a moment and sighed.

Sarah asked, "What? What is it?"

Valerie smiled. "I did some of that myself. When Walter left me, I ran around telling everyone that what galled me most was his lying. *That's* what I minded."

"And that wasn't true?"

"Christ, no. I was married to Walter for twenty years. He'd lied to me plenty of times, and I always forgave him. No, in the end, what hurt most was not *how* he did what he did. It was the simple fact that he had rejected me. That he'd chosen someone else. There's no way I could forgive that."

Sarah said softly, "No, I wouldn't be able to forgive that either."

Valerie sniffed, "Sorry to be so maudlin. This week would have been our twenty-fifth anniversary. I'm feeling sorry for myself."

Sarah reached out, took Valerie's hand, and gave it a gentle squeeze. Valerie went on, "Joseph's mess left Dawn feeling angry and betrayed. So she retaliated."

Sarah asked, "Retaliated? What? Did she have an affair?"

"No, but she might as well have. She got drunk at the Mercy Ball. It's one of the biggest events of the season. And she started flirting with one of the husbands. By the end of the evening, the two of them were kissing on the dance floor. They were pawing at each other like teenagers."

"How did *that* go over?"

"Well, Joseph was devastated."

"And Regina?"

"Regina was over the moon. Dawn handed her a powerful weapon. Think about it. One twenty-minute make-out session transformed Dawn from the victim, the girl whom Joseph had failed, into the tramp who'd cheated on him. Regina had a grand time browbeating Dawn with that. She still does. I think it may be her only hobby. She spends loads of time over at Dawn's place."

"But why does Dawn put up with it?"

"Partly out of remorse. But mostly it's the money. Dawn's addicted to two things: booze and Regina's money. She's not about to go cold turkey on either one."

Sarah shuddered. "Let's change the subject."

Valerie smiled. "No problem."

The two women sat in companionable silence looking out over the ocean. Sarah asked, "Did you ever paint the view from this balcony?" The previous Saturday, Valerie had shown Sarah five canvases. Gorgeous views of La Jolla Cove.

"No, I thought about it, but by the time we moved in here, I'd already given up painting, more or less."

"Why did you give it up?"

Valerie shrugged. "I don't know. There didn't seem to be much point. I'd spend hours each day painting, and after a while it felt like a waste of time. No one cared."

"Is it that important to have an audience?"

Valerie smiled wanly. "For me, it was. La Jolla is all about impressing other people. The cars, the clothes, the houses. That's why I spend twenty minutes applying my makeup every day. That's why I work out six times a week. That's why I had . . . that's why I *considered* plastic surgery, not that I'd ever need it." Valerie winked.

Sarah winked back. "Heaven forbid."

Valerie continued, "Impressing other people takes a lot of work. It's exhausting. Once I realized that my paintings would never be good enough to sell, I lost interest."

Sarah pressed. "But how did you know your paintings wouldn't sell? Did you ever take them to a gallery?"

"No. But Walter had an art dealer look at them. He dragged the poor man over to see my canvases after a dinner party. The man pronounced me a 'very competent amateur.' I took that as code for 'Don't give up your day job.'"

"Do you ever think of going back to it?"

"No. That part of my life is over."

Sarah decided not to keep pressing. Instead the two women moved on to lighter topics. After an interlude, Sarah looked down at her watch and was shocked to find that it was almost three in the afternoon. She would have to leave right away to beat the traffic into LA. She rose and said her good-byes. Then she reached into her purse, drew out a paper bag, and handed it to Valerie. "It's a present."

Valerie opened it and pulled out a set of acrylic paints. "Sarah, it's very sweet of you. But I told you, I don't paint anymore."

Sarah nodded. "I know. I just wanted you to have some fresh paints around. Who knows? You may get inspired."

Valerie regretted making the book club read Walter's favorite novel, Ayn Rand's The Fountainhead. *It wasn't the book's glorification of selfishness that bothered Valerie (though it should have—she would have been less shocked by Walter's treachery later on). No, what hurt Valerie was the scene where the hero's rival—the spineless Peter Keating—takes a late-middle-aged stab at becoming the artist he should have been. Peter makes a few sketches only to be told that it's too late for him to create "real art" because his gifts have languished too long. It took years for Valerie to realize that Ayn Rand might have been wrong about that.*

21

Valerie Begins

After Sarah left, Valerie carried the bag of acrylic paints back to her bedroom and emptied it onto her vanity table: eight tubes of artist-grade Lascaux acrylics, the top of the line. What a waste. Valerie would never paint again. She had *told* Sarah that. Sarah didn't really believe in Valerie's talent. How could she? Unless she didn't know anything about painting. Maybe that was it. Sure, Sarah talked a good game, all that art history business. But that didn't make her an expert. The expert, Walter's expert, had already looked at Valerie's paintings and found them wanting. Case closed.

So either Sarah had bad taste or she was being kind. Probably the latter. She probably thought painting would help Valerie "recover" from her divorce. People could be so naïve. Priscilla had already pushed

Valerie into a bunch of "rejuvenating" activities: pottery classes, ballroom dancing, kayaking. Valerie had diligently tried them all. But none of them took. How the hell could making clay bowls take the place of a twenty-year marriage? The crappiness of the substitutes only underlined what she had lost. She put the paints back in their bag and dropped it all into the wastebasket.

She retrieved the paints the next morning. It was Thursday. A good day. Yes, Valerie felt good. She had risen early, showered, and treated herself to some of Sarah's face cream. In the middle of reading the paper, she remembered the paints. She decided it was wrong to waste them. She should donate them to a school or something. Either that or she should use them herself. Yes, she really *should* use them. What was the harm in trying a little painting? It didn't have to *mean* anything. It could be a hobby. Lots of people used painting as a hobby: Winston Churchill, Bob Dylan, George W. Bush. So why not Valerie Tilmore?

She got dressed, hastily applied her makeup, and headed into town. She needed a canvas. Not a huge one. A small one. That's right. She would start small. Try painting simple subjects: bowls of fruit, a tree, a flower. Then maybe a landscape.

She drove to Aaron Brothers Art & Framing. She intended to buy one or two canvases, but once she got to the store, money flew out of her wallet. She ended up buying eight linen canvases, three flat synthetic brushes, a set of hard bristle brushes, spray bottles, primer, a big water jar to hold brushes, and two painter's cloths. She happily loaded it all into her car. Her purchases made her feel as if she had already achieved great things.

When she got home, she raced inside to her kitchen. She opened the refrigerator and got down on her knees to rifle through the produce drawer. The oranges were all right, but the apples were useless. Valerie couldn't put Red Delicious apples in a painting. They were too pedestrian, too artificial looking. The Barbie doll of the fruit world.

She heard Esperanza trudge up behind her. "Mees Val, what are you doing?"

Still squatting on the floor, Valerie pulled out a bag of grapes and leaned back on her haunches. She held the grapes up so she could see how bruised they were. Not bad. Okay, so she had grapes and oranges. She said, "Espie, can you run out and buy me some apples?"

"But we have—"

"No, not Red Delicious. I want something more authentic. Something a New Englander would eat."

"A New Englander?" Esperanza had never been east of Arizona.

"You know, a Macoun or a McIntosh. Something with character."

Esperanza exhaled loudly. "Okay, an apple weeth a character. No problem. Anytheeng else?"

Valerie had moved on to vegetables. They looked rather good, especially the carrots. But no, she couldn't paint vegetables. The painting would be too much like a nutrition ad. Fruits had sensuality. But vegetables? No. Realizing that Esperanza was still waiting for an answer, Valerie said, "Oh yes. Can you please unload the car?"

"Yes, Mees Val." Esperanza's heavy footsteps retreated slowly from the room. Hearing them made Valerie worry. Esperanza had never been svelte. She had always carried around an extra ten pounds. But the extra weight had suited her. She had been plump, not dumpy. But over the past two years, she had packed on another twenty pounds, far more than her five-foot-four-inch frame could comfortably absorb. Espie had moved beyond being Rubenesque. She was fat now. What if she got diabetes? Or heart disease? They both ran in her family. They didn't just run. They galloped.

Valerie put the grapes and oranges on the counter. She began hunting for a bowl. A wooden one. Wooden bowls always seemed so earthy. A moment later, Esperanza returned. She lugged the canvases across the room and deposited them gently on the kitchen table. She said, "Mees Val . . ."

Valerie looked up. Esperanza stood in a puddle of sunlight next to the kitchen table, the canvases laid out before her. A smile played across her broad face. She asked, "We are painting again?"

Valerie colored but then smiled back. "Yes, Espie, we are painting again."

Espie's grin widened. Then she started moving back across the kitchen. She yelled happily over her shoulder. "I get thee other bags from the car. Then I buy apples for you. Apples with a character!" She disappeared out the side door, moving much more quickly than she had before.

Daphne du Maurier's Rebecca *was the book club pick that got under Kim's skin. She took no pleasure in watching the timid heroine contort herself in a desperate attempt to live up to the memory of her aloof husband's dauntingly beautiful, now-dead first wife. Kim had thrown the book across the room when—hundreds of pages in—the husband revealed that he'd hated his first wife and loved the newbie exactly as she was. Why the fuck hadn't he said so back in chapter one?*

22

Kim's Costco Adventure

Kim stood transfixed. Costco overwhelmed her. There was so much of everything here, *too* much. It made Kim feel tiny and insignificant. Then again, *most* things made her feel that way lately. Trying to reorient herself, Kim once again checked her list—or, more accurately, Priscilla's list. As the ruthlessly efficient head of the Gillespie School's parent association, Priscilla was constantly asking Kim to do errands for this or that function. Today she'd asked if Kim would be a dear and fetch a few things for the Great Artists show. With no job for an alibi, Kim felt she *had* to say yes. After all, her husband, Andrew, had said she should get more involved in their daughters' swanky private school, protect their investment and whatnot. And Andrew was right. He was always right.

So here Kim was. A suburban housewife in tennis whites—her curly long hair shoved back into a low ponytail—wandering in a daze through Costco. As she meandered past a display of skin creams, she remembered another task on her to-do list. An easier task. She rummaged in her purse for her cell phone and the slip of paper Priscilla had given her, the one with Sarah Sloane's number on it.

Priscilla had cornered Kim and Andrew at a dinner party and gone on and on about Sarah's "miracle cream." Kim caught only snippets of Priscilla's patter: "Some French genius created it . . . two thousand a jar . . . Cassandra Blake uses it . . . Hard to get . . . Very exclusive customer list." As usual, when Priscilla spoke, Kim channel surfed inside her head, nodding politely whenever Priscilla paused for breath. But Andrew must have been paying attention, because when Priscilla finished blathering, he insisted that Kim buy some miracle cream for herself.

This shook Kim out of her stupor. "Drew, I don't need two-thousand-dollar face cream."

Andrew waved the objection off. "Honey, no one *needs* two-thousand-dollar face cream. It's a luxury. C'mon, treat yourself. It's not like we can't afford it."

Priscilla, sexy in a low-cut, clingy turquoise dress and silver high heels, laid a hand on Andrew's arm. She purred to Kim, "You've got yourself a good man here. Let him spoil you."

Kim smiled stiffly and counted the seconds until Priscilla removed her hand from Andrew's bicep: fifteen. Was it her imagination or did Andrew flex? Kim told herself that the touch meant nothing. And to Priscilla, it probably did mean nothing. Priscilla liked to touch people, especially people with penises. But Andrew was a different story. Kim had noticed him watching Priscilla, drinking her in. It wasn't that he lusted after her, at least Kim hoped he didn't. He *approved* of her. Priscilla was a blueprint of what a rich wife *should* be: stylishly dressed, impeccably made-up, impossibly thin, excellent at hobnobbing with other richies, and mired in the minutiae of PTA committees. She was a hot grand dame for the La Jolla set. After talking with Priscilla, Andrew always came home with more ideas for how Kim could improve herself.

When Priscilla finally let go of Andrew's bicep, Kim did what she was best at: she gave in. She told Priscilla, "Okay, give me Sarah's number, and I'll call her tomorrow. Scout's honor."

True to her word, Kim stood in the middle of Costco and keyed Sarah's number into her cell phone. Sarah picked up on the second ring. When Kim identified herself, Sarah seemed genuinely pleased to hear from her, and Kim remembered how much she *liked* Sarah Sloane. They arranged to meet on Friday for lunch in La Jolla. Placing her phone back in her purse, Kim felt a little lift at the prospect of maybe, just maybe, making a real friend. Kim had other friends, of course. But they were part of a different world now: the working world. Mostly teachers and administrators at Kim's old school, they were busy working all day.

Besides, on the rare occasions when Kim got together with her old friends, it was awkward. The gulf between their circumstances and Kim's was too great. They were awed by and resentful of her wealth, and she was embarrassed by her sheer inactivity—or, rather, the frivolity of her activity. Keeping up with the La Jolla set required a constant round of pedicures, manicures, facials, hair appointments, exercise sessions, lunches, and on and on. Who knew vanity and self-absorption could be so time-consuming?

Buoyed by the chance to make a new friend, Kim brightened for a few minutes after calling Sarah, but then her mood plunged again. Priscilla's list was demoralizingly long: forty bottles of sparkling cider, ten cheese platters, six tubs of cookies, four fruit platters, two veggie platters. It took forever to find everything in Costco's unmarked rows. And by the time Kim finished, she was starving.

Kim was always starving these days. Andrew had put her on a diet. He wouldn't put it that way, but that was what had happened. It had started a few months back. He and Kim had gone to another of Priscilla's interminable pool parties. Like all La Jolla parties, Priscilla's soirée featured heaps of catered food. The husbands, middle-aged masters of the universe, gorged themselves while their fashionably emaciated wives nibbled servings that would be considered stingy in a POW camp.

Kim had been the exception. Having played tennis for hours that day, she tucked into a plate of ribs. Kim had always been a hearty eater. She'd had to be. As a star tennis player in high school and college, she'd needed big portions to get her through long practices and matches. Later, she cut back, but she didn't have to worry. She'd always been naturally slim. At least, that's what she'd thought.

But Andrew thought otherwise. As he watched scrawny, spray-tanned La Jolla moms prance around Priscilla's pool in hanky-sized bikinis, he got it in his head that maybe Kim should lose a little weight. He could hire a nutritionist for her. Heck, maybe he'd hire a nutritionist for both of them. After all, he could do to lose some weight too. Kim eyed her husband's spare tire and said nothing. Andrew sensed that he'd said the wrong thing, so he quickly changed the subject. Would Kim consider breast enhancement surgery instead? Kim did not just reject that suggestion. She decimated it. She told him that the next time he asked her to get bigger boobs, he'd better be wearing an athletic cup.

But the weight issue lingered. When Kim hugged Andrew, his hands would glide down her sides and make an exploratory pinch, reminding Kim of those metal clamps they used at the gym to measure body fat. When she downed an extra helping of anything but vegetables, he'd raise an eyebrow or say, "You're not going to eat that, are you?"

For the first time in her life, Kim became uncomfortable in her body. Until now, she had been proud of her height and sheer muscularity. But after months of hanging around with Priscilla's crew, she began to perceive her body as huge and ungainly. She wasn't fat—she wasn't, dammit—but there seemed to be *too much* of her. If she slimmed down, if she lost some of her muscle mass, she would fit in better. But that meant dieting. And dieting meant hunger. Perpetual hunger.

As Kim wheeled her jam-packed cart outside, the smells from Costco's concession stand ambushed her. Cinnamon churros, pizza.

Kim fought her impulses, reminding herself that she had a healthy salad and grilled chicken breast waiting for her at home. But her resolve crumbled as soon as she spotted a poster of a hot dog. *That's* what she wanted, a foot-long hot dog loaded with mustard, ketchup, and sauerkraut. And a Coke! None of that diet crap. An honest-to-God soda choked with sugar and caffeine.

She wandered up to the stand in a trance and placed her order. When it came, the hot dog shined with grease. She almost moaned as she bit into it. This was food. She was about to take a second bite when she noticed a black hair dangling from the bun. The hair was kinky; it looked like the world's longest pube. Kim immediately lost her appetite. She rose and dumped the hot dog and her soda into the trash. Instead of being outraged, she felt shabby and ashamed. She deserved what had happened. After all, she had been cheating. The diet gods were not pleased.

Without wiping her greasy hands—she *deserved* to be greasy—she pushed her heavily laden cart out to her car. She began loading wine boxes crammed with sparkling cider into her massive blue Lexus LS hybrid. She loaded the first two crates without difficulty, but the third crate slipped through her oily fingers. Its six glass bottles exploded against the asphalt, sending geysers of fizzy cider in all directions. Much of it splashed onto Kim's legs. Standing there in her short white tennis skirt soaked with yellow cider, she looked like a giant toddler who'd just wet herself.

An old Asian couple and a beefy, bearded man in a Costco apron witnessed the whole thing. The bearded man called out to Kim, "Ma'am, do you need help with anything?"

Through a sob, Kim wailed, "My marriage!"

Annie wasn't sure how she felt about Sheryl Sandberg's Lean In. *On a good day, when Oscar's therapists gave sunny news and Annie happily filled skin cream orders, Annie thought Sandberg was right: she* could *do it all. On bad days, "lean in" sounded an awful lot like "bend over."*

23

Annie Tries to Score

Étinav sales were booming. In brighter moments, Annie felt proud of herself. She felt like a movie character: the plucky entrepreneur, the gal with moxie. She was not just doing well; she was doing good. Annie was a river to her people: providing for her family, seeing Sarah through a rough financial patch, and helping the ladies of La Jolla. Yes, Annie was *helping* them. She was sure of it. Sarah fed this belief by telling Annie about their customers' newfound confidence and the obstacles it had allowed them to overcome. Valerie was painting again. Madge Porter had stood up to her husband and refused to move from the home she loved. And Mrs. Charner had taken up hang gliding!

Annie began to think of herself as a fairy godmother, secretly sprinkling fairy dust over these women's lives. And over Sarah's too. Sarah was not using the cream herself, but selling it made her feel better than she'd felt in years. Sarah enjoyed being the face of the operation, the front woman. And though Sarah would never admit it, Annie knew that Sarah thought *she* was the one who'd made Étinav a hit. Sarah believed it was her charm, her salesmanship, that kept the customers coming. With a gratifying frisson of benevolent condescension, Annie decided to let Sarah go on thinking this. As a mother, Annie knew it was sometimes best to allow sweet, narcissistic thoughts to soar. When Annie's daughter Maddie had been three, Maddie had looked at the full moon outside her car window and announced proudly, "Look, Mom, the moon is following me!" Then, and now with Sarah, Annie nodded and smiled.

Occasionally, anxiety would puncture Annie's fragile serenity. Late at night, she would find herself ripped from her cheerful, industrious mind-set and plunged into a much harsher outlook: a grim mental landscape loaded with angry villagers carrying torches and pitchforks. This was the land of big fear. What if Annie and Sarah got caught? What would happen to them? To Annie's family? What if a client reacted badly to the cream? Alongside these huge fears, another worry lurked like a small parasite on a shark's back: What would happen when Annie ran out of cocaine?

How could a mousy suburban housewife score some blow? Clueless, Annie Googled "cocaine" and "San Diego." Online, she read all about Operation Sudden Fall. Years earlier, the feds had cracked down on drug sales at San Diego State University. They'd arrested 128 people, 95 of them students! The media smirked about how the insular world of the college campus had made drug dealers complacent so that they would sell drugs to practically anyone. All the agents had to do was dress like students, go to a few frat parties, and—bam!—they got all the drugs they wanted. To Annie, it sounded like Eden, Paradise Lost. Reading about the arrests and subsequent shift in culture on the campus, she felt grouchy and cheated. It was like learning about some fabulous clothing sale days after it had ended.

Colleges were out. Annie would have to find another way. On her Mommy's To-Do List app, she typed, "SCORE FOR THE HOME TEAM!"

Kim loved the part in Assassination Vacation *where author Sarah Vowell said she was a verbal Mount Vesuvius in social settings: dormant, dormant, dormant—you could build whole villages on the slopes of her silence—and then* boom*! Words flooded out of her mouth, quieting everything in her wake. Kim stayed dormant most of the time, but then . . .*

24

Ladies Who Lunch

"It wasn't like this in the beginning. I wasn't like this." Tears streamed down Kim's face. She wiped them away with her sleeve and glanced around nervously at the other diners on the terrace. To her immense relief, she didn't see anyone she recognized. Just tourists enjoying a perfect view of La Jolla Cove as they munched on overpriced hash browns.

Sarah handed Kim a Kleenex. "How did your marriage change?"

"I don't know. One minute, we're in college, I'm the tennis star, and he's my lovable, geeky boyfriend. He feels lucky to get me. Then we get married. We have a few kids. I'm teaching. He's working on his startup. We're not loaded or anything, far from it. But we're happy."

"And then?"

"And then his business hits it big. He becomes Mr. CEO. Head of a major company with hundreds of employees. He's rich, and being rich makes him different. He gets used to people obeying him all the time. He starts expecting me to obey him too."

"So do you?"

"Sure, I go along. I'm proud of him, and he's saying all the right things. How we're a team. How his success is my success. But the money changes everything. When his salary explodes, mine becomes totally inconsequential. *I* become inconsequential."

Sarah nodded sympathetically. The pity in her eyes put Kim on the defensive. "I don't want to give you the wrong impression. Andrew isn't a monster. It's just that—"

"He's changed?"

"Yes. He's started hanging out with a different crowd, a richer crowd. The men are all so arrogant. They don't doubt themselves for a minute. They go to work and people agree with them all day long. And then they come home and their wives agree with them too. It's a rarefied group, but—if you hang around with them long enough—it starts to feel like that's how things should be. Regular working families, families where wives are equals, begin to seem like losers. You know the husband would start bossing the wife around if he made enough money, if he was man enough."

Sarah raised an eyebrow. "Man enough?"

"Yes. It's surreal. You've got all these nerdy-looking, chubby men who built their fortunes behind desks. And as soon as they get rich, they start using all this macho language, as if they're gangsters or something. The other day, I heard one of Andrew's partners talking about a competitor starting a price war. He said, 'If those bastards screw with us, we'll take 'em to the mattresses.'"

Sarah caught the *Godfather* reference and smiled. "Yes. I've heard that kind of talk before. Bank account becomes a proxy for dick size."

"Exactly! And what makes all that talk even weirder is that—at the same time Andrew and his buds are becoming hypermale—I get launched into the world of girlie girls. These La Jolla women are all *so* feminine. So put together. The makeup, the clothes. And they all defer to their husbands. It's like being launched back into the 1950s."

Sarah nodded, saying, "So Andrew changed. Did you change too?"

"Yeah. Little changes at first. I started dressing better. I hired a cleaning lady. Stuff like that. But then I started giving in on bigger things. I let Andrew move the girls to a private school because that's where all his friends sent their kids. I gave up my job. I started hanging around with his friends' wives so we'd be more accepted. I went on a diet."

Sarah's eyes widened. "Why would *you* go on a diet?"

Kim colored. "Andrew says I can afford to lose a few pounds."

Sarah shook her head. "No, no. That's completely wrong."

Kim wanted to bear-hug Sarah for saying that, but she'd already been pathetic enough. Kim went on, "Anyway, the changes were gradual but huge. The balance of power in our marriage shifted. It's like every time Andrew succeeds at work, he gets another piece of armor. And every time I give in to him, I take off a piece. And pretty soon it's an armored tank versus me in my birthday suit." Kim started tearing up again. She blew her nose loudly and laughed at herself. "I'm sorry. I swear I usually don't go around bawling."

Sarah shrugged. "You're having a good cry with a girlfriend. There's no shame in that."

Kim sniffed. It was a lie. Sarah wasn't her friend, not yet. She probably wouldn't want to be Kim's friend now. Sarah was a glamorous, smart career woman. Why would she want to hang out with a hysterical housewife? Seeming to sense Kim's thoughts, Sarah said, "Of course, we're not friends yet. But I hope we will be. I liked you as soon as I met you back at book club. To be honest, you were the only person I clicked with."

Kim was shocked. "But you fit in with everyone right away. You seemed so completely at ease."

"Trust me, I felt very much out of place."

"Why?"

"Well, in a lot of ways, I'm like you. Wealth is new to me. I married into money. I didn't grow up with it." Sarah didn't have to explain. By now, everyone in La Jolla had heard her backstory: how she'd married a rich, eccentric professor who was a trust fund baby.

Kim was still skeptical. "You were uncomfortable? But you're used to dealing with all those Hollywood stars?"

"That's different. That's business. With my clients, I have a role to play. I'm there to advise them, not to socialize."

Kim nodded. "God, I miss having a role. A job. It sucks being *me* all the time."

Sarah asked, "You miss teaching?" Kim nodded and sniffed again. Why did her nose have to start running whenever she teared up? Sarah prodded gently, "Why did you stop?"

"I don't know. In the beginning, I had to work. We needed my salary. It wasn't much, but we needed it. But later on, when Andrew's business hit, when the money started coming in, it was different. After a while, it seemed selfish to go on working."

"Did Andrew say you were being selfish?"

"No. He was never that direct about it. He'd talk about how he worried about me whenever I went to work. Why did I have to work in such a rough part of town and all that. He'd talk about how much the girls missed me. If a babysitter messed up, he'd go on and on about it, about how it felt wrong to have his girls being raised by a stranger. He'd talk about how the kids would get so much more out of being with me, a mommy and a teacher."

"Sounds like a lot of guilt. How old are the girls now?"

"Jenna's twelve. Amelia's ten."

Sarah pressed, "Could you maybe teach part time?"

Kim said, "I don't know. I've been out of the game for four years now. Things are tight. Most schools are laying teachers off."

"Even math teachers?"

"I don't know. It's been so long since I checked the want ads. Also, let's face it. I'm getting older. I'm thirty-nine."

Sarah waved this off. "Yes. You're thirty-nine, practically a baby. Lots of people don't even get started on their careers until their late thirties. Heck, Julia Child was almost forty when she took her first cooking class." Thanks to the book club's recent reading of *Julie & Julia*, Sarah and Kim both revered Julia Child.

Kim rolled her eyes. "I'm no Julia Child."

"That's right. You've got a head start on her. You're already certified as a teacher, and you've got years of job experience under your belt."

Kim reflected on this. She ran a finger over the silver lid of the face cream Sarah had sold to her at the start of the meal. Already, it was the best two thousand dollars she had spent in a long time. Kim's smile evaporated when she looked down at her Cobb salad.

Sarah seemed to read Kim's mind, asking, "So, are you gonna share a basket of fries with me or what?"

Sarah was a Kurt Vonnegut fan. She loved the fake religion he created in Cat's Cradle*: Bokononism. When a Bokononist thinks of the elaborate ways events and human relationships interact to mold destiny, the Bokononist will murmur, "Busy, busy, busy."*

25

Sarah's Voice Mail

After stuffing herself, Sarah hugged Kim good-bye and headed out to her car. She checked her voice mail. Three messages. The first was from Sherri, Dr. Alpert's receptionist. Would Sarah please call and confirm her appointment for nine thirty next Wednesday? Determined to behave like a model patient, Sarah immediately keyed in the number. Sherri answered on the second ring. When Sarah identified herself, Sherri dropped her businesslike phone voice and slipped into her Jersey twang. "Long time, no see. Glad to hear you're coming back to us, doll." Sarah had given herself a vacation from fertility treatment ever since she'd quit her job. That had been seven months ago, an eternity in the biological countdown world of fertility clinics. Hearing Sherri's voice after so many months, Sarah smiled. Sherri always called her "doll." The familiarity of Sherri's patter reassured and depressed Sarah. There were certain settings where being a regular is a hallmark of recurrent personal tragedy: fertility clinics, rehab centers, funeral parlors.

After getting off the phone with Sherri, Sarah returned to her voice mail. Her next message came from a stranger, Sylvia Barrington. Mrs. Barrington sounded ancient. She spoke in a faint, ethereal voice, as if she was floating from this life to the next. She explained, "Regina Maris suggested that I call you. She and I are old friends. And she speaks very highly of your beauty treatment. I would very much like to purchase some for myself. Please call me at . . ." Sylvia gave her number slowly. Sarah whipped out a pad and jotted it down.

Sarah clicked on her last message. She recognized the voice immediately. It was Natalie Wilson, Priscilla's soon-to-be-bankrupt "friend." Sarah had ignored Natalie's previous messages. She didn't want to sell her pricey snake oil to a woman about to go broke, especially a woman *who didn't even know* she was about to go broke. But Natalie would not take a hint. In her latest message, Natalie said, with her customary forced brightness, "Hey, Sarah. This is Natalie Wilson. I'm not sure whether you're having problems with your phone or something, but I've actually left you a couple of messages already. Anyhoo, I'm calling because I was hoping to buy a jar of Étinav." Natalie said "anyhoo" a lot. Sarah wondered if she'd picked it up from Priscilla. Even in middle age, Natalie took her cues from the popular girls.

As if reading Sarah's mind, Natalie went on, "Priscilla and Dawn *love* the stuff. It's all they talk about these days. So, anyhoo, if you could call me back, I'd really appreciate it. You can call me *any*time. Day or night. Look forward to talking to you soon. Bye."

Sarah rubbed her temples in frustration. Sighing, she keyed in Natalie's home number. To her relief, she got the woman's answering machine. "Natalie, this is Sarah. I'm sorry it's taken so long for me to get back to you. I would *love* to sell you some cream, but I'm having some problems with supply on my end. That's why I haven't called sooner. I've pressed Dr. Étinav to send me more, but things have stalled. I'll hold on to your number. And when things change, I'll let you know. Take care. Bye."

Putting down her phone, Sarah thought, *There,* that *ought to satisfy her.* Although Sarah loved her new gig as a saleswoman, she sometimes wondered whether she had gotten the short end of the stick. Annie's job seemed so much easier.

Natalie never finagled an invitation to Priscilla's book club, but she'd done plenty of reading over the past year as her friends mysteriously dropped away. She tried Lonely *by some lonesome lady up in Newfoundland. Natalie couldn't take it seriously—of course the woman was lonely. She was in Newfoundland! Natalie also tried Mindy Kaling's* Is Everyone Hanging Out Without Me? *only to find out that Kaling was being facetious.* Everyone *was hanging out with the funny starlet.*

26

Natalie

Natalie Wilson told herself to be patient with Sarah, but she was sick of getting the cold shoulder. She had been shunned all over La Jolla for months, and she still hadn't gotten used to it. She had no idea *why* she was being shunned. She was the only person in La Jolla who didn't know that her husband's business was about to go bust. La Jolla's wealthy denizens did not want to be too close when Natalie's ugly situation imploded; poverty was, quite simply, a downer.

The shunning had started back in November. Priscilla Green *always* invited the Wilsons to go skiing on the weekend after Thanksgiving. Priscilla and her husband had a huge chalet in Aspen, and they loved showing it off. Sometimes they invited other Gillespie couples along too. But as the Greens' dearest friends, the Wilsons were the mainstay. Natalie waited patiently for Priscilla's invitation through September and October. She told herself not to worry. Priscilla was *going* to invite them.

She just hadn't gotten around to it yet. When November rolled around, Natalie's kids started badgering her about the ski trip. Eliza wanted to know if she could please share a room with Priscilla's daughter this year; the girls had always been close. And Grayson asked if he could use his remote-control boat in the Greens' hot tub. Panicking inwardly, Natalie responded with evasive answers and false optimism. She felt like the minister of information for a failing totalitarian regime.

Desperate, she took to loitering around Gillespie in the morning, hoping that she would bump into Priscilla. Thanks to her job as queen of Gillespie's PTA, Priscilla practically lived at the school. But suddenly Priscilla was hard to find. And the few times Natalie caught sight of her, Priscilla always held up a file and protested that she was too busy. In the end, no invitation came. A week after Thanksgiving, Eliza came home in tears. Priscilla's daughter didn't want to be friends with her anymore. As Eliza wept, Natalie cradled her in her arms and mouthed all the lies that you are supposed to tell children: that there was no need to be possessive; that there would always be enough friends to go around. The important thing was for Eliza to hang in there, stay cheerful, and try to make some *new* friends for herself.

Natalie tried to practice what she preached. She tried not to fixate on the Greens. But it was hard. To Natalie, the worst thing about socializing as part of a family was that you could never be wholly honest with the other families in your circle. You couldn't tell your tennis partner that your family had cut her family off because her son was a thug. You couldn't tell Dawn that her husband had made a pass at you in the kitchen during the Super Bowl. Saying such things would make the cozy, fragile civility of the Gillespie School impossible.

And you couldn't demand honesty either. It just wasn't done. Natalie was dying to know why—after five years of joint family vacations; small, intimate birthday parties; and monthly movie nights—the Greens had shut her out. But Natalie knew that if she were to confront Priscilla, to demand an explanation, she would come across as freakishly needy, the equivalent of a homely, hysterical ex-girlfriend banging on her boyfriend's door at two in the morning, yelling, "Why don't you love me anymore?"

News of the confrontation would reverberate through the Gillespie grapevine, making Natalie look lonely and desperate. And Natalie couldn't afford that, especially not now. Natalie knew enough about human nature to realize that it was impossible to attract friends if word got out that you *needed* them. People were like banks; they only wanted to lend affection to people who were already rolling in it.

Natalie turned to her husband, Eric, for solace, but he was no help. He was gone most of the time, running up to Los Angeles or the Bay Area to meet with potential investors. When Natalie had fretted about the Greens back in the fall, Eric had told her she was imagining things. The Greens might drift away for a while, but they'd be back. Later, when even Eric couldn't deny that the Greens had brutally rejected them, he told Natalie not to dwell on it, not to take things so personally. Blubbering, Natalie shot back, "Well, I'm a *person*! How the hell else can I take things?"

Natalie would have bounced back if she'd found someone else to connect with, either by forging new friendships or renovating some old ones. But when she invited new Gillespie moms over, they made vague excuses and never reciprocated her offers. And old friends became scarce. When Natalie invited Walter and hugely pregnant Crystal out to dinner, Crystal pleaded morning sickness. The Praegers claimed to be swamped, and the Stricklands were too. Taken alone, none of these couples was any great loss, not like the Greens, but their sudden, collective desertion had an impact.

Natalie didn't take rejection well. She vacillated among anger, confusion, hope, and despair. She toyed with rebranding herself as a solitary type, a loner content with her own company. But it didn't last. She had a golden retriever's naked need to be liked. But there was nothing she could do. She had to ride it out. That was all she could do.

Or was it? Sure, she couldn't demand that the Greens take her back. She couldn't order the popular kids' moms to invite her kids over. She couldn't force Priscilla to let her into her precious book club. But there was one person Natalie could go after, and that was Sarah Sloane.

At first, Natalie had liked Sarah. When Priscilla brought Sarah over to Natalie's house, Natalie had been almost giddy with excitement. Sarah was so lovely, so poised. It was like having a celebrity come to tea. That visit was Natalie's first social success in months, a success made all the more precious by the fact that Natalie had not arranged it. She had not tainted it with sweat.

When Natalie heard about Sarah's miracle cream, she seized on it as an excuse to wangle her way into Sarah's life. Everyone in La Jolla seemed to be in love with Sarah. Winning Sarah's friendship would be a social coup, a way back in. And besides, Natalie wanted that cream. Everyone else was raving about it. It was the new thing. With fewer emotional ties to lean on, Natalie needed whatever material props she could get.

So she began phoning Sarah. At first, no reply came. Heeding Eric's advice not to take everything so personally, Natalie ignored Sarah's silence and kept calling. Wasn't that a reasonable thing to do? After all, this wasn't a social call. Sarah was a businesswoman. Presumably, she would want whatever new clients she could get. She must be overwhelmed with new customers. Natalie had to be persistent. It was like queuing up at a posh new restaurant. You'd have to fight the crowd to get your name on the list, but eventually you'd get a table.

Natalie was disappointed when she got Sarah's voice mail, explaining that Sarah had fallen short on supplies. But it made sense. Sarah's cream was so popular. And Sarah's message was so polite. She'd promised to get back to Natalie as soon as she got hold of more jars. It was just a matter of time.

Annie had read The Cat in the Hat *to her kids dozens of times. They loved the chaos that resulted when kids let the free-spirited, troublemaking cat enter their house while their mother was out. Annie had a hard time enjoying the book—chaos had reigned in her childhood whenever her mother* was *in.*

27

Annie's Easy Job

Annie was running on less than three hours of sleep. The night before, she had blown two hours sewing Maddie's tree costume for her heavy-handed class play about recycling. Then she'd spent another hour—an hour!—mixing four jars of Étinav. It had taken forever to get the blend just right. She had to keep tweaking the concoction. She couldn't afford to waste a single gram of cocaine.

By the time she managed to get the cocaine to dissolve properly, it was already past two in the morning. She ladled the mixture into four jars, plodded upstairs, and collapsed into bed. An hour later, she woke to the sound of a child wailing. She trudged down the hall to find a fevered Rachel sitting up in her crib, her clothes smattered with vomit. Annie lifted Rachel out, cleaned her up with warm washcloths, and changed the bedding. She had just gotten Rachel back to sleep when Oscar wandered in. Without saying a word, he walked over to Annie, leaned his head against her shoulder, and threw up all over her.

Now Annie had two sick kids and one angry one. Maddie was furious because Annie wouldn't be able to make it to her dreary class propaganda play that evening. Annie tried to soothe her, promising, "But Daddy will be there. He'll take pictures and everything."

Maddie folded her arms tight against her chest and frowned. She looked like an angry genie. "I don't want Daddy there! I want you! Moms are supposed to be at *everything*!"

Annie cooed, "Honey, I would love to be there. Really, I would. But I have to stay here and take care of Rachel and Oscar."

Maddie protested, "It's not fair! You're *always* with Oscar. He goes to the doctor with you all the time! You love him best!"

Just then the phone brayed, saving Annie from regurgitating her spiel about how she loved each of her children immensely but in absolutely equal amounts. Annie picked up the receiver and mumbled hello.

Her mother commanded, "Speak clearly, Annabelle. You must enunciate each syllable. Let your words fill the room!" Although cigarettes had lowered Chloe's voice, she still spoke with the perfect diction and projection she'd mastered in drama school.

Pointedly refusing to take her mother's advice, Annie mumbled, "Wha—is—it, Mom?"

Chloe sighed theatrically. Her pearls of wisdom were wasted. "I was calling to arrange a little visit."

Annie bit down on her lower lip. "Mom, things are so chaotic around here right now. I'm not sure I can handle a houseguest."

Chloe huffed, "Is that all I am to you? A houseguest?"

"No, of course not. It's just that I have a lot on my plate, and—"

"Well, I'm sorry to inconvenience you. I didn't realize that my presence would be such a burden."

Annie lied, "Mom, you are not a burden."

But Chloe was on a roll. "Oh, how sharper than a serpent's tooth is it to have a thankless child!"

"Don't quote Shakespeare at me, Mom. I am not in the mood. You're always welcome here. You know that. It's just that we're going through a rough patch." Annie did not elaborate on Oscar's problems, not with him sitting a few feet away.

Chloe answered, "That's why I want to come. To help with the children."

Annie was skeptical. Chloe had never shown much enthusiasm for child-rearing. She adored her grandchildren. But she loathed the mundane drudgery of actually watching them. Careful not to raise her mother's hackles, Annie said, "Mom, that's very kind of you. But is that the only reason you're coming?"

"No, not the *only* reason. If you must know, I'm having some minor household repairs done."

"What kind of repairs?"

"I'm renovating my living room. I think it's about time, don't you? That Southwestern theme was so dated."

This surprised Annie. Her mother's apartment was dated, but Chloe Baker had always been totally indifferent to décor. Like child-rearing, it bored her. Annie asked, "What are the contractors going to be doing?"

Chloe said, "Oh, I don't know. Pulling out the carpet. Replacing some of the old fixtures. Stripping the paint off the ceiling. That sort of thing."

"Stripping the paint off the ceiling? Is that really necessary?"

Sounding nonchalant, Chloe answered, "I don't know. What do I know about these things? The contractors say they have to do it. I assume they know what they're doing. It is their job, darling."

Annie's antennae went up. "Mom, *why* are they stripping the paint off the ceiling? Did something happen?"

"No, nothing happened."

Annie pressed, "Nothing?"

"Well, nothing important. A little fire in the living room. Nothing major."

Annie balked, "A fire?"

"Yes. A very small one."

"When did this small fire happen?"

"A day or two ago."

"Why didn't you call me?"

Chloe purred, "I didn't want to burden you, darling. As you said, you're going through a rough patch already."

Annie forced herself to sound calm. "How did the fire start, Mom?"

Chloe said airily, "I don't know. Who really knows how these things get started?"

Annie knew exactly how these things got started. Her mother had been drinking and smoking on the couch. She'd spilled some wine on the end table and left her cigarette burning in the ashtray next to it. Then, the way she did most nights, Chloe had passed out. The cigarette had set the wine spill on fire, and soon the whole living room was in flames. She was lucky to be alive. "Mom, are you all right?"

"Thanks so much for finally bothering to ask. Yes, I'm fine. Not a scratch."

"So, how long will it take them to fix up the place?"

"Two months, give or take."

"Two months?"

Chloe said coolly, "Is there an echo on this line, Annabelle?"

Annie sputtered, "No, no. It's just, that's not exactly a little visit."

Chloe said sarcastically, "Thank you so much for that warm welcome."

Trying not to sound too desperate, Annie asked, "What about Jimmy? Did you consider spending part of the time with him?" Chloe had always favored Jimmy. She had made no secret of that. They had so much more in common: acting, a zest for life, drinking, drugs.

"That won't work. These days, Jimmy and I . . . let's just say he has trouble with my lifestyle."

Annie laughed. "And I don't?"

Chloe wasn't amused. "Well, yes, of course, you do. You're always on about the virtues of temperance. It's like having my own personal Eliot Ness. But believe it or not, your brother has become even more tedious on this subject than you are. Every time I talk to him, he tells me all about how Alcoholics Anonymous has saved his life. And then he lectures me about how I need to come back to the program."

Annie was shocked. "I didn't know you used to belong to AA."

Chloe said indignantly, "I have never been to an AA meeting in my life! I have no desire to spill out my troubles to a pack of sanctimonious teetotaling freaks."

"They're not freaks, Mom."

"No, they're worse than that. They're *boring*. Now that your brother's joined that cult, he's completely abandoned his sense of humor. I don't see the two of us getting along very well just now."

Annie conceded, "You have a point."

"So, unless I want to spend the next two months in a hotel, which I absolutely cannot afford to do, I am afraid I will have to inflict my presence upon you, my doting daughter. All right?"

Annie blew her bangs out of her eyes, exhaling loudly. "All right, Mom. No problem. But remember the house rules. No smoking. No drinking."

"Yes. Your house is a joy-free zone. Don't worry. I shall behave myself."

Annie sighed again. Chloe Baker never behaved herself.

As a girl, Valerie got frustrated by L. Frank Baum's The Wonderful Wizard of Oz. *She loved the idea of visiting an all-powerful wizard who could tell her what she was worth and what she should do. But when Baum revealed that the wizard was just some huckster from Omaha, eleven-year-old Valerie had thrown the book against the wall.*

28

Valerie Debuts

The big day had arrived. Valerie was finally going to show her work to an art dealer. And not some small-time shop owner down by La Jolla Cove. No, Valerie had an appointment with David Carson, owner of a high-end gallery in Los Angeles. Sarah had arranged the meeting. She and David had been friends for years. Valerie wasn't surprised. Sarah seemed to know *everyone.* If Valerie were to point out a magazine photo of an Eskimo on an ice floe, Sarah would probably say, "Oh, that's Phil. We were in third grade together."

Sarah had insisted on setting Valerie up with David Carson when she saw Valerie's new canvases. Sarah had come to Valerie's house to drop off another jar of Étinav, and over lunch Valerie shyly admitted that she'd begun painting again. Sarah squealed with delight. She jumped up from the table and threw her arms around Valerie. The gesture made Valerie absurdly happy. It confirmed that two wishes had come true: that she and Sarah had become friends, and that by painting again Valerie had made a momentous positive change in her own life. She wasn't *stuck* anymore. Sarah's hug was a bottle of champagne being smashed against the side of Valerie's ship.

After lunch, Valerie led Sarah to the spare room that she had begun using as her studio. Valerie showed her everything: the fourteen canvases she'd painted over the previous happy, hectic month. Two were still lifes: bowls of fruit. Those had been Valerie's warm-up. The rest of the paintings were landscapes: La Jolla Cove, Seal Beach, the tide pools, the ocean view from Valerie's balcony. Sarah oohed and aahed over all of them. After looking at Valerie's paintings, Sarah spotted a large drawing pad on a desk in the corner. "What's that for?"

"Sketches. They're not much good."

Sarah walked over to the desk and began paging through the sketch pad. Most of the sketches were rough outlines of the paintings Sarah had already seen. She flicked through them quickly. Then she stopped. She stared for a long moment. "Is this Esperanza?"

Valerie walked over to the desk. She looked over Sarah's shoulder. "Yes. It doesn't quite work. I'm afraid I'm not much for portraits."

"Where did you get that idea?"

"My art professor."

"Did you go to art school?"

Valerie laughed. "No, nothing as grand as that. I took a few art electives in college."

"So what did this professor say to you?"

"He told me that I was no good at portraiture." Valerie mimicked her long-ago teacher's English accent: "The human form is beyond you, my dear. I suggest you limit yourself to painting pretty little pictures of pretty little places."

Sarah's brow furrowed. "What an asshole."

Valerie demurred. "To be fair, the portrait I did *was* terrible. It was a nude, a man. He posed for the class. I'd never been in a room with a naked man before. It sounds terribly old-fashioned now, but I was embarrassed. I could barely look at him, let alone paint him. My painting was about as detailed as a chalk outline of a dead body."

"Still, it was one painting. Where did that dolt get off saying *that* to you after one botched painting?"

Valerie shook her head. "It wasn't *that* bad."

"It was bad enough for you to think, twenty years later, that you have no talent for portraiture when clearly"—Sarah gestured at the drawing of Esperanza—"you are terrific at it." From there, Sarah launched into another superlative-laden spiel about how talented Valerie was. She ended her little speech by demanding that Valerie meet with David Carson. Sarah had befriended the art dealer years earlier.

Valerie blustered, "I don't even have a portfolio to show him."

Sarah shot back, "So make one."

Valerie hoped Sarah would forget the whole thing, but she didn't. She phoned Valerie repeatedly over the next few days until Valerie finally agreed to meet the man. So here Valerie was, her brand-new portfolio in the passenger seat next to her as she drove up to Los Angeles. She prayed the portfolio wasn't too amateurish. Its shiny black cover reminded Valerie uncomfortably of the glossy Trapper Keeper she had in elementary school. The portfolio was packed with large color photos of her best paintings and a few of the sketches she'd done of Espie.

Valerie found Carson's gallery easily, smack in the middle of LA's Rodeo Drive. She babied her red Mercedes SL550 up to the curb, turned off the ignition, and checked her reflection in the mirror. She looked good, damned good. She was sure that Sarah's cream had taken five years off her face, maybe ten. Before, Valerie's nipped and tucked skin had seemed tight, somehow pinched. The cream had made it more supple. Yes, she looked younger. She was sure of it.

But even with her improved skin, Valerie never went anywhere without an elaborate carapace of makeup. And today's meeting with David Carson was no exception. She wore her blond hair up in her trademark chignon. She had dressed carefully too. She wore a close-fitting blue-and-yellow Versace print dress and matching blue Manolo stilettos.

Holding her portfolio tightly against her chest, she walked into the gallery and announced herself to the receptionist. The receptionist told her that Mr. Carson would be with her in a moment. Valerie smiled her thanks and drifted away, saying that she wanted to have a look around. What she really wanted was to avoid the receptionist. Valerie was too nervous to make small talk.

Wandering around the gallery, Valerie loved what she saw. The gallery was running a retrospective on a Japanese artist's work: paintings of beautiful, haunted-looking Japanese women done in muted colors. A few desolate urban landscapes. The effect was depressing and vibrant at the same time. After ten minutes, the receptionist approached again, saying that Mr. Carson was ready for her now. Valerie followed the woman down a corridor to his office. The place was a mess, a small, low-ceilinged room with a massive desk covered in a snowdrift of papers. David Carson rose quickly, bumping his knee against his desk and wincing as he did so. Valerie was slightly taken aback. The man was a tree, at least six three, maybe taller. His height seemed ridiculous in such a small space. He looked like a giant inside a hobbit hole. He smiled warmly at Valerie as he shook her comparatively tiny hand in his. He said, "You must be Valerie Tilmore. Thanks for driving up here. Sarah's told me so much about you."

He gestured for Valerie to sit down on the chair across from his desk. Valerie looked over and saw a huge stack of papers on the chair. David reddened. "Sorry, it's such a mess in here. Please dump those papers on the floor."

Valerie picked up the papers and carefully deposited them next to her feet. She smiled at David, unsure of what came next.

He drew her out gently. How was the drive? How long had Valerie known Sarah? How had the two women met? Valerie felt herself calming down as she batted these lobs. David was such a pleasant man. Pleasant to look at too, once she got used to his height. Valerie guessed he had to be about Walter's age, fifty-five or so. She took guilty pleasure in noting that—unlike Walter—David Carson had a full head of wavy gray hair. His features were strong, with sharp cheekbones and an aquiline nose. Evidently, he was not a fan of Botox. The skin around his large brown eyes crinkled when he smiled.

He had good taste too. Stylish and a tad formal. He wore one of the gray wool suits that *Mad Men* had brought back into fashion and a black button-down shirt, left open at the throat. The suit flattered his tall, lean build. Yes, Valerie enjoyed talking to this man.

Her enjoyment reverted to panic when he asked to see her work. Chatting happily, she had almost forgotten the portfolio on her lap. She fumbled with it for a moment before handing it over to him. He laid it across his desk and began to page through it. The man studied each page carefully, but his face gave away nothing. After what felt like an eternity, David looked up and smiled. "Well, I can see why Sarah sent you to me. Your work is very interesting."

Valerie nodded but did not smile back. She recognized faint praise when she heard it. "Interesting"—that's how polite people describe an ugly girl's face. David went on, "Your use of color is very striking."

Valerie murmured, "Thanks." Then, trying not to sound too needy, she asked, "Do you think I could ever sell these paintings?"

David Carson shifted in his chair. "Oh sure. They wouldn't fit with my gallery. But I'm sure you could sell them somewhere. Maybe one of the shops in La Jolla?"

Valerie echoed, "One of the shops in La Jolla?"

"Well, yes. I'm sure they could sell them. There's a lot of foot traffic down there."

Valerie nodded, letting this remark sink in. She knew the man was trying to spare her feelings, but the words still hurt. She pressed, "You mean one of those tourist junk shops? The ones that sell wind chimes and bracelets made of seashells?"

David sighed, his smile vanishing. "You're not going to make this easy for me, are you?"

Valerie shook her head. "That's not my style. So tell me, are any of my paintings good enough to be shown in a real gallery?"

"No, but—"

Valerie nodded. She felt warmth behind her eyes. She had to get away before she started crying. She rose, saying, "Well, thank you for your time."

With new sternness in his voice, David said, "I wasn't finished." He gestured for Valerie to sit down again. And she complied. "The paintings you have in your portfolio, the ones I looked at, they aren't good enough to be sold in an art gallery. But that doesn't mean you don't have potential, serious potential."

Valerie sighed, her shoulders slumping. "I'm a bit old for the 'maybe someday' speech. Don't you think?"

David Carson frowned. "I don't follow you."

Valerie smiled ruefully. "You know, 'maybe someday if I keep painting, if I drink my milk and say my prayers, then maybe, someday, I'll accomplish something.'"

David leaned forward in his chair. "Okay, you want my take. Here it is. Your landscapes are pretty but dull. They're the sort of stuff tourists buy, thinking it will match nicely with the couch when they get home. There's not enough personality there, not enough to captivate a collector. They show you have good technique and a great sense of color. But that's all. Those sketches, the ones of that woman, have a lot more promise. If you want to improve, go find that woman and paint her. Paint her over and over. And then—"

"And then?"

David smiled, his eyes crinkling again. "Then *maybe someday* you'll have a piece of serious art to sell. Okay?"

Valerie sniffed and nodded quickly. She avoided his eyes. "Okay."

"And when you do paint that woman, come back here and give me first crack at what you come up with. Deal?"

Valerie forced herself to be a big girl and look the man in the eye. When she did, she found herself smiling again. "Deal."

Annie raced through Jeanette Walls's The Glass Castle *in a single weekend. Annie had never been trumped before. She thought,* Jeanette, you win—your neglectful, bohemian parents were wayyy worse than mine.

29

Chloe Pitches In

Annie didn't like leaving the girls alone with her mother for five hours, but she had had no choice. A perfect parenting storm had hit. Oscar had speech therapy at one o'clock down at Rady Children's Hospital and group therapy up in Sorrento Valley at three. Annie usually left the girls with a sitter while she chauffeured Oscar on his rounds, but at noon the sitter had called in sick, coughing every two words for effect. Next, Rachel threw a massive tantrum to make it clear that she needed a nap *in her crib* right away. Her Highness refused to nap anywhere else. And then Maddie came down with a fever, scoring a very respectable 102 degrees.

So Annie had to turn to Chloe for help. Chloe heroically donned an apron to get into character. And Annie reminded her mother of the house rules: no sugar, no snacks, no television until after dinner, wake Rachel from her nap at three. "And no smoking."

Chloe put her hand over her heart. "I wouldn't dare."

Annie thanked Chloe and then rushed out to fetch Oscar from preschool. That had been five hours ago. At five thirty, Annie returned.

The foyer was dark. Annie called out tentatively, "We're home!" No one answered.

Annie flipped on the light in the foyer and led Oscar down the hall to the living room. Halfway down the corridor, she realized why no one had answered. The television in the living room was blaring. Annie entered to find Chloe and Maddie curled up on the couch. Still in her apron, Chloe was reading a romance novel, her glasses perched on the end of her nose. Next to her, Maddie was eating a huge bowl of chocolate ice cream while staring mesmerized at the television. Onscreen, Robert De Niro channeled Al Capone, yelling, "You talk to me like that in front of my son? Fuck you and your family!" Annie sprinted to the television and shut it off.

Through a mouthful of ice cream, Maddie whined, "Hey! I was watching that."

Chloe looked up innocently from her book. "How was Oscar's therapy, dear?"

Annie took a moment to assimilate the chaos of her living room. It wasn't the usual kids' mess. It was a catastrophe, the sort of wreckage one might expect at a crime scene. Toys and seat cushions were strewn all over the floor, along with potato chip fragments, raisins, and Magic Markers. A lamp was half knocked over, leaning precariously against an ottoman. Large stick-figure drawings marred the wall next to the bookcase. The coffee table was covered with soda glasses, empty candy boxes, and pretzel sticks. The room was way too cold. Wide open windows admitted the November breeze. Annie said tremulously, "Mom?"

Chloe smiled angelically and launched into her babysitter's report. "Maddie was *very* good."

Maddie announced, "Grandma taught me a trick." Maddie grabbed a pretzel stick from the coffee table and put it in her mouth. Then she mimed lighting it. Leaning back, Maddie drew in a breath of imaginary smoke and then exhaled, languidly tossing her hair about like a glamorous matinee idol. She turned to Annie. "See, Mom? Isn't that great?! We saw it in a movie, *Now* . . ." Maddie faltered.

Chloe piped up, "*Now, Voyager.* We watched it this afternoon." Chloe beamed at Maddie and pushed a stray curl behind the girl's ear. "I know you said no television, Annabelle. But Bette Davis was on. *Every* young girl has to study Ms. Davis. It's part of becoming a woman."

At the mention of becoming a woman, Maddie sat up straighter and took another puff of her imaginary cigarette. "Grandma says she'll buy me some bubblegum cigarettes so I can practice."

Annie repeated, "Mom." Chloe looked up, her face a mask of wholesome concern. Annie marched over to the television and switched on *The Cat in the Hat.* Careful to keep the rage out of her voice, Annie told the kids, "You guys watch this. Grandma and I need to talk in the hallway for a minute." In unconscious imitation of her husband, Annie clenched her jaw and jerked her head for Chloe to follow her.

In the hallway, Chloe whispered, "What is it, dear? Did something bad happen in therapy?" Annie shook her head and glared at her mother wordlessly for a moment. Chloe raised an eyebrow. "Oh wait, don't tell me. I've broken one of your precious rules."

"*One* of my rules? Oh no, try *all* of them!"

Chloe waved her hand in the air, as if trying to shoo away a pest. "What can I say? I thought you wouldn't mind. After all, I don't often get time alone with my granddaughters. It was a special occasion."

Annie shot back, "With you, *every* day is a special occasion."

Chloe colored prettily and smiled. "Thank you, dear."

"It's *not* a compliment."

Chloe shrugged complacently. "All right, so I broke a few tiny rules."

"*Tiny* rules? How about the no-smoking rule, Mom? I'd say that's a big one."

Chloe said, "I did *not* smoke."

"Oh yes you did! That's why you opened the windows—to cover up the smell."

Chloe bluffed, "I opened the windows because I wanted to let some fresh air into this stuffy, overheated house of yours."

"Mom, it's freezing in there."

"I find the breeze invigorating."

Annie pressed, "And I bet you told Maddie not to tell me about your smoking. Didn't you?"

Chloe gaped. "Are you suggesting that I instructed my six-year-old granddaughter to lie?"

"Why not? You did it with me enough times."

"I *never* asked you to lie for me. Oh, maybe once or twice. But after all, everyone lies sometimes. It keeps life interesting."

"So in one afternoon, you smoked, told my daughter to lie to me, and taught her how to smoke too."

"We used pretzel sticks."

Annie went on, "And you let her watch a gangster movie?"

"It was *The Untouchables.* It's an excellent film, Annabelle."

"It's packed with violence and cursing."

Chloe rolled her eyes. "Oh, it's not *that* bad."

"Mom, when I came in, De Niro was shouting the F-word. The F-word!"

Chloe shrugged. "So what? Maddie's bound to hear profanities somewhere. Wouldn't you prefer she heard them when there are responsible adults around?"

Annie was tempted to answer, "Yes—but I left her with *you.*" Instead, Annie closed her eyes for a moment, willing herself to calm down. "Mom, if you had to put the tube on, couldn't you at least put on something appropriate? PBS Kids?"

Chloe wrinkled her nose in disgust. "Now that's what *I* find offensive. That horrid, saccharine pabulum. I don't know how you can stand it."

"It's educational!"

"It's evil! A bunch of puppets talking in overbright voices about the color red or the letter *A*. And the dialogue is terrible. That *Cat in the Hat* show doesn't even rhyme. Seuss would vomit if he ever saw the damned thing!"

Annie opened her mouth to respond, but the doorbell rang. It was Sarah, stopping off on her way back to Los Angeles. Annie turned and trudged to the front door. Chloe followed close behind. Sarah hugged Annie, then spotted Chloe. "Chloe! I had no idea you were visiting. How long has it been?"

Sarah and Chloe hugged. Then Chloe took a step back, purring, "It's been too long, far too long." Chloe and Sarah had always been huge fans of each other. Annie's mother was like a Monet painting, easier to appreciate from a distance.

While Sarah and Chloe chatted, Annie went upstairs to wake Rachel. Thanks to the four-hour nap that Chloe had allowed her, Rachel would keep Annie up well past midnight. Annie lifted Rachel from the crib. She felt her anger ebb as Rachel nuzzled her neck and sighed happily. By the time she returned downstairs, Sarah and Chloe had migrated to the kitchen. They sipped white wine and chatted while Annie threw dinner together. Chloe had made a great show of giving up smoking, but she would never abandon her wine. Annie shot Sarah a warning look when she mentioned Étinav cream. Chloe perked up. "You two are in the beauty business?"

Annie hedged, "We're dabbling."

Chloe said, "Oh, do my ears deceive me? Or am I hearing the hollow tones of false modesty? Come now, you have to tell me *all* about it."

Annie said, "I don't think we should go into this."

Chloe insisted, "Nonsense. Of course, you can tell me. I'm your mother."

Annie said gloomily, "I know."

Sarah said, "I really don't see the harm in telling Chloe about this, Annie. I mean, it's not like we've got anything to hide."

Annie sighed. "Fine, go ahead." She picked up the kids' dinner plates and headed out to the table. Glutted with junk food, Maddie didn't touch her plate, but Oscar and Rachel both tucked in. By the time Annie returned to the kitchen, Sarah had told Chloe all about their business venture—at least the noncriminal aspects of it. Chloe gushed, "Well, I think it's a wonderful idea. I'm so impressed the two of you have been able to get this off the ground. I never thought of my Annabelle as an entrepreneur."

Sarah said, "Oh, but she is. The whole thing was Annie's idea. She came up with the product, the marketing strategy, all of it. She's been so creative." Annie knew she might be imagining it, but she thought she detected a hint of condescension in Sarah's voice. Sarah clearly thought that it was she, not Annie, who was responsible for the cream's success. Sarah assumed that all those customers kept coming back because of her personal charm, her irresistible magnetism. Annie's recipe for the cream didn't matter. Of course, Sarah didn't know what Chef Annie was putting in the special sauce.

Chloe looked at Annie with new interest. "Creative? I'd never thought of you that way, Annabelle. I always thought of you as more of an analytical type. What with the chemistry thing and all . . ."

Annie said defensively, "Chemists *can* be creative, Mom."

"Yes, I suppose. Mad scientists and all that. Well, good for you."

Annie returned to the living room to tend to the kids. When she carried their dinner dishes back into the kitchen, she found Chloe and Sarah talking excitedly. Sarah bubbled, "I've had the best idea. How about we let your mother help us?"

Annie stammered, "I don't think—"

Sarah put her hand on Annie's arm. "Just hear me out. Regina's referred a bunch of elderly women to me. And tomorrow I'm supposed to meet with them down at the Sands." The Sands was a posh retirement home overlooking La Jolla Cove. "This lady, Sylvia Barrington, arranged it. I've never met her face-to-face. But on the phone the woman sounds like she has to be a gazillion years old. And I'm guessing her friends are all in their seventies, at least."

Annie asked, "So?"

"So I'm not sure my pitch will work with them. Usually I'm dealing with women my own age. To women like that, a cream that will take five, maybe ten, years off their faces is worth a lot. It's the difference between middle age and youth. But with Barrington's crowd, setting the clock back five years is nothing. Let's face it, old minus five years is still old." Sarah shot Chloe a cautious look, not wanting to offend her.

Chloe nodded. "Go on, dear. I'm not squeamish."

Sarah continued, "Anyway, if these women are going to fork out two grand a jar, we have to convince them that the cream will make some significant difference in their lives. I can't do that by myself. I won't have any credibility. Understand?"

Chloe said, "Yes! You need someone else, someone closer to their age, to make them understand how rejuvenating the cream is. You need yours truly." Chloe gestured to herself.

Annie shook her head. "I don't think this is such a good idea."

Sarah countered, "C'mon, Annie. Your mother would be a natural. I'm sure those octogenarians would love to look one-tenth as good as she does." Chloe jutted out her chin and beamed. It was true. She was a seventy-year-old knockout. Her high cheekbones, full lips, and big brown eyes made her pretty, but it was her infectious smile and confident way of carrying herself that made her beautiful. Her lifelong habit of avoiding sunshine, often by sleeping through the day in an alcohol-induced stupor, meant that relatively few wrinkles marred her face. And although decades of alcoholism had padded her frame with a few extra pounds, she had retained her enviable curves. Chloe was a living rebuke to public-health ads.

Annie sputtered, "Mom, you look great. But let's face it, you've never done sales before. You're an actress."

Chloe was unfazed. "Darling, that's what a saleswoman is. An actress!"

Chloe turned to Sarah. "You could school me on your sales pitch, and then I could go in and repeat it?"

Sarah beamed. "I don't see why not."

Annie flailed for an objection. "Yeah, well, what if these customers ask something unexpected? What then?"

Chloe smiled and gestured toward Sarah. "Then I will defer to Sarah. After all, she'll be sitting right there. I would never presume to . . ." Annie winced. Chloe Baker was all about presumption.

Sarah put an arm over Chloe's shoulder and told Annie, "Don't worry. I'll school Chloe on what to say. She'll be brilliant."

Chloe beamed. "Yes, and it will be great fun! You've heard of fun, haven't you, Annabelle?"

Sarah didn't know many old people. They just weren't around in her world. They were off hiding somewhere—at senior centers, in Florida, or at home watching Fox News. Sarah guessed they must be like that guy in Tuesdays with Morrie*—slowly dying but full of twinkly-eyed optimism. They'd utter bumper-sticker slogans with enough emphasis to make them sound profound and then complain about not being able to find the remote.*

30

The Sands

Two days later, Sarah and Chloe made their pilgrimage to the Sands.

As always, Sarah had done her homework. She walked Chloe through the retirement home's website. It was bursting with sunshine and activity, featuring loads of happy, hyperkinetic seniors: a silver-haired couple in matching tracksuits strolling briskly next to the ocean; a gaggle of impossibly well-muscled elderly women in swimsuits and bathing caps doing water aerobics; a pair of old men laughing together as they stand astride La Jolla's world-famous Torrey Pines golf course. The Sands promised prospective residents vitality, an endless variety of glamorous pastimes, and all the companionship they could stand. No one was lonely. No one was dying. No, at the Sands, it was spring break forever—but with less-revealing costumes, better music, and far more opulent surroundings.

After reading the Sands's propaganda, Sarah tutored Chloe on her sales patter, and they agreed that Chloe would pose as a customer, a rich woman of leisure.

On the day of what Chloe insisted on calling her performance, Chloe slid into Sarah's car dressed in a silver silk tunic, a blue silk scarf, a matching blue cotton skirt, and heels. She wore her long blond-gray hair up in a messy yet elegant pile, held somehow by a single pearl-encrusted barrette. Her face bore a light dusting of makeup that enhanced her features without making her look too artificial. The total effect was one of stylish, slightly bohemian beauty.

Sarah took the coast road to La Jolla. Chloe rolled down the window and closed her eyes, savoring the breeze against her face. In her throaty stage voice, she thanked Sarah for releasing her from that domestic prison.

Sarah countered, "It's not that bad."

Chloe sniffed, "No smoking, no drinking." Sarah gave Chloe a knowing look. Chloe qualified, "Well, all right, *almost* no drinking. It's like living in a Mormon compound." Chloe withdrew a cigarette case from her purse, then asked, "You don't mind if I smoke, do you?"

Sarah actually did mind. But she shook her head. "No problem. But blow the smoke out the window, okay?"

Chloe lit a cigarette, inhaled deeply, and then exhaled out the window like a good girl. "Ah, free at last, free at last."

"Oh, c'mon, admit it. You're having a great time. You love being around your grandchildren."

Chloe sniffed, "Oh yes. The children are wonderful. It's my daughter who's the difficult one."

"I know Annie's been a bit tense lately, but she's got a lot on her plate."

With genuine pride, Chloe answered, "Yes, and she handles it all brilliantly. My Annabelle is a maternal genius. Lord knows where she gets *that*."

"She gets it from you, doesn't she?"

Chloe laughed. "Good Lord, no. I love my children. But I never had much patience for the day-to-day tedium of raising them. Children are not exactly scintillating company. I mean, how many times can you feign astonishment at the news that dinosaurs were 'really big'? And they're terrible listeners. So horribly self-absorbed. Everything has to be about them, never about you."

Sarah said nothing. She had heard Annie make the same complaint about Chloe more times than she could count.

Chloe went on, "Spend enough time fawning over your children, obsessing about them, and you, their mother, disappear. I was determined not to let that happen to me. I've never had much taste for self-immolation. That's why I only lasted a little while at home. I took three months off when Annie was born, and just six weeks with Jimmy. And each time I went back to work, I found it a huge relief. I wasn't someone's mother. I was me again." Chloe sighed. "But Annabelle is different. She's settled into this grinding, twenty-four-hour version of motherhood. There's no room for anything but duty. She lets the kids have fun. But there's no fun for her."

Sarah countered, "Annie has fun sometimes."

Chloe shook her head. "No, she doesn't. Not really. My daughter has always been uptight. We both know that. But she tempered it with humor. Now that humor, that sense of mischief, is seeping out of her. And because she has decided that her own joy is suspect, she's become intolerant of other adults enjoying themselves."

Sarah said, "That's not true. She's always talking about how hard Harry works, how she wishes he'd relax more."

Chloe smirked. "Oh, she *says* she's worried about him. And maybe she is. But I'm sure if he actually had the temerity to relax—to watch football for a few hours or go out drinking with friends—she would turn on him. They're together in this, you see. They've both decided that they need to be in a perpetual state of anxious industriousness until Oscar gets well."

Sarah recognized the truth in what Chloe was saying, but she couldn't reconcile herself to the bleakness of it. "It's been just a few months since Annie and Harry got the news about Oscar. Once they adjust, I'm sure they'll loosen up again."

Frowning, Chloe said, "I hope so. I really do."

The conversation ceased when La Jolla Cove came into view. Sarah had passed the Cove dozens of times, but its beauty always surprised her: a rocky promontory jutting out into a dazzling blue sea. Seals and sea lions frolicked in its waters, and pelicans roosted on its gray and brown rocks, festooning them with long white streamers of feces. In La Jolla, even bird shit looked good.

The Sands stood on a bluff overlooking this vista. Sarah drove around the back of the facility. She parked next to two white vans embossed with the gold Sands logo. Sarah and Chloe got out of the car and strode into the lobby. Its floors were covered in the same plush beige carpeting that the rest of Southern California used. The residents could have afforded the money for marble floors but not the bruises and broken bones. The rest of the décor made up for the carpeting. High ceilings, pricey artwork, and breathtaking views of the most expensive bit of coastline in the world made it clear that the Sands was not just another retirement home.

Sarah introduced herself to the receptionist and explained that Sylvia Barrington was expecting her. Minutes later, Sylvia appeared. She wasn't at all as Sarah had pictured her. On the phone, Sylvia's voice had sounded ancient, croaky, and faint. It conjured images of a tiny, dried-out crone, a human tumbleweed whom disease could blow off the plane of existence at any moment. But Sylvia Barrington turned out to be tall and sturdy-looking. Her hair was a vibrant red, a shade offered on none of nature's color swatches. The color would have been hideous on most women, but it worked on Sylvia. She wore an expensive blue tracksuit, possibly the same tracksuit the old couple was wearing on the Sands's website. But she dressed it up with a pearl necklace and heavy makeup.

Sarah introduced herself and then Chloe, explaining that she'd brought Chloe along to share the perspective of a "more mature" client. Sylvia protested, "Oh, but we have that already."

Sarah raised an eyebrow. "Do you?"

Sylvia nodded, making the wattles of her neck dance. "Regina, of course."

Sarah answered, "Well, yes. I'm sure Regina's talked to you about our product in the past, but I thought that for *today* it would be—"

Sylvia shook her head again. "Oh, but Regina will be here today. I thought you knew."

Sarah smiled, hoping her irritation didn't show. Although Sarah had been grateful for Regina's referrals, she had no desire to actually see the woman. Sarah said, "No, I knew that Regina referred you, but I didn't realize she was going to be here today. I thought I would be meeting with four *new* clients."

Sylvia's rouged cheeks turned even pinker. "I'm sorry about that. I was sure Regina had spoken to you." She rushed to add, "Of course, it was *my* mistake. Regina never told me she'd talked to you. I just assumed." The hastiness of this qualification suggested that Sylvia, like Dawn, feared Regina Maris.

Sarah shrugged. "No matter. It's always a treat to see Regina. So it will be her, yourself, and two other women, right?"

Sylvia blushed again. "I'm afraid it will just be Regina, Goldie, and me. Estelle was planning to come, but her hip is bothering her."

Sarah nodded sympathetically, as if she didn't mind at all that her prospective profit from this visit had been cut in half. Sylvia led Chloe and Sarah out of the lobby and into one of the Sands's lounges. The room was empty except for a chubby elderly brunette sitting in a cushy white armchair. The brunette was doing a crossword puzzle, her thick horn-rimmed glasses perched on the end of her nose. Sylvia cleared her throat loudly, and the woman looked up.

Sylvia announced, in the loud, carefully enunciated voice that Americans use around foreigners and the slightly deaf, "Goldie, this is Sarah Sloane and her friend, Chloe. They are the women I told you about, the ones who are going to talk to us about Regina's face cream."

Goldie did not rise to greet them, but she smiled a warm smile that lit up her craggy brown eyes. She looked up at Sarah and said, in a thick New York accent, "Oh my Gawd, what a beauty! What a *shayna punim*."

Sarah reached out to shake Goldie's hand, and Goldie cupped Sarah's hand in both of hers, holding Sarah captive for a moment. Using the loud voice that Sylvia had modeled, Sarah said, "Good to meet you, Goldie."

Goldie chided her, "Sweetheart, my hearing's fine. You don't have to shout like I'm at the bottom of a well."

Sarah blushed. "Sorry."

Goldie released Sarah's hand and waved at the air. "Oh, it's fine." Then she turned her gaze on Chloe. "And who's this one?"

Chloe answered, "Chloe Baker. Pleased to meet you."

Goldie raised her eyebrows. "Listen to this one. Such a fancy accent. Like Katharine Hepburn, she talks."

Chloe inclined her head graciously. "I'll take that as a compliment."

Goldie answered, "And so you should." Goldie gestured for the women to sit down in the circle of armchairs next to her. "Sit, already. Sit. I'm getting whiplash from looking up at you."

Once the women had seated themselves, Sarah began, "So I understand that the two of you are interested in buying some Étinav—"

Sylvia interrupted, "Oh, I don't think we should start. Regina's not here yet."

Sarah answered, "Regina's heard all this before. I'm sure she won't mind."

Goldie rolled her eyes. "That one *always* minds."

Sarah wasn't sure how to answer this. Chloe saved her. "Ladies, none of us wants to irritate Regina. So why don't we make a pact? We'll answer any questions you have about the cream. And then, when Regina gets here, my friend Sarah can start her little sales talk as if we'd only just arrived. Sound all right?"

Goldie nodded and pointed to Chloe. "This one, I like. Very shrewd."

Sylvia was more hesitant. Looking around uncertainly, as if Regina's spies might be lurking, Sylvia said, "I guess I don't see the harm in that."

Sarah asked, "So do the two of you have any questions about our product?"

Goldie asked, "Is it really two thousand dollars a jar?"

Sarah nodded. "It is."

Goldie whistled. "What? Is it made of gold or something?"

Sarah shook her head. "No, no gold. The formula is confidential. All I can tell you is that it contains a patented bio-extract that's extremely potent."

Goldie frowned. "You expect us to buy this stuff without knowing the ingredients?"

Sarah smiled and shrugged. "In a word, yes." Goldie and Sylvia exchanged looks.

Chloe broke in, "Let's be honest, ladies. Say Sarah was to give you a long list of chemical ingredients, would the list *mean* anything to you? It certainly wouldn't mean anything to me. I take ten pills every day. All I know about them is that two are blue, four are yellow, and the rest are white."

Goldie conceded, "You're right. The ingredients would mean bupkes to me. In the end, if we buy this stuff, it's because we trust you." Still smiling, Goldie turned to Sarah. "You're a lovely girl. But tell me, why should we trust you? I mean, with my doctor, I know I can trust him. He's got a bunch of degrees from fancy schools up on his wall. But you?"

Sarah smiled, liking Goldie more by the minute. "You're right. Why should you trust me? For me, this is a sideline. I'm a lawyer. One of my clients started buying the cream from Dr. Étinav, and she pulled me in. Now I sell the stuff to my clients and a few friends, mostly as a courtesy. That's why I'm here today—because a friend of a friend asked me to come sell it to you. But I'm no doctor. I can't explain *how* this cream works. All I can say is that it *does* work. Whether you believe me is up to you."

Goldie nodded. Turning back to Chloe, she asked, "So *does* it work?"

Chloe said, "Within limits, yes."

Goldie pressed, "Within limits?"

Chloe elaborated, "Look. If what you want is to eradicate every sag and wrinkle from your face, this cream is *not* the way to go. You should do what many of our peers have done. Go to a dermatologist and tell him to tuck in your face until it's so tight that he can bounce a quarter off it. Your wrinkles will disappear, but at what cost? You can only get so many face-lifts before you start looking like a fun-house mirror version of yourself. Is that what you really want?"

Goldie shook her head. "Oy, no thank you. My friend Norma got another face-lift, and her eyes . . . I swear, one's higher than the other. She looks like a Picasso."

Chloe answered, "Yes, there are plenty of cautionary tales out there. That's what drove me to buy some of the good doctor's cream. I didn't want someone to pin back the fabric of my face. But I knew I could use some sprucing up. I wanted my skin to look fresher, more supple, more the way it used to."

Goldie raised an eyebrow. "And did it work?"

Chloe shrugged. "Well, obviously, I don't look twenty-five years old. Nothing can give me that. But I look much better than I did. And to me that has been worth a great deal."

Goldie asked, "Worth two thousand dollars?"

Chloe answered, "For me, yes. Of course, if my finances were tighter, I would have to answer differently. I am very fortunate. I can drop a few thousand here and there without even feeling it. For me, the question was not *why* to buy the cream. It was *why not.* I wanted a change. I could afford to take a risk that might produce that change. So why the hell not?"

Goldie nodded thoughtfully. After a long moment, she said, "Okay, I'm in."

Sylvia asked, "Are you sure?"

Goldie shrugged. "As the lady said, why the hell not? I'm not asking to be a great beauty. I just want to scrape off a few years." Goldie grinned. "Put the shine back on the apple so Max Pilkus will take a bite."

Chloe raised an eyebrow. "Max Pilkus?"

Goldie's grin broadened. "He's eighty-two, but the man has still got it."

Sylvia put a hand to her face, embarrassed at Goldie's frankness. Chloe asked Sylvia, "And what about you? Do *you* have any questions about the cream?"

Sylvia floundered, "Not really, I just—"

Goldie chided, "Relax, it's not a test."

Sylvia bit down on her bottom lip and then looked to Sarah. "The cream doesn't have any side effects, does it?"

Sarah replied, "No, nothing serious. Some users find the bio-extract a bit stimulating. It's about the same lift you'd get from drinking a cup of coffee."

Sylvia's eyebrows shot up in alarm. "But I don't drink coffee anymore."

Sarah asked, "Do you have a heart condition?"

Sylvia shook her head. "No, but I try to be careful."

Goldie weighed in again, saying affectionately, "She's crazy."

Sarah asked, "What?"

Goldie explained, "Crazy, meshuggener. Sylvie's one of these old people who thinks if she never eats a cookie or drinks a coffee, she'll live forever."

Sylvia bristled, "That's not fair, Goldie. I'm not trying to live forever. I think it's important, at our age, to be as careful as possible. I'm not twenty-five anymore."

Goldie smiled. "Sylvie, you were never twenty-five." Goldie turned to Sarah and Chloe, her audience. "Thirty years I've known this one, and I've never seen her eat a piece of candy or take a drink. It's always 'no thank you' or 'I'll have some later.' I tell her, 'Sylvie, you're seventy-two. What are you waiting for?'"

Sylvie countered, "You want me to buy the cream because *you're* buying it."

Goldie shot back, "Of course that's why I want you to buy it! It's probably a waste of money. But if I'm going to do something stupid, it's always more fun to do it with a friend."

Sylvia smiled in spite of herself. "I guess you have a point." Just then, Regina appeared. Sylvia rose to her feet, saying, "Regina, so good to see you. We were beginning to worry that you wouldn't make it."

Regina smiled. "Yes, I'm sorry to be late. I haven't missed anything, have I?"

Sylvia looked around guiltily so Sarah jumped in. "No, nothing at all. We were getting acquainted. Sylvia thought we should hold off on actually talking about the cream until you got here."

Regina nodded, saying, "Oh, that's sweet of you." She smiled around at the small circle of women, her gaze coming to a rest on Chloe. "I don't believe we've met. I'm Regina Maris. And you are?"

"Chloe Baker. I've been using Dr. Étinav's cream for some time. Sarah brought me along in case these ladies had questions about how well the cream works for—"

Regina interrupted, "For old women."

Chloe inclined her head. "For *more mature* women, yes."

Regina sat down in an armchair next to Sylvia. "Very sensible. Of course, since *I'm* here, there was no need for you to trouble yourself."

"It's no trouble at all. To the contrary, it's been a pleasure." Chloe gestured to Sylvia and Goldie. "It's always a pleasure to meet such charming women."

Regina answered, "Oh yes. They are charming. Sylvia and I go *way* back. Sylvia's husband, Clancy, came to work for *my* husband in . . . Oh, what year was it? Sylvie, when did Clancy's old company fire him? Was it in '83 or '84?"

Sylvia murmured, "Eighty-four."

"Yes. That's right." Regina turned back to Sarah. "I'm afraid I don't have the best head for dates."

Chloe answered, "To the contrary, dear, I suspect you never forget *anything*."

Regina smiled. "No, I suppose I don't. Anyhow, there's no way I could forget Clancy. He worked under my husband for twenty years. Clancy was such a good worker. Not the brightest bulb in the board. Clancy would have admitted as much, don't you think so?" Regina looked to Sylvia.

Sylvia kept her eyes down, but nodded. "Yes, I'm sure he would have."

Regina droned on, "Clancy made CFO at one point, but then he got demoted. Some people aren't meant for upper management." Putting a hand on Sylvia's shoulder, Regina purred, "But still, Clancy did very well for himself. He was a busy worker bee. My husband always said so."

Chloe quipped, "Did he? What marvelous condescension."

This remark diverted Regina's attention from Sylvia and back to Chloe, as Chloe had intended it to. Regina asked Chloe icily, "So, tell me, Chloe, what did *your* husband do, assuming you *had* a husband?"

Chloe answered, "We both worked in the theater. We were actors."

Regina purred, "How charming. Would I have seen you two in anything?"

Chloe shrugged. "I don't know. Did you attend the theater much?"

"I tried to. For years, I made a point of going out to New York to see the big shows. Were you in any major Broadway productions?"

"A few. Mostly Shakespeare."

Regina said, "Odd. I don't recognize you from anything. I suppose my memory for faces is not the best. It's so hard to remember the minor characters. The stars *do* hog the spotlight, don't they? And of course, time changes all of us."

Chloe's voice was hard. "Not *all* of us."

Regina asked, "Come again?"

Chloe leaned forward in her seat. "I never forget a face. In fact, I seem to remember yours from somewhere. Were you ever on the stage?"

Regina smirked. "Oh, I dabbled in the theater for a few years. That was before I met my husband."

Goldie cut in, gesturing to Regina, "Listen to the modesty on this one! Come on, don't be shy, tell the lady about how you worked in show business." Goldie turned to Chloe. "When I told Regina I came from New York, she told me all about how she worked on Broadway. And not in little parts. This one had a big career. She was going places."

Still smirking, Regina said, "Oh, that's ancient history. I gave up the theater when I gave birth to Joseph. It was a tough choice. But I don't have any regrets. I didn't want my children being raised by nannies."

Chloe agreed, "Yes, nannies can be untrustworthy. Sometimes downright naughty." Sarah's eyebrows shot up at this. The remark seemed bizarre coming from Chloe. Chloe pressed on, telling Regina, "So you were in the theater? I knew I recognized you from somewhere. You must tell me what you were in."

Regina laughed nervously. "Oh, I doubt you'd have seen me in anything. It was all so long ago. I was in the chorus of a few shows. Musicals were so big back then."

Chloe grinned. "I see. So you were one of the worker bees in the chorus. There's nothing wrong with that. Not all of us are destined for stardom, or even for speaking parts."

Regina bristled, "I had my share of speaking parts. Singing was never my forte so I only did a few musicals. I preferred more serious work. Dramatic plays."

A strange smile spread across Chloe's face, and Sarah tensed. What was Chloe up to? Playacting at wide-eyed innocence, Chloe asked, "Which dramatic plays were you in? Tennessee Williams? O'Neill, perhaps?"

Regina shook her head. "No, nothing as famous as that. But I had my share of parts in smaller plays, important pieces . . ."

Chloe said, "Yes, I believe I saw one of your important pieces."

Regina's alarm was unmistakable. "You did?"

Chloe smiled serenely. "Oh yes. Like I said, I never forget a face. I saw one of your shows. It was Off-Broadway. A theater down on Fourteenth Street. My husband and I used to run lights for the burlesque houses when acting work dried up. I must have sat through your show dozens of times, maybe even hundreds. I believe it was called *Naughty Nannies*, wasn't it?"

Goldie looked puzzled. "*Naughty Nannies*? That doesn't sound so serious to me."

Chloe answered, "I could be wrong about the title. The show featured a group of women who worked as governesses by day and as prostitutes by night. Am I right, Regina?"

Regina shrugged and looked away. "I can't remember every show I was in, not after all these years."

Chloe pressed, "You don't remember? Well, that *does* surprise me. Not many serious plays give an actress the chance to cavort about the stage wearing nothing but a corset."

Regina colored. "I don't know what you're talking about."

Chloe was relentless. "But dear, you were the lead—the naughtiest nanny of them all, am I right?"

Regina glared at Chloe. "I'm sure you're quite mistaken. I never played anyone like that." She grabbed her purse and stood. "Now, if you'll excuse me, I'm afraid I have to be going. I'm running late for another appointment, an *important* appointment." Regina gave the women a curt nod and strode out of the room.

After a long silence, Sylvia leaned forward. A smile lit her face. She told Sarah, "I'll take two jars."

Years before joining book club, Kim had read the Harry Potter series to her girls. And lately, as Kim grew listless, she began wondering when she'd get her big chance. Where the hell was her letter from Hogwarts?

31

Kim's Mardi Gras

Cajun music blared through the packed hotel ballroom. Onstage, a black seven-man band played accordions, harmonicas, drums, a fiddle, and a washboard, urging the rich white parents of Gillespie School children, "Come on down to Creole Country!" The Gillespie's gala committee had decorated the room's banquet tables in Mardi Gras colors of purple, green, and gold. Along with lavish goody bags, each place setting offered two strands of beads, a sequined mask, a thirty-page program listing the items up for auction, and a bidding paddle.

While Kim's husband, Andrew, and the other parents at the table shouted to each other over the music, Kim retreated behind her red sequined mask and paged through her program. It reported that Theodore and Claudia Garner had donated a weeklong stay at their villa in Tuscany while Michael and Bethany Anderson were offering two weeks at their Aspen ski chalet. The Volkners topped everyone by ponying up an entire month at their beach house in Tahiti. Showoffs. Local merchants had chipped in too. Dr. Stewart Binaid had donated ten Botox sessions. Images Dental offered teeth whitening. And the

Finnington Domestic Arts Institute gave a week with one of its highly trained butlers.

And then there were the teachers' donations. Mrs. Marin, the kindergarten teacher, offered babysitting. Ms. Tanesborough, the tasty young music teacher who guest-starred in the erotic dreams of several Gillespie fathers, offered piano lessons. And Mr. DeSoto, the gym teacher, donated personal training sessions.

Although their donations were welcome at the Gillespie's annual gala, teachers themselves stayed away. They couldn't afford the two-hundred-dollar tickets, let alone to bid on anything. And besides, the gala would have been awkward for them anyway. The gala's main attraction was that it freed Gillespie parents to flash their wads. The grossest displays of ostentation became acceptable, even noble, when done in the name of education. So mothers wore gowns worth several times what a Gillespie teacher made in a month while fathers got into bidding wars over the Gillespie's coveted ten-thousand-dollar parking spots.

Teachers at the Gillespie had an image problem. On the one hand, they wielded tremendous power in the classroom. Indeed, many parents chose the Gillespie School precisely because of its authoritarian style. The teachers' academic toughness freed parents to spoil their children shamelessly at home, and for that the parents were grateful. They deferred to the teachers, analyzing and overanalyzing every teacher comment. Every sticker that graced an assignment was parsed as closely as a newfound segment of the Dead Sea Scrolls.

But Gillespie parents didn't want their children to *become* teachers. Parents delivered this message gently. They handled the unsavory fact of teacher poverty the way other parents treat the question of Santa's existence. A Gillespie parent hoped his child would work out the facts slowly on his own, but if the child didn't, the parent would start dropping hints. Drive a child, especially a boy, past the teachers' parking lot a few times, and the child would quickly get the idea. When pondering what sort of future he wanted, a child would always go for a shiny new Maserati over a beat-up secondhand Subaru.

Skimming through the auction catalog, Kim noticed that someone had drawn a black line through Mrs. Gouvalaris's donation of tutoring. Kim's daughter had had Mrs. Gouvalaris for math the previous year, and the woman was one of Amelia's favorites. Kim decided to ask Priscilla about it. As the dictatorial head of the Gillespie's PTA, Priscilla made it her business to know everything worth knowing about the school, and then some. For months, Kim had avoided Priscilla. Kim shrank from Priscilla's domineering personality. But lately that had begun to change.

Kim had begun to change. She wasn't sure why, but she'd regained some of her confidence. Sarah's cream was part of it. Looking in the mirror, Kim found herself pleased for the first time in years. The cream worked. Her face looked fresher somehow, less haggard. But even more important than the cream was Sarah herself. She and Kim had become good friends. Sarah was a great listener, but more than that, she was a terrific cheerleader. She took Kim's side in every situation, talking up Kim's strengths and downplaying her weaknesses. Just knowing she could call Sarah at any time made Kim feel stronger, less alone.

So Kim rose from her table and walked over to Priscilla. Priscilla wasn't hard to find. Even with the band playing, Priscilla's voice carried through the hall. Kim tapped her on the shoulder, and Priscilla swiveled around. Priscilla said, "Isn't this wonderful? I *knew* the New Orleans theme would work. They almost did it ten years ago. Bought the decorations and everything. But then Katrina hit." Priscilla shook her head. "Well, we couldn't do it *then*. Not with all those bodies floating around the bayou. I was *so* disappointed." Priscilla sighed, obviously counting herself among Katrina's worst victims. "But all's well that ends well, right?"

Kim nodded. "Yes. But can I ask you something? I noticed something odd in the program."

Priscilla's brow furrowed. "If those printers screwed it up again, there'll be hell to pay. I swear, if you want something done right, you have to do it yourself." This was Priscilla's mantra. Like many PTA superwomen, Priscilla viewed herself as a hypercapable beacon in a sea of idiots and laggards.

Kim broke in, "No, it doesn't look like a mistake or anything. I was wondering why Mrs. Gouvalaris's donation is crossed out."

Priscilla smiled with relief. "Oh, that. Hadn't you heard? She's leaving at the end of the month."

"Why?"

"Her husband's been transferred. They're moving to Houston or some God-awful place like that."

"Who's going to take over her class?"

Priscilla shrugged. "I don't know. I'm sure they'll find *someone.* Martha is already working on it." Martha Bisson was the school's headmistress. "Of course, it's not easy finding someone good halfway through the school year. I told Martha that if she wanted *me* to step in and find someone, I would . . ." Priscilla droned on for a while. But Kim heard little of what she said.

Kim wanted that job. She was perfect for it. She'd taught fourth- and fifth-grade math before, and she still had her specialist credential. She'd be at the Gillespie, so she wouldn't have to worry about a long commute. And there would be no problem with her staying late because her girls had both signed up for after-school enrichments. Yes, the job was perfect.

When Kim returned to her table, she found her husband, Andrew, leaning forward in his seat, listening to Bob Morris expound on the merits of electric cars. Bob was one of Andrew's new heroes. He was one of the filthy-rich fiftysomething men of leisure who had traded their old wives in for younger models. These lazy papa bears spent their time loitering around the La Jolla Beach and Tennis Club, tinkering with expensive cars, and tending to their new young families. The lead members of this charmed circle were Bob Morris and Walter Tilmore. Seven years earlier, Bob had dumped his fifty-four-year-old wife for a twentysomething Russian "model/actress" who'd immediately secured her position by giving Bob a son, Dmitri. Meanwhile, Walter, Valerie's ex, was expecting a new baby with his girlfriend, Crystal, any moment.

Kim had heard Bob prattle on about cars before. Too excited to wait, she tapped Andrew on the shoulder, saying, "Honey, I need to—"

Andrew didn't look up at her. He kept his eyes fixed on Bob and held up his index finger for Kim to wait. Kim hated *the finger*. It was the same gesture she'd seen Andrew give his secretary when she interrupted him during an important call, the same gesture he gave his kids when they tried to drag him away from his beloved iPad.

When Bob finally paused for a breath, Kim touched Andrew's knee to get his attention. But instead of turning to her, he gave her the finger again. It infuriated her more than a middle finger would have. Index finger, middle finger . . . they both meant the same thing. Giving Bob Morris his full attention, Andrew made a long speech agreeing with everything Bob had said. Bob loved it. It was like listening to an echo that lasted for five minutes.

When Andrew finished, Kim put a hand on his shoulder and leaned across to Bob, purring, "Sorry to interrupt men's talk, but I'm afraid I need a moment with my husband. After that, he's all yours. I promise." Kim smiled prettily and put her hand on Bob's knee, imitating one of Priscilla's signature moves.

The move worked. Leering at Kim, Bob told Andrew, "Got to give the little woman what she wants, eh?"

Andrew nodded loyally, but Kim caught the flash of annoyance he directed Bob's way. Andrew didn't like anyone ogling his wife. Kim told Andrew that she needed to talk to him in private. She cocked her head at the ballroom's exit. As Andrew rose, he rolled his eyes and said, "Duty calls." Bob laughed.

With a bit more force than necessary, Kim grabbed Andrew by the hand and led him quickly out of the ballroom. When they emerged into the brightly lit hotel lobby, Andrew pulled his hand back, saying, "Easy does it, Tarzan." Andrew made a great show of flexing his fingers, as if they'd been caught in a vise.

Now it was Kim's turn to be annoyed, but she held her tongue. She wanted this conversation to go well. She said, "I'm sorry, honey. It's just that I have some news, and I was excited to tell you."

Andrew looked up at her, his face breaking into a smile. "You've decided to go forward with the surgery?"

Kim blanked. "Surgery?"

"The breast enhancement surgery."

"What?"

Andrew reminded her, "The breast enhancement surgery. You said you needed time to think about it. I thought maybe you'd had an epiphany or something."

Kim gaped. What was he talking about? She hadn't said she'd think about the surgery. She'd turned him down flat. "Drew, I told you. I am *not* getting fake boobs."

Andrew smiled and then said slowly, as if explaining something to a child, "I looked into it, honey. There's no risk. You'd be up and about in a matter of weeks."

Kim felt the blood rush to her face. "I don't want fake boobs. If *you* think they're so great, then *you* get them!" As soon as she said this, Kim's mind flashed on an image of Andrew, Bob Morris, and all their pudgy, prosperous male buddies sitting in a circle playing with their own comically huge fake tits. In a nanosecond, Kim switched from rage to laughter.

Andrew's eyebrows shot up. "All right, I can see you're not thinking rationally. We'll talk about the surgery later, when you've calmed down."

This wasn't good. Kim didn't want to come across as a hysterical housewife. She wanted credibility, dammit. With the rigid concentration of a drunk taking a road test, Kim bit down on her lower lip, and the pain stanched her giggling fit. She said, "I'm fine. Just a bit tired. Drew, my news has nothing to do with surgery. It's a lot more important than that."

"What is it?"

"I want to go back to work."

Andrew shook his head. "We've been through this, Kimberly."

"No, wait, hear me out. I'm not talking about going to work back in National City. I'm talking about a different job. A better one. I'm going to teach at the Gillespie."

Andrew recoiled. "What?"

"The Gillespie. I just heard that Mrs. Gouvalaris is quitting, and they're looking for a replacement."

"Mrs. Gouva-what?"

"Gouvalaris. She was Amelia's math teacher last year. Just like—"

Andrew held up a hand for Kim to stop. "You want to work at the Gillespie?!"

The scorn Andrew pumped into this question made it clear that Kim was in for a fight. "Yes, I want to work at the Gillespie."

Andrew said nothing for a moment. He shook his head. Then he said, "No, honey. I'm afraid not. That would never do."

"Why not?"

"It would place us both in a very awkward position. Don't you see that?"

"Why?"

"You'd be working for our friends. How are our friends going to see you as an equal, or *me* as an equal, if you're one of their employees?"

Kim's brow furrowed. "But I *won't* be working for our friends. I'll be working for the school. I may interact with our friends. I may take *suggestions* from them, but they won't be my bosses."

"Yes, they will. It's the parents who really call the shots at a private school. You *know* that. How are our friends supposed to feel comfortable around you if you're babysitting their kids?"

"I won't be babysitting. I will be teaching. It's very different."

"Is it really?"

"Yes, and the man I married used to know that. I'm going to be teaching mathematics. It's an important job. It's—"

Andrew exhaled loudly. "Please spare me your speech about the sanctity of the teaching profession. I've heard it a thousand times."

Kim's face reddened. "Oh, I'm sorry. Is that the new rule? We only get to talk if we have something brand-new to say? Then I guess I don't have to listen to your speech about how you built your company out of nothing. Or your speech about the importance of associating with the right sort of people. And I never, ever have to listen to you tell me that I should get chemical balls put on my chest!"

"Kim, the only reason I suggested the surgery is that—"

Kim's jaw tightened. She warned him, "Andrew, not—"

"No, you *need* to hear this. The only reason I suggested the surgery is that you've been complaining so much lately about feeling unattractive, about not fitting in. Do *I* think you need new boobs? No. Do I think they might give you a boost in the self-esteem department? Yes."

Kim sneered, "So you think the way for me to boost my self-esteem is to undergo radical, totally unnecessary surgery?"

Andrew threw up his hands. "I was trying to help."

Kim rubbed her temples. "Trying to help? How the hell is getting fake boobs going to help me?" Kim felt her lower lip tremble, always a bad sign. She was losing control. A tear ran down her cheek. She wiped it away quickly.

Andrew stepped forward and hugged her. "Sweetie, please don't take it that way. I don't mean . . . I love you just as you are . . . You used to be so confident, so happy. I want you to feel that way again."

Kim sniffed and met his gaze. "You want me to be happy?"

"Yes, that's *all* I want."

"Then promise me you'll *think* about the Gillespie job. Think about it seriously, okay?"

Andrew nodded. Kim stepped back into his arms. She leaned her head against his shoulder, and he stroked her hair. They stood that way for a long time.

Natalie noticed that—like everybody else—writers were unkind to loners. When loners like Amy in Gone Girl *or Ahab in* Moby-Dick *sought revenge, they came across as creepy and obsessive. But when avengers had pals, like in* The First Wives Club, *it was smiles all around.*

32

One Unhappy Customer

Natalie was fed up with Sarah Sloane. At first, Natalie believed Sarah's lies about not having enough cream for her customers. But then Natalie kept running into more and more people who had tried the stuff. Whenever Dawn or Priscilla deigned to talk to Natalie at the gym, they crowed about how Sarah's cream had revolutionized their lives.

Then, months later, during morning drop-off at the Gillespie, Natalie stopped to chat with sweet, mousy Kim Elliot. Hunting for her car keys, Kim had dumped the contents of her purse onto the hood of her car, and Natalie was shocked to spot a jar of Étinav among the detritus. When Natalie asked her about it, Kim said that she had started using the cream a week ago. Blushing prettily, Kim said, "It seems to be working really well."

Natalie answered, "You're so lucky. I'm still stuck on the waiting list."

Kim's smile faltered. "Waiting list?"

"For Étinav. When did you first order the stuff? Three months ago? Four?"

"No. I called Sarah a few weeks ago. She arranged to meet with me for lunch right away."

Natalie blinked furiously, trying to process this bit of information. Then she recovered herself. "Well, then, Sarah must have gotten a new shipment in. I'll have to call her to remind her about my order." Natalie said her good-byes and hurried back to her car. Slamming her car door shut, she yanked out her phone and called Sarah. Of course, Sarah didn't pick up. Evidently, Sarah had never heard of a little thing called customer service.

So Natalie left Sarah a voice mail for the umpteenth time. But Sarah didn't call back. So, after three days of waiting, Natalie left her another message. Then another one four days after that. Silence.

Natalie fumed. What the hell was this? Who did Sarah think she was? Natalie's money was just as good as anyone else's. If Sarah had decided Natalie wasn't good enough to buy her cream, then Natalie didn't want to buy the stuff anyway.

Natalie told herself that the cream probably didn't even work. It was probably overpriced snake oil. The more Natalie thought about it, the more suspicious it all sounded. Some reclusive French scientist comes up with the secret of everlasting youth, but he doesn't want to sell it on the open market. He doesn't want to get rich off the thing. Oh no! Rather than cashing in by going to the cosmetics companies, this mad genius decides to manufacture the stuff himself and sell it through acquaintances like Sarah? Oh, and nobody, not even Sarah, has any idea what's in the stuff! For all anyone knows, it could be half mayonnaise, half bat guano. Consumers are supposed to trust Dr. Étinav because a few celebrities up in LA vouched for him, as if celebrity endorsements somehow trump FDA approval.

Natalie told herself to forget about Sarah and her cream. But still, it rankled.

Kim said characteristically little when the book club discussed Jonathan Franzen's Freedom. *Franzen's book hit too close for Kim with its main character Patty Berglund, an angst-ridden housewife and faded college athlete. At least, unlike Patty, Kim had not settled for her husband. Like the husband in* Freedom, *Andrew was nerdy and obviously devoted to Kim when they first met, but Kim had fallen for him all the same. She just hadn't realized how much things would change.*

33

Kim's Brunch with a Bastard

Andrew cursed under his breath as he adjusted the passenger seat in his BMW i8, a cramped hybrid two-seater with a six-digit price tag. Waiting behind the wheel, Kim asked, "Are you *sure* we shouldn't take my car?"

Andrew spat back, "Yes, I'm sure. I have to get these crutches in at the right angle, and then I can . . ." Andrew grunted with effort. He wrestled with his crutches, unintentionally bringing one of them down hard on his newly bandaged right foot. "Son of a . . ."

Kim bit the inside of her cheek to stop herself from laughing. She repeated, "Why don't we take my car?"

Andrew fumed. "For the last time, I told you, I want . . . to take . . . the i8." Andrew insisted on referring to his car as "the i8" as if it were a spaceship or some flashy futuristic robot. "I'm already going to be wimping out on Walter's tennis game. I can at least bring the i8 along."

Kim shook her head. "You're not wimping out. You have a broken toe. Walter can't expect—"

Andrew held up his index finger for Kim to be quiet. And she felt the blood rush to her cheeks, but she curbed her temper. She had to. After all, if it weren't for her, Andrew wouldn't have broken his toe in the first place. He'd broken it last night during yet another shouting match. It was the Gillespie job, of course. These days, it was *always* the Gillespie job.

A week earlier, Kim had dropped off her résumé at the Gillespie. Within an hour, the school's headmistress, Martha, had offered her the job, along with a heady bouquet of flattery. How lucky the school was to get such a strong applicant! And in the middle of the school year! Kim was a math goddess! How soon could she start?

Martha gave Kim a week to get back to her. Later, when Andrew got home, the fights began. Or rather, *the* fight began. Because it was the *same* fight over and over. Every night, Kim would start the festivities by saying that she and Andrew needed to talk. Andrew would try to put her off, rubbing his temples and asking her if they could just give it a rest. He wanted to stall. Fans of the status quo always do.

Refusing to be put on hold, Kim reminded Andrew of Martha's deadline, and Andrew rolled his eyes. Then he entered the fray. His opening gambit was always the same. He tried to grab the high ground by talking about how much the girls needed Kim, how important it was that she be there for them. Remember the long hours she used to pull when she worked in National City? Remember how much time the girls used to spend with their nanny? Andrew spat, "For Chrissake, Amelia spoke more Spanish than English!"

This bit of incendiary bullshit needled Kim. True, Amelia had picked up a few Spanish phrases. But knowing how to say *hola* and *gracias* did *not* qualify her to work as a UN interpreter. When Kim corrected Andrew on this, he shrugged his shoulders.

"Okay, fine, so she wasn't *fluent*. My point is that Amelia was spending more time with her nanny than she was *with her mother*." Andrew made this verbal shot to the groin without remorse, cheerfully dipping his toe into the bottomless pit of guilt that working mothers share.

Unwilling to rehash what life had been like for Amelia during the few years when her mother had held down a job, Kim reminded Andrew that the girls were older now. They were off at school most of the day. What good did it do them to have an unemployed mom sitting at home waiting for them like a lonely puppy? What was Kim supposed to do while they were gone? Stare at their photos? Write little poems about how much she missed them?

Last night, as the argument built up steam again, Andrew sputtered, "There's exercise classes, tennis, spa dates . . ."

Kim sneered, "Coloring books, macramé projects . . ."

"Look, I don't know what the other wives do. But *they* keep busy. Priscilla's the head of the PTA. And what's-her-face, Dawn? She's on that board for that thing, right?"

"The truth is you don't give a damn what they do! You don't give a damn what *I* do. All you care about is that I *don't* do anything to embarrass you."

"So I don't want you to embarrass me? Does that make me such a monster?"

"No, but it doesn't make you a—"

Andrew cut her off. "I work hard to provide you with everything a woman could want. Beautiful house, beautiful car . . ."

Kim answered, "Who do you think I am? Malibu Barbie? Am I supposed to walk around 24-7 with a plastic grin because I have all the right accessories?"

"No, but . . . Let's face it, I think most women would jump at the chance to live in a house like this without having to work."

"I'm not *most* women. My life's ambition isn't to live in a posh neighborhood and do nothing all day."

"I'm not saying you should do *nothing*. You should absolutely get out there, maybe take some classes . . ."

Now it was Kim's turn to roll her eyes. "Classes?"

"Sure, there's all kinds of classes you could take. Cooking classes, Pilates, yoga. Hell, if I had the time, I'd *love* to go back to school."

Kim refused to be buried in this avalanche of bullshit. "Then go ahead. Sell the business. We both know you don't *have* to work. Go take a bunch of classes down at the community college for the next few decades."

Andrew countered, "There is no way I could sell the company now, unless I want it to go to some VC firm, some chop shop."

Kim took a deep breath. "Look, I know you've worked hard to build up your company, and I respect that. And I know you've worked hard to give us all this, but I didn't marry you so that you could stick me in a gilded cage. I married you because I love you and respect you. And I *thought* you respected me."

"Of course I do!"

"No, not 'of course.' A big part of respecting me is respecting my need to work."

Andrew couldn't think of an answer to this. Frustrated, he kicked the mahogany coffee table. It was a recent purchase, an antique he had picked up, without consulting Kim, at one of the posh furniture stores on Girard, Seaside Home. The table had cost seven thousand dollars, and Andrew had gotten his money's worth. His kick didn't leave a dent. But Andrew was made of weaker stuff. As soon as his foot connected, he yowled in pain. Twenty minutes later, he and Kim arrived at Scripps Memorial. He'd broken his big toe. It would take weeks to heal.

By the time Kim and Andrew made it home, it was too late to call and cancel the next day's tennis match with Walter. They rang Walter's house the next morning, but no one answered. And Walter didn't carry a cell phone. Walter, Valerie's ex and the nubile Crystal's boyfriend/

baby daddy, didn't believe in cell phones. Walter was a man of strong opinions.

As one of the wealthiest men in California, a man with tentacles in real estate, venture capital, and the tech sector, Walter got plenty of chances to opine. To Walter, a cell phone was a sign of weakness. How could you really be a man, a man of consequence, if anyone could interrupt your life at any time? What sort of a weakling needed such constant contact? Not Walter. Marriage was another sign of weakness. Why would a man tie himself down to one woman? So far as Walter could see, marriage was a way for a woman to hold on to a man long after she'd ceased to attract him. Crystal's pregnancy had done nothing to soften this view.

No, the specter of fatherhood didn't *change* any of Walter's opinions. But it did prompt him to take some *new* ones on board, opinions that he generously shared with impressionable younger bucks like Andrew. At fifty-seven, after a lifetime of Styrofoam cups and gas-guzzling cars, Walter had become an environmentalist.

Walter was the one who convinced Andrew to buy the i8, an outrageously pricey hybrid sports car. Kim was no fan of gas guzzlers, but the i8 was a joke. She'd seen cat boxes with more legroom. The i8 was a car for midgets, not for a five-foot-ten-inch man like Andrew. And certainly not for his five-foot-eleven-inch wife.

After Andrew finally managed to cram his long legs and crutches into the car, Kim drove over to the La Jolla Beach and Tennis Club. Andrew sulked all the way. When they pulled onto the club's circular driveway, he struggled out of the car as fast as he could, ignoring the hovering valet. He yanked his crutches out and charged ahead into the club while Kim fetched her racket from the trunk. She gave the keys, and plenty of apologetic eye contact, to the valet. In the club restaurant, she found Andrew and his posse waiting for her: Walter, the hugely pregnant Crystal, Priscilla, and her husband, Roger. Kim smiled at the diners and settled into the table's one empty seat, next to Andrew.

She listened while Andrew explained how he'd broken his toe. He didn't mention the domestic squabble that had given rise to his accident. And Walter did not pry. Walter wasn't big on questions or on listening. Walter *loved* to talk. He needled Andrew. "So you broke your toe the night before you had to face me on the court. How convenient!"

Andrew smiled sheepishly. "It wasn't convenient. I was looking forward to playing you today. I really was."

Walter smirked and shot a knowing look over at Roger. Roger, a seasoned toady, did not miss his cue. Pointing to the club's menu, Roger asked Andrew, "So what'll you be having today?" He paused theatrically. "I hear the *chicken* is good." Walter, Roger, and Priscilla had a good belly laugh at this while Andrew blushed.

When the laughter trailed off, Walter leaned back in his chair and stretched, puffing out his chest and folding his arms behind his neck. Kim had read somewhere that apes use this same posture to make themselves look bigger, to intimidate. And there was no doubt about it, Walter was one impressive gorilla. His staggering wealth already gave him an aura of invincibility. And his physique added to this. He was tall and thin, about as tall as Kim. He had the ropy muscles and dark tan of a seasoned tennis player. And a booming low voice. Still stretching, Walter smirked. "Don't feel bad, Drew. You're not the first guy to come up with a medical emergency to get out of playing yours truly. For the guys at this club, playing me is like jury duty. You know you'll have to do it sometime, but you put it off as long as you can."

Again, everyone at the table laughed—everyone except Kim. Clumsily changing the subject, Andrew piped up, "I brought the i8 with me."

Walter asked, "Did you?"

Andrew went on, "Yeah, I picked it up two weeks ago." Andrew looked pathetically eager to please, a puppy wagging its tail and waiting for its biscuit.

Walter nodded. "Good for you. Mind you, I'm still holding off on buying one."

Andrew's smile faltered. "But I thought you already ordered one from the dealership."

Walter shook his head. "No. Not yet. Don't want to jump the gun. The i8's a great car. But I heard the interior's a little cramped." Walter chuckled. "Besides, Jag is coming out with a new electric car soon. Fisker's got one too."

Andrew hid his disappointment under a tight smile. Kim couldn't manage even that much. She'd *heard* Walter tell Andrew that he had already ordered an i8 and that Andrew should order one too. Obviously Walter had changed his mind without bothering to update his acolytes. For a moment, Kim wondered who was the bigger asshole: her husband, for following Walter's advice, or Walter, for toying so carelessly with other people. It was no contest. Walter won hands down. Walter Tilmore was the Grand Canyon of assholes.

Having dispensed his latest wisdom on electric cars, Walter returned to bragging about his prowess as a tennis player. He lamented, "I can't get a decent game around this place anymore." He turned to Roger. "You wouldn't be up for a game today, would you?"

Roger smiled and shook his head. "No way. You've embarrassed me enough times. The only way I'm going up against you is if you tie a brick of Kryptonite around your neck."

Walter pressed, "Oh, c'mon. I'll go easy on you."

Roger shook his head. "No, I know where I stand on the food chain. I'm not going up against the top seed in the club."

Kim raised an eyebrow, asking Walter, "Are you *really* the top seed?" It was a sincere question. Kim avoided the club. She didn't like to play there. She preferred pickup matches at the YMCA, matches where she could sweat and hit the ball as hard as she liked without the Priscillas of the world watching.

Walter shrugged. "In my age category, fifty and up. There are a few forty-year-olds around here who can give me a run for my money. But not many. And certainly none of them are seated at this table." Walter winked again. "Yesiree, it's getting so I can't even get a little exercise around here."

Crystal took Walter's hand, purring, "Oh, honey, I'm sure one of the club pros will be in later today. You can play then."

Walter shook his head, instantaneously shifting from smugness to petulance. "I'm tired of playing them. Besides, you have to book them way in advance."

The table fell quiet. Roger and Priscilla shook their bobbleheads in sympathy at Walter's plight while Crystal ran a hand over her vast pregnant belly. Andrew stuck to his tight smile, still pouting over the i8, no doubt. It was Kim who broke the silence. "I'll play you."

Walter said, "Excuse me?"

Kim repeated, "I'll play you."

Walter smiled. "Well, that's very sporting of you. Not to be sexist or anything, but I haven't played against a woman in a long while. I'm afraid my serve might be a little strong for you."

"I'll take my chances."

Plainly amused, Walter raised his eyebrows at Andrew. But Andrew didn't catch Walter's expression. Andrew was too busy staring at Kim, at the determined set of her jaw. With a slight tremor in his voice, Andrew put a hand on Kim's shoulder and said, "Honey, I don't think this is such a good idea."

Kim ignored Andrew. She stared evenly at Walter, sizing him up. She said, "I guess you're right, Walter. It wouldn't be a fair game. I mean, let's face it, you've got a good twenty years on me." Walter leaned forward, his smile gone now. Kim added, "Don't get me wrong. I'm sure you're a terrific player. But . . ." She shrugged good-naturedly. "You're old enough to be my dad." Kim pretended not to notice the jaws dropping around her. She forked a melon ball into her mouth.

Walter said, "Well, that seals it. Now I have to play you."

Kim chirped, "Great. Let's do it. After brunch, of course."

Again, Andrew put a hand on Kim's shoulder. "Sweetie, are you sure you want to do this?"

Still wide-eyed, Kim said, "Oh yes. It'll be great fun. It's just a friendly game."

Andrew started, "But don't you—"

Walter cut him off. "Yes, we can use the court I reserved for my match with Andrew. I think—" Andrew tried to interrupt, but Kim held up her index finger to silence him while Walter spoke. Kim had never given Andrew the finger before. It was delicious.

Kim winced when she read about poor, beautiful Lily Bart losing at cards to a rich society lady in Edith Wharton's The House of Mirth. *For Lily, the loss meant ruin; for the rich lady, it was pocket change.*

34

A Friendly Game

An hour later, Kim and Walter faced off on the tennis court. They bickered for a moment over who'd serve first. Walter smiled wolfishly at Kim. "Ladies first."

Kim waved him off. "Age before beauty. I insist."

So Walter served first. The man hadn't been lying. Thanks to his height and strong arms, he had a powerful serve, one that most club players couldn't have returned. In a burst of speed, Kim shot across the court and batted it back to him. Walter was surprised, but he recovered himself quickly. He won the first game.

With the second game, it was Kim's turn to serve. Feeling playful, she weighed her options. Should she use her first serve, the cannonball? Or should she be ladylike and use her fallback, the serve with the top-spin? Ah, decisions, decisions. Andrew managed to catch her eye from the small set of bleachers beside the court. He mouthed the word *no*.

Kim blew Andrew a kiss and decided to be magnanimous. She used her fallback, the solid serve with just a whiff of topspin. It impressed Walter without scaring him. The second game lasted about as long as the first. This time, Kim won, letting Walter score two points. She made him struggle for each point. Walter huffed as he covered the court, his comb-over flopping askew. Kim had Walter's measure now. He had a strong serve and some wind, but not much. Enough to impress the other fiftysomethings and the flabbier forty-year-olds. But that was all.

With the third game, Walter stepped up to the service line. He didn't bother smiling at Kim. He hit a hard, flat serve and was shocked at the speed with which Kim returned it. His face grew red with exertion as Kim spat back every shot he made, forcing him to run all over the court. At the end of each point, he walked slowly up to the service line, trying to buy time, to get his wind back. But he never did. Kim carried the game easily, breaking his serve.

With the fourth game, Kim decided to stop toying with this mouse and swallow him whole. Really, it was the kindest thing to do. Walter stood far back in the court, waiting for Kim to repeat the ladylike serve she had demonstrated during game two. Kim walked over to the service line and bounced the ball twice. Then she glanced over to the bleachers and caught Andrew's eye again. To Kim's delight, she saw that her husband was smiling proudly.

Turning back to the service line, Kim thought of Al Pacino in *Scarface*, whipping out his machine gun and yelling, "Say hello to my little friend!" Kim smiled. Then she shot her first serve, her cannonball, across the court. Walter didn't return it. He didn't even try to. Instead, he stood stock-still, his mouth agape.

On the bleachers, a bewildered Crystal asked, "What was that?"

Andrew answered smugly, "*That* was an ace."

The rest of the set flew by, with Kim taking game after game. She trounced Walter, winning six games to his one. At the end of the set, they shook hands, and Walter marched sullenly away. His three-man fan base scuttled after him. As Kim came off the court, Andrew rose from his seat, leaning precariously on his crutches. He was beaming at her, but Kim avoided eye contact for a long moment. When she finally met his gaze, she told him, "I'm taking the job."

Andrew nodded. "I know you are." His proud smile didn't falter.

Kim added sharply, "And I *don't* mean the boob job."

"I know." Andrew winced. It was the first time he'd had the good sense to be embarrassed about that little suggestion. "I know, it was a stupid idea. I just, I forgot myself. I forgot us both, I guess." He faltered, then brightened, gesturing back toward the tennis court. "That was amazing, Kimmy." He beamed at her, almost goofy with admiration.

Soon Kim was smiling too. She couldn't help it. Then they both started laughing. They laughed all the way back to the i8. And when Andrew struggled to jam himself into the car again, they laughed even harder.

Years earlier, when Annie read David Sedaris's Me Talk Pretty One Day, *she had laughed smugly at the part where Sedaris's meth dealer abandons him to go to rehab. Afterward, Sedaris suffers sober through a party with his meth-addicted performance artist buddies—all of them hoping in vain to score. Lately, as her coke supply dwindled, Annie had begun wondering where she could meet performance artists.*

35

Annie's Spanish Lessons

Every day, Annie's Mommy's To-Do List app beeped, reminding her to "SCORE FOR THE HOME TEAM!" It didn't take long for her thoughts to turn to Mexico. After all, San Diego was less than ten miles from Tijuana. Rumor had it that anyone could buy drugs there. Buying drugs in TJ was like buying sweaters in Norway, maple syrup in Vermont, or kilts in Scotland. Annie fantasized about quaint roadside stands where sweet-faced Mexican grandmothers sold little cocaine bags decorated with sombreros. Annie would smile and nod, pocketing her drugs and refusing the complimentary churro that accompanied each packet.

But no, Tijuana was not like that. Not anymore. Nowadays, the media was full of reports about the drug war in Mexico. The Mexican government had cracked down, and drug cartels had responded with an orgy of violence. Every day brought news of fresh disasters: kidnappings, shootouts, flamboyantly grotesque murders. Annie had heard that some parts of Mexico were still safe. But she didn't trust herself to differentiate between the "good" Mexico and the hyperviolent part.

Annie decided it would be safer to try her luck in one of San Diego's Hispanic enclaves, Chula Vista or maybe National City. Sure, she had no idea *where* to score drugs in Chula Vista. And okay, Annie's lily-white skin might make her stick out. But maybe she could work that to her advantage. Maybe her whiteness and age would immediately identify her to drug dealers as a potential customer. Maybe, seeing how lost she was, the dealers would come flocking over to her with their wares, like Girl Scouts peddling cookies outside the supermarket.

This fantasy had its appeal. But what if the drug dealers didn't speak any English?

What then? Annie's knowledge of Spanish was limited to what she'd picked up from watching *Dora the Explorer* with her kids, useless unless she ran into a magical talking backpack stuffed with cocaine.

Still, Annie had to try. She rehearsed a few phrases from *Spanish in a Hurry* and set out for Chula Vista. She spent two long mornings casing Chula Vista's strip malls and park benches. Surveying Hispanic faces, Annie felt like Goldilocks. She was looking for someone "just right": sleazy enough to be a drug dealer but wholesome enough not to cheat her. Over and over, she started to approach someone only to turn away at the last minute, afraid she had misread the signals.

Finally, she got up the gumption to approach a thirtysomething Hispanic guy in cargo pants and a white T-shirt. A clean-cut, handsome man, he had one tattoo on his arm—a scarcity of ink that practically qualified him as a Republican in this neighborhood. Annie had watched him for half an hour. He loitered on a street corner next to a traffic light. Car after car approached him. Drivers would roll down their windows, talk to him, hand him something, and then move along.

Copying them, Annie drove up alongside her target. She motioned for him to come over, and he did so, smiling broadly. In her pidgin Spanish, Annie explained what she wanted. The man blinked at her, the way you blink at someone when you want to be pleasant but have no idea what the person has said to you. Then he reached into his pocket and pulled out a white business card. He handed it to Annie. It said, "My name is Miguel Acedro. I am an American citizen. I lost my hearing during a visit to Mexico. Drug gangs shot up my grandmother's house, killing my brother and leaving me deaf. Just say no to drugs. And please give."

Annie turned crimson and handed the card back to the man, along with all the cash she had in her wallet.

Annie would have to look elsewhere.

Middle-aged romance was supposedly in vogue, but Valerie suspected that—even today—a woman's sexuality had a definite expiration date. At some point, a woman had to tastefully drape a dust cover over her vagina or risk becoming ridiculous. How old was the lady of The Bridges of Madison County *anyway?*

36

Valerie's Guest

David Carson didn't give Valerie much warning. On Friday morning, David called Valerie and told her that he would be coming down to La Jolla for the day to see one of his clients. Would Valerie mind if he popped by to see what she was working on? A little bird—Sarah—told him that Valerie had painted some portraits of her maid. "Esperanza, wasn't it?"

Valerie nodded. Then, realizing David couldn't hear a nod over the phone, she stammered, "Yes, Esperanza. I've done four, I mean three, three canvases of her."

Valerie could hear the amusement in David's voice as he asked, "Which is it?"

"Excuse me?"

"Are you going to show me three canvases? Or will I get to see all four?"

Valerie smiled. "Depends on my mood."

They agreed he could come by her place around five o'clock. He proved to be unfashionably punctual, arriving at five on the dot. Valerie sat upstairs, listening as Esperanza answered the door and showed him into the living room. Needing a moment to work up her courage, Valerie inspected her reflection. Thanks to Sarah's miracle cream, Valerie's skin looked radiant these days. But she applied her usual heavy dose of makeup. Valerie felt that only women in their twenties and thirties could afford to take chances with their appearances. After that, it was best to leave the roulette table and stick to what worked. For Valerie, that meant heavy makeup and blond hair worn up in a tight chignon.

Valerie had dressed with care: a close-fitting white sleeveless dress with elaborate blue beading at the neckline, matching blue stilettos, and her white enamel CJ Charles bracelet. It was the same bracelet she'd worn to her first meeting with David, the bracelet that she hoped would become her good-luck charm.

Valerie had a strong superstitious streak. For years, she'd treasured her blue sapphire necklace as a talisman. Walter had given the necklace to her for their third anniversary, a blue sapphire pendant suspended in a white platinum setting with a matching thick white platinum chain. She'd worn it on opening day at the Del Mar races every year, and she'd always come out ahead at the betting booth. She'd worn it, tucked discreetly underneath her tennis whites, whenever Walter had a particularly grueling match, and he had always won. The necklace had brought Valerie luck until she made the mistake of wearing it to Walter's fiftieth birthday party. She'd planned the whole affair, two hundred people on a ninety-foot yacht. Walter had enjoyed himself tremendously: drinking, joking, and flirting the night away. At the end of the evening, when they disembarked, he kissed Valerie on the nose and told her he wanted a divorce. After that, the necklace stayed in its box.

Now, her nerves humming, Valerie noticed that a few strands of hair had come loose from her chignon. Hurrying, she pulled the pins out of her hair, planning to wrestle her mane back into submission. But then, seeing her shiny blond hair fall in waves around her shoulders, Valerie thought better of it. Maybe she wasn't too old to gamble after all.

She entered the living room as Espie was leaving. Espie's eyes drifted up to Valerie's hair, and a mischievous smile spread across her face. Valerie felt herself color but strove to ignore it. She walked across the room toward the gallery owner. Just feet away from David Carson, Valerie was stunned all over again by his height. A lifetime with Walter had gotten her used to tall men, but this one was a sequoia. Six three at least. And so handsome. Sometimes, Valerie's memory airbrushed the looks of people she met, recasting them with the better-looking actors who might play them on television. But not David Carson. He was exactly as she remembered him: full head of wavy gray hair, sharp cheekbones, aquiline nose, and large warm brown eyes.

He stood smiling at Valerie, not saying anything. With a start, Valerie realized that it was her turn to take the lead. This time, *she* was the host. She flailed, "So, um, you were with a client today here in La Jolla all day today?" Christ, could she use the word *today* any more times in a sentence today?

David nodded. "Yes. She bought a house down here. *Another* house. And she wanted my advice."

Valerie smiled. "Advice on which artwork would match the rugs?"

David shrugged. "You got it. Usually, I don't do the interior decorator thing, but this woman has been a very good customer. So when she snaps her fingers, I'm there."

"May I ask her name?"

"Lenora Ryland."

Valerie's eyebrows shot up. She'd read about the aging heiress in *Vanity Fair*. "Ryland has a home in La Jolla?"

David shrugged again, coloring slightly. "Well, not exactly. But it's close by. Rancho Santa Fe." Rancho Santa Fe was La Jolla's opulent neighbor to the north. It lacked La Jolla's gorgeous seaside views but offered more room to build. If La Jolla's ten-thousand-square-foot mansions left a tycoon feeling cramped, he could always go and spread his wings on the Rancho, along with Bill Gates, Janet Jackson, and Jenny Craig. Plenty of room for personal tennis courts, polo fields, and private movie theaters up there.

Valerie ran some quick calculations in her head. David was based up in LA. It would have taken him at least an hour and a half to get down to Rancho Santa Fe. By coming south from the Rancho to see Valerie in La Jolla, he'd added a solid thirty minutes to his trip, both ways. An hour and a half, if you counted traffic. So much for popping by.

Changing the subject, David asked, "So, can I see your latest work?"

"Follow me." Valerie led him up the stairs to her studio. Her latest painting of Esperanza stood perched on an easel. Valerie had laid the other three canvases out on her work table.

David spent a long time studying the canvases, his face impassive. Valerie stood awkwardly by the window, not knowing what to do with her arms. Arms crossed seemed too defensive, arms down too listless. She was grateful when David ended her suffering. He pointed to the painting on the easel. It showed Esperanza straightening her son Carlos's collar as he modeled his new army uniform. In his raw youth, Carlos seemed both formidable and achingly vulnerable. Esperanza had to stand on her tiptoes to reach his collar. She stared intently at the brown fabric, willing the uniform to protect her son and knowing that it couldn't.

Pointing at the painting, David said, "That one, that's the one I want."

Valerie swallowed hard. "You think it would work in your gallery?"

David nodded. "Oh yes. It would work anywhere. It's terrific."

Valerie didn't know what to say. What did one say at a moment like this? She had to be professional, because that's what she was now, a professional artist. She said tentatively, as if talking was new to her, "I think it would work very well in your gallery."

"So you'd be willing to sell it?"

Valerie nodded quickly, a radiant smile spreading across her face. Then, trying to look serious, she said, "For a price, of course."

David grinned. "Of course."

Lightheartedly, she and David tossed the question of price around for a few minutes like a beach ball. They resolved nothing but that was all right. They both knew that money wasn't the point of this moment. The point was to make happy noises at each other in celebration of Valerie's triumph. After half an hour, Valerie led David back down the stairs into the foyer. He fished his keys out of his pocket and jangled them in his right hand for a moment. Then he asked if he could take Valerie out to dinner that night. Surprised, Valerie asked dumbly, "Dinner?"

"Yes, dinner. You know, the last meal of the day." Feigning nonchalance, David tossed his keys in the air but dropped them on the way down. They clattered noisily against the marble floor of the foyer. He scrambled to retrieve them.

When he stood, Valerie told him, "Yes, dinner would be lovely."

Annie was too savvy to waste money on face cream, but she was a sucker for diet books: The Paleo Diet, Skinny Bitch in the Kitch, The Dukan Diet, *Scarsdale, Atkins,* Fit for Life. *She read them all . . . usually late at night over a bowl of ice cream.*

37

Ice Cream for Two

Annie surrendered to her insomnia at one o'clock in the morning. She rose from bed and swaddled herself in her purple fleece robe. Then she tiptoed down through the dark house to her kitchen pantry. When she opened the door, the pantry's dim overhead light switched on. She climbed the step stool and reached for the Band-Aid tin that she kept on the top shelf. She flicked the tin open. Ta-da! Ladies and gentlemen, no cocaine left. How did the nursery rhyme go? "Old Mother Hubbard went to her cupboard and found she was fresh out of blow." Something like that.

Annie put the Band-Aid tin back in its spot on the top shelf. What the hell was she going to do now? Earlier that day, she'd forced herself to call Jimmy. For the first time in her life, Annie had hoped that her brother would answer the phone stoned. But Jimmy hadn't sounded stoned. Far from it: he'd gotten back from another Narcotics Anonymous meeting. He was taking life one day at a time and sponsoring two new members, fledglings in the program. They would be going on a nature hike this weekend. Annie pictured the wholesome trio hiking merrily through the foothills of LA, high on God, program, and wheatgrass juice. Uck.

Annie climbed down from the step stool. She was feeling them again, butterflies. Not in her stomach but high in her chest. She knew butterflies couldn't talk, but these seemed to sing in high-pitched voices, "You're screwed, you're screwed." There was only one thing that could stop the butterflies. Annie walked over to the refrigerator and pulled out a half gallon of chocolate ice cream. She fished a spoon out of the utensil drawer. Then she stood at the counter, popped the top off the ice cream, and dug in.

The ice cream was beginning to work its magic when the overhead lights came on. Sarah had flicked the switch. Sarah had arranged to crash at Annie's place after a late night out in La Jolla with her clients. Annie had forgotten all about it, and now here Sarah stood in the kitchen doorway, a look of undisguised shock on her face. Annie colored, embarrassed at the tableau she presented: a housewife furtively eating a half gallon of ice cream next to the kitchen sink. And she looked a mess too. She had a bright pink heat rash on her left cheek from where her face had pressed too hard against her pillow, her curly hair was askew, and a fresh brown chocolate stain marred her baggy robe. Annie usually didn't put much effort into her appearance, but there were certain mental snapshots of her that she didn't want anyone carrying around.

As usual, Sarah tried to put Annie at ease. Sarah put on her best unthreatening smile, the smile a veterinarian might give to a skittish animal. "Got any ice cream left for me?"

Annie mumbled, "You startled me."

"Sorry. I just got in. I let myself in as quietly as I could. I didn't want to wake the kids."

Annie nodded sheepishly and felt her cheeks return to their normal color. She walked over to the fridge and fetched a pint of Ben & Jerry's Chunky Monkey. She plopped down at the kitchen table, placing her half gallon of Breyers in front of her and the comparatively ladylike pint in front of Sarah. Sarah gracefully hitched up the sides of her sheer gold-sequined Oscar de la Renta evening gown so that it would not wrinkle. She deposited herself carefully on the chair.

Annie asked, "So how was the ball?" Hoping to drum up business, Sarah had spent the evening at the Mercy Ball, the swankiest event on San Diego's social calendar. She would sleep at Annie's place and return to Los Angeles in the morning.

Sarah smiled. "Great, for the most part."

"For the most part?"

Sarah sighed. "There was some strangeness with Natalie Wilson. I told you about her, right? She's the one who wants to buy cream but can't afford it. Only she doesn't *know* she can't afford it. Everyone in town knows her husband's business is tanking, except her. Anyway, the first time she asked to buy some cream, I put her off by telling her I was running low on supplies."

Annie winced, thinking that Sarah would have to go around telling that to a lot more customers soon. Annie had only six more jars of Étinav left.

Sarah went on, "And Natalie seemed to believe me. But tonight, at the ball, it was really awkward. There were all these women giving me their numbers and placing orders. I think Natalie got suspicious. She shot me a dirty look. It's crazy. I mean, here I am trying to save her from wasting her last two grand, and she's glaring at me. Oh well, no good deed goes unpunished."

Annie pressed, "But other than Natalie, the evening went well?"

Sarah beamed. "Very well. I ran into plenty of rich ladies who had heard of us."

Annie corrected her, "Heard of *you. You're* the face of this business." After assisting at Sarah's book club debut, Annie had stopped going to meetings. Sarah handled the book club ladies quite capably on her own.

Sarah shrugged this off. "Anyhow, they all wanted to buy some Étinav. I have a dozen phone numbers in my purse." Sarah took a small, demure bite of ice cream. She always took small, demure bites. That must be the secret of her perfect figure: tiny bites and discreet, grueling daily workouts at her gym up in Los Angeles. Even Sarah couldn't look this good at forty without making sacrifices.

Annie suddenly became aware of the grim contrast she and Sarah made: the haggard, chubby housewife and the glamorous movie star. Annie spooned ice cream into her mouth and garbled, "You look beautiful." Only it came out "bootiful."

Sarah murmured, "Thanks." Then she gave Annie one of her soulful "let's talk" looks. Annie felt her back go up. Sarah asked, "So, do you want to tell me what's worrying you?"

Annie was tempted to blurt out the truth. *"Oh, don't mind me. I'm in a funk because we're fresh out of cocaine. That's the secret ingredient in that goo you've been peddling all over town."* But Annie wasn't ready to go down that road, not yet. Time for a diversion. Annie said wearily, "Oh, it's the same old thing. Oscar's therapy . . ." Then she stuffed another spoonful of ice cream into her mouth, hoping she wouldn't have to answer any more questions.

But Sarah wouldn't let it go. "Oscar's making progress, isn't he?"

Annie hedged. The truth was that Oscar was doing amazingly well. All his therapists said the same thing: he was a star patient. His unflagging eagerness to please, along with Annie's relentless reinforcement at home, yielded terrific results. Oscar still had problems. His therapists ferreted out new ones all the time. But his problems were tractable; they had solutions. Yes, Oscar would be all right so long as his mommy kept bringing in lots of money to pay for his therapies. Annie struck a tragic pose—she wasn't Chloe Baker's daughter for nothing. "It's hard to gauge. This autism thing is like Whack-a-Mole. Every time we smash one problem down, two more pop up in its place. Get rid of the eye-contact thing, and now you've got to focus on how bad he is at reading other kids' expressions. That sort of thing."

Sarah said, "I can't imagine how hard all of this must be for you. But you're doing a great job." Annie raised an eyebrow. Sarah went on, "No, really. You're the one who paid for Oscar's therapy. You're the one who schleps him there, and you're the one who reinforces it at home. You've been so ballsy in standing up to this thing."

Annie surprised herself by getting choked up. It was true. She had come through for Oscar. But what if she couldn't keep coming through for him? What if the Étinav money spigot ran dry? What then? Annie wasn't like Sarah. Annie couldn't go off and start all over again with some big, flashy new job. Oscar needed Annie at home. Expensive as it was, his therapy only did 10 percent of the work. The rest of the heavy lifting had to be done at home, by Annie. Oscar's formal therapy sessions were like piano lessons. They gave Oscar new tools, but he would only get better if he practiced using those tools. And because Oscar's problems were social in nature, he could not drill by himself. He needed a skilled partner—his mother, someone to make sure he hit the right notes. So Annie had to be at home, but she also had to make money, lots of it. Even with his recent promotion, Harry's salary would not be enough.

Starting to tear up, Annie felt her anxiety peak and then turn to resentment. This resentment was a fresh pimple on the face of her emotional life. Annie had resented no one when her cocaine larder was full. Back then, she'd been pathetically grateful to Sarah for hawking her wares. And everything had been right with the world. The money came pouring in. Oscar got all the therapy he needed. And Annie got a head rush from being both a supermom and an entrepreneur. Things had gotten better with Harry too. Once he saw how much money his wife's little beauty business was bringing in, he became more than tolerant of it; he became downright grateful. He started to relax for the first time in months.

Now those heady times were about to come to an end. And Annie was the only one who knew it. The secret was crushing her. So she started to resent the very people whom she had deceived by omission, Harry and Sarah. How nice it must be for Harry! To enjoy all the benefits of an at-home wife *and* a second income. To sleep soundly every night without a clue as to what chemical trick was making it all possible.

And Sarah! How easy it was for her! To have no kids to worry about. To walk around with a well-toned rump in gorgeous evening gowns and hobnob with the rich. How lovely it must be to rake in thousands of dollars for face cream without the slightest idea as to why people were willing to pay that much. Oh sure, Sarah had her theories. She never admitted it. Sarah was too faux humble for that. But Annie knew that Sarah thought she was the secret ingredient. Sarah thought her customers kept coming back because she was such a huge treat to be around: so charming and charismatic. The ultimate saleswoman. Sarah had no idea that the cream itself, with its subtle, carefully calibrated cocaine high, was the real reason customers kept coming back. Lucky, carefree Sarah. Just think, she got to pull down a full half share of the proceeds without even a twinge of guilt. A full half share! Annie smirked, "Nice dress. Must have cost a fortune."

Sarah was caught off guard by the bitterness in Annie's voice. "Are you mad at me?"

Annie shook her head. "Why would I be mad at you?"

Sarah raised her eyebrows. "You sound like you're mad at me."

"Well, I'm not."

"Good."

Annie said crisply, "Good."

Sarah took a deep breath and exhaled. "Okay, this is bullshit. Why are you mad at me?"

"I'm not mad at you. I just get a little jealous sometimes."

"Jealous of what?"

Annie rolled her eyes. "Oh, you know."

"No, I don't know."

Annie flailed. She knew she was being awful, but she was too tired and irritated to hold back. "It's just that, sometimes, I can't help noticing how easy life is for some people."

"Meaning me?"

Annie huffed, "Meaning some people. No money troubles. No autistic kids to worry about. No demanding mothers to contend with. No real problems."

Sarah answered, "Annie, I know my life—and the lives of our clients—must seem perfect to you sometimes. But you know that's not true. We all have our struggles."

Folding her arms against her chest, Annie said, "No, we don't."

"I see. So you're the only person on the planet with real problems? Is that it?"

"No, not the only person. There are plenty of other people with real problems. Just none of those rich idiots you hang out with."

That did it. Sarah exploded, "You are so full of it! You think Oscar gives you a right to sulk and moan all day long. Everybody else's pain is inferior. Well, screw you! Whether you accept it or not, there are plenty of people out there suffering, rich and poor. We may not dress like crap or stuff ourselves with ice cream every night. We may not lash out at every sucker who stumbles by, but we still are suffering."

Annie sniffed, "How are you suffering?"

Sarah's chin trembled slightly. "You know exactly how."

And suddenly Annie did remember. She remembered all of it. Of course, she knew about Sarah's fertility problems, knew about them in excruciating detail. But Sarah hadn't mentioned them in months. And Annie had stupidly thought that because Sarah seemed so happy, she must be happy. Annie had forgotten one of the biggest differences between her and Sarah: Sarah's stoicism. Sarah had not been raised by Chloe Baker. Sarah had grown up with stoic parents who believed in keeping a stiff upper lip. So Sarah held back her own grief, but never for a moment had she made Annie feel embarrassed or maudlin for voicing her own troubles. Chagrined, Annie said, "Oh Christ, I'm sorry. It's just that you keep going on and on about how much you love selling, how much fun you're having. You never talk about . . ."

A tear slinked down Sarah's heavily made-up face. "About the baby?" Annie nodded. Sarah took another bite of ice cream, a big one this time. "Honestly, I was having a good time. I treated myself to a nice long vacation. No visits to Dr. Alpert. I got to dress up, try my hand at something new, and I was good it. It felt wonderful to succeed like that after so many years of failing."

"And now?"

"Vacation's over. We raised enough so I could go back to Alpert. So it's started all over again. Back to taking hormone shots every day. Back to feeling crazy half the time. I lurch from worrying about what I'll do if this round doesn't work to daydreaming about what it'd be like if it does work. Only now it's worse. My daydreams are so much more vivid. Watching you with your kids has filled in all the hazy blank spaces in my fantasy life. And it's made the wanting worse."

Annie felt guilt rip through her. "Oh, sweetie, I'm sorry. It's so crazy around here. It never even occurred to me that anyone would—"

"Would want what you have?" Annie nodded. Sarah smiled ruefully. "Look, I know you feel invisible because you're an at-home mom. I know you feel like everyone looks down on you. But I don't. And your kids certainly don't. To them, you're the center of the universe. And that's what I want. That kind of connection. That kind of meaning. Who gives a damn if I look good in an evening gown? What's the point if I can't have a child?"

"Sarah, your life is not meaningless."

"Not meaningless. Just not as important."

"You are important! You mean the world to me! And Michael! Don't forget about Michael!"

Sarah sniffed, "What about him?"

Annie countered, "What about him? The man worships you!" Sarah said nothing. Annie asked, "I'm right about that. Aren't I?"

"Yes, Michael loves me, but . . ."

"But what?"

Sarah said, almost in a whisper, "But I'm not enough."

Annie darkened. "What do you mean? Are you saying Michael will leave you if you can't have children? Because if he does, then he's a complete bastard. I'll kill him! I swear I will—"

"Down, Fido. I'm not saying Michael would leave me. It's just that we had a deal. He got to gallivant all over the world hunting dinosaur bones, and I got to work 24-7 at the firm. We both liked it that way. And we both agreed that that would have to change when we had kids. And now I don't want to be stuck in some law firm all day. I want to be at home, not full time, but enough to *enjoy* my home. Only I don't know if I can get Michael to slow down if it's just for me. I mean, what's he supposed to do? Sit around gazing at me while I do housework? I can't see him being happy with that, not when there are so many fun things to dig up."

"Sare, you don't have to have children to demand that your husband be around once in a while. You have rights, you know."

Sarah shrugged. "I know. But let's face it, the home front becomes a lot more compelling when there are kids around. Kids are the whole point. I know that's not a very modern thing to say."

Annie risked a smile. "Yes, I'm deeply offended."

Sarah continued, "I know Michael won't leave me if I don't have a child. I know I can survive without having one, but I want one so much. You know?"

Annie whispered, "I know." She handed Sarah a napkin, and Sarah dabbed at her tears.

Sarah went on, "Anyhow, I'm going in for a round of IVF later this week. So I'll be out of the loop for a few days. I'm going to treat myself to a full media blackout: no voice mails, no e-mails, nothing. My outgoing message says I'll be in Europe for the week. Doesn't that sound wonderful?"

"Enchanting."

Sarah said, "When I get back, we can rev up our engines and start selling again. Okay?"

Annie nodded. "Sounds great." So Annie had one week, one week to stock up on cocaine. She could do it. She'd reload her Band-Aid tin, and they'd be back in business.

Josephine Brearly never joined a book club. An outdoorsy, athletic woman for most of her long life, Josephine preferred boating, skiing, and hiking to the sedentary tedium of reading or the even worse tedium of talking *about reading. Most days, Josephine read nothing beyond her morning newspaper—though she did have a weakness for books about dogs.* Old Yeller *and* Marley & Me *had both reduced her to soppy tears.*

38

Aunt Josephine

Josephine Brearly was a shrewd old woman. She knew why her nieces and nephews had stepped up their visits. It was the stroke, of course. One stroke and the piñata of Josephine's vast wealth had been lowered to make it an easier target. So her nieces and nephews—greedy, sticky-fingered children at heart—were jockeying for position. When Josephine died, they would elbow each other out of the way, grabbing for whatever they could.

To be fair, there was a lot at stake. Josephine was an immensely wealthy woman. She had married wisely and often. Her husbands had never been foolish enough to reproduce, so their money had flowed down to Josephine free of encumbrances. A child of the Depression, Josephine hoarded every penny. Her money sat untouched in bank accounts, blue-chip stocks, and bonds. Josephine lived handsomely off interest payments and dividends, never dipping a toe into the principal.

The prospect of so much wealth must have been maddening for her nieces and nephews. But Josephine knew that when the time came, her so-called progeny would be disappointed. There would be some money for them. She had to leave them something. But it would be "go away" money, enough to keep them from suing her estate. It would be enough to make it clear that she had thought of them, she just hadn't thought much of them. Josephine didn't love them. There was only one thing Josephine loved: dogs. Or, to be more specific, her dogs. If Josephine could have left her entire fortune to her two corgis, Duchess and Witchie, she would have done so. But her lawyers had told her that that was impossible. So she settled for the next best thing. She donated the bulk of her money to the Carlyle Canine Trust, a charity that worked to advance the interests of purebred pooches everywhere. Josephine would leave another large pile of money to one of her vulture-like relatives on the condition that he or she pamper Josephine's beloved pups into their dotage.

But who should Josephine pick? That was the question that kept her up nights. She'd disqualified her two nephews because—although they stooped and bowed to Josephine—they never paid an iota of attention to Duchess or Witchie. Even worse, her nephew Tobias had two cats of his own. Josephine felt nothing but contempt for cat people. Cat people were a freakish tribe, as reclusive and unreliable as their chosen familiars. No, no. Tobias was out.

That left her nieces: Belinda and Natalie. For a while, Belinda had been the front-runner. Belinda reminded Josephine of a Weimaraner, a breed that Josephine had admired briefly before settling on corgis as the pinnacle of dogdom. Belinda was tall, lean, and athletic, an elegant brunette with icy blue eyes. Like Josephine, Belinda had married well, but not as well as Josephine had. Belinda's husband had made money in real estate but not enough to outshine, or even compare with, Josephine's fortune.

Belinda had visited once a month before Josephine had her stroke, and then once a week thereafter. Her visits lasted an hour, short enough for Belinda to keep up a charming patter. Most important for Josephine, Belinda was a dog person. She gossiped knowledgeably about Westminster and Crufts. And she always fussed over Josephine's dogs, rubbing them behind their ears and addressing them in a high-pitched, affectionate tone. And Duchess and Witchie adored Belinda too. They rubbed against her trouser legs and licked her fingers.

Josephine had been about to settle on Belinda as the one when Belinda ruined everything. Belinda had left after one of her visits. And Josephine migrated over to her kitchen window, which overlooked the Sands's parking lot two floors below. Josephine watched Belinda march out to her car and prop her purse on the hood. Then Belinda opened the purse and withdrew a lint roller from it. She ran the roller up and down her clothes over and over. Next, pursing her pretty lips in disgust, Belinda plucked the hair-covered strip of lint tape from the roller and threw it to the ground. Josephine thought things couldn't get any worse from there, but they did. Belinda removed a tiny vial of fluid from her bag. She tipped the vial into her hands and then rubbed them together vigorously. Josephine didn't need to see the vial's label. She knew what it was: Purell. The force of that knowledge hit Josephine like a slap across the face. No real dog lover would use that stuff after petting two clean purebred pups. Belinda was out.

So now Natalie was Josephine's only hope, her best shot at placing Witchie and Duchess within the family. Like Belinda, Natalie visited Josephine once a week. But Natalie was not as appealing as her cousin. If Belinda was a Weimaraner, Natalie was a pug, short and stocky with a round, smiling face. Josephine had never liked pugs much; they made too much noise, always breathing so loudly through their mashed-up noses. Natalie made too much noise too. The woman prattled on and on about her children, her husband, her weight problem, and her "creative outlets." Photography and whatnot. So far as Josephine could tell, it did not take much creativity to point and shoot a camera.

But now, as Natalie entered Josephine's large, airy apartment at the Sands, she had her aunt's full attention. Natalie got off to a good start, giving Josephine a perfunctory hug and then going down on her chubby haunches to greet Witchie and Duchess. The dogs followed at Natalie's heels as Josephine led her into the living room. The two women settled on the couch, and Josephine noted the way Natalie absentmindedly caressed Duchess's magnificent head as she droned on. But Natalie did drone on. As Natalie blathered about what a fabulous time she'd had the night before at the Mercy Ball, Josephine felt her mind slip its leash and begin to wander. To Josephine, the greatest advantage of having suffered a stroke was that it freed her from San Diego's endless cycle of galas. She had hated parading about in evening gowns while her beloved dogs were trapped at home.

Josephine's attention snapped back to the conversation at the mention of Sarah Sloane. Surprised, Josephine asked, "Sarah was at the Mercy Ball?"

Natalie nodded. "Yes, do you know her?"

Josephine smiled warmly. "Everyone around here knows her. She's a lovely girl." Sarah had immediately won Josephine's favor by recognizing Duchess and Witchie as Cardigan Welsh corgis. People, even supposed dog lovers, constantly mistook the bitches for their more common tailless cousins, the Pembrokes.

Natalie's eyes widened. "What has Sarah been doing around here? Does she have relatives at the Sands?"

Josephine shook her head. "No, at least I don't think so. She and Chloe come around once or twice a month."

"Chloe?"

"Yes, Chloe Baker. She's an older woman. A helluva lot of fun."

"Does Chloe have relatives here?"

Josephine waved this off. "No, Chloe and Sarah don't come to visit. They come to drop off that cream of theirs. What is it? Epinate or Étinav? Something like that."

Natalie paled. "They've been selling Étinav at the Sands?"

"Oh yes. They're like a cosmetologist's version of the Good Humor man. They come around and all the old birds flock down to the lobby with their purses."

Natalie blinked furiously, struggling to process this news. "But I'd heard Sarah was running low on supplies. She's very picky about who she takes on as a customer."

Josephine shrugged. "She didn't seem that picky to me."

Her nostrils flaring, Natalie asked, "Sarah has sold Étinav to you?"

"Yes, she sold me some a few weeks back. Mind you, I can't say whether it works or not. I keep forgetting to put it on in the morning."

Natalie pursed her thin lips together, making them disappear. Then she leaped to her feet. "May I use your bathroom for a moment?"

Josephine nodded. "Of course."

Natalie strode over to the bathroom, and Josephine, always sensitive to body language, noticed a stiffness in her niece's gait. Replaying the Belinda debacle in her mind, Josephine wondered whether Natalie planned to scrub the dog hair off her hands. As soon as the bathroom door swung shut, Josephine walked quietly over to the bathroom, holding up a finger for the corgis to stay. Josephine hovered outside the door, waiting for the telltale sound of the faucet. If she heard it, the sound of her niece scouring her hands, Natalie would be out of the running. Josephine didn't know what she would do. Maybe give Tobias a second look? The thought of her corgis cohabiting with her nephew's felines made her shudder.

But the sound of the faucet didn't come. There was just a flush and the click of the door opening. Natalie hadn't even rinsed her hands! While that omission might disqualify Natalie from working in a restaurant, it raised her standing a thousandfold in her aunt's eyes. Natalie reemerged with the jar of Étinav in her right hand. She asked if she might borrow the cream for a few days. "I want to try a little of it. I'm thinking of buying some for myself. And I figure—"

Josephine cut her off. "Of course! Keep it. Like I said, I never remember to use the stuff."

Natalie followed Josephine back into the living room. Sitting down, Natalie placed the jar of Étinav inside her purse. Then she withdrew a large manila envelope from her bag. Natalie held up the envelope, announcing, "And I have something for you! I know you're not into photography, but I thought you might like these shots I took of the girls."

Natalie handed over the envelope, and Josephine opened it. Inside were glossy black-and-white photos of Witchie and Duchess: Duchess leaping over a small white fence; Witchie basking in the sunlight on the Sands's great lawn; the two dogs running side-by-side down a garden path. Josephine studied the photos for a long time. When she finally looked up at Natalie, her eyes were moist. These pictures settled it. Natalie was the one.

In that moment, Natalie pulled herself and her family back from the financial brink without ever realizing that they had ever been in danger. Had Natalie known what was at stake, she would have wept with relief. But sitting there on Josephine's couch, Natalie was oblivious to her husband's financial peril and her aunt's plans. Instead, Natalie focused on one thing: how Sarah had slighted her.

In Stephen King's Carrie, *a rejected and bullied teenager uses her telekinetic powers to kill everyone at her school prom. Natalie sympathized, but she had to admit—it was a bit much.*

39

A Woman Scorned

Natalie had had enough. She was tired of feeling lonely and powerless. She couldn't force her way into the La Jolla book club. She couldn't make Priscilla Green rekindle their old friendship. Hell, she couldn't even get Walter and his bimbo to come to dinner anymore. There was nothing Natalie could do to dispel whatever taint was on her, but there was one thing Natalie could do: retaliate against Sarah Sloane.

Sarah's ramblings about supply problems and waiting lists had been bullshit. Natalie had known this ever since Kim Elliot opened her yap in the Gillespie parking lot. Yes, Natalie had known, but she'd managed to put it out of her mind. She'd told herself that it didn't matter. Maybe Kim's connections had allowed her to jump the line. Maybe Sarah had taken pity on Kim. It was paranoid for Natalie to assume that Sarah had anything against her, right?

Wrong. Even paranoids have real enemies. After languishing on Sarah's "waiting list" for months, Natalie had found out—from dowdy Aunt Josephine of all people!—that all the wizened crones up at the Sands have been slathering themselves with Sarah's glop all along. Sarah had charmed the old bags as easily as she had the rest of La Jolla. Oh yes, everybody loved Sarah.

Well, screw that.

Natalie knew exactly where to go. She had used Peeky Labs once before, to screen a nanny's urine sample for drugs. That's what Peeky Labs did. It analyzed samples. Broke them down and figured them out. The day after visiting Aunt Josephine, Natalie marched into Peeky Labs and gave them a sample of Étinav. She explained that it was a new face cream she was thinking of using, but she had lots of allergies and couldn't put just anything on her skin. She would need a list of the cream's components. Unlike Sarah, the folks at Peeky Labs were very happy to accept Natalie's money. They said they'd get the results back for her in fifteen days.

Natalie planned to take the list of ingredients and post them on the web, anonymously, of course. She couldn't wait to see how La Jolla's in crowd would take it when they found out that they'd been shucking out two grand a jar for a mixture of Pond's and powdered sugar, or whatever other crap was in this stuff.

Sarah Sloane had messed with the wrong woman.

Annie idolized Lisbeth Salander, heroine of The Girl with the Dragon Tattoo. *Annie lost herself reading about Lisbeth's adventures: hacking into government computer networks, taking revenge on her rapist, and disguising herself so that she could steal millions in plain sight. Annie could never be that daring.*

40

Annie Shoots, She . . .

Annie was desperate now. The cupboard was bare. She had to find some cocaine, and fast. Where should she look next?

Frustrated, Annie turned to the San Diego District Attorney's website for guidance. Sure enough, the DA had posted press releases touting drug busts in Imperial Beach, Pacific Beach, and other seedy beach areas. What was it with drug dealers and beaches? Did they surf? The police had arrested dozens of drug dealers operating out of the beaches' tattoo parlors.

Annie decided to try Pacific Beach, PB for short. It was familiar territory. She had taken her kids to a slew of birthday parties at PB's My Gym, an island of wholesomeness in a sea of sleaze. She'd driven past PB's sex shops, tattoo parlors, and run-down bars enough times for them to seem kitschy rather than threatening. Also, Annie figured she might be able to blend in because PB was mostly white.

Yes, Annie would go to PB. But first she needed a disguise. Annie chose tight jeans, red high heels, and a black top that bared her chubby midriff, an alabaster body part that had not seen the light of day since the Reagan administration. Striving to mimic the unhealthy pallor of a druggie, she put on loads of eyeliner and dark lipstick but no blush. A nose ring would have helped, but she wasn't ready to go that far. So instead she opted for temporary tattoos. She had a box of them, leftover kid party favors. She rifled past the Disney princesses and Lightning McQueens until she found a Chinese dragon. True, it looked a bit more cheerful than Annie would have liked. It was winking. But Annie figured it would pass as a proper tramp stamp from a distance. She wet it and rubbed it onto the middle of her spine, just above the waistband of her low-slung pants.

Driving to PB, Annie tried to get into character; she practiced talking to her reflection in the rearview mirror. She abandoned her fast-talking, slightly nasal East Coast twang in favor of a native Californian's slow drawl, the foggy, vaguely out-of-it voice that she used before she'd had her coffee in the morning. She rehearsed a groggy stoner look, her mouth slightly open, her lids at half-mast, her eyebrows relaxed. She told her reflection that she was looking to score, to cop, to connect. She said that she was hunting the Big C, that she wanted to go for a sleigh ride, that she needed some Bolivian marching powder.

She cruised around PB for thirty minutes until she came to the most run-down tattoo parlor she could find, Murder Ink. The black "M" in the store's sign hung askew, and the sea-green paint on its façade was peeling. Annie parked and inspected her reflection one last time. She wished her eyes were more bloodshot. That would have been a nice touch. Then she remembered the AOSept solution in her purse. She whipped out the miniature bottle of contact lens cleaner and put a drop in each eye. Just as she had remembered, the stuff turned the whites of her eyes a gratifying pink. What she hadn't remembered was the burning sensation. She rubbed furiously at her tearing eyes.

When the burning eased, she got out of her car and stepped up to the pavement. She reminded herself not to walk too fast. She slouched and tried to copy a slacker's loping gait. The interior of Murder Ink was gratifyingly empty, just a pale, thin blonde sitting behind a counter. When the blonde looked up, Annie said, "Hey."

The blonde answered, "You here for a tattoo?"

Annie nodded. "I heard you guys were the best." Where would she have heard that? Was there a *Consumer Reports* for sleaze?

The blonde asked, "What'd you have in mind?"

Annie hadn't thought of this. She had no cover story. She stammered, "I, uh, I like dragons." Christ, she sounded like a four-year-old boy.

Blondie asked, "Dragons?" Annie nodded dumbly. The blonde reached beneath the counter and brought up a thick three-ring notebook. "Jazz does dragons all the time. You want to pick one out?"

Annie nodded again. She studied the book's pages for a moment, not knowing how to proceed. Suddenly, she heard a mechanical whirring sound coming from the back of the store. The blonde gestured at the dark blue curtain behind her, explaining, "Jazz has been working on that guy all morning."

Annie shrugged and tried to mirror the blonde's blasé expression, but this became harder as Annie skimmed through the tattoo book: dragons, daggers, curse words. Annie felt her square persona taking over and decided she had to act fast. She had to get this drug deal moving. She cleared her throat and leaned forward against the counter, saying, "Actually, I'm not here for a tattoo."

"Oh?"

"Nah. I, um, well, I heard that Jazz sells more than just tattoos, if you know what I mean."

The blonde's face was stubbornly blank. "What?"

Annie forged ahead, saying, "I was hoping Jazz might be able to hook me up."

"Hook you up?" Blondie wasn't making this easy.

Annie persisted, "You know, hook me up. Help me score."

Comprehension dawned on the blonde's face. "You were hoping Jazz would help you to *score*? What did you have in mind?"

Annie decided she'd come too far to play coy now. Her voice breaking like a thirteen-year-old boy's, she squeaked, "I was hoping to score some blow."

The blonde nodded. "I see." She pointed to the curtain behind the counter. "Give me a second to talk to Jazz." She disappeared behind the curtain, and a moment later, the whirring noise of whatever tool Jazz had been using came to a stop. Annie heard voices murmuring.

Then a large bald man came out from behind the curtain with the blonde in tow. Although middle-aged, Jazz was almost comically muscular. His pectoral muscles strained against the fabric of his white T-shirt. He folded his arms across his broad chest and glowered down at Annie like an angry Mr. Clean. Annie gazed hopefully up at him, shifting from foot to foot. Jazz jerked his head at the blonde. "Jeannie tells me you came here to buy some cocaine." His voice was low and raspy, the voice of a heavy smoker.

Gulping hard, Annie said, "Yup, yes sir. Cocaine, that's right."

Jazz studied Annie for long moment. Then he said, "I think I can help you." Annie felt relief rush through her. This was going to work. Jazz went on, "How much are you looking to buy? A gram? An eight-ball?"

Talk of quantities made Annie relax. She'd done her homework and knew that an eight-ball was three and a half grams of cocaine. The Internet said that lots of cocaine users bought cocaine by the eight-ball; it was cocaine's equivalent of a gallon of milk. But Annie didn't want to have to go shopping again too soon. She wanted to stock up. She said, "I was hoping to pick up ten grams. Um, three eight-balls."

Jazz looked impressed. "Ten grams? You a dealer?"

Annie shook her head. She said, "No, no. It's for me. I like knowing that I have enough set aside for—"

"A rainy day?"

Annie laughed nervously. "Something like that."

"Like I said, I think I can help you." Jazz bent and reached beneath the counter. He pulled out a yellow sheet of paper. A price sheet? Did drug dealers keep price sheets? Annie stepped forward, and Jazz pushed the paper across the counter toward her. At the top, in bold letters, it said, "Narcotics Anonymous."

Annie felt the color rush to her cheeks. She shook her head. "No, this isn't—"

Jazz held up his hand for her to stop. He said, "I know. This isn't what you were expecting when you came in here."

Annie flailed, "No, you don't understand. I'm not—"

His voice heavy with sarcasm, Jazz said, "Let me guess. You're not an addict. You don't *need* a twelve-step group. You got it all under control."

Annie put her hand to her forehead, mortified. Jazz went on, "You look in the mirror and you don't see a junkie, right? Well, let me tell you what I see. I see a woman with bloodshot eyes, a woman so hopped up on coke that she probably hasn't slept in days." Annie cursed her AOSept trick.

Jazz continued, "I see a woman so desperate for drugs that she'll go up to strangers trying to score. Cocaine has made her so stupid that she'll risk getting busted for God knows how long just so she can get high one more time." Annie's blush deepened. That stupid remark hurt.

She looked helplessly over at Jeannie, hoping for an ally. No help there. The girl's expression was a mask of pity mingled with disgust. There was no way Annie could talk herself out of this one. There was nothing to do but surrender. She listened patiently as Jazz told her all about how he'd hit bottom. He had been a family man: a wife, kid, big house on the beach, the works. He snorted his paycheck, his kid's college fund, his mortgage payments. Then he started stealing to pay for his habit. He got busted, did hard time in jail. When he got out, his wife had left him, and he didn't have a penny to his name. That's when he joined Narcotics Anonymous, and he'd been there ever since. He lectured Annie on the twelve steps and urged her to get her tail over to a meeting. The Narcotics Anonymous flyer he'd handed her was a meeting list. He wrote his phone number at the bottom of it, telling her she could call him anytime, day or night.

Annie thanked him meekly and backed out of the store. When she opened the front door, Jazz called out, "Hey . . ." His face softened for the first time. "You don't have to use drugs to have fun in this life. Next weekend, NA is holding a big bowling tournament up in Mira Mesa. You should come." Annie smiled weakly and escaped out the door.

Now a hard-core believer in the program, Jimmy made Annie read the AA's Big Book *so that she could understand his journey. The book preached against egotistical self-reliance. To move forward, an addict had to admit helplessness and reach out to others for help. Annie knew she would cave soon. She needed help—getting cocaine.*

41

Chloe to the Rescue

Later that night, Annie broke down. She was playing with Oscar on the floor. Maddie and Rachel were curled up on the couch next to Chloe watching figure skating. Maddie's favorite was on, an Olympic hopeful named Sue Kim Soo, alias Sue2. Coming into the long program, Sue2 had been the overwhelming favorite. But just seconds into her routine, she fell smack on her bottom. She finished the rest of her routine without a glitch. At the end of it, Chloe wolf-whistled and exclaimed, "Brilliant!"

Maddie objected, "Gramma, she wasn't brilliant. She fell on her butt."

"Ah, yes. She fell, but then she got up. Do you have any idea what it takes to do that? To get up in front of millions of people who've just seen you fall and complete a performance with grace and style? My dear, she was positively heroic!"

From her seat on the floor next to Oscar, Annie watched Sue2 skate around the rink, gathering up the flowers that the crowd had thrown down to her. A coltish girl, Sue2 smiled hard through her tears. Watching her, Annie burst into tears—great, racking sobs. The kids turned and stared, not knowing what to make of their bawling mother. Rachel was the first to spring into action. She toddled across the rug and put her small arms around Annie's shoulders, murmuring, "There, there." An unconscious, spot-on imitation of Annie.

Maddie came over next. She put a hand on Annie's shoulder and said, "It's all right, Mom. Sue2 just made a mistake. They aren't going to shoot her. It's not like with the horses."

Oscar said nothing. He stared at Annie, his mouth slightly agape. Annie struggled hard to regain control of herself. Covering for Annie, Chloe said breezily, "Oh, Mommy's just tired. Adults cry sometimes when they're really tired just like children do." The kids looked to their mother for confirmation. Annie nodded her head. Chloe went on, "So why don't we give Mommy a little break. Tonight, I will do stories."

The kids gathered their books and settled next to Chloe on the couch while Annie snuck upstairs to wash her face. After story time, the two women joined forces, brushing teeth and cramming the sleepy children into their pajamas. Then Annie and Chloe migrated downstairs. Annie was loading the dishwasher when Chloe came up behind her. "So, Annabelle, are you going to volunteer what is wrong with you? Or are you going to make me sniff the trouble out like a bloodhound?"

Avoiding eye contact, Annie said, "Mom, it's nothing. I'm just tired."

Chloe raised an eyebrow. "I see. So we're going with bloodhound." She mused, "Let's start with the usual suspects. What makes a grown woman cry? Are you pregnant?"

"No." Annie shut the dishwasher to punctuate her point.

Chloe eyed Annie suspiciously. "Women often weep during the first blush of pregnancy."

"Mom, I've already got three kids." Annie walked purposefully toward the kitchen, hoping to telegraph industriousness. Industriousness was one of Chloe's turnoffs.

Chloe was relentless. She trailed Annie. "All the more reason to cry if you're pregnant again. Three children make for a lively household. Four children, well, that's pandemonium."

"Mom, I'm *not* pregnant."

Chloe nodded. "I see. Is it an affair?"

"What?"

"Is Harry having an affair?"

Annie said, "No! Harry would never do something like that."

Chloe shrugged. "I admit. Harry *seems* like the faithful type. But let's face it, dull as Harry may be, he's still a man. A man's libido is like a volcano. It can be dormant for years of domestic bliss and then, suddenly, boom."

"Mom, I promise, Harry is not having an affair." Annie started wiping down the kitchen table.

Undeterred, Chloe asked, "What about you?"

"Me?"

"Are *you* having an affair, Annabelle?" Chloe narrowed her eyes and flared her nostrils, a penetrating expression she had mastered when she'd played a detective in the Arlington Playhouse's production of *Murder Most Foul.*

Annie laughed. "You think *I'm* having an affair?"

Chloe bristled, "I don't see anything outlandish about the notion."

"Mom, I'm not up on infidelity. But from what I hear, I would have to attract a flesh-and-blood man if I was going to have an affair. And I'm not exactly in my prime."

Indignant, Chloe blustered, "Nonsense! You're a very lovely woman, Annabelle. All you lack is confidence. If you put yourself out there, really made an effort, I have no doubt you could attract a lover."

"Well, thanks, Mom. It's good to know you have faith in me."

"All right, so it's not pregnancy, not infidelity . . ." Chloe drummed her fingers against the kitchen counter as her mind raced. Then disappointment overtook her face. "It's not money, is it? *Please* tell me it's not money. That's such a bourgeois reason to get upset."

"No, it's not money. Well, not directly . . ."

The bloodhound smelled blood. "But indirectly?"

Annie closed her eyes. She shook her head, and Chloe moved in. "What is it, Annabelle? What's going on?" Annie's lower lip trembled. She felt tears coming again. Chloe repeated, "What *is* it?"

Annie stammered, "It's, it's cocaine."

Chloe gaped. "You're using cocaine?"

"No, well, I was, but . . ."

"But what?"

Her face buckling, Annie wailed, "But now I can't find any more!"

"What?"

And so it all came out. Sitting across from each other at the kitchen table—as if they were swapping recipes, for Chrissake!—Annie told Chloe through tears about how she'd confiscated cocaine from Jimmy. Then a few weeks later, she used it to whip up her first batch of Étinav. Annie put just enough in each jar to give the customer a slight high, a confidence boost. The customer would look in the mirror and think she looked better because she *felt* better. And Étinav would get the credit. Annie explained, "I know it was wrong to spike the stuff with cocaine. But everyone seemed so happy. The customers, Sarah, my kids, even Harry. I was—"

"You were inspired!"

Annie did a double take. "What?"

Her eyes misty with pride, Chloe repeated, "You were inspired!"

"You're not repulsed by what I did?"

"Absolutely not."

"But Mom, I drugged a bunch of women."

"Oh, Annabelle, you know I've always believed in living better pharmacologically. You were doing those women a favor. They needed to be drugged."

"Mom, no one needs to be drugged."

Chloe warmed to her theme. "To the contrary, most people need to be drugged at some point or another in their lives. They need to soar on chemical wings."

Annie put her hand to her forehead. She pleaded, "Mom . . ."

Chloe went on, "Think of it! Think of all the great plays and films where some drug allows the protagonist to break free and embark on some grand adventure. *The Philadelphia Story, Cat on a Hot Tin Roof, American Beauty, Alice in Wonderland.* Even Dumbo had to become inebriated before he flew for the first time."

Annie rolled her eyes. "Dumbo?"

"Make fun of me if you wish, Annabelle. But your plan was pure genius. These women who buy your cream, by definition they lack confidence. They're terrified of what they see in the mirror, trapped by it. With your little chemical trick, you freed them from that terror. You made them love their own reflections. Brilliant!"

Annie had no answer to this. She was surprised to find herself moved by her mother's little speech. For months, she'd suffered under the weight of her secret, expecting people to recoil if they ever found her out. And now here was her mother praising her. Annie felt relief, even a little pride. The pride evaporated with Chloe's next question. "But darling, does Sarah know about the cocaine?"

Annie shook her head. "No. She never would have gone along with it. Besides, it'd be wrong to tell her."

"Wrong?"

Annie explained, "Yeah, I figure I was protecting her by keeping her in the dark. If Sarah sells the stuff knowing it's cocaine, then the government can throw her in jail for selling drugs. But if she has no idea about the coke, then they can't prosecute her. She's a dupe, not a criminal."

Chloe cocked an eyebrow. "Where did you learn that?"

"I saw a thing on *Law & Order* about it. They couldn't convict the drug mule because the guy didn't know he was carrying drugs. He thought it was powdered sugar."

Chloe nodded, impressed with Annie's answer. Like many Americans, Chloe believed most of the legal claptrap she'd seen on *Law & Order*. The ominous voice-overs, the chuh-chink sound . . . it had to be true. "I see. Well, that makes sense to me, but I'm afraid you're still going to have to tell her."

"But—"

Chloe held up a hand. "Legally, you may be right. It might be better for her not to know. But we have to be practical. Sarah is going to learn your secret. It's just a matter of time. Better she hears it from you than from someone else."

Annie flailed, "But if I tell her, she might never forgive me. Hell, she might even turn me in."

"I can't see Sarah ever turning you in, dear."

Annie shot back, sullenly, "I bet you couldn't see me peddling cocaine either."

Chloe smiled. "True enough, but I still say Sarah won't turn you in. She's too loyal for that. She might be angry at you for a while, maybe even forever. But I don't think she'd ever seriously hurt you. She loves you too much for that. And you love her too much not to come clean with her."

Annie sighed. "You're right."

"Oh, Annabelle, don't be so grim. Sarah might surprise you. She might find your plan as compelling as I do. And if she doesn't, if she bows out, I can be your new pitchperson. I've gotten a good deal of practice going to the Sands every week."

"Thanks, Mom." Annie squeezed her mother's hand. Then her situation came crashing back down on her. "Mom, I'm finished anyway." Annie explained that she had run out of cocaine. She might keep business afloat for a little bit, hawking bland stuff and milking the Étinav name. But eventually word would get out. Old customers would sense that something was missing, and new customers would wonder what all the fuss had been about. Sales would dry up.

Chloe asked, “And where will that leave you and Sarah?”

“Well, if Sarah gets lucky, if she gets pregnant on this round of IVF, then she won’t need the Étinav money. She’ll be set.”

“And what about you?”

“The way I see it, I’m screwed. I’ve stashed away enough to pay for Oscar’s therapy for a few more months. But after that . . .” Annie exhaled loudly. “The bills will keep coming in.”

Chloe gave Annie’s hand a squeeze. “Well, then, we’ll have to get you some cocaine.”

“How are we going to do that?”

Chloe smiled at her daughter. “Oh, Annabelle, it can’t be that hard to purchase cocaine. Millions of people do it every day.”

Folding her arms against her chest, Annie said defensively, “It’s harder than you think.” She told Chloe about Chula Vista and her disastrous encounter with Jazz. Annie whined, “Even back in college, no one ever offered me drugs. I don’t know why.” She sounded like a kid complaining that no one would play with her.

Chloe reached over and pushed a stray curl out of Annie’s eyes. “Of course they didn’t offer you drugs.”

Petulantly, Annie asked, “Why not?”

“Annabelle, please don’t take this the wrong way, but there’s something very moral about you. You’re like an Amish woman with an invisible prayer bonnet on your head. People don’t need to see the bonnet on you. They can *sense* it. If I were a casting agent, I’d put you up for all the prim and proper parts: the jury member who gasps when a witness uses an off-color expression, that sort of thing.”

Annie opened her mouth to object. But Chloe cut her off. “I’m not saying you *are* like that. I mean, of course, compared to me you are. But let’s be honest, compared to me *most* people seem excessively moralistic. I was always at the other end of the casting continuum. I cannot count how many times I've played the whore with the heart of gold, the drunken houseguest. I'm not any of those things in real life. At least, I haven't done any whoring. But still I give off the impression that I could be a whore. And to the audience, that's all that matters."

Annie smiled, knowing her mother was right. "So what do we do? You may be great at giving off the lawless vibe, but I don't think anyone in PB will want to sell drugs to a woman in her seventies."

"You're probably right. It's discrimination. Ageism, I think they call it. It's a sorry world when an elderly woman cannot get her drug of choice."

"And I don't have any connections. The strongest thing my friends use is coffee. And there's no way Jimmy will help us."

"Yes. Your brother's rehabilitation has come at a rather inconvenient juncture." Chloe shook her head gravely. Then a smile spread slowly across her face. "But I see no reason why we can't go to one of Jimmy's friends."

Annie raised an eyebrow. "You're in touch with Jimmy's old drug buddies?"

Chloe grinned. "With *one* of them, yes. Do you remember Stephanie?"

"Stephanie Davis?"

Chloe beamed. "Yes. She and Jimmy used to go 'round together. To be honest, I was hoping your brother would settle down with her. Such a lovely girl. Don't you think so?"

Annie nodded wordlessly. Stephanie was undeniably attractive, but not in a way that would appeal to most prospective mothers-in-law. She had played bit parts in a dozen pornographic movies. The woman oozed sex. God had blessed her with sleepy, hooded eyes, a husky voice, and almost comically sensuous lips, and a plastic surgeon had added two massive silicone balls to her chest. This was Chloe's ideal daughter-in-law? Chloe's chronic disappointment in Harry was a relief. Annie asked, "Is Stephanie a drug dealer?"

Chloe flinched. "No, nothing as sordid as that. But she's connected. She can get drugs and sell them to us."

"You think she'd sell drugs to us?"

"Not to you, darling. I'm afraid you didn't make a very good impression on Stephanie. You weren't very congenial."

Annie said, "I was so! I offered her drinks. I tried to make small talk."

Chloe nodded. "I know. As usual, you got all the formalities right. No, the problem was your expression. The way you stared at her chest, it was as if you'd never seen breasts before. It reminded me of that photograph of Sophia Loren sitting next to Jayne Mansfield. There Jayne is, in all her glory, her splendid cleavage spilling out of her tiny dress, and the look of disgust on Sophia's face . . . what a wonderful photograph!"

Annie colored. "I wasn't *that* bad. Was I?"

"Oh, I'm afraid you were, my dear. Still, that doesn't matter now. What matters is that Stephanie and I built up a rapport. She wants to be a legitimate actress. She calls me all the time for advice. It's rather flattering."

"Is she talented?"

Chloe wrinkled her nose. "No. She's terrible. But she tries so hard. It's moving, valiant in its own way."

"So you'll call her?"

"Yes, in fact, I'll telephone her right now." Chloe rose from the table and walked over to her purse. She pulled out her cell phone and called Stephanie. The two women immediately lapsed into talk about "the craft." Annie tuned out for the drama chat but she perked up when Chloe announced that she needed to get hold of some cocaine for a friend. Could Stephanie help her? She could? How marvelous. Chloe purred into the phone, "Yes, yes. No problem . . . How soon do you think you can get it for me, dear? . . . Stupendous! I'll drive up on Friday then. We can make a day of it if you'd like . . . All right, see you Friday." Chloe snapped her cell phone shut. She turned to Annie in triumph. "It's done!"

Annie hugged her mother tightly, murmuring, "Thanks, Mom."

Chloe hugged back. "Oh, sweetie, that's what moms are for."

Thanks to her parents' atheism, Sarah did not read the Bible until taking a lit course in college. She quickly forgot the Good Book's many rules and begats. *But the story of her biblical namesake stayed with her. Sarah, Abraham's wife, was barren and sat in mute assent when Abraham fathered a child with another woman. When Sarah was in her nineties, a visitor told her that she would have a son, and Sarah laughed at the idea. Sarah was the only woman in the Bible to laugh. A year later, she gave birth to Isaac.*

42

Sarah's Little Indians

Sarah checked her watch again. Eleven seventeen. Where was her husband?

Sarah's appointment with Dr. Alpert was set for eleven o'clock. Sitting in the great doctor's waiting room with an ancient copy of *Good Housekeeping* in her lap, Sarah fished her cell phone out of her purse and called Michael. His phone sent her straight to voice mail. Michael's genial baritone told her to leave a message, and Sarah whispered through clenched teeth, "Where are you, honey?"

Michael had promised he would come. He'd already missed every other phase of in vitro attempt number three. On extraction day, when Dr. Alpert went in like a reverse Easter Bunny to take away Sarah's eggs, Michael had been stuck at a paleontologists' conference in Madison, Wisconsin. Sarah had lain on the table, woozy from a mild sedative, while Dr. Alpert used a tube to suck thirteen viable eggs out of her. Thirteen!

She'd been so pumped up with fertility drugs that in one month her body had produced thirteen times a normal woman's egg count. She'd gotten up from the table, bleary from the sedative and feeling a distant soreness in her crotch. It had been Annie, not Michael, who had chauffeured Sarah home from the appointment and put her to bed with a cold washcloth across her forehead.

Afterward, Michael apologized by phone but said he would really try to make it to embryo day. That was when Sarah would meet with Alpert's embryologist. At the last moment, Michael had missed this meeting too. He'd been on a dig in Utah, and his team had unearthed some fascinating remains. Skull fragments from an apatosaurus! He couldn't possibly leave Utah now. Sarah asked, "Why not? What's so great about Utah? We've got plenty of dead stuff here. Just look in my womb."

Michael pleaded, "Honey, of course I want to be there. But I'm the head of the team. And this could be a major find, a career maker. I can't possibly leave now. And besides, it's not like I'd be able to do anything there. The embryos are either viable or they're not." And that was the rub. Like most men, Michael didn't want to be around for horrible news unless he could do something about it, something macho and proactive. Build a fort, kick someone's butt, buy a big-screen TV.

Sarah closed her eyes and took a deep breath. "There's plenty for you to do here. You can hold my hand. You can make sure I don't have to face bad news alone."

Michael chided her, "Who says it will be bad news? It might be great news. For all we know, we could have a dozen embryos."

"Don't get greedy."

"I'm not greedy. Just one baby would be a miracle. Hell, having you is a miracle."

Sarah bristled, "A miracle you take for granted."

Michael sighed. "Look, I know it's lousy I'm not there for embryo day. But I'll make it up to you, I promise."

So Sarah faced embryo day alone. But the news was good. Michael's sperm had teamed up with her eggs to produce seven viable embryos. Seven! Three days later, Dr. Alpert cherry-picked the three biggest, heartiest-looking embryos of the batch and implanted them in Sarah's womb.

Three little Indians. But would any of them take root? Today, one week after implantation, Sarah would find out. She told herself that she could handle bad news. She'd lived through it before. But failing at IVF on the third try would not be like failing after the first try. The first time, there was still hope. Your body had failed you, but that didn't mean it would always fail you. By the third time around, your body had declared its intentions. Your womb wasn't under renovations. It had gone out of business.

Sarah didn't want to face that news alone. She glanced down at her watch again. Eleven nineteen. Where was he? She was about to call him again when Michael strode into the waiting room, his battered green canvas duffel bag slung over his shoulder. He had two weeks' worth of stubble on his cheeks, his jeans were dirty, and his hiking boots were caked with mud. Sunburned and filthy, the man looked like he had walked across the desert to get home. Plopping down in the seat next to Sarah, he kissed her cheek. "Hello, beautiful."

Sarah kept her arms crossed tightly against her chest. She whispered, "You were supposed to be home by nine this morning. You're two hours late."

Michael smiled. "I wanted to make an entrance."

"Well, you certainly did that." She glanced around at the well-dressed, affluent couples scattered throughout the waiting room with its blush-pink walls and hotel décor. "Couldn't you have taken a bath before you came? You look like Indiana Jones on a bad day."

Clearly pleased, Michael sat up straighter. "Indiana Jones? Really?"

Sarah tried to hold on to her anger. He was two hours late, dammit. But she was too relieved to see him. Softening, she said, "Maybe more like Pigpen."

Michael nodded. "I can accept that. Pigpen was a good guy. Not much with the ladies, but still a good guy." Then, looking genuinely penitent, Michael leaned in closer to Sarah and whispered, "I'm sorry I'm late. My flight was delayed, and my cell phone conked out."

On the verge of tears—damned fertility drugs!—Sarah said nothing. She squeezed his hand. Then the ultrasound technician, Audra, called them in. Looking as frightened as Hansel and Gretel lost in the black forest, Sarah and Michael held hands as they followed Audra down a corridor to the dimly lit ultrasound room.

Audra was a short, plump brunette. Her '80s-style glasses made her eyes appear huge and owlish. Blinking up at Sarah, the white-coated gnome ordered Sarah to undress from the waist down; she held out a thin paper sheet for Sarah to use as a drape. While Sarah disrobed, Audra snapped a fresh condom onto the ultrasound's wand, and Michael sat down next to the head of the exam table.

When Sarah was settled on the table, her feet suspended in black plastic stirrups, Audra gently inserted the wand up inside her. Bracing one hand against Sarah's abdomen, Audra used her other hand to maneuver the wand. Audra's large eyes stared at the machine's monitor. Michael and Sarah stared at the monitor too, but its grainy black-and-white images told them nothing. Audra moved the wand slowly inside Sarah, back and forth—sweeping Sarah's womb like a metal detector seeking treasure. And then suddenly Audra stopped. Holding the wand in one hand, she used her other hand to type on the machine's keyboard. The caption "4X" appeared on the bottom of the monitor. Audra hit "Return," and the grainy landscape Sarah and Michael had been looking at disappeared. A new vista leaped into focus, more detailed but still indecipherable to Sarah's eyes.

Her voice just above a whisper, Audra asked, "They implanted three embryos, right?"

Sarah murmured, "Right."

Her face giving away nothing, Audra leaned back and withdrew the wand from Sarah's uterus. She pulled off her gloves and announced that she would be back in a moment with Dr. Alpert. As soon as she left the room, Michael leaned forward and kissed Sarah's cheek. "You all right?"

Sarah gave a quick nod, and then Audra returned with Dr. Alpert. The technician donned fresh gloves and repeated her scan of Sarah's womb, settling again on the same patch of terrain. Audra nodded at Dr. Alpert, and he stepped forward to study the monitor. For a moment, his figure blocked the monitor from Sarah's view. But then he stepped back. He gestured to two small circular shapes on the screen and asked, "So, Sarah, how does it feel to be carrying twins?"

Sarah struggled to catch up. "Twins?" Michael leaned over and gave her a huge kiss on the mouth. When he pulled back, Sarah saw that there were tears in his eyes. Then she looked past him at the two tiny ovals pulsating on the screen. Beaming, she told Dr. Alpert that she felt fan-fucking-tastic.

Sarah loved Simon Brett's witty British-on-steroids cynicism. When she read Brett's A Shock to the System, *she smiled at his description of the protagonist's sullen teenage children, children who had "lost the charm that smallness had imparted." Sarah told herself what all would-be parents do: "My children will be different."*

43

Sarah's Good News

As soon as Sarah got out of Alpert's office, she called Annie. Annie had been on standby for hours, so she picked up on the first ring. The bleating of traffic horns told Sarah that Annie was stuck in traffic with the speakerphone blaring. Before Sarah could get a word out, Maddie yelled, "Mom, Oscar's bothering me!"

Oscar answered, "Am not!"

"Are too!"

Annie purred to Sarah, "Sorry, Sare. Give me a second." Then Annie bellowed, "Be quiet! Mommy has a very important call from Aunt Sarah! I need to hear this." Taking the volume back down, Annie asked, "Okay, okay, so what did Alpert say?"

Beaming, Sarah said, "Yes!"

"Yes, you're pregnant? Or yes, you'll need to try again?"

"Pregnant!"

Annie let out a huge whoop of joy. Smiling, Sarah held the phone away from her ear for a moment. Annie had serious pipes. "Oh, Sare, congratulations! You're going to be a mommy!"

"It looks that way. But it's still early in the game." Sarah didn't want to tempt fate; she was terrified of a miscarriage.

Annie grew quiet for a moment, but only a moment. Her optimism was like a kid who's been scolded for running by the pool. It slowed for a second or two before breaking again into an exuberant run. "You're right. We'll have to tiptoe around for the first three months. But still! Pregnant! You, Sarah Sloane, are pregnant! Officially with child. Banged up. Expecting. Bun in the oven."

Maddie asked, "What's in the oven?"

Annie crowed, "Aunt Sarah is going to have a baby! Oh shit, sorry, Sarah, I shouldn't have told them yet. Oh shit, I'm sorry, kids, I shouldn't have said *shit*."

Sarah laughed. "I haven't told you the best part yet."

"There's a best part? What could be better than having a baby?"

"Having two."

Annie squealed again. "Twins? You're having twins? Kids, Auntie Sarah is having twins!"

Maddie announced, "A woman gets twins in her belly if she has sex for two days."

Annie gaped. "What?"

Rachel weighed in. "I want Old McDonald's!"

Annie answered, "No, sweetie, not now, after Maddie's soccer practice."

Rachel screeched, "I want Old McDonald's *now*!"

Annie hollered, "Not now! You kids are behaving like monsters. *You don't deserve food!*" Then, her voice suddenly warm, Annie told Sarah, "Sare, I'm going to have to get off the phone. But that's great news. I'm so happy for you. Children are such a blessing."

Annie had no trouble forgiving Les Misérables' *Jean Valjean for stealing a loaf of bread. But she didn't buy into forgiveness for bigger crimes like the double homicide in Sister Prejean's* Dead Man Walking *or the pedophilia in Nabokov's* Lolita. *Annie figured spiking face cream with coke was more on the loaf-of-bread end of the spectrum. She hoped Sarah would see it the same way.*

44

Annie's Bad News

When Sarah arrived at Annie's house on Tuesday morning, Annie ambushed her with three boxes of baby paraphernalia. Annie had stuffed two boxes with lightly used unisex yellow onesies and blankets. But when Sarah opened the third box, she found new gear: a Winnie the Pooh mobile, teddy bears, a stuffed ducky. Holding the ducky in her hand, Sarah asked, "Why are the tags still on these?"

"Those are my wish gifts."

"Wish gifts?"

"I bought them when you first started trying and then again each time you went in for IVF." Annie added quickly, "I *know* you hate to jinx things. But I didn't buy them assuming that I'd be able to give them to you right away. I bought them as a sort of a prayer. An offering to the gods of retail. Is that okay?"

Sarah smiled and nuzzled the ducky. "I don't mind."

"Some of them are a little girlie. The pink Webkinz. I kept the receipts if you want to exchange them. They're in an envelope at the bottom of the box."

Still holding the ducky, Sarah shrugged. "That's okay. I don't think a baby boy will mind having one or two pink toys."

They meandered into Annie's kitchen. Sarah asked, "What's that smell?"

Annie beamed. "Peanut butter cookies." Sarah plopped down at the kitchen table, and Annie set the cookies out on a plate with two glasses of milk. Annie watched Sarah nibble at the cookies. Annie knew it was time to tell her. No more pussyfooting around. Annie cleared her throat. "I have some news of my own."

Her mouth full of cookie, Sarah garbled, "Go on."

"It's about Étinav. The formulation. Um, you know how I told you the cream needed something to give it some kick?"

Sarah licked crumbs off her finger and nodded. "You put caffeine in there, right?"

Annie colored. "Not exactly."

Still munching on a cookie, Sarah said, "So what then?"

Talking quickly, almost manically, Annie said, "Well, I *thought* about using caffeine. I really did. It tightens the pores. But it doesn't have enough kick. It doesn't lift the user's mood. I played with a bunch of ingredients. I really did. I even ground up some antidepressants to see if they'd do the trick. But that didn't work either. You have to have tons of Prozac in your system for it to work, and we needed something that kicked in fast. So the customers could feel it working, feel the cream working, you know what I mean?"

Sarah put down her cookie. Annie had her full attention now. "Annie, what are you trying to tell me?"

Annie let out a strange high-pitched laugh. "I was only able to find one ingredient that did everything I needed it to do. It could be absorbed through the skin, and a small dose could give a solid high, a confidence boost. To make the customer *feel* like the cream was working."

Sarah paled. "Did you spike the cream with some kind of drug?"

Annie nodded. Sarah's mouth fell open. Then she leaned forward and put her face in her hands. Through her fingers, she said, "I think I'm going to be sick." She ran for the bathroom, slamming the door behind her. Annie hovered in the hallway, listening to Sarah retch. Next came the sound of water running in the sink. After what felt like an eternity, Sarah emerged from the bathroom.

Annie said, "I'm so sorry. I should have told you sooner. But I thought—"

Glaring, Sarah held up her hand to silence Annie. She gestured toward the kitchen table and commanded, "Sit down. Do not say another word until I ask you to." Annie rushed obediently to her chair.

Sarah sat down across from Annie. Her voice stern, Sarah said, "I'm going to ask you some questions. I want you to answer yes or no. I want no extra details. Volunteer nothing. Do you understand?"

Annie bobbed her head. "Yes."

Sarah started, "You know that I'm an attorney, don't you?"

Annie bobbed her head again. "Yes, of course. Why are you—"

Sarah repeated, "Just answer yes or no."

"Yes, I know you're an attorney."

"And in the past, from time to time, you have come to me for legal advice. Is that correct?"

Annie thought back. At first, she drew a blank. But then she remembered. There was the time she and Harry asked Sarah about drawing up a will. And the other time when Jimmy had gotten himself arrested. Annie stammered, "Y-yes. You've given me legal advice before."

"And you've heard about the attorney-client privilege, haven't you?" Sarah was talking slowly now, almost rhythmically. She might as well have been swinging a pocket watch in front of Annie's eyes.

As if in a trance, Annie said mechanically, "The attorney-client privilege, yes."

Sarah went on, "To refresh your memory, if you come to me strictly as a friend and tell me something, then I can be asked about that conversation in a court of law. The conversation is not privileged, not confidential. Do you understand?"

"Yes, I understand."

"But if you come to me and tell me something because you are seeking legal advice, then it's different. Then, even if I wanted to, I couldn't testify about that conversation. Whatever you say to me would be privileged. Do you understand?"

"Yes." Annie nodded, wanting desperately to ingratiate herself.

"Good. So let's take this one step at a time. Up until today, you have never indicated to me that Étinav contained any illegal components, is that correct?"

"Yes. I mean no. I never said it had anything—"

Sarah cut her off. "And today, you are coming to me not as a friend but as a client. Is that true?"

It wasn't true. But it *should* have been. Why hadn't Annie thought this through? Annie bobbed her head. "Yes."

Sarah went on, "You are coming to me because you want to learn the legal consequences of using certain ingredients in your face cream, is that right?"

Annie didn't like hearing Sarah call it "your" face cream. Wasn't it "our" face cream? But Annie deserved it. Her lies had made Étinav all her own. Sheepishly, Annie said, "Yes."

"So with all that in mind, tell me: What did you put in the cream?"

Annie stammered, "StriVectin, Pond's, some rosemary for smell, and cocaine."

Sarah gaped. "Cocaine?"

Annie nodded.

Sarah closed her eyes for a moment, processing the bad news. Sighing, she asked, "How much cocaine in each jar?"

"Just a smidgen."

An edge in her voice, Sarah repeated, "How much, Annie?"

"One gram. Just enough to give the cream a kick."

"And how long have you been spiking the cream with cocaine?"

"A while."

"Don't play with me, Annie."

"Since the beginning."

"Back in July?"

"Uh-huh."

"So there's been cocaine in every single jar of Étinav that you have ever made. Is that what you're telling me?"

"Uh-huh."

"And you didn't tell me this before because . . . ?"

"I didn't want to incriminate you."

"Let me get this straight. You sent me all over La Jolla peddling jars full of cocaine, but you didn't want to incriminate me?"

"I figured you'd be in the clear."

"And how did you figure that, Annie?"

"I saw an episode of *Law & Order.* They arrested this guy for being a drug mule. But they couldn't make the charges stick because the guy didn't know he was carrying cocaine. He thought—"

"So you felt confident about sending me out to sell cocaine because you saw a TV show?"

Annie flailed. Sarah put her face in her hands again. The kitchen fell silent. Annie pleaded, "I'm sorry I didn't tell you. I did it to protect you."

"Oh, please, Annie, don't lie to me."

"What do you mean?"

Sarah took her hands away from her face and glared at Annie. "You knew there was no way I would have gone along with this."

"I thought—"

"You needed me to sell this stuff. That's all you cared about. And you knew I would have said no if you'd told me about the cocaine. You weren't protecting me. You were using me, plain and simple."

"That's not true!"

"Really?" Sarah shot her a withering stare.

Annie gulped. "Not entirely true. I just . . . At first, when we came up with the idea of selling cream, I *planned* to use legitimate ingredients. I swear. But as I tinkered with the formula, I grew convinced—no, I *knew* that we had to have something extra. Something to hook people. So I put in some cocaine I'd gotten from Jimmy. Just a little. At first I couldn't believe I was doing it. I thought of it as an experiment. But it worked! The clients loved the stuff. We were making good money. It was a win-win all around. I figured the risk was worth it."

Sarah laughed bitterly. "Do you have any idea how many times I've heard that?"

"Heard what?"

Sarah mimicked Annie's whine perfectly, "'I figured the risk was worth it.' Every white-collar criminal says that. No one's ever honest about the damage they're doing. They all have special circumstances, some precious bullshit excuse."

Annie fumbled, "But I do have special circumstances. So do you."

"No, we don't. Not under the law."

"Well, maybe not under the law, but—"

"But what, Annie? What's so goddamned special about our needs?"

Annie shot back, "Oscar is autistic. He needs treatment!"

"Yes, Oscar needs treatment. Does that mean every parent with a sick kid can go out and break the law? If my little Timmy needs an operation, do I get to knock over a liquor store?"

"We didn't knock over a liquor store. We didn't pull a gun on anyone. We sold some overpriced cream to a bunch of women who have more money than they can possibly need."

"And we used cocaine to do it. We exposed every single one of our customers to cocaine. And we did it without their consent. Do you have any idea how crazy that is? How lucky we've been? What if someone had a heart attack? What if someone overdosed? What if your brother's powder had been cut with something horrible?"

"It wasn't!"

"How do you know, Annie?"

Annie huffed, "The Internet says most cutting agents are perfectly harmless. Sugars, laxatives, baking powder . . ."

"Ever hear of dealers cutting cocaine with crystal meth?"

Annie gaped. "What?"

"That's right, Annie. Some dealers cut cocaine with crystal meth. Meth is a helluva lot cheaper than coke, and it's just as strong. What if one of our old ladies at the Sands had keeled over from that crap? What then, Annie?"

Annie said feebly, "But no one *did* keel over . . ."

Sarah leaned back in her chair. She tilted her head back and stared at the ceiling, exhaling loudly. Annie tolerated the quiet for as long as she could. Then she asked plaintively, "What are you going to do?"

"I don't know. All I know is I'm out."

"Out?"

"That's right. I'm out. It's what we lawyers call withdrawing from the conspiracy. I'm not selling another jar of that stuff."

"But what about our customers?"

Sarah closed her eyes again. She thought of Valerie, of Kim, of all the other women who had become more than just customers, who had become friends. She hated abandoning them without an explanation, but she couldn't see any other way out. Sarah sighed, her eyes filling with tears. "Tell them whatever you want to tell them. I had to leave town. A family crisis came up. Whatever works for you."

"And what about us?"

"Us?"

Annie's chin trembled. She tried not to sound pathetic, but it was hard. "Are we still going to be friends?"

Sarah studied Annie for a long moment. "I don't know, Annie. This is a lot to take in, a lot to forgive. I would never turn you in, but I don't know. I just don't know. Plus, things are different now. It's not just my ass on the line."

Annie nodded, her eyes filling with tears. "I know, you're a mother now. You have to do whatever's best for you and your babies. I get that."

After a long silence, the two women rose from the table. Annie insisted on carrying the three boxes out to the car. She said Sarah shouldn't lift anything, not in her condition. Annie loaded the car, and the two women hugged, saying nothing. Then Sarah got in and drove away.

Sarah only made it a few blocks before she had to pull over. Crying and raging at the same time, she reached over into the box on the passenger seat, the box loaded with new stuffed animals. She reached down to the bottom of the box and quickly found what she was looking for: the envelope Annie had told her about, the one loaded with receipts.

Sarah had to know. Had Annie really bought the toys one by one? As an offering to the gods of retail each time Sarah was waiting for another delayed period? Another IVF treatment? Or was that a lie too? Maybe Annie had bought all the toys over the past few days, hoping to soften Sarah up for the big news. If so, it would have been stupid to put the receipts in the box. But plenty of Sarah's clients had made even dumber mistakes.

Going through the envelope, Sarah got her answer. Annie had gotten the blue elephant just a few months after Sarah had gotten married, back when Sarah and Michael first started trying. She'd bought the pink giraffe a year later, when Sarah had her first false alarm, a late period. She'd bought the two brown teddy bears a year after that, when Sarah tried IVF for the first time. And the white puppy dog right around IVF attempt number two. The ducky was the most recent purchase, bought just days ago.

Sarah hugged the ducky tightly against her chest. She missed Annie already.

A hardworking, seasoned prosecutor, Oliver Thatch thought book clubs were for bored menopausal housewives. Thatch hadn't cracked a novel in more than twenty years. On his few vacations, he binged on gritty tell-alls about organized crime. His favorite was Killing Pablo*—about the rise of Colombian drug lord Pablo Escobar and the lone brave police colonel who brought him down.*

45

Tattletale

Oliver Thatch did not want to take this meeting. He'd been with the San Diego District Attorney's Office for ten years, seven in the narcotics unit. He was too senior to babysit some spoiled socialite. He didn't care which higher-up played golf with her husband. He didn't have time for this crap.

Thatch knew what his ex-wife, Brenda, would have said: that he lacked ambition, that he wasn't politically savvy enough to get ahead, that socialites were the sort of people he should *want* to meet. In her flat Midwestern twang, Brenda had scolded him, "Ollie"—he hated being called Ollie—"you'll never get anywhere sitting in that office listening to wiretaps. Oh sure, the cops may love you. Big deal! When the DA chooses who to bring up, he's not going to ask a bunch of cops who reek of BO and stale doughnuts." The hag had a point. Thatch hadn't been promoted in three years. He'd put away dozens of drug dealers, but no one high-profile. No high-profile cases meant no press, and no press meant no promotions. Press and personal connections, those were the only ways to get ahead.

Oliver Thatch knew all this, but he resented it. Even after three years without moving up, he mulishly stuck to his quiet—but important!—cases and refused to network. So he was in a sour mood when he entered the conference room to meet with Natalie Wilson. Thatch didn't know much about the woman. What was there to know? Those rich La Jolla women were all the same: big fancy houses, one or two pampered brats with last names as first names, high-end cars, and an army of Chicanas to make everything run like clockwork.

Natalie Wilson fit the mold perfectly. Thatch didn't know who had designed her green silk dress, but he knew it was expensive. Probably cost more than he took home in a month. The gold bangles on her wrists didn't come cheap either. And her wedding ring! It was huge. Not a rock, a boulder. A short, stocky blonde, Natalie Wilson had buff arms and legs that attested she spent half her day at the gym. Thatch sucked in his hefty gut as he studied her. It wasn't fair. The only people with enough time to stay in shape these days were spoiled women like this one and the thugs Thatch sent to jail.

Shutting the conference room door behind him, Thatch reached across the table and shook Natalie Wilson's manicured hand. She smiled up at him. Thatch nodded to the room's only other occupant, Maria Rodriguez. A smart, hardworking cop, Rodriguez had been bumped up to detective two years earlier. She'd made a name for herself busting drug dealers in National City. She loved working the streets, but pregnancy had benched her. She resented it. Most female cops did, but what else could the bosses do? Rodriguez was a tiny thing: barely five feet tall, thin and wiry. But at seven months pregnant, her belly was huge. She looked like an eighth grader smuggling a watermelon under her shirt. Rodriguez was probably just as annoyed as Thatch was to be doing an intake session with a rich brat.

Sitting down, Thatch introduced himself. "I'm Oliver Thatch. I'm a prosecutor with the narcotics division. I'm guessing you've met my colleague here, Maria Rodriguez. She's a detective, also with the drug unit."

Natalie Wilson nodded eagerly. She had that same wide-eyed, "golly gee whillikers, this is just like TV" look that all those society types got whenever they condescended to visit a police station. The rich always got a kick out of the station's battered metal file cabinets, ugly fluorescent lighting, and Office Max décor. So gritty!

Thatch forged ahead. "So, my unit chief told me that you wanted to report a crime."

Again, Natalie's perfectly coiffed blond head bobbed. "That's right." She leaned forward in her chair, as if about to share a particularly juicy bit of gossip. "There's been a crime, right in *my* neighborhood. Can you *believe* it?"

Thatch knew the answer, but he asked anyway, "And what neighborhood is that?"

Natalie answered, "La Jolla. I found someone selling drugs right in the middle of La Jolla. Can you imagine?"

"What kind of drugs are we talking about?"

"Cocaine."

Thatch said sarcastically, "My goodness. Rich people taking cocaine? That is a shock." Rodriguez grinned.

But Natalie didn't detect any mockery. Rich people seldom did; they weren't on guard for it. Natalie plowed ahead, "Omigosh, the worst part is that the customers don't even know they're taking cocaine. They have no idea."

Now *that* was interesting. Thatch asked, "What? Do they think they're getting meth?" It made no sense. Meth was cheaper than cocaine. Dealers used meth to cut cocaine, not the other way around.

Natalie's carefully plucked eyebrows shot up in bewilderment. She echoed, "Meth?"

Rodriguez explained, “Crystal meth. It’s an amphetamine. Very popular street drug.”

Natalie shook her head. “Oh no, these ladies would never go for something like that. No, they’re not buying, um, meth. They’re buying face cream.”

Now Thatch was lost. “Face cream?”

Natalie Wilson nodded. “Yes, a high-end face cream called Étinav. This woman, Sarah Sloane, that’s S-L-O-A-N-E, she’s been selling the stuff all over La Jolla. She says all the movie stars use it.”

Thatch repeated, “Face cream?”

Natalie nodded again. “Yah-huh, that’s right. Sarah has been selling it for two thousand dollars a jar.”

Thatch goggled. “Two thousand dollars a jar? How big are these jars?” He pictured a vat or at least a mayonnaise jar.

“One or two ounces.”

Thatch still didn’t get it. “So these women are paying two thousand dollars a pop for tiny jars of face cream?”

“Yes, that’s right.”

Thatch pressed, “And they’ve got no idea that this face cream has got cocaine in it?”

Natalie’s head bobbed again. “Yes. I mean no, no idea.”

Thatch sneaked a look over at Rodriguez. She shrugged. Thatch prodded, “What do they think is in the stuff? Gold dust? Shredded platinum?”

Natalie explained, “Sarah tells them that it’s got some kind of patented bio-extract. She says some French doctor came up with it.”

Thatch asked, “So these ladies plunk down two g’s for face cream without having any clue what’s in it?”

“Yes.”

Thatch turned to Rodriguez, saying, “They have to know it’s got coke in it. Who the hell pays two g’s a jar for face cream?” Again,

Rodriguez shrugged. Thatch could tell she had an opinion on this, but she was too smart to voice it in front of Natalie Wilson.

Changing tacks, Thatch asked Natalie, "How do you know this face cream has coke in it?"

Natalie announced, "I had it tested." She dug inside her purse and pulled out a computer printout embossed with the Peeky Labs logo. She flattened the printout and pushed it across the table to Thatch. He scanned the list of components: water, glycerin, EDTA, and there, plain as day, cocaine. An estimated one gram per forty-gram jar. Thatch handed the paper to Rodriguez.

Thatch asked Natalie, "Do you still have the sample?"

Natalie nodded again. She reached inside her purse and pulled out a small white glass jar with a silver top. Rodriguez leaned forward. Saying nothing, Rodriguez picked the jar up from the table and examined it. Then she laughed.

Thatch asked, "What's so funny?"

Rodriguez shook her head. "I've seen this jar before. My *abuela* has a few of them around. She buys the stuff down in Tijuana. Only her jars are loaded with bunion cream."

Thatch said, "So this Sarah person is going down to TJ to buy bunion cream, emptying out the jars, and then filling them with lotion and cocaine?"

Rodriguez smiled. "Looks like it."

Rodriguez's grin was infectious. Thatch felt the corners of his mouth go up. This was going to be fun. And with La Jolla ladies on the hook, it would be high-profile too, media catnip.

And this time, Thatch would make sure he got credit. He'd leak the story himself. He didn't have much experience with the press, but he knew such things were done. He'd just have to be careful. A few well-placed calls, and he'd finally graduate from line prosecutor to management nirvana.

Chloe wasn't much for reading, but she'd adored Larry McMurtry's Terms of Endearment. *She had no trouble understanding the prickly but loving relationship between the adult daughter Emma and her aging—but still vibrantly sexual!—mother, Aurora. Both Emma and Annie struggled against their mothers' surpluses of personality.*

46

Busted

Chloe felt marvelous. For the first time in decades, Annie was letting Chloe mother her. With Sarah having stomped off in a huff, Annie needed Chloe. She needed someone to confide in, someone to soothe her, someone to build her back up. And for once Chloe knew what to say to her daughter. Chloe was wonderful at validating people, at explaining away their less fortunate moments and highlighting their triumphs. Chloe had played more than her fair share of whores and murderesses precisely because she could sympathize with just about anyone. *"Well, of course you murdered him. He forgot your birthday!" "Sit in LA traffic long enough, and anyone's thoughts will turn to matricide." "They call it stalking, but I think it's sweet."*

Chloe spent days coaxing her daughter out of a guilt-induced stupor. Yes, Annie had lied to her best friend. And sure, she'd exposed dozens of women to cocaine. But she'd had an excellent reason! She had done it to pay for Oscar's therapy, to make him well. What mother bear wouldn't break a few laws to protect her cub?

Annie should be proud of what she'd done. She hadn't harmed anyone. She had kept the cocaine dose responsibly low so that no one would become addicted. Big tobacco couldn't claim as much; neither could Sara Lee or McDonald's! What's more, Annie hadn't allowed any pregnant women or cardiac patients to use her product. She was that concerned with public health.

Annie had done her customers a favor. In exchange for a measly few thousand dollars—a pittance to them!—Annie had given them new confidence. She had imbued their shuffling existence with swagger. She'd given them the boost that women of a certain age need. And that boost had changed their lives for the better. Kim returned to teaching. Valerie started painting again, sold her work, and got a new man in the bargain. And over at the Sands, the aged Goldie managed to seduce the even more aged Max Pilkus.

Annie had made all this possible. She was not the villain of the piece! She was not the ruthless, swindling tailor from *The Emperor's New Clothes*. No, she was more like the fairy godmother in *Cinderella*, sprinkling her customers with magic confidence-inducing powder so they could finally enjoy the ball that their lives should be.

And her work was not done yet! Oscar's therapy still had to be paid for, and there were still plenty of women out there who could benefit from Annie's cream. The show must go on! Chloe would take Sarah's place. After months of going to the Sands, Chloe had the product spiel down pat. And the customers, the ones at the Sands anyway, knew Chloe. They felt comfortable with her. Yes, Chloe was confident she'd be able to rebuild Annie's client base.

It took a few days, but eventually Annie let herself be persuaded. The Étinav business would not collapse. Sarah wouldn't stay mad forever. Annie gave Chloe her last four jars of Étinav and wished her well as she set off for the Sands.

Chloe wasn't planning to make her rounds. Not this time. She would meet with a few customers: first, the dog lover Josephine; next, Sylvia and Goldie; and then, perhaps, the ancient Norma Jenkins.

When she entered the Sands's foyer, Chloe waved to the receptionist and took the elevator up to Josephine's place. She was surprised when an immensely pregnant Chicana opened the door. From her surgical scrubs, Chloe guessed the woman was a nurse. That was odd. Chloe had never seen Josephine with a nurse before. The residents who needed nursing stuck to the top two floors of the Sands's continuing care unit.

The Chicana beckoned Chloe in, saying, in heavily accented English, "You must be Mees Baker. Mees Josephine ees expecting you."

Chloe smiled and followed the nurse into Josephine's living room. Josephine was perched on a cushy blue velvet armchair. Her left foot was propped up on a matching ottoman; it was encased in a white plaster cast. Coming to Josephine's side, Chloe cooed, "Darling, what happened to you?"

Josephine sulked. "I tripped over a rock while I was out for a walk with my babies. Broke one of the bones in my foot."

"That must have been horrible for you. And your poor pups! Is there anything I can get you?"

"No, no. That's what I've got Maria for." Josephine gestured at the nurse hovering discreetly on a chair in the corner. At the mention of her name, she looked up from a magazine and smiled.

Chloe asked, "Does it hurt terribly?"

Josephine shrugged. "No, not really. I've been through much worse. Please, sit down."

Chloe sat down on Josephine's expensive, dog-hair-matted couch. "So how *are* Duchess and Witchie? Come to think of it, where are they?"

Josephine squirmed in her chair for a moment. Was Chloe imagining things or was the woman avoiding eye contact? Josephine explained, "They're out with the dog walker. They should be back in half an hour."

"Oh, good. I love these new photos of them." Chloe gestured to the large, blown-up black-and-white portraits hanging over the mantelpiece.

Still avoiding eye contact, Josephine said, "Yes. My niece did those."

"Your niece? Well, she's very talented."

"Yes. I think so too." Josephine studied the photos for a long moment. Then, clearing her throat, she asked, "So, did you get my phone message? Have you brought me some cream today?"

"Yes, of course." Chloe patted her purse. "It's right here." Chloe reached into her bag and withdrew a jar. She crossed the room and handed it to Josephine. Josephine pressed a roll of sweat-covered hundred-dollar bills into her hand. The cash surprised Chloe; customers always paid by check. But she took the money without protest and returned to the couch. With false brightness, Chloe said, "Pleasure doing business with you."

Chloe bent down and tucked the wad of cash inside her purse. When she looked up again, Josephine was staring at her, her expression pained. "I'm sorry, Chloe. I didn't want to do this. But my niece, well, she was so determined. And I need her to watch my babies when I'm gone."

Chloe didn't understand. Then the Chicana nurse stepped forward. Her heavy Spanish accent suddenly gone, the woman flashed a badge at Chloe, saying, "Detective Rodriguez, San Diego PD. Chloe Baker, you are under arrest for distribution of narcotics." Chloe rose numbly to her feet. The policewoman/nurse navigated her gently but firmly away from the couch, saying, "You have the right to remain silent. Anything you say can and will be used against you in a court of law. You have the right to an attorney . . ."

When Chloe reached the front door, she turned back to Josephine. "This is why you kept the dogs away, isn't it?"

Josephine nodded. "I couldn't bear to have them be a part of this."

Chloe smiled. "I understand."

When Sarah finally got pregnant, she was determined to be ruthlessly positive about it. She would not jinx her twins by complaining about minor inconveniences. No, she would remain sunny. She read all the feel-good books she could find on pregnancy and child-rearing, blocking out dark thoughts by force of will. But as the days wore on and her nausea went from bad to worse, one book kept bobbing up in Sarah's consciousness: Rosemary's Baby, *Ira Levin's tale about Satan's mother. Rosemary had had morning sickness too, right?*

47

Sarah's Visitors

Sarah was in her bathroom, vomiting for the second time that morning, when she heard a knock at her door. She called out, "Just a minute!" and splashed cold water on her face. The knocking got louder. She wiped her face on a towel and winced at her reflection in the mirror. She was a mess: red hair tousled, huge bags under her eyes, a small vomit stain on her gray T-shirt. Again, she heard knocking. Rushing to the door, she called out, "All right, I'm coming!"

She opened the door without bothering to look through the peephole, her first big mistake of the day. In stepped two uniformed policemen. They barked, "LAPD."

A balding detective in a rumpled gray suit came in after them. He flashed his badge. "Detective Brandl, San Diego PD. Are you Sarah Sloane?"

Sarah nodded, her sluggish, sleep-deprived mind suddenly coming wide awake. San Diego PD with an LAPD escort. So San Diego was leading the investigation, and it had already lined up help from the LA police. That meant San Diego was taking this thing very seriously, not a good sign. Sarah mumbled, "Yes, I'm Sarah Sloane."

Flashing a folded document at her, Detective Brandl announced, "We have a warrant to search the premises." He jammed the warrant quickly back into his pocket and gestured for the uniforms to get started.

Suddenly, the lawyerly side of Sarah's brain revved like a rusty but still powerful engine. She held up her hand for the uniforms to stay where they were. "One moment, gentlemen. May I see the search warrant?"

Detective Brandl rolled his eyes and sighed theatrically. Police shows had made life so tedious. These days, everybody was insisting on their rights. He handed Sarah the crumpled warrant and waited while she looked through it.

Sarah took her time reading through the warrant. Then she handed it back to Detective Brandl. "Everything seems to be in order." She gestured for the two uniforms to enter and then turned back to Brandl. "Now, if you don't mind, I would like to call my attorney. I think he would want to be here for this."

Again, Brandl rolled his eyes. "Fine, but you know we don't have to wait for him before we get started."

"I know. Don't worry, he'll be quick." Sarah strode into the living room with Brandl trailing close behind her.

She reached for her phone and keyed in her old boss's number. After a pause, Marty's secretary put her through. Before Sarah could get a word out, Marty said, "Sarah Sloane! How the hell are you? Had any good sandwiches lately?"

Sarah took a deep breath and prayed that she knew Marty as well as she thought she did. He might be a shit to everyone else but not to his clients. For his clients, he was a fierce white knight, a savior with a bottomless briefcase of tricks. "Marty, I'm in a bind. The police are searching my apartment. Can you get over here?"

There was silence on the other end of the line. Then Marty said, "I'll be there in ten minutes." He hung up.

Sarah held the receiver to her chest for a moment. Marty would be here. Everything would be all right. He would make it right. Relief turned to panic as Sarah felt a wave of nausea wash over her. Turning to Brandl, she begged, "I need to go to the bathroom."

Brandl folded his arms across his chest. "And flush a kilo down the toilet? I don't think so."

Sarah opened her mouth to protest. But her eloquence was cut off by a torrent of vomit, most of it landing on Brandl's shoes. When she was done, she wiped her mouth on her sleeve. Her eyes were tearing. "I'm so sorry. It's morning sickness. I'm pregnant."

Wiping his shoe off on the carpet, Brandl smirked. "Congratulations."

Annie always got annoyed at the cryptic warnings in Shakespeare: "Beware the ides of March, Caesar!" "Hey, Macbeth, look out for those woods moving on Dunsinane!" Skip the poetic language. Annie liked her warnings nice and clear: "The British are coming!" There, was that so hard?

48

Chloe Calls

Annie was dyeing her hair with Miss Clairol "Roasted Chestnut," number six, when Chloe called on the house landline. Sitting in her bathroom with a plastic grocery bag tied around her head, Annie let the call go to her answering machine. After the beep, Chloe's voice boomed, "Hello, Annabelle. I thought you should know that I have been arrested. I'm in the lockup at the police station downtown. When you get a chance, please be a dear and come down to bail me out. Although my cellmate recommends King Stahlman Bail Bonds, I prefer to go with family."

Annie ran into the bedroom and grabbed the receiver. "Mom?"

"Oh, marvelous. You're home. I know it's old-fashioned of me, but I loathe answering machines. They're so impersonal."

"You're in jail?"

Chloe sighed. "Yes, I'm afraid so."

"What happened?"

"Oh, it's a long story. I was down at the Sands, meeting with a customer, and an undercover police officer arrested me for selling drugs." Chloe sounded nonchalant, almost bored by Annie's questions. Moodwise, Chloe had always been a contrarian. She loved to jazz up the mundane with histrionics, but she remained remarkably calm in a crisis.

Annie sat down hard on her bed, the wind knocked out of her. "You were arrested for selling drugs?"

"Yes, I'm afraid so. Terrible mix-up. I can't go into details right now. The police clerk, a very considerate young man, informed me that this call might be recorded. Please come as soon as you can."

Her adrenaline rushing, Annie said, "Of course. I'll be right there, Mom."

"Oh, and one last thing, be a dear and bring my other handbag along, the red one. I have a splitting headache, and it's got my Advil in it. At least I think it does. Please check and make sure my Advil's in there before you leave the house."

"Okay, yeah, sure."

Her voice suddenly stern, Chloe said, "I *mean* it, Annabelle. I *have* to have that Advil. You have to check my purse for it."

"Fine, sure." Annie hung up the phone. She ran to the hallway for her purse and was about to head out the door when she remembered the hair dye and plastic baggie on her head. She raced back up the stairs, falling and smacking her knee on the top step. Cursing, she showered and rinsed the dye out of her hair. Then she dressed and headed out the door.

She was halfway down her front walk when she remembered Chloe's handbag. Damn! She ran back to the house, grabbed the handbag from the guest room, and checked to make sure it had Advil inside it. It didn't. Instead, it contained a hairbrush, a lipstick, and three eight-balls of cocaine in small clear plastic bags. These were the drugs that Chloe had just bought from Stephanie for the family business. *This* was what Chloe had wanted Annie to take care of. Annie got a mental runner's cramp as her brain raced to catch up with reality. Chloe had been warning Annie to get rid of the drugs before the police arrived.

Hands shaking, Annie opened the three baggies and dumped their contents into the toilet in the guest bathroom. This was a crime too, wasn't it? *Law & Order* said so. "Obstruction of evidence," "destruction of justice"—something like that, right? Annie flushed the toilet twice. Then she rushed off to bail out her mother.

When Annie read The Lion, the Witch and the Wardrobe *in fourth grade, she couldn't understand why the Pevensie children had forgiven their creepy brother Edmund. The kid had sold out his own siblings—his own blood! And for what? A few bars of Turkish delight? Annie had rushed down to the candy store to try some. It tasted like feet, evil feet. Annie wasn't big on forgiveness, so asking it from someone else was scary.*

49

Chloe's Grand Sacrifice

Annie had so little to offer to Sarah: just apologies, a plate full of peanut butter cookies, and a promise to do whatever she could to clean up the mess she'd made. Annie followed behind her mother as they entered Sarah's apartment. She watched jealously as Sarah and Chloe hugged each other with real warmth. Then, with a shaky smile, Annie stepped forward and handed her plate of cookies to Sarah, saying, "I made these for you."

Unsmiling, Sarah set the plate on the table in the foyer. "Thanks, but I'm having trouble keeping anything down these days."

Chloe said, "Ah, nausea. The curse of the expectant mother."

"And the recently arrested," Sarah griped, shooting a dirty look at Annie.

Chloe mused, "Did getting arrested make you nauseous, dear? I myself found it invigorating. I've never felt quite so alive as I did when the police placed those handcuffs on me. It made me understand the appeal of S&M, not that I'd try it myself. At least, I don't think I would."

Annie said, "Um, well, maybe Michael can have the cookies." She looked around nervously. "Is he here?" She dreaded facing Sarah's husband. She suspected he was no longer a fan. Hell, even Annie wasn't Annie's fan anymore.

Sensing Annie's anxiety, Sarah said, "No, you can relax. He's out getting groceries."

Being told she could relax did not relax Annie at all. "I guess he must hate me now." Annie's own husband was furious at her. But his anger was tempered by his fear of her going to jail, of losing her. Also, and Annie hadn't expected this, Harry said he understood why she'd done it. She was a mama bear protecting her cubs—okay, swindling people for her cubs, whatever.

Sarah said, "No, Michael's given you a full pardon, and me too. He's saving his anger for the criminal justice system. He thinks most drugs should be legal, says we didn't do anything wrong." Sarah shook her head, not quite believing her luck. She was grateful for her husband's socially liberal, pro-pothead, pro-Sarah take on things. But she still couldn't believe how supportive Michael was being, how, for the first time, he was completely there for her—now, when she didn't even deserve it. But did anyone really get what they deserved? No. Sarah still couldn't quite wrap her mind around the fact that she'd been screwed by someone she'd tried to help: Natalie. Sarah's good deed had bitten her in the ass.

She led Chloe and Annie into her living room. She gestured toward the couch. "Please, sit down." Looking only at Chloe, Sarah asked, "Can I get you anything? Water, juice, soda?"

Chloe asked, "Do you have anything stronger than that, dear?"

Sarah smiled. "I have white wine."

Chloe answered, "Wonderful, I'd love a glass. Make it two."

Annie objected, "Mom, I can't. I have to drive."

Chloe smiled placidly, explaining, "Both glasses are for me, dear. With you driving and our beloved Sarah pregnant, I'm afraid I'll have to drink for all of us." Chloe winked. Her recent arrest and Annie's resulting guilt had bought Chloe full immunity from Annie's tedious rules. Sarah fetched two glasses of wine and carried them over to Chloe. Chloe set one glass down on the coffee table. She cradled the other in her right hand, saying, "Ah, chardonnay, every year is a good one."

Settling in an armchair, Sarah used the remote to turn on the television. "My lawyer said we should expect to see a piece about ourselves on the six o'clock news."

Chloe leaned forward, her eyes wide with excitement. "Really?"

Sarah nodded. "Marty got a call from Chuck Sanders over at Channel Three."

Annie gaped. "Marty is your lawyer? But he was awful to you. He—"

Sarah interrupted, "He's my new best friend."

Chastened, Annie nodded. Chloe said, "Oh yes, you must thank Marty for me. I simply adore the lawyer he found for me."

Sarah asked, "He sent you to Frank Peterson, right?"

Chloe said dreamily, "Yes. The man is a legal genius. You should've seen the way he handled my arraignment. He has the most marvelous head of silver hair. And that voice! So commanding!"

Sarah said, "I'm glad Peterson is working out so well."

Laying a hand on Sarah's knee, Chloe cooed, "And you, Sarah dear, how did your arraignment go?" From Chloe's casual girlishness, she might have been asking about a hair appointment.

Sarah blushed. "It was mortifying. That ADA, Thatch, asked for five hundred thousand dollars in bail."

Annie said hopefully, "But Marty shot him down, right?"

Sarah rolled her eyes. "Oh sure, but only after I agreed to surrender my passport and wear a leg bracelet." Sarah raised her right ankle, showing off the bulky black contraption. It was the nastiest bit of jewelry she had ever worn.

Chloe shook her head in disgust. "That Thatch character is a menace. He demanded three hundred thousand bail for me. Fortunately, Frank was able to make the judge see sense." Chloe sighed, a seventy-year-old woman with a schoolgirl crush.

Chloe's eyes were suddenly drawn to the television. Anchorman Chuck Sanders's basso profundo filled the apartment. Sanders announced, "And just south of our fair city, officials in San Diego have uncovered a major drug ring operating in the exclusive, upscale neighborhood of La Jolla. A drug ring with a twist . . ."

The camera cut from Sanders to a series of shots showcasing La Jolla: the Cove, the Ferrari dealership, the jewelry stores on Girard Avenue, the Torrey Pines golf course. Sanders droned, "Famous for its panoramic views, high-end boutiques, spas, and world-class golf courses, La Jolla is a magnet for tourists. It is also home to some of the wealthiest people in the world. Politicos like Mitt Romney and John McCain. Movie stars like Raquel Welch and NFL greats. And now, according to sources at the San Diego District Attorney's Office, La Jolla has become a hunting ground for sophisticated criminals. Just as Bernie Madoff preyed upon greedy financial investors . . ." The camera showed Bernie Madoff doing his perp walk down the streets of New York flanked by dozens of reporters.

Sarah murmured, "Oh shit . . ."

The screen switched back to a slide show of La Jolla's mansions. Sanders went on, "A small group of female con artists preyed upon the vanity of La Jolla's richest women, getting them to pay two thousand dollars a jar for face cream spiked with cocaine. We go now to field reporter Stacey Sagher in San Diego."

Stacey Sagher smiled from the steps of the state courthouse. "Thanks, Chuck. I'm here with Assistant District Attorney Oliver

Thatch, the lead prosecutor on the case." Sagher turned to Thatch. "Tell me, why did these con artists put cocaine in their face cream?"

Thatch shook his head gravely, as if personally aggrieved by all the evil in the world. "Well, Stacey, these con artists preyed upon aging wealthy women. They told their victims that this cream would take years off their faces. Best I can tell, they spiked the cream with cocaine because they wanted their victims to become addicted to the stuff. That way, the victims would buy more."

Sagher marveled, "At two thousand dollars a jar?"

"That's right, Stacey."

"And has your office taken any action against the perpetrators?"

"Well, our investigation is ongoing. But I can report that we have charged the two leaders of the conspiracy: Sarah Sloane and Chloe Baker. We expect more arrests to follow."

Sagher thanked Thatch and then turned back to the camera. "I'm Stacey Sagher, reporting from downtown San Diego. Back to you, Chuck."

The camera returned to Chuck Sanders sitting behind the anchor desk. "Thanks, Stacey." Then, as if taking Thatch's cue, Sanders shook his head, musing soulfully, "Two thousand dollars a jar for face cream . . . the pressure society puts on women to look good has really gotten out of control." Then abruptly Sanders brightened. "Up next, the new Brazilian blowout. Is the hair treatment worth the high price tag? And what are the risks?"

Sarah switched off the television. "This is bad. This is really bad."

Chloe answered, "Oh, don't be so gloomy."

Sarah countered, "They're comparing us to Bernie Madoff!"

Chloe shrugged. "Yes, all right, that bit was bad. But I thought the rest was fairly innocuous. So we sold some cream with cocaine in it to some wealthy women? Is that really such a crime?"

Sarah said, "Yes, it is!" Sarah's eyes began to water, and her chin trembled. "Worst part is, I can't even apologize to them. Valerie, Kim, all of my old clients have been calling. You wouldn't believe the messages I've been getting."

Chloe asked gently, "Nasty stuff?"

Sarah sniffed back a tear. "No . . . Yes . . . It's a mix. Most are furious. Some are just confused and hurt. Kim was actually worried about me, if you can believe that."

"Did you call any of them back?" asked Annie.

"No. I can't. Marty says I can't talk to any of the victims in the case. It's the old anything I say 'can and will be used against me in a court of law.'" Annie nodded. She'd heard that line a gazillion times on her beloved cop shows.

Annie rushed to reassure her friend. "Sarah, it's going to be all right."

Sarah winced. "Easy for you to say. You haven't even been charged yet." The police had enough to charge Sarah and Chloe with distributing narcotics because they'd been the ones to actually deliver the cream. Annie'd been arrested. And thanks to *Breaking Bad*, they suspected their little chemist might be the mastermind, but couldn't prove it yet.

Annie said, "I'll talk to the police. I'll say that you knew nothing about the cocaine. I'll say it was all my idea."

"It *was* all your idea!" Sarah's eyes filled with tears.

Annie said, "I know. I'll just be telling them the truth. But it *is* the truth. That's got to count for something."

Sarah sniffed and wiped her eyes. "Like any of that matters."

Annie flailed, "But it does matter. They'll have to believe us. They can't prove you knew about the cocaine because you didn't."

Sarah blew her nose loudly. "Don't you get it, Annie? No one is going to believe anything I say. Thatch will drag me into court, charge me with drug dealing, and then—when I deny it—he'll destroy my credibility. He'll put up dozens of witnesses who'll say that I told them all sorts of lies about our cream. All that crap about Cassandra Blake and our 'patented bio-extract,' not to mention the great Dr. Étinav.

Étinav—*vanité* spelled backward—very cute. The jury will figure that if I lied about all that other stuff, I must be lying about cocaine too."

Chloe said airily, "Yes, people are so strange about lying. So judgmental. You'd think they'd be more forgiving. After all, everyone lies every day. You'd assume a jury could differentiate between little harmless lies and the larger terrible ones. But they can't." Chloe shook her head and took another long sip of wine. She disapproved of disapproval.

Annie pressed on, "Sarah, if I tell them you didn't know anything about the cocaine, that's got to count for something. Right now, they think I'm some dopey housewife, that I was completely out of the loop. I can change that. I can make them see that I was the mastermind behind the whole thing. I'll flash my chemistry PhD at them. I'll explain how I came up with the idea to use cocaine, how I fixed the dosage. If I build myself up, maybe they won't be so fixated on you."

Sarah said bleakly, "Maybe, but I wouldn't count on it. I think we'd both end up going to jail."

Putting her wineglass down, Chloe announced, "Neither of you is going to jail. I won't allow it."

Sarah said, "I'm afraid it's not going to be up to you, Chloe."

Jutting out her chin, Chloe insisted, "Oh yes, it will be. Sarah, darling, I may not know anything about the law, but I do know human nature. This Thatch character is a fool. He's making the same mistake I've seen dozens of directors make. He's overpromising."

"Overpromising?"

Chloe nodded sagely. "Oh yes. Directors do it all the time. They start a production with grand ambitions. They go on and on about how revolutionary the show will be, how transcendent. But then reality gets in the way. Time runs out; funds dry up. Big ideas fall away. The director gives up his grand vision and lowers his sights, realizing he'll be lucky if he can put up the same hackneyed show that his predecessors did."

Annie said gently, "Mom, Thatch isn't putting on a show. He's putting a criminal case together."

Chloe countered, "Darling, a criminal case is just like a show. If Thatch intends to fight our version of events, if he won't settle for one of us coming forward and pleading guilty, then he will have to put on a show. He'll have to find witnesses to prove that Sarah knew about the cocaine. He'll have to document every sale, tie every knot. That is a lot of work and resources, especially for a case involving small amounts of cocaine and not very much money. The two of you raised less than two hundred thousand dollars. And you used less than two hundred grams of cocaine. That's not much for San Diego. Frank told me that millions of dollars' worth of cocaine passes through the city every month. The San Diego police can barely keep up with it. Do you really think they're going to waste tons of money prosecuting us when they have real crimes to solve?"

Annie countered, "Mom, I keep telling you, what I did was a real crime."

Chloe batted this argument away with a wave of her hand, saying, "Yes. Technically speaking, it was a crime. And I am positive this Thatch person has worked himself into a lather about it. But I doubt his superiors will want to pull out all the stops and take this case to trial, not in this political climate."

Annie asked, "Political?"

"Yes, of course. You and Sarah were taking what was rightfully yours. You were proletarian heroes siphoning wealth from the filthy rich, the top 1 percent. To them, the money they spent was nothing but pocket change. To you, it was . . ." Chloe faltered for a moment, then eyed Sarah's swollen abdomen. "To you, it was *life*."

Annie said, "Mom, I don't—"

But Sarah cut in, "Wait a minute, Annie. Chloe may have a point. This case would be a PR nightmare. The government might walk away if one of us pleads out."

Annie nodded. "Good, so I'll take the plea. And if I'm lucky—"

Chloe said sharply, "You will do nothing of the sort, Annabelle."

"Mom, it's the only way—"

"No, it's not the only way. And you both know it." Her voice softening, Chloe told Annie, "I know you want to make amends to Sarah. You're desperate to make amends. But this is not the way to do it. Neither of you can afford to go to prison. You are both too important."

Annie echoed, "Too important?"

Chloe explained, "You're both mothers now, mothers with young children. For those children, you are the most important person in the world." Focusing on Annie, Chloe went on, "You may think a brief stint in jail, a few months apart, will leave them unscathed, but you'd be wrong. Trust me, I know. I spent most of your childhood on the road. I thought you'd be fine without me so long as I left you with an acceptable substitute: your father, a nanny. But sometimes there are no acceptable substitutes. Children need their mothers."

Annie paled. She'd never spoken to Chloe about her long absences. She thought that Chloe had been oblivious to the pain they had caused. Chloe went on, "No, I will be the one to go to jail. You and Sarah have no business there."

Sarah said, "Chloe, that's sweet of you to offer. But how are you going to get them to believe that you were in charge of all this?"

Chloe smiled. "Sarah, darling, you've never seen me onstage, but trust me, I can be very convincing. Thanks to my work at the Sands, the police already have a large group of witnesses against me. The Sands crowd will be a prosecutor's delight. They're easy to locate. They have plenty of time on their hands. And being a witness will be just about the most exciting thing some of those old biddies have done in years. What's more, I can finally put my decades of struggling with pills and alcohol to good use. I can flash my certificates from the Betty Ford Clinic and all those other useless rehabs to establish my credentials as an addict. I'll tell the police that I spiked my daughter's face cream with cocaine to give it some zazz, and the police will believe me because . . . well, a junkie will add cocaine to just about anything. We use it the way

Italians use basil. I'll say that I kept the two of you in the dark because you're both so prudish about drugs."

Sarah gaped. "You really think you can make them buy all that?"

Chloe repeated, "Darling, I am a magnificent actress."

Annie said proudly, "She is."

Chloe turned to Sarah. "I just want one thing in exchange."

"What?"

"I want you to forgive my daughter. I want the two of you to make peace with each other."

Sarah pursed her lips together, considering Chloe's demand. Then she said, "It's hard to forgive . . ."

Chloe waved this off. "Darling, forgiving Annie may be hard, but replacing her is impossible. She's been your best friend for twenty years, and she has only failed you once. That's a pretty impressive record. Forgive her. You won't regret it."

Sarah looked over at Annie. "I think I can forgive you, but first . . ."

Annie asked, "First?"

Sarah smiled. "First, I'll need you to bring those cookies in from the foyer. I'm starving." Annie jumped up quickly to fetch the cookies. When she returned with them, tears were running down her face. Sarah asked, "Why are you crying?"

Annie put the cookies on the coffee table and swabbed away her tears. "I'm just so relieved." She looked down at Sarah. "Why are *you* crying?"

"I'm pregnant." The two friends hugged, and a moment later a crying Chloe joined them on the couch. Annie and Sarah drew back at the sight of Chloe's tears.

Chloe explained, "I love to cry too. It's just so dramatic!"

Oliver Thatch loved the prosecutor from the true-crime bestseller Fatal Vision. *Years after reading it, Thatch still remembered how the drab but dogged prosecutor worked for over a decade to bring a triple murderer to justice. What Thatch didn't remember was that* Fatal Vision*'s author, Joe McGinniss, had originally been brought in by the murderer's defense team to write a piece exonerating him. McGinniss, like many journalists before him, had slipped his leash and gone where he wasn't supposed to go.*

50

The Price of Fame

Thatch watched his star on the rise. Thanks to his information, the *Union-Tribune* led with a teaser on page one, followed by a full spread on page five. It was all there: the two-thousand-dollar price tag, the cocaine, the bogus story about the reclusive French genius, the equally bogus rumors about movie stars using the cream. The *Trib* even got aging screen siren Cassandra Blake to go on record claiming that she'd never heard of Dr. Étinav or his cream. The *Trib* gave the story sex appeal by throwing in glossy color photos of Blake and dishy defendant Sarah Sloane. Best of all, the *Trib* added gratifyingly long quotes from Thatch, the lead prosecutor on the case.

The *Trib* article was just the beginning. Everyone was talking about Thatch's big case. The *La Jolla Light* and the *La Jolla Village News* focused on the all-important question of how the scandal would impact La Jolla's real estate prices. The editors concluded that crime waves were usually bad news, but the glamour of this particular scam might actually enhance La Jolla's prestige. After all, La Jolla had been targeted precisely because its residents could afford to buy just about anything at any price. Not bad PR. Hadn't Madoff's scams reminded the world yet again of the opulence of Manhattan's Upper East Side?

And now the nationals were beginning to call. AARP's magazine wanted to explore the plight of elderly victims over at the Sands. *Allure, Marie Claire,* and lesser beauty rags tut-tutted over how the Baker case had undermined consumers' faith in beauty creams. Most exciting of all, Thatch had started getting voice mails from the heavy hitters: the *New York Times,* the *Los Angeles Times,* even *People* magazine.

Yesiree, Oliver Thatch was coming up in the world. He could feel it. When his boss, Brian McCafferty, summoned Thatch to his office on Wednesday morning, Thatch practically danced his way up to the nineteenth floor.

When Thatch entered McCafferty's office, he was surprised to find Maria Rodriguez sitting in one of the chairs opposite the great man's desk. The hugely pregnant detective nodded to Thatch but didn't smile. McCafferty wasn't smiling either. He gestured for Thatch to sit. Thatch sat down and looked expectantly at his boss, but McCafferty said nothing. Instead, McCafferty flipped through a pile of newspapers strewn across his desk: the *Union-Tribune*, the *La Jolla Village News,* the *Del Mar Times*. McCafferty studied the newspapers in silence while Thatch resisted the urge to bite at his cuticles. Thatch smiled at Rodriguez, but she avoided his gaze.

Finally, McCafferty broke the silence. "Your La Jolla case has been getting a lot of press attention."

Thatch ventured a smile. "Yes, sir."

McCafferty looked up from his newspapers, his icy blue eyes focusing on Thatch. For a millisecond, Thatch felt an absurd impulse to protect his groin. McCafferty said, "You've been showboating with reporters, haven't you?"

Thatch colored. "I wouldn't call it showboating. I've taken a few calls, that's all. Answered a few questions." Thatch laughed nervously. "Mostly just fact-checking."

"When you were on Channel Three last night, was that just fact-checking?"

Thatch flailed. "No, of course not. I, uh—"

McCafferty cut him off. "You've been with this office for ten years. Right, Thatch?"

"Eleven, this spring."

"So you know that we have a PR staff up in the front office, don't you?"

"Yes, but—" Thatch's antennae were up; McCafferty was cross-examining him.

McCafferty went on, "And the whole point of that press staff—the only reason we pay their salaries—is to make sure that we get our stories out there when and how we want them out there. You realize that, right?" Thatch nodded. McCafferty continued, "Because if we don't control the stories, then we don't control our cases. Release information too early and you can run into all kinds of problems: witnesses get scared off; evidence gets destroyed; defendants lawyer up too soon. You've heard of that sort of stuff happening, haven't you?"

"Yes, sir, but in this case—"

McCafferty said sharply, "In this case what?"

Thatch fumbled. "We don't have to worry about witnesses getting scared off. These perps aren't violent drug lords. They're a couple of women selling face cream. And these victims aren't exactly meek. These are rich, sophisticated women. They're not scared of being arrested or deported."

"So tell me, Thatch, what are they scared of?"

"Excuse me?"

"What are rich La Jolla socialites scared of?" McCafferty waited for an answer. When he didn't get one, he forged ahead, "Impropriety, damage to their precious reputations."

Thatch countered, "But they haven't done anything wrong. They didn't know the cocaine was in the cream. Why should they—"

"You're asking me *why* a La Jolla matron wouldn't want the rest of the world to find out that she has been using cocaine?"

"But these women didn't know about the coke. They have nothing to be ashamed of."

"That's right. So why should they be made to suffer?"

Thatch said, "But they're not going to suffer. They come in, testify about buying the cream, and they're done. None of them is going to jail . . ."

"I'm not talking about jail, you idiot. I'm talking about embarrassment."

Thatch was lost. "Embarrassment?"

"You ever heard of the Bigboy case?"

Thatch shook his head. McCafferty smiled. "Great little case. The feds had it. Bigboy was a male enhancement drug. It was supposed to put the ram back in your rod. The drug company ran a gazillion ads on late-night TV for the stuff. Remember Happy Harvey? The guy with the megawatt smile, the '50s décor, and that banjo music in the background? That ad was for Bigboy. The company got thousands of guys to send in for the stuff. Only problem was . . . it didn't do anything. These guys were as impotent as ever, only they were out a few hundred bucks. When the feds tried to go after the company for fraud, they figured they had an airtight case. Blatant lies, a drug that does nothing, the works. But there was one problem. None of the customers wanted to testify. No one wanted to stand up in open court and admit that he ordered this stuff because he couldn't get it up. Nobody wanted to come forward as Captain Flaccid."

Thatch gulped but fought on. "But this isn't like that. This isn't embarrassing—"

McCafferty cut in, "Not embarrassing? Are you nuts? Every victim you put on the stand will have to admit that she was using cocaine for months, that she was, on some level, a doper. She'll also have to admit that she was a fool, that she was gullible enough to buy all that crap about Dr. Étinav. And on top of that, she'll have to cop to being totally obsessed with looking young."

"These victims aren't exactly alone on that. Loads of women get plastic surgery."

"Yes, but they don't go around bragging about it."

Thatch countered, "I see what you're saying, but I don't think we have to worry about this. I mean, the press stories on this case have been very sympathetic to the victims."

"So far."

Thatch winced. "You think that will change?"

"It already is changing. That's how the press operates. It bites away at one side of a story until it gets bored, and then it chews on the other side of the story. That's why timing is everything when you're dealing with these guys. Your little piece in the *Trib* may have sympathized with the victims. But these later pieces don't. Already, you've got the *Reader* making fun of the victims for being dupes. You've got the religious magazines talking about the sin of vanity. And soon the nationals will get into it. The bloggers will have a great time talking about how rich and superficial the victims were, how shallow. How they deserved to be tricked out of their money—"

"Okay, so the vics might get some bad press. But they'll still have to testify. I can make them testify. I'll subpoena them."

McCafferty smirked. "You think subpoenas can fix this?"

Thatch swallowed. "Well, sure, we do it all the time on drug cases . . ."

McCafferty shook his head. "This isn't one of your little drug cases. These are white-collar folks, with white-collar resources. You subpoena them and they'll lawyer up. Hell, they already have lawyered up."

Thatch repeated helplessly, "But they didn't do anything wrong!"

"They used cocaine, didn't they? Last time I checked, that's a no-no. Certainly a good enough basis for taking the Fifth."

Thatch countered, "I'll immunize them! They can't take the Fifth if I promise not to prosecute them."

"Oh, sure. You'll promise, but what about the feds? The feds can still go after them."

"The feds wouldn't do that!"

"Of course they wouldn't. But that won't stop these ladies' lawyers from arguing otherwise. These aren't public defenders, Thatch. These are high-priced lawyers who bill by the hour. They'll paper us to death. Anything to stop their precious clients from embarrassing themselves."

"We don't know that that's how things will play out. We can't know—"

"Oh yes, we do. Rodriguez is already running into walls."

Thatch looked over at Rodriguez. He finally understood why she was here. She had the good grace to squirm slightly in her chair. "It's true. I can't get through to any of the victims. Even those old bats at the home are referring me to their lawyers."

McCafferty scowled. "And I've gotten a dozen calls from eminent husbands telling me that our office should stop harassing their wives or else."

Thatch gaped. "Or else what?"

"Or else they'll sue. That's what rich people do when you annoy them. They sue you."

Thatch sunk back in his chair, thoroughly deflated. For the first time that morning, McCafferty looked at Thatch with something approaching sympathy. McCafferty said, "I know. You wanted to get out front of the story. You wanted a little glory for yourself. Lots of prosecutors do." McCafferty shook his head. "But, my friend, you screwed up big-time. If you'd waited, we could have lined up our witnesses before the press got hold of it. We could have quietly built up a case, forced the defendants to plead out and do serious time, and then—when we had our stiff sentences all lined up—then we could have taken our bows in the papers. The problem isn't what you did, but when you did it. And now . . ."

Thatch asked, "And now?"

McCafferty shrugged. "Now you're like those Bigboy customers. An impotent shmuck."

Chloe never understood why the heroine of Dickens's A Tale of Two Cities *chose the boringly moralistic Charles Darnay over the cynical, witty Sydney Carton. True, Carton drank too much, but that was a sign of personal depth, wasn't it? And who couldn't love the way Carton sacrificed himself, allowing himself to be executed so that the woman he loved wouldn't lose her dull hubby? And what an exit line: "It is a far, far better thing that I do, than I have ever done before." And then there was some stuff about Jesus. Yes, Carton had gotten religion in the end. But oh well, no one was perfect.*

51

Chloe Takes the Stand

Overnight, Sarah and Chloe morphed from drug-peddling pariahs into national heroines. At first, the press focused on Sarah. Her gorgeous face and Harvard pedigree made her media catnip. She became the ultimate best friend. She had risked everything to help pay her best friend's son's medical bills. What a pal! *People, Access Hollywood,* and *More* magazine used Sarah's ten minutes of fame as an excuse to run top-ten lists of female friendships, real and fictional. Annie and Sarah came in ahead of the *Sex and the City* girls but behind Jennifer Aniston and Courteney Cox.

When the press tired of the good-friend angle, Marty Goldstein fed them an even better one. Sitting down with Ellen on *Ellen*, Marty explained that Sarah loved Annie's little boy, the photogenic, apple-cheeked Oscar. He was like a son to her. That connection was everything to Sarah because—hold on to your Kleenex, ladies!—Sarah had been struggling for years to have a child of her own. She wanted a baby more than anything else in the world. Could Ellen understand that? Of course, she could. Ellen understood everything. And, there, on *Ellen*, Marty was happy to reveal the good news. After six years of trying, Sarah had finally gotten pregnant, with twins! Ellen was so excited. Wasn't this exciting! Ellen insisted on leading Marty and her studio audience in one of her trademark happy dances. The episode ended with a very plump Marty Goldstein doing the worm across the studio floor, a visual that became a YouTube sensation.

When the press finally calmed down about Sarah's twins, it was Chloe's turn. Chloe had a more complex image. Although nerdy chemist Annie had mixed the creams, it was Chloe who—without telling anyone!—had spiked the concoction with cocaine. So Chloe started out in the public mind as a drug pusher.

Frank Peterson began rehabilitating his client by having her come out as an addict. Chloe had spent her entire life battling alcohol, pills, and—yes—cocaine. She'd done time at the Betty Ford Clinic and other rehabs, but none of them cured her. She was a lost soul, helpless against her own demons. Drugging the good women of La Jolla had been a mistake. On the E! network, Frank Peterson shook his head, explaining, "To err is human. And my client is very human."

Now Chloe was full of remorse, so much remorse that she'd finally managed to get clean. Her son, a recovering addict and a very promising actor, had talked her into joining Narcotics Anonymous *and* Alcoholics Anonymous—a "double winner." Chloe had not used cocaine or alcohol in months. She had gotten in touch with her higher power and was working the steps, taking life one day at a time.

When a few news cycles had passed and Chloe had done enough repenting for her sins, Frank Peterson moved on to phase two: turning her from a recovering sinner into a saint. In a brilliant PR move, he co-opted the elderly press. *AARP, Active Over 50, and Reminisce* had all encountered a crotchety wall of silence at the Sands. The Sands's well-heeled matrons had images to think of, legacies to protect. These women had donated thousands, even millions, to charities so that their names would live on forever atop hospitals, schools, and community centers. Unlike everyone else in America, they did not want ten minutes of cheap fame. They wanted decades of high-end respect. Patrons of the arts? Yes. Cocaine users? No.

The senior rags ran their stories anyway, along with tip lists on how seniors could avoid being victims ("that understanding stranger who claims to have known you at school might not be who he says he is"). But their stories lacked the personal angle that magazines thrive on. Chloe's lawyer came to the rescue, giving them full access to his client. Chloe instantly became "America's Grandma." After all, she'd done everything for her grandson! Chloe proved that grandparents were not just bit players in their grandchildren's lives. Grandparents were—sniff, sniff—the "grandest parents" a child would ever have. They offered unbridled love coupled with decades of hard-won wisdom. Just a month after running their pieces on elder crime, the senior press made Chloe their cover girl. And Chloe did not disappoint. The magazines put her quotes in boldface: "I'd do anything for my grandchild: cheat, steal, even move to Pittsburgh!" "Boundaries are for crime scenes, not one's flesh and blood!" "Let's face it, young parents often have no idea what they're doing. When it comes to child-rearing or sex, I'll take the wizened old pro over the perky novice any day!"

On the day of Chloe's sentencing, the courtroom was packed with paparazzi and fans. Sarah and Annie sat with their families in the front row. Chloe's lawyer had been very clear on the importance of presenting a united front. Chloe's people—especially her three photogenic grandchildren—had to be out front and center. Their presence would remind everyone how much the little tykes would miss their beloved granny if the judge sent her away to prison. Oscar and Rachel were too young and bored to understand the proceedings, but theatrical Maddie had the time of her life posing demurely for the press. And of course Sarah had to be there—her massively pregnant belly punctuated the point that Chloe had sinned "for the children." And Annie was there too, prettily wholesome in a blue flowered dress that Sarah had chosen for her. Annie fidgeted nervously as Oscar and Rachel squirmed on her and Harry's laps, and Sarah gave her hand a reassuring squeeze.

Fortunately for Chloe, most of her "victims" did not show up in the courtroom. The Priscillas and Reginas of La Jolla didn't want anyone knowing that they'd used cocaine, albeit unwittingly. Though worried about Sarah, Valerie was still too hurt to come to court, and Kim was busy teaching.

Chloe's plan had worked. Oliver Thatch could insinuate all he wanted, but he couldn't prove that Sarah knew about the cocaine. So in the end he dropped the charges against her. He never even bothered opening a dossier against Annie. And his case against Chloe was weak. With no witnesses except Natalie Wilson and her reluctant Aunt Josephine, Thatch couldn't even make the five-gram requirement for a single count of distributing narcotics. Instead, he had to settle for charging Chloe with that great prosecutorial catchall—fraud (for lying about the contents of the cream). Chloe had pled guilty and now faced up to three years in jail.

Standing before the court, Thatch argued that Chloe should receive the maximum. But it was a halfhearted performance. Thatch wanted this case over. He no longer craved advancement. He wanted to crawl into his office and go back to working on his low-profile wiretap cases.

When Thatch finished, it was Frank Peterson's turn. Peterson reminded the court of how remorseful Chloe was. He launched into the extraordinary circumstances that had lured her into committing her crime: her need to pay for little Oscar's treatment. He stressed that while no one deserves to be tricked, Chloe had chosen only to victimize people who could afford to lose a few thousand dollars. She did not prey upon the most vulnerable members of society, only upon the wealthy and healthy.

When Peterson finished his speech, the courtroom burst into applause, and the judge asked that the defendant please rise. Glowering at Chloe, the judge said, "You have pled guilty to one count of fraud, a very serious charge. Before I sentence you, do you have anything to say?"

Chloe smiled. "Your Honor, I always have something to say. I stand before you today because I am a deeply flawed person. I feel tremendous remorse for my crime. It was wrong, horribly wrong, for me to expose other people to cocaine. As an addict, I was in denial about the power of that drug. My past few months in Narcotics Anonymous have made me see the error of my ways." Chloe batted her eyelashes appealingly. Yes, she had been a very bad girl.

She went on, "All I can say in my defense is that everything I did, I did out of love. Love for my grandson, Oscar. He is an extraordinary boy, one of the great loves of my life. His situation was simple: he needed treatment, and the insurance companies would not pay for it. Now, I know what I was supposed to do. I was supposed to sit on the sidelines, offer what little financial and emotional support I could, and hope for the best. But I'm afraid I'm not built that way. I've never managed to embrace the role of impotent bystander. I had to do something.

"My daughter, Annie, felt the same way. She couldn't sit there and watch her son deteriorate. So she launched him into treatment, devoted all of her energy to his care, and set up a business to fund the effort. I thought her plan to sell face cream was brave and creative. I still do. My daughter is one of the few heroes I know. Her quiet endurance, brains, and sheer gall are amazing. She figured out that her rich neighbors, the women of La Jolla, were willing to pay huge amounts of money for face cream, so she launched a business to net as much of that money as she could. She was a commercial Robin Hood: taking money from the rich so that she could fund the treatment of her poor son. I cannot begin to tell you how proud I am of my daughter, how much I love her and wish I could be like her.

"But, alas, I am not like her. Audacious as she was, Annie always acted within the bounds of the law. I was the one who spiced up her innocuous face cream with cocaine. The plan was all my own. I did so because I thought the cream wouldn't sell otherwise. What I did was wrong. But I acted out of love. Love for my grandson and my daughter.

"And, believe it or not, I also acted out of love for the women of La Jolla. I loved those women because I shared their pain: the pain of aging; the pain of becoming invisible, asexual, and irrelevant. Time is unkind to all of us, but it is particularly sadistic to women. A man's physical prowess may dwindle with time, but he has compensations: stature, wealth, eminence. Men grow distinguished while women simply grow old.

"But it doesn't have to be this way. Women can refuse to fade away. We can refuse to be less than we are. We can sag and wrinkle without losing our essential beauty. We have to redefine what beauty means to us. We have to choose to love who we are and what we are becoming.

"By putting cocaine into my daughter's face cream, I hoped to make the women of La Jolla love themselves just a little more. I didn't think I was distorting their view of themselves. If anything, I was restoring proper focus. They are beautiful. They are capable. I wanted them to see what I see when I look at them. And for a time, they did. Many of them changed their lives: began new careers, new relationships, new adventures. My greatest hope is that they will continue down the roads they started. I wish those women nothing but the best. And to the extent that I harmed any of them, I am profoundly sorry.

"And that, Your Honor, is all I have to say."

Epilogue

The judge sentenced Chloe to thirty days in jail. Chloe did not sit idle in prison. She had one of her new fans create a website on which people could donate money for Oscar's medical treatment. Grandmothers across the country dug deep into their pockets, and Oscar soon had enough to buy all the treatment he would ever need. On Chloe's release, ABC announced that she would join that season's *Dancing with the Stars.* From then on, her career went from strength to strength: a stint as Mama Morton on Broadway in *Chicago*, ads for adult remedies like Maalox and Metamucil. And the men! First there was her brief affair with Frank Peterson; then a December-May romance with her *Chicago* costar. Finally, a whirlwind courtship with an obscure Swedish royal almost led to an engagement. When interviewed, Chloe played coy on the subject of romance. She told interviewers that her heart was already taken by her grandchildren; her son, Jimmy; and her daughter, Annie. And, for once, Chloe was telling the truth.

With Chloe firmly in her corner and Oscar's treatment paid for, Annie finally clawed her way out of her depression. She continued to work with Oscar every day, but the toil seemed lighter now, less daunting. Oscar was flourishing, and so were the girls. When Rachel finished preschool, Annie returned to work at one of UC San Diego's laboratories. The lab was quiet, often tedious, and packed with awkward coworkers, but Annie loved every minute of it. And Harry finally had his happy wife back. Harry relaxed, as much as Harry could do such a thing.

Sarah relaxed too. Days after Chloe's release from prison, Sarah gave birth to fraternal twins: Gideon and Gracie. Sarah stayed home with them for a year. She turned down Marty's offer to take her back at the firm and instead went off to UCLA to earn a degree in marketing. She watched the twins during the afternoons, and Michael joined her at night, every night.

Sarah remained close to Valerie and Kim. She had a front-row seat at Valerie's wedding. Valerie married David Carson on a grassy spot overlooking La Jolla Cove. The wedding party was small: the bride and groom with two attendants, David's brother as best man, and Esperanza as the matron of honor. Valerie and David spent six weeks honeymooning in Europe before returning to work: he to the gallery and she to her easel.

Meanwhile, Kim continued teaching at the Gillespie School. She developed a reputation as one of the school's toughest, and best, math teachers. She and Andrew played a great deal of tennis together. When tipsy, Kim credited the game with reviving their sex life.

Walter, Valerie's ex-husband, did not have much sex after his newborn son arrived. After Crystal gave birth, she suddenly lost all interest in sex. And between midnight feedings and Gymboree classes, Walter did not have all that much interest in sex either. He was too tired.

Natalie was not tired anymore. Thanks to the Sarah Sloane affair, Natalie went from being blacklisted as a potential pauper to being blacklisted as a high-end narc. To Natalie, the change made little difference. What did make a difference was her Aunt Josephine's money. When Natalie's husband, Eric, finally came clean and admitted that their finances were in ruins, Aunt Josephine came to the rescue. She gave Natalie a healthy advance on her inheritance. Natalie and Eric used that money to move to Los Angeles. Natalie loved it there. She finally found people who appreciated her: "creative" types like herself. She still traveled south to La Jolla once a week to visit Aunt Josephine and the dogs.

Priscilla's book club went on meeting once a month in La Jolla. They lost a few members—Valerie, Kim, and Sarah—but they found eager newbies to replace them. The book club continued to read significant works of fiction, but they rarely discussed any of them.

Acknowledgments

Boy, I owe a lot of people! Thanks to my brilliant, funny husband, Johnny Chen, for supporting me emotionally and financially throughout this process. Thanks to my friend Anna De Angelis for fantastic edits, relentless cheerleading, and expert chemist's advice. Thanks also to my enormously talented friends Deborah Cunningham and Tami Sagher (future Oscar winner) for their terrific edits and insights too. And thanks to my friend Kate MacPhail for talking me off the ledge and never letting me quit.

Endless gratitude to my sister, Jessica Cooperman, for her advice, support, and years of unpaid babysitting services (I hope to reciprocate soon!). And thanks to my parents, Mort and Ingrid Cooperman. I literally wouldn't be here or anywhere else without them.

More thanks to my fiercely honest, endlessly supportive dynamo of an agent Amy Tipton (Signature Literary). And thanks to my witty, wise editor, Jodi Warshaw, and the other kind folks at Lake Union Publishing (Amazon). Thanks also to Jay Schaefer and Caroline Tolley for their editorial guidance.

Another round of thanks to Lee Saara Bickley, Nicole Smokler-Monsowitz, Sandy Smokler, Jen Charat, Arielle Eckstut, Audra Grim, Steve Martin, Sasha Raskin, Julie Schwartz, John Grossman, Mark Gerson, Anna Gouvalaris, Katharyn Feldsott Canfield, Wendy Wardlow, Nataliya Telerman, and Kinky Friedman.

Finally, thanks to my children, Jacob, Lily, Daisy, and Oliver (I've listed you in order by age—no favoritism here!—I love all of you equally and endlessly). Without you and the love you inspire in me, I never would have written this book.

About the Author

Photo © 2016 Jaime Moore

Kathy Cooperman spent four years performing improvisational comedy, then decided to do something less fun with her life. After graduating from Yale Law School, she went into criminal law, defending "innocent" (rich) clients. These days, she lives in Del Mar, California, with her husband and four challenging young children. Crimes Against a Book Club is her first novel. Follow her on Twitter @Kathy_Cooperman.